ALIEN™

OUT OF THE SHADOWS

A L I E N

OUT OF THE SHADOWS

TIM LEBBON

TITAN BOOKS

ALIEN™: OUT OF THE SHADOWS

Print edition ISBN: 9781783292820
E-book edition ISBN: 9781781162699

Published by Titan Books
A division of Titan Publishing Group Ltd
144 Southwark Street, London SE1 0UP

First edition: January 2014
5 7 9 10 8 6 4

A CIP catalogue record for this title is available from the British Library.

Printed and bound in Great Britain by CPI Group Ltd.

Did you enjoy this book?
We love to hear from our readers. Please email us at readerfeedback@titanemail.com or write to us at Reader Feedback at the above address.

To receive advance information, news, competitions, and exclusive offers online, please sign up for the Titan newsletter on our website
www.titanbooks.com

"The universe seems neither benign
nor hostile, merely indifferent."
CARL SAGAN

YEARLY PROGRESS REPORT:

To: Weyland-Yutani Corporation, Science Division
(Ref: code 937)

Date (unspecified)

Transmission (pending)

My search continues.

PART 1

DREAMING OF
MONSTERS

1

MARION

Chris Hooper dreamed of monsters.

As a youngster they'd fascinated him, as they did all children. But unlike children born generations before him, there were places he could go, destinations he could explore, where he might just find them. No longer restricted to the pages of fairy tales or the digital imagery of imaginative moviemakers, humankind's forays into space had opened up a whole galaxy of possibilities.

So from a young age he looked to the stars, and those dreams persisted.

In his early twenties he'd worked for a year on Callisto, one of Jupiter's moons. They'd been hauling ores from several miles below the surface, and in a nearby mine a Chinese team had broken through into a sub-surface sea. There had been crustaceans and shrimp, tiny pilot fish and delicate frond-like creatures a hundred feet long. But no monsters to set his imagination on fire.

When he'd left the solar system to work in deep space, traveling as engineer on various haulage, exploration, and mining ships, he'd eagerly sought out tales of alien life forms encountered on those distant asteroids, planets, and moons. Though adulthood had diluted his youngster's vivid imagination with more mundane concerns—family estrangement, income, and well-being—he still told himself stories. But over the years, none of what he'd found had lived up to the fictions he'd created.

As time passed he'd come to terms with the fact that monsters were only monsters before they were found, and perhaps the universe wasn't quite so remarkable as he'd once hoped.

Certainly not here.

Working in one of the *Marion*'s four docking bays, he paused to look down at the planet below with a mixture of distaste and boredom. LV178. Such an inhospitable, storm-scoured, sand-blasted hell of a rock that they hadn't even bothered to give it a proper name. He'd spent three long years here, making lots of money he had no opportunity to spend.

Trimonite was the hardest, strongest material known to man, and when a seam as rich as this one was found, it paid to mine it out. One day he'd head home, he promised himself at the end of every fifty-day shift. Home to the two boys and wife he'd run away from seven years before. One day. But he was beginning to fear that this life had become a habit, and the longer it continued, the harder it might be to break.

"Hoop!" The voice startled him, and as he spun around Jordan was already chuckling.

He and the captain had been involved briefly, a year before. These confined quarters and stressful work conditions meant that such liaisons were frequent, and inevitably brief. But Hoop liked the fact that they had remained close. Once they'd got the screwing out of the way, they'd become the best of friends.

"Lucy, you scared the shit out of me."

"That's Captain Jordan to you." She examined the machinery he'd been working on, without even glancing at the viewing window. "All good here?"

"Yeah, heat baffles need replacing, but I'll get Powell and Welford onto that."

"The terrible twins," Jordan said, smiling. Powell was close to six foot six, tall, black, and slim as a pole. Welford was more than a foot shorter, white, and twice as heavy. As different as could be, yet the ship's engineers were both smartasses.

"Still no contact?" Hoop asked.

Jordan frowned briefly. It wasn't unusual to lose touch with the surface, but not for two days running.

"Storms down there are the worst I've seen," she said, nodding at the window. From three hundred miles up, the planet's surface looked even more inhospitable than usual—a smear of burnt oranges and yellows, browns and blood-reds, with the circling eyes of countless sandstorms raging across the equatorial regions. "They've gotta abate soon. I'm not too worried yet, but I'll be happy when we can talk to the dropships again."

"Yeah, you and me both. The *Marion* feels like a derelict when we're between shifts."

Jordan nodded. She was obviously concerned, and for an awkward, silent moment Hoop thought he should say something more to comfort her. But she was the captain because she could handle situations like this. That, and because she was a badass.

"Lachance is doing spaghetti again tonight," she said.

"For a Frenchman, he sure can cook Italian."

Jordan chuckled, but he could feel her tension.

"Lucy, it's just the storms," Hoop said. He was sure of that. But he was equally sure that "just storms" could easily cause disaster. Out here in the furthest quadrants of known space—pushing the limits of technology, knowledge, and understanding, and doing their best to deal with the corners cut by the Kelland Mining Company—it didn't take much for things to go wrong.

Hoop had never met a ship's engineer better than him, and that was why he was here. Jordan was an experienced flight captain, knowledgeable and wise. Lachance, cynical and gruff, was an excellent pilot who had a healthy respect for space and all it could throw at them. And the rest of their team, though a mixed bunch, were all more than capable at their jobs. The miners themselves were a hardy breed, many of them experienced from stints on Jupiter's and Neptune's moons. Mean bastards, with streaks of sick humor, most were as hard as the trimonite they sought.

But no experience, no confidence or hardness or pig-headedness, could dodge fate. They all knew how dangerous it was. Most of them had grown used to living with the danger, and the close proximity of death.

Only seven months ago they'd lost three miners in an accident in Bay One as the dropship *Samson* came in to dock. No one's fault, really. Just eagerness to be back on board in relative comfort, after fifty days down the mine. The airlock hadn't sealed properly, an indicator had malfunctioned, and the two men and a woman had suffocated.

Hoop knew that Jordan still had sleepless nights over that. For three days after transmitting her condolences to the miners' families, she hadn't left her cabin. As far as Hoop was concerned, that was what made her a great captain—she was a badass who cared.

"Just the storms," she echoed. She leaned past Hoop and rested against the bulkhead, looking down through the window. Despite the violence, from up here the planet looked almost beautiful, an artist's palette of autumnal colors. "I fucking hate this place."

"Pays the bills."

"Ha! Bills…" She seemed in a maudlin mood, and Hoop didn't like her like this. Perhaps that was a price of their closeness—he got to see a side of her the rest of the crew never would.

"Almost finished," he said, nudging some loose ducting with his foot. "Meet you in the rec room in an hour. Shoot some pool?"

Jordan raised an eyebrow. "Another rematch?"

"You've got to let me win sometime."

"You've never, *ever* beaten me at pool."

"But I used to let you play with my cue."

"As your captain, I could put you in the brig for such comments."

"Yeah. Right. You and which army?"

Jordan turned her back on Hoop. "Stop wasting time and get back to work, chief engineer."

"Yes, captain." He watched her walk away along the dusky corridor and through a sliding door, and then he was alone again.

Alone with the atmosphere, the sounds, the smells of the ship…

The stench of space-flea piss from the small, annoying mites that managed to multiply, however many times the crew tried to purge them. They were tiny, but a million fleas pissing produced a sharp, rank odor that clung to the air.

The constant background hum of machinery was inaudible unless Hoop really listened for it, because it was so ever-present. There were distant thuds, echoing grinds, the whisper of air movement encouraged by conditioning fans and baffles, the occasional creak of the ship's huge bulk settling and shifting. Some of the noises he could identify because he knew them so well, and on occasion he perceived problems simply through hearing or *not* hearing them—sticking doors, worn bearings in air duct seals, faulty transmissions.

But there were also mysterious sounds that vibrated through the ship now and then, like hesitant, heavy footsteps in distant corridors, or someone screaming from a level or two away. He'd never figured those out. Lachance liked to say it was the ship screaming in boredom.

He hoped that was all they were.

The vessel was huge and would take him half an hour to walk from nose to tail, and yet it was a speck in the vastness of space. The void exerted a negative pressure on him, and if he thought about it too much, he thought he would explode—be ripped apart, cell by cell, molecule by molecule, spread to the cosmos from which he had originally come. He was the stuff of the stars, and when he was a young boy—dreaming of monsters, and looking to space in the hope that he would find them—that had made him feel special.

Now, it only made him feel small.

However close they all lived together on the *Marion*, they were alone out here.

Shaking away the thoughts, he bent to work again, making more noise than was necessary—a clatter to keep him company. He was looking forward to shooting some pool with Jordan and having her whip his ass again. There were colleagues and acquaintances aplenty, but she was the closest thing he had to a good friend.

The recreation room was actually a block of four compartments to the rear of the *Marion*'s accommodations hub. There was a movie theater with a large screen and an array of seating, a music library with various listening posts, a reading room with comfortable chairs and reading devices—and then there was Baxter's Bar, better known as BeeBee's. Josh Baxter was the ship's communications officer, but he also acted as their barman. He mixed a mean cocktail.

Though it was sandwiched back between the accommodations hub and the sectioned holds, BeeBee's was the social center of the ship. There were two pool tables, table tennis, a selection of faux-antique computer game consoles, and the bar area with tables and chairs scattered in casual abandon. It had not been viewed as a priority by the company that paid the ship's designers, so the ceiling was a mass of exposed service pipework, the floor textured metal, the walls bare and unpainted. However, those using BeeBee's had done their best to make it more comfortable. Seats were padded, lighting was low and moody, and many miners and crew had copied Baxter's idea of hanging decorated blankets from the walls. Some painted the blankets, others tore and tied. Each of them was distinct. It gave the whole rec room a casual, almost arty air.

Miners had fifty days between shifts on the planet, so they often spent much of their off-time here, and though alcohol distribution was strictly regulated, it still made for some raucous nights.

Captain Jordan allowed that. In fact, she positively encouraged it, because it was a release of tension that the ship would otherwise barely contain. It wasn't possible to communicate with any of their loved ones back home. Distances were so vast, time so extended, that any meaningful contact was impossible. They needed somewhere to feel at home, and BeeBee's provided just that.

When Hoop entered, it was all but deserted. These quiet times between shift changes gave Baxter time to clear out the bar stock, tidy the room, and prepare for the next onslaught. He worked quietly behind the bar, stocking bottled beer and preparing a selection of dehydrated snacks. Water on the ship always tasted vaguely metallic, so he rehydrated many of the treats in stale beer. No one complained.

"And here he is," Jordan said. She was sitting on a stool by one of the pool tables, bottle in hand. "Back for another beating. What do you think, Baxter?"

Baxter nodded a greeting to Hoop.

"Sucker for punishment," he agreed.

"Yep. Sucker."

"Well if you don't *want* to play…" Hoop said.

Jordan slid from her stool, plucked a cue from the rack and lobbed it at him. As he caught it out of the air, the ship's intercom chimed.

"Oh, now, what the hell?" Jordan sighed.

Baxter leaned across the bar and hit the intercom.

"Captain! *Anyone!*" It was their pilot, Lachance. "Get up to the bridge, now. We've got incoming from one of the dropships." His French accent was much more acute than normal. That happened when he was upset or stressed, neither of which occurred very often.

Jordan dashed to the bar and pressed the transmit button.

"Which one?"

"The *Samson*. But it's fucked up."

"What do you mean?" In the background, behind Lachance's confused words and the sounds of chaos from the bridge, Hoop heard static-tinged screaming. He and Jordan locked eyes.

Then they ran, and Baxter followed.

The *Marion* was a big ship, far more suited to massive deep-ore mining than trimonite extrusion, and it took them a few minutes to make their way to the bridge. Along the curved corridor that wound around the accommodations hub, then up three levels by elevator. By the time they bumped into Garcia and Kasyanov, everyone else was there.

"What's going on?" Jordan demanded. Baxter rushed across to the communications center, and Lachance stood gratefully to vacate his chair. Baxter slipped on a pair of headphones, and his left hand hovered over an array of dials and switches.

"Heard something coming through static a few minutes ago," Lachance said. "The higher they climb, the clearer it gets." They called him "No-Chance" Lachance because of his laconic pessimism, but in truth he was one of the most level-headed among them. Now, Hoop could see by his expression that something had him very rattled.

From loudspeakers around the bridge, frantic breathing crackled.

"*Samson*, Captain Jordan is now on the bridge," Baxter said. "Please give us your—"

"I don't have time to fucking give you anything, just get the med pods fired up!" The voice was so distorted that they couldn't tell who it was.

Jordan grabbed a headset from beside Baxter. Hoop looked around at the others, all of them standing around the communications area. The bridge was large, but they were all bunched in close. They showed the tension they had to be feeling, even the usually unflappable science officer, Karen Sneddon. The thin, severe-faced woman had been to more planets, asteroids, and moons than all of them put together. But there was fear in her eyes.

"*Samson*, this is Captain Jordan. What's happening? What's going on down at the mine?"

"… creatures! We've—"

The contact cut out abruptly, leaving the bridge ringingly silent.

Wide viewing windows looked out onto the familiar view of space and an arc of the planet below, as if nothing had changed. The low-level hum of machinery was complemented by agitated breathing.

"Baxter," Jordan said softly, "I'd like them back online."

"I'm doing my best," he replied.

"Creatures?" The ship's medic Garcia tapped nervously at her chin. "No one's ever seen *creatures* down the mine, have they?"

"There's nothing living on that rock, other than bacteria," Sneddon said. She was shifting from foot to foot. "Maybe that's not what they said. Maybe they said fissures, or something."

"Have we got them on scanner yet?" Jordan asked.

Baxter waved to his left, where three screens were set aslant in the control panel. One was backlit a dull green, and it showed two small points of light moving quickly toward them. Interference from electrical storms in the upper atmosphere sparked across the screen. But the points were firm, their movement defined.

"Which is the *Samson*?" Hoop asked.

"Lead ship is *Samson*," Lachance said. "The *Delilah* follows."

"Maybe ten minutes out," Jordan said. "Any communication from *Delilah*?"

No one answered. Answer enough.

"I'm not sure we can—" Hoop began, then the speakers burst back into life. *Let them dock,* he was going to say.

"—stuck to their faces!" the voice said. It was still unrecognizable.

Baxter turned some dials, and then a larger screen above his station flickered to life. The *Samson*'s pilot, Vic Jones, appeared as a blurred image. Hoop tried to see past him to the inner cabin of the dropship, but the vibration of their steep ascent out of LV178's atmosphere made a mess out of everything.

"How many with you?" Hoop asked.

"Hoop? That you?"

"Yeah."

"The other shift found something. Something horrible. Few of them… " He faded out again, his image stuttering and flickering as atmospherics caused more chaos.

"Kasyanov, you and Garcia get to sick bay and fire up the med pods," Jordan said to the doctor and her medic.

"You can't be serious," Hoop said. As Jordan turned on him, Jones's voice crackled in again.

"—all four, only me and Sticky untouched. They're okay right now, but… to shiver and spit. Just get… to dock!"

"They might be *infected*!" Hoop said.

"Which is why we'll get them straight to sick bay."

"This is fucking serious." Hoop nodded at the screen where Jones's image continued to flicker and dance, his voice cutting in and out. Most of what Jones said made little sense, but they could all hear his terror. "He's shitting himself!"

Kasyanov and Garcia hustled from the bridge, and Hoop looked to Sneddon for support. But the science officer was leaning over the back of Baxter's chair, frowning as she tried to make out whatever else Jones was saying.

"Jones, what about the *Delilah*?" Jordan said into her headset. "Jones?"

"...left the same time... something got on board, and... "

"*What* got on board?"

The screen snowed, the comm link fuzzed with static, and those remaining on the bridge stood staring at each other for a loaded, terrible few seconds.

"I'm getting down to the docking level," Jordan said. "Cornell, with me. Baxter, tell them Bay Three."

Hoop coughed a disbelieving laugh.

"You're taking *him* to back you up?"

"He's security officer, Hoop."

"He's a drunk!" Cornell didn't even meet Hoop's stare, let alone respond.

"He has a gun," Jordan said. "You stay here, supervise the bridge. Lachance, help guide them in. Remote pilot the dropships if you have to."

"If we can even get a link to them," Lachance said.

"Assume we can, and do it!" Jordan snapped. She took a few deep breaths, and Hoop could almost hear her thoughts. *Never figured it would fuck up this bad, gotta be calm, gotta be in control.* He knew she was thinking about those three miners she'd lost, and dreading the idea of losing more. She looked straight at him. He frowned, but she turned and left the bridge before he could object again.

There was no way they should be letting the *Samson* dock, Hoop knew. Or if it did dock, they had to sever all external operation of the airlock until they knew it was safe. There had been twenty miners taken down to the surface, and twenty more scheduled to return in the dropships. Two shifts of twenty men and women—but right now, the ten people still on the *Marion* had to be the priority.

He moved to Baxter's communication panel and checked the radar scanner again. The *Samson* had been tagged with its name now, and it looked to be performing a textbook approach, arcing up out of the atmosphere and approaching the orbiting *Marion* from the sunward side.

"Lachance?" Hoop asked, pointing at the screen.

"It's climbing steeply. Jones is pushing it as hard and as fast as he can."

"Keen to reach the *Marion*."

"But that's not right…" Lachance muttered.

"What?" Hoop asked.

"*Delilah*. She's changing direction."

"Baxter," Hoop said, "plot a course trace on the *Delilah*."

Baxter hit some buttons and the screen flickered as it changed. The *Delilah* grew a tail of blue dots, and its projected course appeared as a hazy fan.

"Who's piloting *Delilah* this drop?"

"Gemma Keech," Welford said. "She's a good pilot."

"Not today she isn't. Baxter, we need to talk to *Delilah*, or see what's happening on board."

"I'm doing what I can."

"Yeah." Hoop had a lot of respect for Baxter. He was a strange guy, not really a mixer at all—probably why he spent more of his time behind the bar than in front of it—but he was a whiz when it came to communications tech. If things went wrong, he was their potential lifeline to home, and as such one of the most important people on the *Marion*.

"We have no idea what they've got on board," Powell said. "Could be anything."

"Did he say there's only six of them on the *Samson*?" Welford asked. "What about all the others?"

Hoop shrugged. Each ship held twenty people and a pilot. If the *Samson* was returning less than half full—and they had no idea how many were on *Delilah*—then what had happened to the rest of them?

He closed his eyes briefly, trying to gather himself.

"I've got visual on *Delilah*!" Baxter said. He clicked a few more keys on his computer keyboard, then switched on one of the blank screens. "No audio, and there's no response to my hails. Maybe…" But his voice trailed off.

They all saw what was happening inside *Delilah*.

The pilot, Gemma Keech, was screaming in her seat, terrified and determined, eyes glued to the window before her. It was haunting witnessing such fear in utter silence. Behind her, shadows thrashed and twisted.

"Baxter," Hoop whispered. "Camera."

Baxter stroked his keyboard and the view switched to a camera above and behind Keech's head. It was a widescreen, compressing the image but taking in the entire passenger compartment.

And there was blood.

Three miners were kneeling directly behind the pilot. Two of them held spiked sand-picks, light alloy tools used for breaking through compacted sandstones. They were waving and lashing at something, but their target was just out of sight. The miner in the middle held a plasma torch.

"He can't use that in there," Powell said. "If he does he'll... he'll... what the *fuck*?"

Several miners seemed to have been strapped into their seats. Their heads were tilted back, chests a mess of blood and ripped clothing, protruding ribs and flesh. One of them still writhed and shook, and there was something coming out of her chest. Pulling itself out. A smooth curved surface glimmering with artificial light, it shone with her blood.

Other miners were splayed on the floor of the cabin, and seemed to be dead. Shapes darted between them, slicing and slashing, and blood was splashed across the floor, up the walls. It dripped from the ceiling.

At the back of the passenger cabin, three small shapes were charging again and again at a closed door. There was a small bathroom back there, Hoop knew, just two stalls and a washbasin. And there was something in there the things wanted.

Those things.

Each was the size of a small cat, and looked to be a deep ochre color, glittering with the wetness of their unnatural births. They were somehow sharp-looking, like giant beetles or scorpions back home.

The bathroom door was already heavily dented, and one side of it seemed to be caving in.

"That's two inch steel," Hoop said.

"We've got to help them," Welford said.

"I think they're beyond that," Sneddon said, and for a moment Hoop wanted to punch her. But she was right. Keech's silent screaming bore testament to that. Whatever else they had seen, whatever the pilot already knew, the hopelessness of the *Delilah*'s situation was evident in her eyes.

"Turn it off," Hoop said, but Baxter could not comply. And all six of them on the bridge continued to watch.

The creatures smashed through the bathroom door and squeezed inside, and figures jerked and thrashed.

One of the miners holding a sand-pick flipped up and forward as if his legs had been knocked from beneath him. The man with the plasma torch slumped to the right, away from the struggling figure. Something many-legged scuttled across the camera, blotting everything from view for a blessed moment.

When the camera was clear again, the plasma torch was already alight.

"Oh, no," Powell said.

The flare was blinding white. It surged across the cabin, and for a terrible few seconds the strapped-down miners' bodies were sizzling and flaming, clothes burning and flesh flowing. Only one of them writhed in his bindings, and the thing protruding from his chest burst aside, becoming a mass of fire streaking across the cabin.

Then the plasma jet suddenly swept back and around, and everything went white.

Baxter hit his keyboard, going back to the cockpit view, and Gemma Keech was on fire.

He switched it off then. Even though everything they'd seen had been soundless, losing the image seemed to drop an awful silence across the bridge.

It was Hoop who moved first. He hit the AllShip intercom button and winced at the whine of crackling feedback.

"Lucy, we can't let those ships dock," he said into the microphone. "You hear me? The *Delilah* is… there are things on board. Monsters."

He closed his eyes, mourning his childhood's lost innocence. "Everyone's dead."

"Oh, *no*!" Lachance said.

Hoop looked at him, and the Frenchman was staring down at the radar screen.

"Too late," Lachance whispered. Hoop saw, and cursed himself. He should have thought of this! He struck the button again and started shouting.

"Jordan, Cornell, get out of there, get away from the docking level, far away as you can, run, *run*!" He only hoped they heard and took heed. But a moment later he realized it really didn't matter.

The stricken *Delilah* ploughed into the *Marion*, and the impact and explosion knocked them all from their feet.

2

SAMSON

Everyone and everything was screaming.

Several warning sirens blasted their individual songs—proximity alert; damage indicator; hull breach. People shouted in panic, confusion, and fear. And behind it all was a deep, rumbling roar from the ship itself. The *Marion* was in pain, and its vast bulk was grinding itself apart.

Lucy and Cornell, Hoop thought from his position on the floor. But whether they were alive or dead didn't change anything right now. He was senior officer on the bridge. As scared and shocked as all of them, but he had to take charge.

He grabbed a fixed seat and hauled himself upright. Lights flashed. Cords, paneling, and strip-lights swung where they had been knocked from their mountings. Artificial gravity still worked, at least. He closed his eyes and breathed deeply, trying to recall his training. There had been an in-depth module in their pre-flight sessions, called "Massive Damage Control," and their guide—a grizzled old veteran of seven solar system moon habitations and three deep space exploration flights—had finished each talk with, *But don't forget YTF*.

It took Hoop until the last talk to ask what he meant.

"Don't forget…" the vet said, *"you're truly fucked."*

Everyone knew that a disaster like this meant the end. But that didn't mean they wouldn't fight until the last.

"Lachance!" Hoop said, but the pilot was already strapping himself into the flight seat that faced the largest window. His hands worked expertly across the controls, and if it weren't for the insistent warning buzzers and sirens, Hoop might have been comforted.

"What about Captain Jordan and Cornell?" Powell asked.

"Not now," Hoop said. "Is everyone all right?" He looked around the bridge. Baxter was strapping himself tight into his seat, dabbing at a bloodied nose. Welford and Powell held each other up against the curved wall at the bridge's rear. Sneddon was on her hands and knees, blood dripping onto the floor beneath her.

She was shaking.

"Sneddon?" Hoop said.

"Yeah." She looked up at him. There was a deep cut across her right cheek and nose. Her eyes were hazy and unfocussed.

Hoop went to her and helped her up, and Powell came with a first aid kit.

The *Marion* was juddering. A new siren had started blaring, and in the confusion Hoop couldn't identify it.

"Lachance?"

"Atmosphere venting," he said. "Hang on." He scanned his instruments, tapping keyboards, tracing patterns on screens that would mean little to anyone else. Jordan could pilot the *Marion* if she absolutely had to. But Lachance was the most experienced astronaut among them.

"We're screwed," Powell said.

"Shut it," Welford told him.

"That's it," Powell responded. "We're screwed. Game over."

"Just shut up!" Welford shouted.

"We should get to the escape pods!" Powell said.

Hoop tried not to listen to the exchange. He focussed on Lachance, strapped tightly into the pilot's seat and doing his best to ignore the rhythmic shuddering emanating from somewhere deep in the ship. *That doesn't feel good*, he thought.

The four docking bays were in a protruding level beneath the ship's nose, more than five hundred yards from the engine room. Yet an impact like that could have caused catastrophic structural damage throughout the ship. The surest way to see the damage would be to view it firsthand, but the quickest assessment would come from their pilot and his instruments.

"Get out," Powell continued, "get away before the *Marion* breaks up, down to the surface and—"

"And what?" Hoop snapped without turning around. "Survive on sand for the two years it'll take a rescue mission to reach us? *If* the company even decides a rescue is feasible," he added. "Now *shut it*!"

"Okay," Lachance said. He rested his hands on the flight stick, and Hoop could almost feel him holding his breath. Hoop had always been amazed that such a huge vessel could be controlled via this one small control.

Lachance called it The Jesus Stick.

"Okay," the pilot said again. "Looks like the *Delilah* took out the port arm of the docking level, Bays One and Two. Three might be damaged, can't tell, sensors there are screwed. Four seems to be untouched. Atmosphere is venting from levels three, four, and five. All bulkhead doors have closed, but some secondary safety seals have malfunctioned and are still leaking."

"So the rest of the *Marion* is airtight for now?" Hoop asked.

"For now, yes." Lachance pointed at a schematic of the ship on one of his screens. "There's still stuff going on at the crash site, though. I can't see what, but I suspect there's lots of debris moving around down there. Any part of that could do more damage to the ship. Rad levels seem constant, so I don't think the *Delilah*'s fuel cell was compromised. But if its containment core is floating around down there..." He trailed off.

"So what's the *good* news?" Sneddon asked.

"That *was* the good news," Lachance said. "*Marion*'s lost two of her lateral dampers, three out of seven starboard sub-thrusters are out of action. And there's this." He pointed at another screen where lines danced and crossed.

"Orbital map?" Hoop asked.

"Right. We've been nudged out of orbit. And with those dampers and subs wasted, there's no way to fix it."

"How long?" Powell asked.

Lachance shrugged his muscular shoulders.

"Not quick. I'll have to run some calculations."

"But we're all right for now?" Hoop asked. "The next minute, the next hour?"

"As far as I can see, yes."

Hoop nodded and turned to the others. They were staring at him, and he was sure he returned their fear and shock. But he had to get a grip, and keep it. Move past this initial panic, shift into post-crash mode as quickly as he could.

"Kasyanov and Garcia?" he asked, looking at Baxter.

Baxter nodded and hit AllShip on the intercom.

"Kasyanov? Garcia?"

Nothing.

"Maybe the med bay vented," Powell said. "It's forward from here, not far above the docking bays."

"Try on their personal comms," Hoop said.

Baxter tapped keyboards and donned his headpiece again.

"Kasyanov, Garcia, you there?" He winced, then threw a switch that put what he heard on loudspeaker. There was a whine, interrupted by staccato ragged thudding.

"What the hell...?" they heard Kasyanov say, and everyone sighed with relief.

"You both okay?" Baxter asked.

"Fine. Trapped by... but okay. What happened?"

"*Delilah* hit us." Baxter glanced up at Hoop.

"Tell them to stay where they are for now," Hoop said. "Let's stabilize things before we start moving around anymore."

Baxter spoke again, and then just as Hoop thought of the second dropship, Sneddon asked, "What about the *Samson*?"

"Can you hail them?" Hoop asked.

Baxter tried several times, but was greeted only by static.

"Cameras," Sneddon said.

"I've got no contact with them at all."

"No, switch to the cameras in Bay Three," Sneddon replied. "If they're still coming in, and Jones sees the damage, he'll aim for there."

Baxter nodded, his hands drifting across the control panels.

A screen flickered into life. The picture jumped, but it showed a clear view out from the end of Bay Three's docking arm.

"Shit" Hoop muttered.

The *Samson* was less than a minute away.

"But those things…" Sneddon said.

I wish you were still here, Lucy, Hoop thought. But Lucy and Cornell had to be dead. He was in charge. And now, with the *Marion* fatally damaged, an even more pressing danger was manifesting.

"We've got to get down there," Hoop said. "Sneddon, Welford, with me. Let's suit up."

As Welford broke out the emergency space suits from units at the rear of the bridge, Hoop and Lachance exchanged glances. If anything happened to Hoop, Lachance was next in charge. But if it got to that stage, there'd be very little left for him to command.

"We'll stay in contact all the time," Hoop said.

"Great, that'll help." Lachance smiled and nodded.

As the three of them pulled on the atmosphere suits, the *Marion* shuddered one more time.

"*Samson* is docking," Baxter said.

"Keep everything locked," Hoop said. "*Everything*. Docking arm, airlock, inner vestibule."

"Tight as a shark's arse," Lachance said.

We should be assessing damage, Hoop thought. *Making sure the distress signal has transmitted, getting down to med bay, doing any emergency repairs that might give us more time.*

But the *Samson* held dangers that were still very much a threat.

That was priority one.

Though he was now in command, Hoop couldn't help viewing things through the eyes of chief engineer. Lights flickered on and off, indicating damaged ducting and cabling on several of the electrical loops. Suit sensors showed that atmosphere was relatively stable, though he had already told Sneddon and Welford that they were to keep their helmets locked on. Damage to the *Marion* might well be an ongoing process.

They eschewed the elevator to climb down two levels via the large central staircase. The ship still juddered, and now and then a deeper, heavier thud rattled in from somewhere far away. Hoop didn't have a clue what it might be. The huge engines were isolated for now, never in use while they were in orbit. The life support generators were situated far toward the rear of the ship, close to the recreation rooms. All he could think was that the superstructure had been weakened so much in the crash that damage was spreading. Cracks forming. Airtight compartments being compromised and venting explosively to space.

If that was the case, they needn't worry about their decaying orbit.

"*Samson*'s initiating the automatic docking sequence," Baxter said through their suits' comm link.

"Can you view on board?" Hoop asked.

"Negative. I'm still trying to get contact back online. *Samson* has gone quiet."

"Keep us informed," Hoop said. "We'll be there soon."

"What do we do when we get there?" Welford asked from behind him.

"Make sure everything's locked up tight," Sneddon said.

"Right," Hoop agreed. "Sneddon, did you recognize those things we saw on the *Delilah*?" He said no more, and his companions' breathing rattled in his headset.

"No," Sneddon said. Her voice was low, quiet. "I've never seen or heard of anything like them."

"It's like they were hatching from inside the miners' chests."

"I've read everything I can about alien life-forms," Sneddon said. "The first was discovered more than eighty years ago, and since then everything discovered through official missions has been reported, categorized wherever possible, captured, and analyzed. Nothing like this. Just… nothing. The closest analogy I can offer is a parasitic insect."

"So if they hatched from the miners, what laid the eggs?" Welford asked. But Sneddon didn't answer, and it was a question that didn't bear thinking about right then.

"Whatever it was, we can't let them on board," Hoop said, more determined than ever. "They're not that big—we lose one on the *Marion*, and we'll never find it again."

"Until it gets hungry," Welford said.

"Is that what they were doing?" Hoop asked. "Eating?"

"Not sure," Sneddon said.

They moved on silently, as if wrestling with thoughts about those strange, horrific alien creatures. Finally Hoop broke the silence.

"Well, Karen, if we get out of this, you'll have something to report," he said.

"I've already started making notes." Sneddon's voice sounded suddenly distant and strange, and Hoop thought there might be something wrong with his suit's intercom.

"You're just spooky," Welford said, and the science officer chuckled.

"Come on," Hoop said. "We're getting close to the docking level. Keep your eyes open." Another thud shook through the ship. If it really was an explosive decompression—one in a series—then keeping their eyes open would merely enable them to witness their doom as a bulkhead exploded, they were sucked out into space, and the force of the vented air shoved them away from the *Marion*.

He'd read about astronauts being blasted into space. Given a shove, they'd keep moving away from their ship, drifting until their air ran out and they suffocated. But worse were the cases of people who, for some reason—a badly connected tether, a stumble—drifted only slowly, so slowly, away from their craft, unable to return, dying while home was still within sight.

Sometimes a spacesuit's air could last for up to two days.

They reached the end of the entry corridor leading down into the docking level. A bulkhead door had closed, and Hoop took a moment to check sensors. The atmosphere beyond seemed normal, so he input the override code and the locking mechanism whispered open.

A soft hiss, and the door slid into the wall.

The left branch led to Bays One and Two, the right to Three and Four. Ten yards along the left corridor, Hoop saw the blood.

"Oh, shit," Welford said.

The wet splash on the wall spur beside the blast door was the size of a dinner plate. The blood had run, forming spidery lines toward the floor. It glistened, still wet.

"Let's check," Hoop said, but he was already quite certain what they would find. The door sensors had been damaged, but a quick look through the spy hole confirmed his suspicions. Beyond the door was vacuum. Wall paneling and systems ducting had been stripped away by the storm of air being sucked out. If the person who had left that blood spatter had been able to hang on until the blast doors automatically slammed shut…

But they were out there now, beyond the *Marion*, lost.

"One and Two definitely out of action," Hoop said. "Blast doors seem to be holding well. Powell, don't budge from that panel, and make sure all the doors behind us are locked up tight."

"You're sure?" Powell said in their headsets. "You'll be trapped down there."

"If compartments are still failing, it could fuck the whole ship," Hoop said. "Yeah, I'm sure."

He turned to the others. Sneddon was looking past him at the blood spatter, her eyes wide behind the suit glass.

"Hey," Hoop said.

"Yeah." She looked at him. Glanced away again. "I'm sorry, Hoop."

"We've all lost friends. Let's make sure we don't lose any more." They headed back along the opposite corridor, toward Bays Three and Four.

"*Samson* has docked," Baxter said through the comm.

"On automatic?"

"Affirmative." Most docking procedures were performed automatically, but Hoop knew that Vic Jones occasionally liked to fly manually. Not this time.

"Any contact?"

"Nothing. But I think I just saw a flicker on the screen. I'm working to get visual back, if nothing else."

"Keep me posted. We need to know what's going on inside that ship." Hoop led the way. The blast door leading to Bays One and Two was still open, and they moved quickly through toward the undamaged docking areas.

Another vibration rumbled through the ship, transmitted up through the floor. Hoop pressed his gloved hand hard against the wall, leaning in, trying to feel the echoes of the mysterious impact. But they had already faded.

"Lachance, any idea what's causing those impacts?"

"Negative. The ship seems steady."

"Compartments failing, you think?"

"I don't think so. If that was happening we'd be venting air to space, and that would act as thrust. I'd see movement in the *Marion*. As it is, her flight pattern seems to have stabilized into the slowly decaying orbit we talked about. We're no longer geo-stationary, but we're moving very slowly in comparison with the surface. Maybe ten miles per hour."

"Okay. Something else, then. Something loose."

"Take care down there," Lachance said. He wasn't usually one to offer platitudes.

They passed through two more bulkhead doors, checking the sensors both times to ensure that the compartments on the other side were still pressurized. As they neared bays Three and Four, Hoop knew they'd have a visual on the damage.

The docking bays were contained in two projections from the underside of the *Marion*. One and Two were contained in the port projection, Three and Four in the starboard. As they neared the corridor leading into bays Three and Four, there were viewing windows on both sides.

"Oh, hell," Hoop muttered. He was the first to see, and he heard shocked gasps from Sneddon and Welford.

The front third of the port projection, including the docking arms and parts of the airlock structures, had been swept away as if by a giant hand. Bay One was completely gone, torn aside to leave a ragged wound behind. Parts of Bay Two were still intact, including one long shred of the docking arm which was the source of the intermittent impacts—snagged on the end of the loose reach of torn metal and sparking cables was a chunk of the *Delilah*. The size of several people, weighing maybe ten tons, the unidentifiable mass of metal, paneling, and electrics bounced from the underside of the *Marion*, swept down, ricocheted from the ruined superstructure of Bay Two, then bounced back up again.

Each strike gave it the momentum to return. It moved slowly, but such was its weight that the impact when it came was still enough to send vibrations through the entire belly of the ship.

The *Delilah* had all but disintegrated when it hit. Detritus from the crash still drifted with the *Marion*, and in the distance, silhouetted against the planet's stormy surface, Hoop could see larger chunks slowly moving away from them.

"That's a person out there," Welford said quietly, pointing. Hoop saw the shape pressed against the remains of Bay Two, impaled on some of the torn metal superstructure. He couldn't tell the sex. The body was badly mutilated, naked, and most of its head was missing.

"I hope they all died quickly," Sneddon said.

"They were already dead!" Hoop snapped. He sighed, and raised a hand in apology. His heart was racing. Seventeen years in space and he'd never seen anything like this. People died all the time, of course, because space was such an inimical environment. Accidents were common, and it was the larger disasters that gained notoriety. The passenger ship *Archimedes*, struck by a hail of micro meteors on its way to Alpha Centurai, with the loss of seven hundred passengers and crew. The Colonial Marine base on a large moon in the Outer Rim, its environmental systems sabotaged, resulting in the loss of over a thousand personnel.

Even further back, in the fledgling days of space travel, the research station *Nephilim* orbiting Ganymede suffered stabilizer malfunction and spun down onto the moon's surface. That one was still taught to anyone planning a career in space exploration, because every one of the three hundred people on board had continued with their experiments, transmitting data and messages of hope until the very last moment. It had been a symbol of humankind's determination to edge out past the confines of their own planet, and eventually their own system.

In the scheme of things, this tragedy was small. But Hoop had known every one of those people on board the *Delilah*. And even though he couldn't identify the frozen, ruined body stuck against the wrecked docking bay structure, he knew that he had spoken, joked, and laughed with them.

"We'll have to cut that free," Welford said, and at first Hoop thought he was talking about the corpse. But the engineer was watching the slowly drifting mass of metal as it moved back toward the shattered docking bays.

"We've got to do that and a *lot* more," Hoop said. If they were to survive—if they got past this initial chaos, secured the *Samson*, figured out what the fuck was going on—he, Welford, and Powell needed to pull some miracles out of somewhere. "Gonna earn our pay now, guys."

"Hoop, the *Samson*," Baxter muttered in his ear.

"What is it?" They couldn't yet see the ship where it was now static on the other side of the starboard docking arm.

"I've got it… a picture, up on screen." His voice sounded hollow, empty.

"And?" Sneddon asked.

"And you don't want to open it up. Ever. Don't even go near it."

Hoop wished he could see, though part of him was glad that he couldn't.

"What's happening in there?" Sneddon asked.

"They've… they've *hatched*," Baxter said. "And they're just… waiting. Those things, just sort of crouched there beside the bodies."

"What about Jones and Sticky?"

"Sticky's dead. Jones isn't." That flat tone again, so that Hoop didn't really want to ask any more. But Sneddon did. Maybe it was her science officer's curiosity.

"What's happening to Jones?" she asked.

"Nothing. He's… I can see him, just at the bottom of the picture. He's just sitting there, seat turned around, back against the control panel. Shaking and crying."

They haven't killed him yet, Hoop thought.

"We have to seal this up," he said. "All the doors are locked down anyway, but we have to disable all of the manual controls."

"You think those things can open doors?" Welford asked.

"Hoop's right," Sneddon said. "We must assume the worst."

"Can't we just cut the *Samson* loose?"

Hoop had already thought of that. But despite the danger, they might still need the dropship. The *Marion*'s orbit was still decaying. There were escape pods, but their targeting was uncertain. If they used them, they'd end up scattered across the surface of the planet.

The *Samson* might be their only hope of survival.

"We do that and it might drift with us for days," Lachance said, his voice coming through a hail of static. "Impact the *Marion*, cause more damage. We're in bad enough shape as it is."

"Baxter, we're losing you," Hoop said.

"…damaged," Baxter said. "Lachance?"

"He's right," Lachance responded. "Indicators are flagging up more damage every minute that goes by. Comms, environmental, remote system. We need to start fixing things."

"Got to fix this first," Hoop said. "We go through the vestibule, into the docking arm for Bay Three, then into the airlock. Then from there we work back out, disabling manual controls and shutting everything down."

"We could purge the airlock, too," Welford said.

"Good idea. If anything does escape from the *Samson*, it won't be able to breathe."

"Who's to say that they breathe at all?" Sneddon said. "We don't know what they are, where they come from. Mammal, insectile, reptilian, something else. Don't know *anything*!" Her voice was tinged with panic.

"And it's going to stay that way," Hoop said. "First chance we get, we kill them. All of them."

He wanted support from someone, but no one replied. He expected disagreement from Sneddon—as science officer, she'd see past the chaos and death to what these creatures might mean for science. But she said nothing, just stared at him, her eyes bruised, cut nose swelling.

I really am in charge now, he thought. It weighed heavy.

"Right," he said. "Let's get to it."

They followed Hoop's plan.

In through the vestibule that served bays Three and Four, through the docking arm, then through the airlock to the outer hatch. Hoop and Welford went ahead, leaving Sneddon to close the doors behind them, and at the end of the docking arm the two men paused. Beyond the closed hatch lay a narrow gap, and then the *Samson*'s outer airlock door. There was a small viewing window in both hatch and door.

The inside of the *Samson*'s window was steamed up.

Hoop wondered whether the things knew they were there, so close. He thought of asking Baxter, but silence seemed wisest. Silence, and speed.

They quickly dismantled the hatch's locking mechanism and disabled it, disconnecting the power source. It would need to be repaired before the hatch could be opened again. *Much stronger than the bathroom door on the* Delilah. The thought didn't comfort Hoop as much as it should have.

They worked backward, and when they'd disabled the door mechanism between docking arm and vestibule, Welford purged the atmosphere. The doors creaked slightly under the altered pressures.

Outside the vestibule, Sneddon waited.

"Done?" she asked.

"Just this last door," Hoop said. Welford went to work.

Five minutes later they were making their way back toward the bridge. There were now four sealed and locked doors standing between the *Samson* and the *Marion*, as well as a vacuum in the airlock.

He should have felt safer.

"Baxter, you still got a feed from the *Samson*?" he asked.

"Yeah. Not much change, those things are just sitting there. One of them… it sort of stretched for a while, like shadows were growing out of it. Weird lighting in there, and the picture's not great, but it looked like it was shedding its skin."

Another voice muttered something that Hoop missed.

"What was that?" he said.

"I said it looks like it's *grown*," Powell said. "The one that shed its skin. It's bigger."

"What about Jones?" Hoop asked, deeply troubled. *Bigger?* Impossible in such a short time, surely.

"Still there," Baxter said. "I can only see his arm, shoulder, head. He's still shaking."

"Record the images," Sneddon said.

"For later viewing pleasure?" Lachance asked, but no one replied. No time for humor, even if it was tinged with sarcasm.

"We'll be back in a few minutes," Hoop said. "Lachance, get the computer to categorize damage. I'll prioritize when we get there, then we'll pull together a work schedule. Baxter, has a distress signal gone out?"

"Oh, yeah, that's the other fun bit," Baxter said. "Some of the wreckage must have fucked the antenna array. So the computer says the signal is transmitting, but I don't think it is."

"Right. Great. Fucking wonderful." Hoop shook his head. "Any meteors heading toward us? Black holes opening up? Anything else to worry about?"

"The bridge's coffee carafe was smashed," Powell said, his voice deep and deadly serious.

Hoop started laughing. By the time he got his hysteria under control, tears smeared the inside of his helmet's visor.

By the time they reached the bridge, Kasyanov and Garcia had made their way back from the medical bay. The few personnel left aboard the *Marion* were either dead or sporting minor injuries, so there was little for them to do down there.

"It was creepy, just the two of us," Garcia said. "So we shut everything down. Figured it would be safer up here, with everyone together."

Just how safe that might be, Lachance revealed to them all.

"The only blessing is that the *Delilah*'s fuel core wasn't compromised during the crash," he said.

"So where is it?" Hoop asked.

Lachance was still in his pilot's seat. "Out there somewhere," he said, "floating around." He waved his hand, a cigar clutched between two fingers. Hoop and most of the others hated the stink of the things. But with everything that had happened, it seemed almost comical to ask him to put it out.

"We saw plenty of wreckage close to the ship," Welford said. "Maybe it *was* compromised and it's just floating somewhere nearby, overheating and ready to blow."

"In which case, *c'est la vie*," Lachance said. "Unless you want to throw on a suit and take a space walk." Welford looked away, and Lachance smiled. "And anyway, we have more immediate concerns—things we *can* do something about."

"The *Samson*?" Powell asked.

Hoop looked at the screens. The interior of the dropship was unchanged: shadows. Shadows flickered, Jones shook. They all wanted to turn it off, but Hoop had insisted keeping it on. They needed to know.

Lachance shrugged.

"We have to consider that safe, for now. But the sensors have identified atmosphere leaks in five blast doors, which probably means another five we don't know about. Decks five and six have vented completely into space, and the damage will need to be isolated and repaired. The chunk of the *Delilah* that's caught onto the ruin of the docking bays needs freeing and sending on its way. Otherwise it'll cause more damage."

"And the *Marion*'s positioning?" Hoop asked.

"Decaying. I'm… not sure there's much we can do about it. The crash has damaged more of the ship than we can see. I suspect there's some severe structural trauma. And it appears as if both fuel cell coolant systems have been damaged."

"Oh, great," Powell said.

"How bad?" Hoop asked.

"That's something that needs checking manually," Lachance said. "But there's more. Heaven has been corrupted."

"What with?" Hoop asked. His heart sank. Heaven was their bio pod, a small but lush food-growing compound in the *Marion*'s nose section, where many of the miners and crew went for their green therapy. After years in space—and working down in the sterile, sand-blasted hell of LV178—the sight of a carrot head or a wall of green beans did more than any drug cocktail to alleviate depression.

"I'm not sure yet," Lachance said. "Jordan was the one who…"

Lucy loved her gardening, Hoop thought. They'd made love in Heaven once, down on the damp soil with only the fruit trees and vegetable patches bearing witness.

"We have dried foods," Hoop said. "Is the water storage undamaged?"

"As far as I can tell."

"Okay, then." He looked around at the remainder of *Marion*'s crew. They were all shocked by how quickly and badly everything had gone to shit. But they were also hard, adaptable people, used to living with constant dangers and ready to confront the impossible to survive. "Welford, Powell, get the full damage report from Lachance and prioritize. We'll need help. All of you can use spanners and push welding kit."

"But there's something else to do first," Baxter said.

"Yep. And that's down to me. I'll record the distress signal, then you do everything you can to make sure it's sent."

Looking across Baxter's control panel, Hoop's gaze rested on the screen that was still showing the *Samson*'s interior. Jones's shoulder and head was the only thing moving, shivering in the bottom left corner. Beyond lay the motionless shadows of dead people. Sitting beside them, those small, indistinct aliens.

"And I think you can turn that off," Hoop said. "For now."

3

R I P L E Y

PROGRESS REPORT:
To: Weyland-Yutani Corporation, Science Division
(Ref: code 937)
Date (unspecified)
Transmission (pending)

Distress signal received. Sufficiently relevant to divert.
Expected travel time to LV178:
Current speed: 4,423 days.
Full speed: 77 days.
Fuel inventory: 92%
Initiating thrust.

She dreams of monsters.

Sharp, black, chitinous, sleek, vicious, hiding in shadows and pouncing, seeding themselves in people she loved—her ex-husband, her sweet daughter—and then bursting forth in showers of far too much blood. They expand too quickly, as if rapidly brought in close from distances she can barely comprehend. And as they are drawn nearer through the voids of deep space they are growing, growing—the size of a ship, a moon, a planet, and then larger still.

They will swallow the universe, and yet they will still leave her alive to witness its consumption.

She dreams of monsters, stalking the corridors of her mind and wiping faces from memory before she can even remember their names.

In between these dreams lies a simple void of shadows. But it offers no respite, because there is always a before to mourn, and an after to dread.

When she starts to wake at last, Ripley's nightmares scuttle back into the shadows and begin to fade away. But only partly. Even as light dawns across her dreams, the shadows remain.

Waiting.

"Dallas," Ripley said.

"What?"

She smacked her lips together, tried to cough past her dry throat, and realized that it couldn't be. Dallas was dead. The alien had taken him.

The face before her was thin, bearded, and troubled. Unknown.

He stared at her.

"Dallas, as in Texas?" he asked.

"Texas?" Her thoughts were a mess. A stew of random memories, some of which she recognized, some she did not. She struggled to pull them together, desperate for a clue as to who and where she was. She felt disassociated from her body. Floating impressions trying to find a home, her physical self a cold, loose thing over which she had no control.

Behind everything loomed a shadow… huge, insidious.

"Great," the man said. "Just fucking great."

"Huh?" Was she back on *Nostromo*? But then she remembered the blazing star that massive salvage ship had become. Rescue, then?

Someone had found her. The shuttle had been retrieved and boarded. She was saved.

She was Ellen Ripley, and soon she'd be reunited with—

Something moved across her stomach. A flood of images assaulted her, so vivid compared to those she'd had since waking that they startled her into movement and kicked her senses alive—

—*Kane thrashing, his chest ripping and bursting open, that thing emerging*—

—and she reached to her own chest, ready to feel the stretching skin and the agony of ribs rupturing outward.

"Hey, hey," the man said, reaching for her.

Don't you understand what's going to happen? She wanted to shout, but her voice was trapped, her mouth so dry that her tongue felt like a swollen, sand-coated slug. He held her shoulders and stroked her chin with both thumbs. It was such a gentle, intimate gesture that she paused in her writhing.

"You've got a cat," he said, smiling. The smile suited his face, yet it looked uncomfortable, as if he rarely used it.

"Jonesy," Ripley rasped painfully, and the cat crawled up from her stomach to her chest. It stood there, swaying slightly, then arched its back and clenched its claws. They scratched Ripley's skin through her thin vest and she winced, but it was a good feeling. A pain that told her she was still alive.

She reached for Jonesy, and as she stroked him a feeling of immense well-being came over her. She had risen up out of the shadows, and now that she was home—or near to home, if she had been recovered by a larger ship—then she would do her best to leave them behind. The terrible, mournful memories were already crowding in, but they were just that. Memories.

The future was a wide-open place.

"They found us," she whispered to the cat as he growled softly in his throat. Her arms barely felt like her own, but she could feel fur against her fingertips and palms. Jonesy stretched against her. She wondered if cats could have nightmares.

"We're safe now…"

She thought of Amanda, her daughter, and how pleased they would be to see each other. Had Ripley missed her eleventh birthday? She sincerely hoped not, because she hated breaking a promise.

Sitting up slowly, the man helping her, she groaned as her nerves came to life. It was the worst case of pins and needles ever, far worse than she'd ever had following any previous hypersleep. Upright, she sat as motionless as possible as the circulation returned, her singing nerve endings finally falling silent.

And then the man spoke.

"Actually… you're not really that safe, to be honest."

"What?"

"I mean, we're not a rescue ship. We thought *you* were the rescue ship when we first saw you on our scopes. Thought maybe you'd answered our distress signal. But…" He trailed off, and when Ripley looked up she saw two other figures behind him in the shuttle's confined interior. They stood back against the wall, warily eyeing her and the stasis pod.

"You're kidding me," one of them, a woman, said.

"Can it, Sneddon." The man held out his hand. "My name's Hoop. Can you stand?"

"Where am I?" Ripley asked.

"Nowhere you want to be, that's for sure," the man behind Hoop said. He was very tall, thin, gaunt. "Go back to sleep, Miss. Sweet dreams."

"And that's Powell," Hoop said. "Don't mind them. Let's get you to med bay. Garcia can clean you up and check you over. Looks like you need feeding, too."

Ripley frowned, and her mouth instantly grew dry again. Her stomach rumbled. She felt dizzy. She grabbed the side of the stasis pod, and as she slowly slung her leg over the rim and tried to stand, Hoop held her arm. His hand seems incredibly warm, wonderfully real. But his words hung with her.

Jonesy snuggled back down into the foot of the stasis pod, as if eager to find sleep again. *Maybe cats really do know everything*, she mused.

"Where…?" Ripley asked again, but then the shuttle began to spin, and as she fainted the shadows closed in once more.

Garcia was a small, attractive woman who had a habit of laughing softly after everything she said. But Ripley didn't think it was an endemic shyness. The ship's medic was nervous.

"You're on the *Marion*," she said. "Orbital mining freighter. We work for the Kelland Mining Company. They're owned by Prospectia, who are a sub-division of San Rei Corporation, who are—like pretty much everything—owned by Weyland-Yutani." She shrugged, chuckled. "Our ship's built for harvesting large core deposits, really—the holds are huge and there are four extendable towing decks stacked back beneath the engine room. But we mine trimonite. Hardest substance known to man. It's fifteen times harder than diamond, and extremely rare. We have little more than three tons of it on board."

"What's the problem with the ship?" Ripley asked. She was still tired, and feeling sick, but she had her wits about her again. And she knew something here was very wrong.

Garcia glanced aside, her laughter almost silent.

"Couple of mechanical issues." She reached for some more sterile gel and started rubbing it along Ripley's forearm.

"Are we heading home?"

"Home?" Garcia asked.

"The solar system. Earth."

The medic suddenly looked scared. She shook her head.

"Hoop said to treat you, that's all." She started working on Ripley again, chattering away to cover her nervousness, talking inconsequentialities, and Ripley let her. If Garcia could somehow make her stop feeling so shitty, it was a small price to pay.

Time to rest a little, perhaps, before she found out what the hell was going on.

"Saline drip," Garcia said, picking up a needle. "Old world medicine, but it'll aid rehydration and have you feeling much more energetic in half an hour. Small scratch." She slid the needle expertly into a vein on Ripley's arm and taped it in place. "I'd recommend small amounts of liquid food to begin with—your stomach hasn't dealt with food for so long, and its lining has become quite sensitive."

"So long?" Ripley asked.

A pause, a small laugh.

"Soup. Lachance makes a good soup, for such a cynical bastard.

He's in the galley now." She went to a cupboard and brought back a white bag. "We have some clothes for you. I had to dispose of your underwear, I'm afraid."

Ripley lifted the sheet covering her and realized she was naked. On purpose? Maybe they didn't want her just getting up and running around.

"Thanks," she said. "I'll dress now."

"Not yet," Garcia said, dropping the bag and shoving it beneath the bed with her foot. "More tests. I'm still checking your liver and kidney functions. Your pulse seems fine but your lung capacity appears to be reduced, probably due to holding a sleep pattern for so…" She turned away again to a medicine table. "I have some pills and medicines for you to take."

"What for?"

"To make you better."

"I'm not ill." Ripley looked past Garcia and around the med bay. It was small, only six beds, and some of it looked basic. But there were also several hi-tech pieces of equipment that she didn't recognize, including one sizeable medical pod in the center of the room bearing a familiar name badge on the side.

A cold hand closed around Ripley's heart.

I was expendable, she thought. She felt a fierce pride, and an anger, at being the only survivor.

"You didn't say you were actually a Weyland-Yutani vessel."

"What?" She followed Ripley's gaze. "Oh, no, we're not. Not officially. I told you, our company is Kelland Mining, an offshoot of San Rei. But Weyland-Yutani makes a lot of equipment used in deep space exploration. Difficult to find a ship without something of theirs on it. And to be honest, their med pods are just about the best I've ever seen. They can do amazing stuff, we once had a miner with—"

"They're a big company?"

"The biggest," Garcia said. "They practically *own* space. The parent company owns countless others, and San Rei was bought up by them… don't know, maybe twelve years ago? I was working at Kelland's Io headquarters then, hadn't gone out on any flights.

It didn't change much, but it did open our eyes to all the diverse missions that were being launched." She chattered on as she prepared medicines, counted out pills, and Ripley let her.

"They're investing in terraforming companies now, you know? They set up massive atmosphere processing plants on suitable planets, do something to the air—clean it, treat it, I don't know, I'm a medic—and it takes decades. Then there's materials acquisition, prospecting, mining. I've heard they've built massive ships, miles long, that catch and tow small asteroids. Loads of research stations, too. Medical, scientific, military. Weyland-Yutani have their fingers in lots of pies."

Maybe times haven't changed so much, Ripley thought, and it was the measure of "times" that was bothering her. She sat up and slipped one leg out of bed, pushing Garcia aside.

"I feel fine," she insisted. The sheet dropped from her and Garcia looked away, embarrassed. Ripley used the advantage and stood, reaching down for the bag of clothes.

"Oh…" A voice said. She looked up. Hoop stood at the entrance to the medical bay, staring at her nakedness for just a few seconds too long before looking away. "Shit, sorry, I thought you were—"

"Safe in bed where you want me?" Ripley said. "Asking no questions?"

"Please," Hoop said without turning. He didn't elaborate, but Ripley sat back down. In truth, she did so before she fell down, because she still felt like crap. She propped up the pillow and tucked the sheet beneath her arms.

"You're safe to look now," she said.

Hoop smiled and came to sit on the foot of her bed.

"How are you feeling?"

"Tell me what's going on, and I'll decide."

Hoop glanced at Garcia, who nodded.

"Yeah, she's fine," the medic acknowledged.

"See?" Ripley said. *Fine,* apart from the sick feeling of dread in her stomach.

"Okay," Hoop said. "So, here it is. You've hardly been rescued. We spotted your shuttle on our scanners just over fifteen hours ago. You were on a controlled approach."

"Controlled by whom?"

Hoop shrugged.

"You drifted in, circled the *Marion* once, then docked at the one docking arm we have left." Something passed across his face then.

That's something else to ask about, Ripley thought, *if he doesn't volunteer it. The docking arm.*

"The shuttle has proximity protocols," she said.

"Auto docking?"

"If it's programed to do so."

"Okay, well, that's academic now. Our situation—and now yours—is... pretty grim." He paused, as if to gather his thoughts. "We suffered a collision eleven weeks ago. Lost a lot of our people. It's knocked us out of geostationary orbit, and we're now in a decaying pattern. We figure less than fifteen days before we start burning up in the atmosphere."

"Atmosphere of what?"

"LV178. A rock."

"The planet you're mining for trimonite," Ripley said, and she was amused at the look Hoop threw Garcia. "It's okay, she didn't tell me anything else. Like, anything important."

Hoop held out his hands.

"That's it. Our antenna array was damaged, so we couldn't send any long-distance distress signals. But after the collision we sent a call for help on a high frequency transmitter, and it's still being transmitted on a loop. Hoping it would be picked up by someone within rescue distance." He frowned. "You didn't hear it?"

"Sorry," she replied. "I was taking a nap."

"Of course." Hoop looked away, stroking his hands together. Two other people entered med bay, both of them ragged, unkempt. She recognized Kasyanov, the dark-skinned ship's doctor who had given her the initial examination. But the man she didn't know. Heavily built, a sad, saggy face—his name tag said Baxter. He sat on another bed and stared at her.

"Hi," she said. He only nodded.

"So what happened to you?" Hoop asked.

Ripley closed her eyes and a rush of memories flooded in—the planet, Kane, the alien's birth, its rapid growth, and then the terror and loss on the *Nostromo* before her escape in the shuttle. That final confrontation with the devil. The memories shocked her with their violence, their immediacy. It was as if the past was more real than the present.

"I was on a towing vessel," she said. "Crew died in an accident, the ship's core went into meltdown. I'm the only one who got away."

"*Nostromo*," Hoop said.

"How do you know that?"

"I accessed the shuttle's computer. I remember reading about your ship, actually, when I was a kid. It's gone down in the 'lost without trace' files."

Ripley blinked.

"How long was I out there?" But she already knew the answer was going to be difficult. She'd seen that in Garcia's reaction, and saw it again now in Hoop.

"Thirty-seven years."

Ripley looked down at her hands, the needles in her forearms.

I haven't aged a day, she thought. And then she pictured Amanda, her sweet daughter who'd hated the idea that she was going away, even for seventeen months. *It'll make things so easy for us when I get back*, Ripley had told her, hugging her tight. *Here, look*. She'd pointed at Amanda's computer screen and scrolled through a calendar there. *Your eleventh birthday. I'll be back for that, and I'll buy you the best present ever*.

"Going to tell her about *Samson*?" Baxter said.

Ripley looked around the room.

"Who's Samson?"

No one replied.

Baxter shrugged and walked across to her bed, laying a tablet computer on the sheet.

"Fine," he said. "Easier to show her, anyway." He tapped an icon.

"The *Samson* is locked into our other surviving docking arm. Has been for seventy-seven days. It's sealed. These things are inside, and they're also the reason we're fucked."

He swiped the screen.

At that moment, Ripley doubted everything. The fact that she was awake. Her being there, the feel of sheets against her skin, and the sharp prick of needles in her arms. She doubted the idea that she had survived at all, and hoped that this was simply her dying nightmare.

"Oh, no," she breathed, and the atmosphere in the room changed instantly.

She started to shake. When she blinked her dreams were close again, the shadowy monsters the size of the stars. *So was it just a dream?* she wondered. *A nightmare?* She looked around at these people she did not know, and as panic bit in she wondered where they could have come from.

"No," she said, her dry throat burning. "Not here!"

Kasyanov shouted something, Garcia held her down, and another sharp pain bit into the back of her hand.

But even as everything faded away, there was no peace to be found.

"She knew what they were," Hoop said.

They were back on the bridge. Kasyanov and Garcia had remained in med bay to keep Ripley under observation, with orders to call him back down the moment she stirred. He wanted to be there for her. Such an ordeal she'd suffered, and now she'd woken into something worse.

Besides that, she might be able to help.

"Maybe she'll know how to kill them," Baxter said.

"Maybe," Hoop said. "Maybe not. At the very least, she recognized them from that." He nodded at the monitor. It held the final image they'd gleaned from the *Samson*'s internal camera. Then they'd lost contact, thirty days ago.

Jones had been long-dead by then. The things had dragged him back into the passenger hold and killed him. They'd grown into dark, shadowy shapes that none of them could quite make out. The size of a person, maybe even larger, the four shapes remained all but motionless. It made them even more difficult to see on the badly lit image.

Baxter scrolled back through the views of Bay Three—images they'd all come to know so well. The trio of cameras Welford and Powell had set up showed the same as ever—no movement, no sign of disturbance. The doors remained locked and solid. Microphones picked up no noise. They'd lost view of the inside of *Samson*, but at least they could still keep watch.

And if those things did smash through the doors, and burst out of the docking bay? They had a plan. But none of them had much faith in it.

"I'll go and see how Powell and Welford are getting on," Hoop said. "Shout if there's anything from med bay."

"Why do you think she came here?" Baxter said.

"I'm not sure she knows." Hoop picked up the plasma torch he'd taken to carrying, slung it over his shoulder, and left the bridge.

The torch was a small, handheld version, used in the mines for melting and hardening sand deposits. The biggest ones they had down there ran on rails, and were used for forming the solid walls of new mine shafts—blast the sand, melt it, and it hardened again into ten-inch-thick slabs. The smaller torches could be wielded by a miner to fix breaches.

Or, Hoop thought, to drive away unwanted guests.

He didn't know if it would work, and he'd seen the effects when one had been discharged in the *Delilah*. But in the larger confines of *Marion*, if one of those things came at him, he'd be ready.

Sneddon was in the science lab. She spent a lot of time in there now, and sometimes when Hoop paid her a visit he felt as if he was intruding. She'd always been a quiet woman, and quietly attractive, and Hoop had often enjoyed talking to her about the scientific aspects of their work. She'd once worked for Weyland-Yutani on one of their research bases orbiting Proxima Centauri. Though she didn't work directly for them any more, the company still funded science officers on many ships, and for any sub-divisional company who wanted them. The funding was very generous, and it would often go a large way toward bankrolling a mission.

He liked Sneddon. He liked her dedication to her work, and her apparent love of it. *It's an endless, wonderful playground out there*, she'd said once when he asked her what she hoped to find. *Anything is possible.*

Now Sneddon's childlike imagination had taken a hit.

At the same time, Hoop's childhood dreams had found reality.

When he reached the lab, Sneddon was sitting on a stool at the large central island. There were a couple of tablet computers in front of her, and a steaming mug of coffee. She held her head in her hands, elbows resting on the counter top.

"Hey," Hoop said.

She looked up, startled.

"Oh. Didn't hear you."

"Everything cool?"

Sneddon smiled softly. "Despite the fact that we're slowly spiraling to our deaths, set to crash on a lifeless sand-hell of a planet? Yes, everything's cool."

He smiled wryly.

"So what do you think about Ripley?"

"It's obvious she's seen these things before," Sneddon replied, a frown wrinkling her forehead. "Where, how, when, why, I haven't got the faintest clue. But I'd like to talk to her."

"If you think it'll help."

"Help?" Sneddon asked. She looked confused.

"You know what I mean," Hoop said. He laid the plasma torch gently on the bench.

"Well, I've been thinking about that," she said, smiling. "I know you're in charge, and I'm pretty sure I know what you've been thinking these past few days."

"Do you, now?" Hoop asked, amused. He liked that she smiled. There were far too few smiles nowadays.

"Escape pods," Sneddon said. "Maybe try to regulate their nav computers, land within walking distance of each other and the mine."

Hoop drummed his fingers on the bench.

"Reach there together, there'll be enough food and supplies down there for a couple of years."

"And those things, too."

"Forewarned is forearmed," Hoop said.

"With that?" Sneddon said, nudging the plasma torch. Her bitter laugh wiped the smile from her face.

"There might not be any more things down there at all. They might have all come up on the *Delilah*."

"Or there might be a dozen, or more." Sneddon stood and started pacing. "Think about it. They were hatching from the miners. We saw that. Just… breaking out of them. Implanted by those things attached to their faces, perhaps. I don't know. But if that is the case, we have to assume that anyone left behind was infected."

"Sixteen on the *Delilah*. Six on the *Samson*."

Sneddon nodded.

"So eighteen left in the mine," Hoop said.

"I'd rather go down on the *Marion*," Sneddon said, "if it came to that. But now it doesn't have to."

"You know something I don't?"

"No, but maybe I'm thinking about things in a different way."

Hoop frowned, held out his hands.

"And?"

"Her shuttle. It's a deep space shuttle! Used for short-distance transfers of personnel, or as a long-term lifeboat."

"And one stasis pod for nine of us."

"Doesn't matter," Sneddon said. "Look." She slid one of the tablets across to Hoop. At first he didn't really understand what he was seeing. It was an old, old image of a lifeboat. Lost at sea back on Earth, crammed with survivors, a sail rigged from shirts and broken oars, wretched people hanging over the side, or eating fish, or squeezing drinking water from hastily rigged moisture catchers.

"Today, I'm stupid," Hoop said. "In charge, yes. But stupid. So just tell me."

"One stasis pod between the nine of us," Sneddon said. "But we pack the shuttle with as many supplies as we can. Program a course toward Earth, or at the very least the outer rim. Fire the engines until the fuel's out and we're traveling as fast as we can. A good proportion of light speed. Then… take turns in the stasis pod."

"Take turns?" he said. "She's been drifting out there for thirty-seven years!"

"Yeah, but something's very wrong with that. I haven't checked yet, but the shuttle computer must have malfunctioned."

"There was no indication of that when I checked its log."

"You didn't go deep enough, Hoop. The point is, we can *survive* like that. Six months at a time, one of us in stasis, eight others… surviving."

"Six months in a tightly confined space? That shuttle's designed for five people, max, for short trips. Eight of us? We'll end up killing each other." He shook his head. "And how long do you figure it'll take?"

Sneddon raised an eyebrow.

"Well… years."

"Years?"

"Maybe three until we reach the outer rim, and then—"

"It's impossible!" he said.

Sneddon tapped the tablet's screen again, and Hoop looked. She'd certainly done her homework. Examples manifested and faded on the screen—lifeboats at sea, strandings on damaged orbitals, miraculous survivals dotting the history of space disasters. None of the timescales were quite what Sneddon was describing, but each story testified to the will of desperate people to survive, whatever the situation.

However hopeless.

"We'd need to check the shuttle's systems," he said. "Fuel cell, life support."

"And you're chief engineer, aren't you?"

Hoop laughed. "You're serious about this."

"Yes."

He stared at her for a while, trying to deny the shred of hope she'd planted in him. He couldn't afford to grab hold of it.

"Rescue isn't coming, Hoop," she said. "Not in time."

"Yeah," he said. "I know."

"So you'll—"

"Hoop!" Kasyanov's voice cut in over the intercom. "Ripley's stirring. I could sedate her again, but I really don't want to pump her full of any more drugs."

Hoop leapt to the wall and hit the intercom button.

"No, don't. She's slept enough. I'll be right down." He smiled at Sneddon, and then nodded. "I'll speak to Ripley, get her access codes."

As he left the science lab and headed for med bay, the ship's corridors seemed lighter than they had in a long time.

4

9 3 7

Not only was she still light years from home, but she'd docked with a damaged ship in a decaying orbit around a hellhole of a planet, alongside a dropship full of the monsters that haunted her nightmares.

Ripley might have laughed at the irony.

She'd successfully shaken the idea that it was a dream, or a nightmare—it had taken time, and convincing herself hadn't been easy—but the explanation still eluded her.

How was this all possible?

Perhaps the answers were on her shuttle.

"Really, I'm ready to walk," she said. Kasyanov—a tall, fit woman who obviously looked after herself—shot her a disapproving look, but Ripley could see that the doctor held a grudging respect for her patient's stubbornness.

"You've barely walked for thirty-seven years," Kasyanov protested.

"Thanks for reminding me. But as far as my body's concerned, it was yesterday." She'd already stood from her bed and dressed while Kasyanov and Garcia were elsewhere, determined to prove herself to them. And she'd been pleased at how good she actually felt. The sedative was still wearing off, but beneath that she was starting to feel her old self again. Whatever Garcia had done for her—the saline drip, the other drugs—was working.

"Patients," Kasyanov said, rolling her eyes.

"Yeah, who'd be one, right?" Ripley stood from the bed, and as she was tying the boots that had been given to her, Hoop breezed into the bay.

"Oh, you're dressed." He feigned disappointment, then said, "You're looking good!"

Ripley looked up and raised an eyebrow. "I'm twice your age."

"I've had a few long trips myself, you know," he replied without missing a beat. "Maybe one day we can have a drink, compare sleeps?" He smiled as he spoke, but maybe he was a little bit serious, too.

Ripley laughed despite herself. Then she remembered. The image was never far away, but for a few seconds here and there she could forget. A burst of laughter, a smile, a friendly comment would hide the memory beneath the mundane.

"I'd like to take a look at the *Narcissus*," Hoop said.

"You and me both."

"You haven't spent long enough in it already?"

Ripley stood and stretched. She was tall, lithe, and she enjoyed the feel of her muscles finding their flexibility again. The aches and pains meant she was awake and mobile.

"I've got some questions for the computer," she said. "Like why the hell it brought me to this shit hole."

"Thanks," Hoop said.

"You're welcome."

Ripley saw the doctor and medic exchange glances, but couldn't quite read them. She hadn't yet worked out the dynamic there. Kasyanov, as the doctor, was clearly in charge of med bay. But she also appeared nervous, scared, and Garcia seemed to be the one most at ease.

"Come on," Hoop said. "I'll walk you to the docking bay."

They left med bay together, and Hoop remained silent. *Waiting for my questions*, Ripley thought. She had so many. But she was afraid that once she started asking, none of the answers could satisfy, and nothing he said would be good.

"You say you don't know why you docked with us?" Hoop asked finally.

"I was asleep when the shuttle docked, you know that." Something troubled Ripley, nudging at her consciousness like a memory trying to nose its way in. A suspicion. An explanation. But her mind still hadn't completely recovered from hypersleep, and she didn't think she'd like what it had to say. "What's that?" she asked, nodding at the heavy object draped over Hoop's shoulder. It looked like a stumpy, box-shaped gun.

"Plasma torch," he said. "In case they get free."

Ripley laughed. It burst from her in a rush, like she was vomiting disbelief, and she couldn't stop. Her eyes burned. Tears ran down her face. She thought of Hoop trying to scorch an alien with his box-gun, and the laughter turned hysterical. Between breaths it sounded like she was trying to scream, and when she felt Hoop's hands on her shoulders she lashed out at him, seeing only his shadow through tear-distorted eyes—long arms, spiky edges.

She saw an alien bearing down and clasping her to its chest, that long curved head raising, mouth sprouting the silvery, deadly teeth that would smash through her skull and free her at last from her nightmares.

"Ripley!" Hoop shouted.

She knew who he was, where she was, but the shakes had set in. Trying to believe they were physiological, she knew the truth. She was scared. Properly, completely fucking terrified.

"That?" she said, gasping and swiping at the plasma torch. "You really think…? Have you seen one of them, close up?"

"No," he said softly. "None of us have."

"No, of course not," Ripley said. "You're still alive." The hands squeezed harder and she leaned into him. To her own surprise, she welcomed his embrace, his smell, the feel of his rough beard against her neck and cheek. She took great comfort from the contact. It made her think of Dallas.

"But you have," he said.

Ripley remembered the time in the shuttle, moments after the

Nostromo had bloomed into nuclear nothingness and she'd believed it was all over. The alien, slow and lazy for reasons she didn't understand, but for which she gave thanks. *Because it's just fed?* she'd wondered at the time, Parker and Lambert fresh in her mind. *Because it thinks it's safe?*

She nodded against his shoulder.

"Where?" he asked, quietly but with urgency. "When?"

"I can't answer that right now," she whispered. "I... I don't understand. But soon I will." She pulled back from him, wiped angrily at her eyes. It wasn't appearing weak in front of him that troubled her—it was feeling weak in *herself*. She'd seen that thing off, blasted it into space, and she should no longer be afraid. "The shuttle. There are answers there."

"Okay," Hoop said. He looked down at the plasma torch, went to shrug it off.

"No," Ripley said, pressing her hand over his on the torch's barrel. "It *might* help."

Hoop nodded, frowning. *He's seen some stuff himself*, she thought. Maybe once she'd found out exactly how and why she was here, the two of them could talk properly.

"Right," he said. "Besides, we're passing close to the docked dropship."

"But everything's secure," Ripley said. "Isn't it?"

"We're keeping a close eye on things," Hoop said, nodding. "The image we showed you is the last we've seen inside the *Samson*. But it's safe."

"Safe," Ripley said, trying the word. On this dying ship it seemed so out of place.

Hoop led the way, and at the end of a corridor they turned to go right. He nodded to the left, where a heavy bulkhead door had been welded shut with a dri-metal seal. "The *Delilah* crashed into the ship through there, taking out Bays One and Two. We were lucky the fuel cell didn't rupture, but we had to cut it loose afterward. It was snagged on the wrecked superstructure, wrapped up a load of other tattered ship parts. Me, Welford, and Powell went out there and spent three hours with cutting torches. Shoved it aside. When we came back inside we watched for an hour while it floated away."

"And this way?" Ripley asked, pointing right. They continued, and she noticed Hoop taking a tighter grip on the plasma torch.

"Bay Three's through there," he said, nodding toward a door. Its control panel had been removed and wires and connectors hung loose.

"What's with that?" Ripley asked.

"No way of opening it without fixing the controls."

"Or smashing the door down."

"That's six-inch triple-layered polymer-inlaid steel," Hoop said. "And there are three more doors and a vented airlock between here and the *Samson*."

Ripley only nodded. But the word "safe" still eluded her.

"Come on," Hoop said. "Your shuttle's through here."

Ripley was surprised at how comforted she felt, ducking through Bay Four's open airlock and entering the *Narcissus*. She had no good memories of the vessel—only of the alien, and her terror that it would take her, too. But Jonesy was there, snuggled up in the open stasis pod as if still in hypersleep. And there were memories of the *Nostromo* and her crew. Dead for almost four decades, now, but to Ripley it felt like yesterday.

Parker, slaughtered on the floor. Lambert, hanging where the alien had slung her after ripping a hole through her face. All that blood.

"You okay?" Hoop asked.

Ripley nodded. Then she moved through the cramped shuttle and sat in the pilot's seat. She was aware of Hoop walking, slowly, around the shuttle as she ran her fingers across the keyboard and initiated the computer. Mother was gone, but the *Narcissus*'s computers still had a similarly constructed interface, designed so that the user felt as if they were actually talking to a friend. With technologies that could make an android like Ash, it had always seemed strange to Ripley giving a faceless computer a human voice.

She entered her access code. *Morning, Narcissus*, she typed. The reply appeared onscreen.

Good morning, Warrant Officer Ripley.

Request reason for Narcissus's *change of course.*

Information withheld.

"Huh," Ripley said.

"Everything okay?" Hoop asked. He was examining the stasis pod she'd spent so long in, stroking Jonesy who was slinking back and forth with his back arched, tail stretched. He might well have been the oldest cat in the galaxy.

"Sure," she replied.

Hoop nodded, glanced toward the computer screen, and then started looking around the rest of the shuttle's interior.

Request records of incoming signals received over the past one thousand days. Ripley expected a streaming list of information—space was filled with beamed communications, and most ship's computers logged and discarded them if they were not relevant.

That information also withheld.

Request replay of distress signal received from Deep Space Mining Orbital Marion.

That information also withheld.

"Fuck you very much," Ripley muttered as she typed, *Because of Special Order 937?*

That reference does not compute.

Emergency Command Override 100375.

I'm afraid that Override code is no longer valid.

61

Ripley frowned. Tapped her fingers beside the keyboard. Stared at the words on the screen. Even Mother had never communicated in such a conversational tone. And this was just the shuttle's computer. Weird.

Request data of timescales and travel distances since Nostromo's *detonation?*

`That data unavailable.`

Unavailable or withheld?

The computer did not reply.

Such evasiveness wasn't possible from this machine. Not on its own. It was a functional system, not an AI like Mother. And Mother was gone.

The only other person who'd had access to Mother was Dallas. Dallas and…

…and after Dallas had been taken, and she'd quizzed Mother herself, she remembered her shock at that other presence in the computer room.

Screw you, Ash, Ripley typed.

The cursor blinked.

But the computer didn't respond. Not even a "Does not compute."

Ripley gasped. She hit the shutdown, and the text on the screen faded to a soft, background glow. Yet still she felt as if she was being watched. The computer's arrogant silence seemed to ring through the interior of the shuttle, almost mocking.

"What was in your distress signal?" Ripley asked abruptly.

Hoop was rooting around in the rear of the shuttle, examining the space suits still hanging in the locker back there.

"Huh?"

"The distress signal you sent after the crash!" Ripley said. "Did you mention those things? The creatures? Did you say what they were like, what they did?"

"I… Yeah, I think so."

"You *think* so?"

"It was more than ten weeks ago, Ripley. I recorded it hours after I'd seen lots of friends die, and witnessed what happened—"

"I need to hear it."

"What's wrong?"

She stood and backed away from the interface. It was stupid—there was no camera there—but she felt observed. She took off her jacket and dropped it across the screen.

"The alien on my ship wasn't an accident," she said. "And I don't think it's an accident that I've come here, either. But I need to know. I need to hear the signal."

Hoop nodded and came toward her.

"I can patch in from here," he said, nodding down at where her jacket covered the keyboard.

"You can?"

"I'm chief engineer on this jaunt, and that covers all the infotech systems, too."

Ripley stepped aside and watched as Hoop moved the jacket, sat, and worked at the interface. The words she saw on the screen—the interaction—seemed innocent enough.

Hoop chuckled.

"What is it?"

"These systems. Pretty old. I had more computing power than this to play VR games, when I was a kid."

"You don't see anything odd with the computer?"

"Odd?" He didn't look up, and Ripley didn't elaborate. "Here we are," he said. "I've patched into *Marion*'s computer, and here's the message. It's on a loop." He scanned the control panel, and Ripley leaned forward to switch to loudspeaker.

Hoop's voice came through. There was an edgy tone to it—the fear was palpable.

"… decaying orbit. Second dropship *Samson* is docked and isolated, those things in there hopefully contained. They… laid infants or eggs inside the miners, burst from their chests. We are not contaminated, repeat, *not* contaminated. Estimate ninety days until we hit LV178's atmosphere. All channels open, please respond. Ends.

"This is DSMO *Marion*, of the Kelland Company, registration HGY-64678, requesting immediate aid. Crew and mining teams down to eight surviving members. Miners discovered something on the surface of LV178, attacked, dropship *Delilah* crashed the *Marion*. Many systems damaged, environment stable but we are now in a decaying orbit. Second dropship *Samson* is docked and isolated…"

Hoop tapped the keyboard to turn off the replay, then glanced back at Ripley.

"Ash," she whispered.

"What's Ash?"

"Android. Weyland-Yutani. He was tasked with finding any alien life forms that might have been of interest to the company. His orders… crew expendable. My crew. Me." She stared at the computer again until Hoop dropped her jacket back across it. "He's gone, but he must have transferred part of his AI programing to the *Narcissus*.

He's here. He's in *here* now, and he brought me to you because of those aliens."

"I'm not sure it's possible that an AI could—"

"I should have been home," Ripley said, thinking of Amanda and her sad, wet eyes when she'd watched her mother leave. She hated herself for that. Even though she should have been home with her daughter for her eleventh birthday, and nothing that had happened was her fault, Ripley hated herself. "I should have never left."

"Well, maybe some good can come of this," Hoop said.

"Good?" Ripley said.

"Your shuttle. Sneddon and I think we can get away on it, all of us. And that'll leave the *Marion* and those fuckers on the *Samson* to burn up in the planet's atmosphere."

Ripley knew that for any extended voyage the shuttle was only suitable for one, with only a single stasis pod. But she didn't care. Any way to distance herself from those aliens—any way to deny Ash from fulfilling his Special Order—was good for her.

"Maybe," she said. "I'll run a systems check."

"You're not alone anymore, Ripley," Hoop said.

She blinked quickly, and nodded her thanks. Somehow, he seemed to know just what to say.

"You'll stay here with me for a while?"

Hoop feigned surprise.

"Do you have coffee?"

"No."

"Then my time here is limited." He stood away from the control desk and started looking around the shuttle again. It was cramped, confined—and way, way too small.

Ignoring the computer, Ripley started manual processing of systems information.

It only took three minutes to realize how screwed they were.

5

NARCISSUS

Hoop had worked with androids before. In the deep asteroid mines of Wilson's Scarps, they were often the first ones down and the last ones back. They'd been perfectly reasonable, amenable, quiet, honest, and strong. Safe. He couldn't say he'd liked them, exactly, but they'd never been dangerous or intimidating. Never scheming.

Occasionally he'd heard of malfunctions in some of the earlier military-grade androids, and there were unconfirmed reports—little more than rumors, really—that the military had suffered human losses as a result. But they were a different breed of android, designed for strength but with a built-in expiration date. They were easy to spot. Their designers hadn't been too concerned with aesthetics.

That must have been the case on *Nostromo*. And now, assuming Ripley was right, the AI had somehow followed her, and was still using her for its programed mission. As his team discussed their options, she looked wretched—taking in the conversation, looking at each crew member who expressed an opinion, and yet remaining silent. She smoked cigarette after cigarette, and drank coffee.

She must think she's still dreaming, he mused, *consumed by nightmares*. And every now and then she glanced across at him as if checking that he was on board with all of this.

Because it turned out that they were more royally screwed than any of them had thought.

The plan they were slowly forming—crazy as it was—seemed to be the only way out. It was a last chance, and they had no option but to grab it.

"You're sure about the timescales?" Powell asked. "Only a few days until we start skimming the atmosphere?"

"Sure as I can be," Lachance replied.

"I thought we had a couple of *weeks* left," Kasyanov said, voice raised as fear clasped her.

"Sorry. I lost my crystal ball in the collision." Lachance rested in the pilot's chair, turned around to face them all. The rest sat or stood around the bridge, in seats or leaning against equipment terminals. It was the first time Ripley had been with all eight of them together, but Hoop couldn't sense any nervousness in her. If anything, she was too distracted for that.

"And there's nothing you guys can do?" Kasyanov said, looking at Powell, Welford, and then Hoop. He didn't like the accusation in her eyes, as if they hadn't done their best. "I mean, you're engineers."

"Kasyanov, I think I've made it pretty clear," Lachance said. "Our attitude control is damaged beyond repair, retro capability is down to thirty percent. Several containment bulkheads are cracked, and there's a good chance if we initiate thrust we'll just flash-fry ourselves with radiation." He paused briefly.

"We *do* still have coffee, though. That's one positive."

"How do we know all that's true?" Kasyanov asked. "It's getting desperate here. We should go outside, look again at all the damage."

"You know because I'm the best pilot who's ever worked for Kelland," Lachance said. "And the fact that Hoop, Welford, and Powell have kept us all alive for this long is a fucking miracle. Fixing the hull breaches, repressurizing the vented sections of the ship. *That's* why you know it's true."

Kasyanov started to say some more, but Garcia put a hand on her arm. Hoop didn't think she even squeezed—just the contact was enough to silence the doctor.

"However much we wish it wasn't true, it is," Hoop said. "And we've got no more time to waste. We think we have a plan, but it's not going to be easy."

"Who's 'we'?" Kasyanov asked.

"Me, Sneddon, Ripley."

"Ripley? The stranger who just woke up from half-a-century of snoozing? What's *she* got to do with this?"

Ripley glanced across at Kasyanov, then away again, looking down at the coffee cup in her hand. Hoop waited for her to speak, but she remained silent.

"This isn't a conspiracy, Kasyanov," he said. "Hear us out."

The doctor drew in a breath and seemed to puff herself up, ready to say something else, challenge him some more. But then she nodded.

"I'm sorry, Hoop... everyone. Just so strung out." She and Ripley exchanged weak smiles.

"We all are," Hoop said. "It's been over seventy days, waiting for some sign that our signal's been picked up, acknowledged and relayed onward, and that someone's coming for us. Maybe the frequency's been frazzled, and we're just coming through as background fuzz. Or maybe someone's heard us, but we're too far out, and it's too expensive to mount a rescue."

"Or there's just not the time," Baxter said. "Changing course, plotting a route, estimating the fuel requirements. Anyone who did catch the signal would have a lot to do before they even got here."

"Right," Hoop said. "So we're running out of time, and now we've got to help ourselves. More than we have been. More than just patching up problems while we wait."

"Escape pods?" Powell asked.

"We've talked about that," Lachance said, waving the suggestion aside.

"Yeah," Sneddon said. "That's just a slow death. We're in a drifting orbit now, and even if we could rig a way to steer the pods more accurately, to land as close to the mine as possible, we could still go down miles away. We'd be scattered, alone, and vulnerable."

"The *Samson*, then." Baxter had mentioned this before, putting it forward as their only real option, if the individual escape pods wouldn't work. They could open the doors, kill the aliens, then take the *Samson* away from LV178.

But it was a dropship, built for short-distance transport to and from the surface of a planet. It wasn't equipped for deep space travel. No stasis pods, no recycling environmental systems. It was a no-go.

"We'd starve to death, suffocate, or end up murdering each other," Lachance said. He looked at Baxter, wearing a deadpan face. "I'd kill you first, you know."

"You'd try," Baxter muttered.

"Yeah, sure, the *Samson*," Powell said. "And who's going to stand by those doors when we open them? We can't see what those things are doing inside."

"We can't escape on the *Samson*," Hoop said. "But that doesn't mean we don't need it. Ripley?" She looked uncertain, but she stood, stubbed out her cigarette, and lit another.

"Hoop and Sneddon came up with this," she said, taking the first drag. "It might work. The *Narcissus* is a lifeboat as well as a deep space shuttle. Environmental systems, carbon dioxide recycling capability."

"But for nine of us?" Welford asked.

"We take turns in the stasis pod," Ripley said. "But that's getting ahead of ourselves. There's another problem."

"Of course there is," Powell said. "Why should anything be easy?"

"What's the problem?" Lachance asked.

"The shuttle's fuel cell is degraded," Ripley said. "Less than ten percent charge left, which is nowhere near enough."

"Enough to get us away from the *Marion*, surely," Kasyanov said.

"I've run the figures," Hoop said. "Lachance, Sneddon, I'd like you both to check them. But we need enough power to get the overloaded shuttle away from *Marion*, out of orbit, and accelerated to a speed that'll get us back within the outer rim before we've died of old age. I figure we need eighty percent of a full charge, at least. Any more than that just means we can accelerate to a faster speed, get there quicker."

Welford snorted, but then Ripley spoke again.

"It'll be real-time," she said. "Even sharing the stasis pod means there'll be eight people at a time just… sitting around. Growing older."

"We estimate eighty percent cell charge will get us past the outer rim within six years," Hoop said. "Give or take."

There was a stunned silence.

"So I *do* get to murder Baxter," Lachance said.

"Fucking hell," Powell said.

"Yeah," Kasyanov agreed. Her voice shook.

"Welford's feet smell," Garcia said. "Lachance farts. Hell, we won't survive a year."

No one laughed.

"Is there a precedent?" Lachance asked.

"We'd be setting it," Sneddon said.

The bridge was silent for a time while they all thought about what it really meant.

"You said we still need the *Samson*," Lachance said. "For its fuel cells?"

Hoop shook his head, and looked to Ripley again.

"Won't power my shuttle," she said. "Completely different system design. The *Marion*'s might, but Hoop tells me they're damaged and dangerous. He says there are more down in the mine, though— spares, stored remotely, just in case. So we have to take the *Samson* down to the surface. We bring a couple back up, adapt one, and fix it into the *Narcissus*. Load the shuttle up with as many supplies as we can, then blast off before your ship starts to burn."

More silence.

Ripley smiled. "Then all we need is a deck of cards."

"Piece o' cake," Lachance said.

"Yeah," Powell said, voice quavering with panic, "no problem. Easy!"

"Well…" Hoop said. "There's more."

Powell muttered something, Kasyanov threw up her hands.

"What?" Lachance said. "Another problem? Don't tell me. The shuttle's made of cheese."

"It seems Ripley's been having some computer malfunctions," Hoop said. "Maybe it's best if I let her tell you about it."

Ripley raised her cup of cold coffee in a toast. He shrugged apologetically. *Sorry*, he mouthed. She gave him the finger.

He liked Ripley. She was strong, attractive, confident in the same self-deprecating way Lucy Jordan had been.

Damn it.

"Ash," Ripley said. "He was an android aboard my ship."

She told the entire story, and something about it felt so unreal. It wasn't the strangeness of the story itself—she'd witnessed everything, knew it all to be true. It was the idea that Ash had *followed* her. He'd expressed his sympathies, and Parker had burned off his face, but by then he must have already insinuated himself into the shuttle's computer, just in case things went wrong aboard *Nostromo*. How could he have been so prepared? What sort of paranoid programing had he been given?

She spoke about him now as if he could hear every word. She was only sorry that he couldn't feel shame.

"So as far as I can tell, he's the reason I'm here," she concluded. "And he's not going to be happy unless I bring one of those things back with me."

"That's just really fucking dandy," Powell said. "So we clear one ship of fucking great big rib-busting monsters so we can escape on another ship piloted by a psychotic AI. Wonderful. My life is complete."

"I don't think it's that much of a problem anymore," Ripley said. She lit another cigarette. The smoke burned her throat. They were harsh Russian cigarettes, brought along by Kasyanov. Of the *Marion's* crew that survived, only the doctor smoked. "Because of Ash, I'm here instead of home. I haven't been able to access detailed flight logs yet, but… it could be he's just kept me floating around out here. Waiting for another sign that these aliens are still around."

"But why keep you alive, if that's the case?" Sneddon asked.

"Because he needs someone for the alien to impregnate. He's seen how violent the fully-grown creature is, there's no way he could get one back to Weyland-Yutani. Not on board the *Narcissus*." She exhaled smoke and waved it away. "Anyway, that's beside the point. Can't undo what that bastard has done. But back then he was mobile, tactile. Hell, we all thought he was human. He interfered in our decision-making, steered events toward his secret agenda. And when things got out of his control, he went on the rampage.

"Now… he's not really here anymore. He's just code. Ethereal." She blew smoke again, but this time didn't wave it away. "And we know where to find him."

"So we just shut down Ripley's shuttle's computer until we're ready to go," Hoop said. "Then when we're underway, and before we initiate main thrust, I'll do my best to purge Ash from the systems. Or at least to isolate him to certain drives."

"God knows you'll have plenty of time," Powell said.

"Right," Ripley said. "And there'll always be someone awake, to monitor any changes in the shuttle's programed flight. Incoming signals. Whatever."

"So Ash is just floundering," Sneddon said. "Following his programing, but without a plan."

Ripley shrugged. She wasn't sure. He'd been so deceitful, so scheming back on *Nostromo*, that she didn't want to underestimate him now. But whatever part of Ash still survived, he could no longer intrude in their actions. Not physically, at least.

Soon, she would return to the *Narcissus* to find out more.

"So that's the plan," Hoop said. "Lachance, I need you to plot the *Marion*'s trajectory around the planet; let us know when we'll be closest to the mine. But it's gotta be soon, like in the next couple of days. Powell, Welford, I need you to gather as much of the mining equipment as you can. We need plasma torches, sand picks, anything else you can find."

"There are the thumpers," Garcia said. "They use them to fire charges deep into loose sand."

Hoop nodded.

"Can we really use them in the *Samson*?" Baxter asked.

"We don't have to use the explosive charges," Welford said. "Substitute bolts, or something, and you have a pretty good projectile weapon."

Ripley was looking into her cup of cold coffee, listening to the discussion, trying to take it all in. But her mind was elsewhere. Somewhere dark, claustrophobic. Stalking the steam-filled corridors where lighting flashed, the countdown siren wailed, and the alien could have been waiting around any corner.

"How many are in there?" she asked. The conversation was too loud, so no one heard her. She tried again. "*Hey!*" That quieted them down. "How many are in the *Samson*?"

"We think four," Hoop said.

"Fully grown?"

He shrugged. Looked around.

"Last time we saw, they looked big," Baxter said. "Just shadows, really. They were still, hunkered down at the back of the passenger compartment."

"Maybe they were dead," Kasyanov said hopefully. Nobody responded to that. Their luck wasn't going that way.

"They have acid for blood," Ripley said.

"What?" Sneddon asked.

"Dallas—our captain—said it was molecular acid of some sort. It ate through two decks before its effect slowed down."

"Oh, man," Powell said, laughing in disbelief. "Do they fire lightning out of their asses, too? Do they cum nuclear jelly? What else, huh?"

"Ripley, that's..." Sneddon stopped, and shook her head. Ripley looked up in time to see her glance at the others, eyebrows raised.

"I'm not making this up," Ripley said.

"No one said you were," Hoop said.

"Hoop, come on!" Sneddon said. "Acid for blood?"

There was a long silence on the bridge. Ripley smoked the last of her cigarette and dropped the butt into her coffee mug. It sizzled out. She was feeling an increasingly urgent need to get back to the *Narcissus*, alone, find her own space. Talk with Ash. She wasn't sure it would solve anything, but it might make her sense of betrayal easier to bear.

She'd promised Amanda she'd be home.

Closing her eyes, she willed back the tears. She'd already cried too much. Now it was time to survive.

"If you want to use the *Samson*, best draw them out before you kill them," she said. "That's all I'm saying."

"We'll work on a plan," Hoop said. "In the meantime—"

"Good. I'm going back to my shuttle." Ripley stood, but the science officer blocked her path.

"Now wait," Sneddon said. She was six inches shorter than Ripley, but she stood her ground. Ripley respected that. "None of us knows you. You come here for whatever reason, start telling us these stories about rogue AIs and aliens with acid for blood. And now you want to go back to your shuttle?"

"Yeah, why?" Powell asked. "Hoop, we can't just let her wander round."

"What, you're afraid I'm going to damage your perfect little ship?" Ripley asked. "God knows, we wouldn't want to scratch the paint."

"Let's just chill," Hoop said. But Sneddon's blood was up.

"What are you going back for?" she demanded. "You've just come from there with Hoop."

"You're welcome to come," Ripley said. She was staring Sneddon down. She waited until the shorter woman averted her gaze, then smiled. "I'm just going to feed my cat."

As it turned out, Jonesy wasn't hungry. Ripley laid out some reconstituted chicken, and though he crept from the stasis pod and sniffed at it, he turned his nose up and slinked away. But he stayed in the shuttle.

Maybe he can smell them out there, Ripley thought. *Maybe he knows more than the rest of us.*

The acid-for-blood thing troubled her. What she'd witnessed had been just a drop, spilled from the thing hugging Kane's face when Ash and Dallas tried cutting it off. She didn't know whether the fully-grown alien carried the same blood, or whether wounding one would result in a similar effect. Really, she knew so little. But though the reality of her experience had been terrifying, the alien had taken on larger, darker connotations in her sleep.

Thirty-seven years of nightmares, she thought. *And now that I'm awake, the nightmare has woken with me.*

She moved around the cramped space, again wondering just how the hell nine people would survive in here. Even with one in the stasis pod, there'd barely be room for the rest to sit down. There was a small bathroom behind the equipment locker, so at least there'd be privacy for toilet and limited washing. But existing together here for more than a few days hardly bore thinking about.

For months? Years?

She finally found Jonesy again in the suit locker, snuggled down in one of the big EVA boots. He took some coaxing, but eventually he miaowed and climbed out, letting Ripley pick him up and hug him to her. He was her link to the past, and the only solid proof that any of it had actually happened. She didn't really require such proof—she was confident that she could distinguish reality from nightmare—but the cat was a comfort nonetheless.

"Come on then, you little bastard," she said. "You gonna help me?" She held the cat up and looked into his eyes. "So why didn't you spot anything wrong with that bastard Ash? Damn fine ship's cat *you* are."

She sat in the pilot's seat, Jonesy on her lap, and rested her fingers on the keyboard. She took a deep breath. Ash had tried to kill her, but he was just a machine. An AI, true. Created to think for himself, process data and make his own decisions, act on programed responses and write and install new programs based on experience—essentially learning. But a machine nevertheless. Designed, manufactured, given android life in the labs of Weyland-Yutani.

Suddenly Ripley felt a rush of hatred for the company. They had decided she and her crew were expendable, and four decades later they were still fucking with her life.

It was time for that to stop.

Hello Ash, she typed. The words appeared on the screen before her, flashing green, the cursor passing the time as a response was considered. She didn't actually expect one, assuming a resounding silence as the AI strived to hide its continued existence. Instead, the reply was almost instant.

```
Hello Ripley.
```

She sat back in her seat, stroking the cat. The sensation returned—the feeling of being watched. She didn't like it.

You brought us here in response to the Marion's *distress signal?*

```
That's right.
```

Crew still expendable in accordance with special order 937?

```
You're the last of the Nostromo's crew.
```

Answer the question, Ash.

```
Yes. Crew expendable.
```

"Nice," she breathed. Jonesy purred in her lap. *But I know where you are now, Ash. You can't control things anymore. You're without purpose.*

```
I did my best.
```

Ripley looked at those words and thought about what they meant. The *Nostromo*'s crew, brutally killed by the thing Ash had allowed on board. Her decades in hypersleep, away from her daughter and home.

Fuck you, Ash, she typed.

The cursor blinked back.

Ripley punched the computer off and then sat back in the chair. Jonesy stretched and allowed himself to be scratched.

6

FAMILY

The *Marion* drifted, Lachance computed, and he decided that four days after Ripley's arrival would be the optimum time to drop back down to the mine. It would entail a thousand-mile, three-hour drop, four hours at the mine retrieving the spare fuel cells, and then an hour's blast back into orbit. If all went well they'd be away from *Marion* for around eight hours. If all didn't go well...

Everyone knew what the results of that would be.

Hoop suggested that they open up the *Samson* a day before they were due to drop. That would give them time to tackle the creatures inside, clear out the ship, and prep it for travel. If there was damage, they could do their best to repair it.

No one mentioned the possibility that it might be damaged beyond their ability to repair. There were so many things that could go wrong that they didn't bear discussing, and as such the survivors lived in a miasma of false positivity. The only talk was good talk. Everyone kept bad thoughts to themselves.

Baxter was the only one who was openly pessimistic, but then they were used to that with him. Nothing new.

Hoop was becoming more and more impressed with Ripley. That first day she'd been woozy and uncertain, but she soon found her feet. She came across as strong, resilient, yet damaged—tortured by what she had experienced. She'd once mentioned her daughter, but never again. He could see the pain in her eyes, but also the hope that she would see her child again.

Hope in the face of hopelessness, he supposed, was what kept them all going.

And she was attractive. He couldn't get away from that. She looked to him first when they had group conversations, and he didn't think it was because he was ostensibly in command. Maybe it was because, having both lost their children, they had something in common.

Hoop often thought about his two sons, and how he and their mother had watched a marriage dissolve around them. Neither of them had been able to rescue it. His job was the prime cause, she'd told him. *It's dangerous*, she said. *You're away for a year at a time.* But he'd refused to accept all of the blame.

It's well-paid, had been his response. *One more long job, then we'll be able to buy our own business back on Earth, be self-sufficient.*

And so it had spiraled, until eventually he had retreated to the one thing he knew was utterly indifferent, not caring how and what he was.

Space.

I ran away. The thought dogged him constantly, and it was the last thing the woman he loved had said. *You're running away.*

Ripley's presence made him feel more guilty than before, because in his case it had been a willing decision. She should only have been away for eighteen months.

He and Ripley spent some more time in the *Narcissus*, talking about the journey they would undertake together, being positive, discussing how nine people could live in a shuttle designed for three or four, at most. For years. Perhaps many years.

All the time there was a quiet hysteria lurking behind everything they said, a shared understanding that this was a crazy, unworkable idea. But it was their *only* idea. Sometimes it felt cramped with just the two of them in the shuttle, although Hoop wondered whether that was just him.

They also discussed their families. Hesitatingly at first, but then with an increasing openness. They talked of guilt, and how incredible distances did nothing to dull the sense of loss. He didn't pity her, and he thought she was thankful for that. She gave him understanding, and he was grateful. They were both cursed by distance and time, and the staggering loneliness that both could instill in a person. They were getting to know each other. And while it was a good feeling, there was also something delicate about every connection made.

They were both tentative, guarded. Their situation meant that they could be ripped apart at any moment.

They also talked about Ash. Hoop was quite the computer expert, and he didn't mind saying it. But though he was relatively confident about being able to purge Ash's AI from the shuttle's computer— or at very least, compartmentalize it so that it could no longer exert any control—he and Ripley decided that he should wait until they were away from the *Marion* and headed home. They would need the computer untouched and undamaged in order to program their route, and it was possible—albeit remotely—that his efforts to remove Ash might corrupt a wider swathe of the systems.

Besides, the disembodied Ash could do them no harm.

Those three days passed quickly, and there were tensions in the group. There always had been, and those that were familiar Hoop cast to one side. The relationship between the doc and Garcia was weird—he thought they were probably lovers, as well as colleagues— but they were always efficient, and professional when it was needed. Powell complained. Sneddon was quiet and steadfast, a gentle bravery shining through. She would be a rock for them all.

The others bickered, though no more than usual. But it was Ripley's presence that caused the greatest waves.

"But I can't help being fascinated by them," Sneddon said. She was scrolling through stills from inside the *Samson* again, the tablet propped against her coffee mug. It had been almost three weeks since they'd last seen inside the dropship. None of them knew what to expect when they opened it up.

"They're monsters," Ripley said. She was leaning against a work counter. The science lab was small and compact, and with the three of them in there it was already growing warm. Hoop had suggested that they conserve power and turn off any unnecessary environmental systems.

"We're not catching them, Sneddon," Hoop said. "That door opens and we kill them."

"Oh, yeah, sure," Sneddon replied without looking up. "But have you considered just how?"

"Of course. The plasma torches, sand picks, and charge thumpers."

"Right," Sneddon said. "So torch them with plasma and their skin, or whatever they have, bursts open. Acid spills. Sand picks hack at them... open them up. Fire projectiles with the charge thumpers... more acid."

"What else do you suggest?" Ripley asked, an edge to her voice.

"I suggest that we come up with something else," Sneddon said. "Trap them somehow. Hold them until we can—"

"We need to kill them, or they'll kill *us*," Ripley said. "If they're anything like the one we had on *Nostromo* they'll be eight, nine feet tall, incredibly fast and strong, and utterly vicious. And you want to trap them? How? You got a box we can bait with some cheese?"

Sneddon sat back, looking calm and composed. She glanced at Ripley, then looked squarely at Hoop.

"Is she safe?" she asked.

"Safe as any of us are right now," Hoop said. He looked at Ripley, frowned, tried to warn her off. But he could see that her outburst was driven by fear, not anger. For a moment it seemed as if she was seeing something very far away, and he wondered yet again at the nightmares she must still suffer. She'd told him about each of her dead crewmates—some of them her friends, the captain her occasional lover.

"Cargo netting," Sneddon said.

Ripley coughed something between a laugh and a gasp.

"It's strong enough to pack tons of equipment in the holds," Sneddon went on. "Twisted steel core. It'll hold them long enough for us to decide what to do with them."

"How do you know it will work?" Ripley asked.

"How do you know it won't?" Sneddon countered. "At least this way we don't risk burning a hole right through the hull. If what you say about acid is true..."

"It's true," Ripley said. "What, you don't believe me now?"

Sneddon sighed, swinging back in her chair. "I think we just need to be—"

"Who appointed you science officer?" Ripley asked.

"The company. Kelland."

"Which is owned by Weyland-Yutani."

"Very distantly, yes," Sneddon replied. "So?"

"And you worked for Weyland-Yutani before that?"

"I served my apprenticeship with them, on Mars, yes."

"Ripley?" Hoop asked. She seemed to be losing control, panicking. He didn't like that. More than anything, it made his own subsumed panic start to simmer again. Without even realizing it, he thought perhaps he'd taken Ripley's strength to feed his own.

"Don't wrap me in your conspiracies," Sneddon said quietly.

"This isn't about gathering specimens," Ripley said. "It's about surviving!"

"I didn't say I wanted to gather anything."

"But you find them fascinating—you said so yourself."

"And you don't?" Sneddon asked. She slid the tablet across the bench, but Ripley looked away.

"No," she said. "Horrifying. Repulsive. But not fascinating."

Knowing what Ripley had told him about Ash, Hoop supposed he should have seen this coming. He wanted to defuse the situation, bring it back onto a calm footing. It had started as a friendly discussion about how the creatures could be tackled, but had descended into a standoff. He took a breath, ready to speak.

But Sneddon's actions spoke for him.

She slid open an equipment drawer, plucked out a scalpel and nicked the top of her thumb. She squeezed the digit and smeared a droplet of blood across the white bench surface. Then she looked at Ripley.

Ripley sighed. "Sorry," she said. "Really."

Sneddon smiled. "Hey, I can't blame you. Truth is, I've never liked androids myself."

"Really?" Ripley said.

"I'm a science officer, but my basis is in biology." She picked up a piece of gauze, and held it firmly over the cut. "I find them unnatural."

"And now we can all be friends," Hoop said. His own sigh of relief was unfeigned, and both Ripley and Sneddon laughed.

"So, these nets," Ripley said. "Take me to see them."

Even before Ripley arrived, they had taken to spending most of their time on the bridge. It was a large enough area to feel comfortable, with the various workstations, well-designed and spread out, but still small enough to talk with each other without having to shout. At least three of the surviving members of the *Marion* needed to be there at any one time, and each of them preferred being close to one another. Most of the time, at least. On those few occasions when tensions rose and tempers flared, they all had their individual cabins in the accommodations hub.

The rec room became dusty and unused, and on those few occasions when Hoop had cause to visit, the sight of it made him unbearably sad. He had never believed in ghosts, but he felt the echo of every dead friend in that silent room so used to laughter.

Six hours before they were planning on opening the *Samson*, they stood or sat around the bridge, all eyes focussed on him. He felt the weight of responsibility, even though they were all making the decisions now. He hadn't forced his notional position of command on them. Since the disaster, he had simply been guiding, advising, and standing there to be shouted and screamed at if the stresses got too great.

Now, the pressure was almost unbearable. He knew that every single one of them felt it, because he could see it in their eyes, their taut expressions. He knew all of them so much more deeply than he had just seventy days before. Trauma had thrown them closer together, and now the time had come to try and make things better.

Hours of planning, scheming, suggestions and disagreements, drawing plans, and sick humor had led to this.

"We're ready," Hoop said. "We know that Baxter hasn't managed to establish any visual connection back to the *Samson*, so there's no saying what we'll be facing when the doors open. Maybe those bastard things will have starved. Maybe they'll be asleep, or hibernating, and we can just gather them up and blast them into space. Could be they'll come out fighting. In which case we'll be ready." He nodded at the array of mining tools. "So, anything else? Have we missed anything? Any more questions, speak up now."

None of them spoke. He looked around the bridge, giving them all a chance. His gaze rested on Ripley, and he saw something there that continued to give him hope—resilience, determination…

Anger.

"Okay," he said. "You all know what to do."

The vestibule to Bay Three was circular and fifty feet across, lined with ranks of dusty seating interspersed with equipment racks for those awaiting a dropship. Its smoothly curved side walls were partly glazed, and offered views over the destroyed Bays One and Two on the port side. The *Narcissus* was docked at Bay Four, off to starboard.

Through a heavy door at the far end was the airlock, a space large enough for ten people at a time to be strapped in and decontaminated while it was pressurized or vented. At the other end of it, another door led into the docking arm. This was a space only ten feet long, partly flexible, that fixed directly to the surround around the dropship's outer hull hatch.

Baxter and Lachance remained on the bridge, Lachance to oversee master controls—airlock operation, environmental, and remote opening of the *Samson*'s hatch—and Baxter to ensure that communication channels were kept open. Everyone wore a headset and microphone, and they could all hear one another. For the moment, though, they were maintaining strict silence.

Hoop was in command, reasoning that someone needed to oversee the operation, and no one had objected. Ripley suggested that most of them were relieved it wasn't them.

No one disagreed.

They waited nervously in the vestibule while Powell and Welford repaired the disconnected door mechanism leading into the airlock. Through the viewing windows, Ripley could see the flanks of the *Samson* about thirty feet away. The ship looked innocent enough. But what she knew, the images she had seen, were enough to make her terrified of it. That motionless, silent ship contained her nightmares, and they were preparing to let them out.

She was chilled with nervous perspiration, trying to level her breathing. She didn't want them all to hear her fear.

She pulled her gaze away and looked to her left, toward the ruins of docking bays One and Two. Hoop had already shown her this, but it was still a sad, shocking sight. So many had died there. She was amazed the disaster hadn't taken out the whole ship. Yet in a way it had, the ripples and effects of the crash still being felt at a much slower pace.

"Welford?" Hoop asked.

"Not long," the engineer replied. "Lachance, ready to pressurize?"

"Ready," Lachance said from the bridge.

"Like I said," Hoop said, "as slow as you can. Don't want to make any more noise than is necessary."

In case they hear us, Ripley thought. Her heart hammered, and drips of sweat trickled down her back. Kasyanov had given her some spare clothing, and Ripley knew from its fit that they didn't belong to the doctor. She wondered whose it had been. The shirt and trousers were tight but not uncomfortable, the jacket snug beneath the arms and across her back. She wore her own boots from the *Nostromo*. Probably collector's items now.

The two engineers worked at the door, both efficient and quiet. Ripley had seen them arguing, and Powell more than anyone seemed to exude negativity. But they worked as a team, and there was something almost balletic about their movement, as if they were one body split in two. She wondered how long they had been working together out here. She should have asked. She should have got to know them better, before—

She took a deep breath to compose herself, and Hoop glanced across at her. He'd heard through her microphone. She didn't return his glance, didn't want him to see how afraid she was. She needed to be strong. Always had been, working with the crew of the *Nostromo*, most of them men. It was a trait she liked in herself, and she hated that fear was picking at its edges.

Ripley stood against the left wall of the vestibule, Hoop was in the middle, and Kasyanov and Garcia were to the right. Hoop carried the plasma torch—a serious bit of kit, he'd said—leaving her with a sand pick and the medics with charge thumpers. They were large and unwieldy, but packed a lot of punch. Sneddon was with the engineers, heavy cargo netting piled around her feet.

Ripley had examined the cargo netting, and it was stronger than she'd expected. Triple-core steel wrapped in epoxy-molded carbon fiber, and wound in compressed nylon strands. There were special cutting tools they used to slice the netting if they had to. She'd nodded, but had advised a healthy skepticism. They couldn't assume that *anything* would hold the beasts.

"Done," Welford said. "Lachance?"

"Pressurizing."

There was an almost sub-audible hum as the airlock beyond the vestibule was filled once more with air. The lights above the heavy doors flickered softly, and after a minute all three glowed a soft green.

"Okay," Lachance said. "Just check the pressures there, would you?"

Powell looked at the gauges beside the door. He held up his thumb.

"Open it up," Hoop said.

Welford stroked a pressure pad, and the doors slid apart. Despite their care and the readings, there was still a sigh as the doors opened. Ripley swallowed and her ears popped. She looked across at Hoop, but he seemed unconcerned.

"Okay guys," Hoop said, "slow and quiet."

Nervously, Welford and Powell entered the airlock. Ripley moved sideways, so that she could see them inside. As soon as they reached the far door they started repairing the dismantled door mechanism.

Garcia and Sneddon went to work rigging the heavy cargo netting around the door that led from the airlock into the vestibule, leaving one side loose for the engineers to slip past once they were done.

Ripley frowned. No matter how she looked at it, the plan was as loose and woolly as ever. Remote-open the *Samson*, wait until the aliens came through and got caught in the netting. Use sand picks to hook the netting and drag them back through the vestibule and along the corridor to the ruined docking bays. Open the inner door, shove the creatures through, lock the door again. Blast them into space.

It was like catching a shark in a goldfish net.

Yet there were so many ways the aliens might not play ball. *What if they stay in the* Samson? Ripley had asked. Welford had suggested a remote drone they used for deep mine exploration. Sending it in, luring them out.

So woolly. So loose.

The others seemed just as nervous. Some of them had seen these things in action—on monitors, on the destroyed dropship, and aboard the *Samson*. But the ones they'd seen had been small. Not much bigger than the bastard that had burst from Kane at their last meal together. The grown ones, the adults, had existed on their screens as little more than ambiguous shadows.

She shook her head. Her breathing came heavier.

"This won't work," she said.

"Ripley," Hoop whispered.

The others were looking at her, eyes wide.

"Not four of them," she said. She hefted the sand pick. It was heavy, its end viciously barbed, but it felt insufficient. She swung it too slowly. Her shoulders already ached from holding it.

"We should think of something else," she said.

"Damn it, Ripley!" Lachance said.

"Quiet!" Baxter hissed. "Welford and Powell have a headset, too!"

She knew they were right. The engineers were almost within

touching distance of the dropship, and soon they'd have the last door ready to open.

They couldn't change their minds now.

And the aliens had been in there for more than seventy days. Their only food source—the bodies of the six miners and dropship crew—had been rotting the entire time. Little food, no water. Nowhere to move and stretch. Maybe they would be tired and weak, and easy to drag away.

Maybe.

Ripley nodded to let the others know she had her fears under control. But really, she didn't. Hoop knew that—she could see it when he looked across at her. *He's as scared as me.*

Perhaps they all were.

But they were also desperate.

Welford and Powell retreated back through the airlock, ducking around the heavy netting that had been hung across the inner door. Welford nodded to Hoop.

"Okay, Lachance, airlock outer door ready to open."

Ripley heard someone take in a sharp breath, then through the airlock she saw the docking arm's outer door slide open into the wall. Beyond lay the *Samson*'s outer hatch. It was dusty, scratched, and docked perfectly central to the airlock.

"Last check," Hoop said. "Baxter, no view or sound from inside?"

"Still nothing," Baxter said.

"Welford, Powell, either side of the netting with the plasma torches. Remember, only blast them if you have to. Kasyanov, wait over there with the charge thumper. Ripley, you okay?"

She nodded.

"Good. Sneddon, Garcia, back through the doors into the corridor behind the vestibule. Once we start dragging them in the net, you lead the way to Bays One and Two. Open the blast doors as quickly as you can, then get ready to close them again. Lachance, once we've shut them in there, you remote-open the door leading to the ruined docking bays."

"Easy," Ripley said. Someone laughed. Someone else started

swearing quietly, voice so soft that she couldn't even tell whether it was a man or woman.

Wait! she wanted to say. *Wait, we still have time, we can come up with something else!* But she knew that they *didn't* have time. That bastard Ash had brought her to this doomed ship, and now she was going to face them again.

The monsters from her nightmares.

Hoop whispered, "Go." The *Samson*'s outer hatch squealed open, and the shadows came.

7

SHADOWS

Between blinks, Ripley's world turned to chaos.

As soon as the *Samson*'s hatch was open the aliens surged out. They were so fast, so silent and furious, that she didn't have time to count. Their limbs powered them along the docking arm and through the airlock, skittering on the metallic surfaces. Someone shouted in surprise, and then the creatures struck the heavy netting.

Ripley crouched down clutching her sand pick, ready to drag the creatures toward the vestibule's rear doors. But something was wrong with the net. It held two of them tightly in a tangled jumble, but two more thrashed violently, limbs waving and slashing, tails lashing out, and those terrible teeth clacking together and driving ice-cold fear through her veins.

"Careful, they're—" she shouted.

And then they were through.

The tightly coiled metal-cored netting ruptured, high-tension wiring thrashing at the air with a high-pitched whipping sound. Welford screamed as his features blurred. Blood splashed across the vestibule, painting the harsh white surfaces a startling shade of red.

Hoop shouted as he ignited his plasma torch. One alien surged at him, then kicked sideways against a rank of fixed seating, veering away from the waving flame.

Directly toward Ripley.

She crouched against the bulkhead and propped the long pick's handle beside her, pointing it up and away from her at an angle. The alien—tall, spiked, chitinous, with razor nails and the curved head and extruding mouth that had haunted her for so long—skidded toward her, claws scoring ruts in the flooring as it tried to slow. But not quite quickly enough.

It squealed as the point penetrated its body somewhere just above it legs.

An acrid stench made Ripley gag. She heard fluid spattering onto metal, and then she smelled burning.

"Acid!" she shouted. She shoved forward with the sand pick. The alien stood its ground, crouched down with its hands clawed and waving, mouth snapping forward. But it was playing for distraction. Ripley heard the soft *whoosh!* of its tail, and ducked just in time.

The pick was snatched from her hands and sent clattering across the vestibule.

Ripley feinted left toward the airlock, then leapt to the right, following the curved wall toward the rear doors. She sensed the thing following her, and as she approached the doors Hoop shouted.

"Ripley, *down!*"

She dropped without hesitation. A roar burst all around her and she smelled hair singeing, felt the skin on the back of her neck and scalp and arms stretching as an unbelievable heat scorched the air above and behind her.

The alien squealed, high and agonized.

Ripley looked toward the open exit doors just as another shadow powered out through them. From beyond she heard an impact—wet, meaty, a thud and a grunt. Someone screamed.

Something grasped her hand and she cried out, rolled, kicking out, her heavy boot connecting with Hoop's thigh. He gasped, then grabbed her tighter and dragged her across the vestibule.

The alien was still squealing as it burned, thrashing back along the curved bulkhead toward the airlock doors.

And toward Powell. He was standing over the two aliens still struggling in the net, aiming his charge thumper. There was something wrong with his face. Ripley saw the splash of blood across his chest and neck, saw it dripping from his features. He was totally expressionless. He waved the thumper back and forth, but didn't seem to be seeing anything.

She glanced aside from him and saw what had become of Welford. He was meat.

"Powell!" she shouted. "Eyes right!"

Powell lifted his head. But instead of looking right at the blazing alien that was staggering toward him, he looked left at his dead friend.

Kasyanov leapt across two rows of seats, braced her legs, and fired her charge thumper at the burning alien. The shot was deafening, pulsing in Ripley's ears and blowing the flames back from the creature's sizzling hide.

It screeched louder. But it continued on toward Powell, falling on him, and Ripley didn't quite close her eyes in time. She saw Powell's head erupt beneath the impact of the burning thing's silvery mouth.

"What the fuck?" Hoop shouted.

Kasyanov fired the thumper again, two more times, shattering the alien's head and spreading its burning parts across the floor and wall on that side of the vestibule. Flames curved across the windows, smoke formed intricate patterns, and an acidic haze rose.

Hissing. Smoking.

"We need to get out!" Ripley said.

"Where's the other one?" Hoop asked.

"Through the door. But the acid will—"

"Kasyanov, out!" Hoop shouted.

Kasyanov came for them. Ripley saw her disbelief, but also the determination that had smothered her terror. That was good. They'd need that.

One of the aliens trapped in the netting broke free, streaking toward them across the vestibule. It knocked seating aside, jumped over the back of a row of fixed equipment racks, and bore down on Kasyanov.

Hoop raised the plasma torch. But if he fired this close he'd fry the doctor as well.

"No!" Ripley said. "Hoop!" She sidestepped to the left, never taking her eyes off the alien. It paused briefly, and her selfish thought was, *Not me, don't come at me.* Fear drove that idea, and moments later—as the alien leapt and Hoop fried it with the plasma torch—she felt a flush of shame.

But Kasyanov was alive because of Ripley's quick decision. She'd acted on instinct, and her baser thoughts, more taken with self-preservation, had needed a moment to catch up.

The Russian nodded once at her.

Then one of the acid-splashed windows blew out.

The storm was instantaneous. Anything not fixed down was picked up and blasted toward the ruptured window, carried by the atmosphere gushing out into space under massive pressure. Broken chairs, dropped weapons, wall paneling powered across the vestibule and jammed against the window and bulkhead. The noise was incredible, a roar that threatened to suck Ripley's eardrums from her skull. She tried to breathe, but couldn't pull air into her lungs. She held onto a floor fixing for a row of chairs with one hand, reaching for Hoop with the other.

Hoop clung onto the door frame, Kasyanov clasping onto his flapping jacket.

Ripley looked over her shoulder. Two tattered bodies—all that remained of Welford and Powell—were pressed hard against the broken window, the two dead, burned aliens almost merged with them. The surviving creature, still tangled in netting, was clasping onto the airlock doorway, but as she watched its grip slipped and it impacted against its dead brethren. Things were drawn through the airlock and whipped around toward the breach—clothing, body parts, other objects she couldn't identify from inside the *Samson*.

She saw Powell's right arm and chest sizzling and flowing from spilled acid.

"We don't have long!" she tried to shout. She barely even heard herself, but she could see from Kasyanov's expression that she knew the terrible danger they were in.

For a moment, the storm abated a little. The blown window was clogged with furniture, body parts, and bulkhead paneling. Ripley felt the pressure on her ears and the tugging at her limbs lessening, so she started pulling herself along the floor fixings toward the doorway. With the acid eating away at the detritus, the calmer period wouldn't last for long.

Hoop hauled himself through, helped by hands from the other side. Kasyanov went with him. Then they both turned back for her.

Jammed against the door frame and held from behind, Hoop reached for Ripley.

As he looked over her shoulders and his eyes widened, she got her feet under her and pushed.

Hoop grabbed her arms and squeezed, so tight that she saw blood pooling around where his fingernails bit into her wrists.

The entire bulkhead surrounding the shattered window gave way.

With a shout Ripley barely heard, Hoop pulled her toward him. The doors were already closing, and she was tugged through the opening moments before the edges met.

There was a loud, long whine, a metallic groaning, and then the growl of racing air fell immediately away. Beyond the door was chaos. But here, for a few seconds, it was almost silent.

Then Ripley's hearing faded back in. She heard panting and groaning, and Hoop's muttered curses when he saw Garcia's mutilated body jammed through a doorway across the corridor. Her chest was a bloodied mess, bones glinting with dripping blood.

"One... one came through," Ripley said, looking at Sneddon. The science officer nodded and pointed along the corridor.

"Into the ship," she said. "It moved so fast. And it was huge. *Huge!*"

"We've got to find it," Ripley said.

"The others?" Sneddon asked.

Hoop shook his head. "Welford. Powell. Gone."

The chaos beyond the doors ended as quickly as it had begun.

Ripley stood up, shaking, looking around at the others—Hoop, Kasyanov, Sneddon. She tried not to look at Garcia's damaged, pathetic body, because it reminded her so much of Lambert, hanging there with her arm still swinging, blood still dripping.

"We've got to track it down," Ripley said again.

"Baxter, Lachance!" Hoop said. "One got free on the ship. You hear me?"

No reply.

"The decompression must have screwed the com connection," Sneddon said.

Ripley reached for her headset, but it was gone. Ripped off in the violence.

"The bridge," Hoop said. "All of us. We need to stay together, get up there as quickly as possible. Warn them. Then we decide what to do. But *only* after we're all together. Agreed?"

Ripley nodded.

"Yeah," Sneddon said.

Hoop took the last remaining charge thumper from Sneddon, and led the way.

They'd moved so quickly! Even after being trapped in the *Samson* for seventy days, they'd stormed out of there faster than Ripley could have imagined. She wasn't really sure what she'd been expecting… To find that it had all been a bad dream, perhaps. To discover that the things in there weren't really related in any way to the monster that had killed her crew, thirty-seven years before.

But it hadn't been, and they were. *Exactly* the same. Giant, insectile, reptilian things, yet with a body that in certain light, from certain angles, could have been humanoid.

That head… those teeth…

Hoop held out his hand, palm up toward them. Ripley stopped and repeated the signal so that Sneddon could see, and behind her Kasyanov.

They were at a junction in the corridor. Across the junction was the door that led into the ruined docking bays, still solid and secure. Around the corner lay the route up into the main body of the *Marion*.

Hoop stood motionless, the charge thumper held across his body. It was long, unwieldy, and to aim it ahead of him as he stepped around, he'd have to move across the corridor.

The alien could have been *anywhere*. Any corner. Any shadow in the corridor walls, open doorway, hatch, side room. She'd seen it rush from the vestibule, heard it pause just long enough to kill Garcia, and then it had gone, ignoring Sneddon altogether. Maybe because she carried a weapon. But more likely, Ripley thought, because it sensed the vast ship to which it now had unrestricted access.

Maybe it had stopped a dozen steps away and was waiting for them. Drooling, hissing softly, anticipating its first real meal in so long.

Or perhaps it had dashed headlong into the depths of the ship, losing itself in unlit, unheated rooms, where it could plan what to do next.

Hoop slipped around the corner and Ripley paused for a second, holding her breath. But there was no explosion of violence, and she followed, drawing close to him once again.

They reached the end of the docking section and climbed a wide staircase into the main ship. She kept her eyes on the head of the staircase. It was well lit up there, yet she still expected to see the shimmering silhouette, all spiked limbs and curved head.

But they were alone.

Hoop glanced back, face tense. Ripley smiled and nodded encouragingly, and he returned her smile.

Behind her, Sneddon and Kasyanov remained close, but not so close that they might interrupt each other's movements. Even though she'd lost her headset, Ripley could still hear their heavy breathing—part exertion, mostly terror. No one spoke. The shock of what had happened was still circling, held at bay by the adrenalin rush.

Soon it'll hit us, Ripley thought, remembering the crunching sound as the alien bit into Powell's head, the hissing, acidic stench as the destroyed creature's blood splashed down across Powell's and Welford's ruined corpses.

Soon it'll really hit us.

Hoop led them through a wider, better-lit corridor stretching toward a central circulation area. From there other corridors led off, as well as an elevator that rose up through the decks. Three doors were securely closed, shutting off deck areas that had decompressed during the initial disaster, all of which were now out of bounds. The other corridors, all leading toward the rear of the ship, were still open.

From where they stood they could see part of the way along each one. Doors stood in shadows. Staircases rose out of sight. Lights flickered from weak or interrupted power supplies, causing flinching movement where there was none.

Hoop indicated the elevator. Sneddon moved forward, quickly and silently, and pressed the call button.

"Baxter?" Hoop whispered again into his microphone. "Lachance?" He looked at Sneddon, then back at Kasyanov. They both shook their heads.

The lights above the elevator shone a flat red.

"Stairs?" Ripley asked.

Hoop nodded and pointed the way. They moved behind the elevator bank and toward the bottom of the widest staircase. Hoop immediately started climbing, charge thumper aimed up and ahead of him.

Ripley and the others followed. They trod quietly, moving as quickly as they dared, and at the next half-landing Hoop paused and peered around the corner. He moved on. The ship hummed and throbbed around them with familiar sounds and sensations.

At the next landing Hoop stopped again, staring, frozen.

Ripley moved up beside him. She was ready to act quickly—grab him, fall back and down if the alien pounced. But to begin with she couldn't see anything out of place, and she touched his shoulder and squeezed to get his attention.

Hoop swung the charge thumper around and down, pointing its wide barrel at something on the landing. A clear, viscous slime, splashed down on the landing and the first tread of the next flight, then smeared across the textured metal.

"Which level is the bridge?" she whispered in his ear. She was confused, lost.

He pointed up, held up one finger.

"We have to get out of the stairwell," she said. "Get up there some other—"

Hoop ran. He pushed off with a grunt, leaping up the staircase two at a time, weapon held out before him. He moved so quickly that he took Ripley and the others by surprise, and by the time she started after him he was already on the next half-landing, swinging around the corner without pause. She grabbed the handrail and pulled herself up.

We should be going slow and quiet! she thought. But she also knew exactly what Hoop was feeling. He wanted to get to the bridge and warn Lachance and Baxter before the alien got there. And if they arrived and the other two had already been slaughtered, he wanted to kill the fucking thing.

Ripley saw him pause briefly at the doorway leading onto the next deck, then he touched the pressure pad and the door whispered open. He pushed through, crouched down low, looking all around as Ripley and the others closed on him. With a quick glance back at them, he moved on.

Ripley finally recognized where they were. As they approached the main entrance that led onto the bridge she dashed on ahead, pausing by the doors and listening, one hand hovering over the pressure pad. She couldn't hear anything from inside, but then perhaps the doors were soundproofed. Maybe the screaming was contained.

Nodding to Hoop, she counted down with her fingers.

Three... two... one...

She stroked the pad and the door whispered open. They went in together, Hoop on the left, Ripley on the right, and the joy and relief was almost overwhelming when she saw Lachance and Baxter huddled around the communications desk.

"What the fuck?" Baxter asked, standing and sending his chair spinning across the floor. "We lost contact and..." He saw their faces then, and read the terror.

"What happened?" Lachance asked.

"Secure the bridge," Hoop said to Sneddon and Kasyanov. "Lock the doors. All of them."

"What about the others?" Baxter asked.

"How long ago did you lose contact?"

"Just when they—when you were opening up the airlock," Baxter said. "I was about to come down, but…"

"There *are* no others," Hoop said. "Secure the bridge. Then we'll decide what the hell to do next."

Their grief was palpable.

They'd already lost so many friends and colleagues, but these eight survivors had existed together for more than seventy days, striving to make the *Marion* safe, hoping that their distress signal would be picked up by another ship. Living day by day with the constant, hanging threat of further mechanical malfunction, or a break-out of those monsters from the *Samson*. Fighting against the odds, their determination had seen them through. Perhaps they hadn't all liked each other, but what group of people could claim that? Especially under such stress.

Yet they had been the survivors. And now three of them were gone, slaughtered in a matter of moments by those bastard creatures.

Ripley gave them their silence, retreating to a control panel and sitting in the upholstered chair. It was a navigational control point. She browsed the system, noting the other planets and their distances, orbits, make-up. The sun at the system's center was almost half a billion miles away.

No wonder it feels so fucking cold.

"We've got to find it," Sneddon said. "Track it down and kill it."

"Track it down how?" Kasyanov asked. "It could be hiding away anywhere on the *Marion*. It'll take us forever, and we only have days."

"I saw it," Sneddon said. At the sound of her voice—so filled with dreadful awe, quavering in fear—everyone grew quiet, still. "It came out like… like a living shadow. Garcia didn't even know what hit her, I don't think. She didn't scream, didn't have time. Just a grunt. Like she was disagreeing with something. Just that, and then it killed her and ran. Just… brutalized her, for no reason."

"They don't reason," Ripley said. "They kill and feed. And if there's no time to feed, they just kill."

"But that's not natural," Sneddon said. "Animals kill for a purpose."

"Some do," Ripley said. "Humans don't."

"What is and isn't natural out here?" Hoop asked, and he sounded angry. "Doesn't matter. What matters is what we do."

"Track it down," Sneddon said.

"There's no time!" Kasyanov said.

"That acid ate through the vestibule windows and floor in no time," Hoop said. "We're lucky the doors are holding—they're blast doors, not proper external doors."

"So how the hell do we get to the *Samson* now?" Lachance asked.

"That's another problem." Hoop was the center of attention. Not only in command, he was the only engineer left alive.

"Suit up," Lachance said.

"Exactly what I was thinking," Hoop said.

"Yeah," Baxter agreed. "The *Samson*'s environmental systems will recompress, once we're inside."

"We'll need to form another airlock," Hoop said.

"But we can't just leave that thing roaming around the ship!" Kasyanov shouted. She was standing, fists clenched at her sides. "It could chew through cables, smash doors. Do god-knows-what sort of damage."

"We can leave it." Hoop looked at Ripley, as if seeking her agreement. And suddenly the others were watching her, as well.

Ripley nodded.

"Yeah. It's either that, or we hunt the thing through the ship and put everyone at risk. At least this way we have a chance."

"Yeah, a chance," Kasyanov scoffed. "What are the odds? I'm taking bets. Anyone?"

"I don't gamble," Ripley said. "Listen, if three of us keep watch while the other three work, it'll still take a while to get into the *Samson*. Then when we return, straight into my shuttle and away."

"What about supplies?" Baxter asked. "Food, water. Lube for all that lovin' we'll be doing."

"Are there stocks down at the mine?" Ripley asked Hoop.

"Yep."

"But that's where *they* came from!" Sneddon said.

Ripley nodded. No one else spoke. *Yeah, we've all been thinking about that, too*, she thought.

"Right, so I'll call it," Hoop said. "I've got an idea of how we can get through the decompressed rooms to the *Samson*. We all go, and follow the plan. And if that thing causes us problems when we come back, we deal with it then."

"One cataclysm at a time, eh?" Baxter said.

"Something like that."

"We need more weapons," Ripley said. "We lost most of them down there when…"

"We can divert to Hold 2 on the way down," Sneddon said. "Plenty of charge thumpers and plasma torches there."

"Easy," Lachance said.

"A walk in the park," Baxter agreed.

"We're all going to die," Kasyanov said. And she meant it. She wasn't making a joke. Ripley had been impressed when she leaped into action in the docking arm, but now she was the voice of pessimism once again.

"Not today," Ripley replied. Kasyanov snorted. No one else replied.

They moved, but not too quickly. On the relative safety of the bridge, they each took a few moments to compose their thoughts.

Beyond the doors lay only danger.

8

VACUUM

They made sure that the bridge was properly sealed before they left.

There was brief discussion that Lachance and Baxter might remain behind, but it was quickly dismissed, and they didn't need much persuading that they should go with the others. Neither liked the idea of being left alone with the creature, especially if something went wrong on the planetary surface. Better that they all remain together. Besides, there was little that they could do aboard the orbiting ship, other than track its doomed trajectory.

Just before they left the bridge level, Hoop watched as Kasyanov approached Ripley, stretched on tiptoes, and planted a kiss on her cheek. She didn't speak—perhaps words of thanks would have been redundant, or might have lessened the moment—but she and Ripley locked glances for a moment, and then both nodded.

"If you ladies are done smooching, maybe it's time to get the fuck off this ship," Baxter said. With the bridge doors locked and their mechanisms disabled, the six survivors moved off toward Hold 2. Sneddon volunteered to go first, asking for Hoop's charge thumper. He didn't object. They were all in this together.

They circled back around the accommodations hub, watching each door in the inner wall of the curved corridor. There were almost a hundred separate bunk rooms in the hub, and the alien could be hiding in any of them. Access doors were recessed into the gray metal wall and difficult to see, and subdued lighting gave the shadows added depth. It was a stressful journey. They took it slowly and reached Hold 2 without incident.

It was a huge space—high ceilinged, cavernous and partly filled with spare mining equipment. Two massive ground transport vehicles were chained down to the floor, and several smaller trucks had moved around during and immediately following the *Delilah*'s crash. Other equipment lay stacked or scattered. There were metal transport crates, tool racks, supply tanks and boxes, and all manner of smaller items. It formed a complex maze of walkways and dead ends, and Hoop suddenly wanted to turn and go back the way they'd come.

But they needed weapons. Not just in case they came across that bastard thing in the *Marion*'s corridors, but to face whatever they might find down on the planet. The miners had unearthed something dreadful down there, and there was no telling how many of the things might be waiting for them.

The thought almost paralyzed him with a sense of hopelessness. But he had to shake his doubts and hide them away beneath the stark knowledge that they had no other options.

He motioned the others close, and he led the way along the hold's outer wall. When he reached a heavy green door he entered an access code. The door whispered open, and automatic lighting flickered on inside.

"All in," he murmured.

They filed past him, Ripley bringing up the rear.

"What's this?" she asked.

"Workshop," Hoop said. He was the last inside, backing in, watching the hold as he closed the door behind him. Only then did he turn around and relax.

Powell stood by the welding rig over in the far corner, complaining about something Welford had done, or something that grumpy bastard Baxter had said in the rec room, or maybe just finding an aspect of his own appearance to whinge about. Welford sat at the electronics island bench, goggles up on his forehead. He smiled at Powell's constant, monotonous drone. A massive coffee mug emblazoned with the words "Engineers are always screwing" steamed by his elbow as he waxed lyrical on some subject or another, his voice a constant background buzz, a counterpoint to Powell's deep tones.

Hoop blinked. He never thought he'd miss those two, not really. They'd died badly. He couldn't hold back the memories. He'd spent so long down here with them, working on various repair and maintenance jobs, and although they'd been more friendly with each other than with him—his superior ranking, he thought, or perhaps just that the two of them were more alike—they'd still been a team of three.

"What a dump," Baxter said.

"Fuck you," Hoop said.

"Nice place you've got here..." Ripley smiled, and she seemed to understand. Maybe she'd seen it in his expression.

Hoop sniffed and pointed.

"There's some stuff racked in the cupboards back there. Baxter, why don't you and Lachance check it out? Sneddon, Kasyanov, come with me and Ripley."

"Where?"

"Through there." He pointed at a door in the side wall, closed and marked with a *Hazardous Materials* symbol.

"What's in there?" Ripley asked.

"I'll show you," he said, smiling. "Wondering if we can fight fire with fire."

Hoop punched in the access code and the door slid open. Lighting flickered on inside, illuminating a small, sterile-looking room, more like a research lab than the workshop that led to it. He'd spent quite a bit of time in here, toying with chemicals and developing various application methods. Jordan had always turned a blind eye to the engineers' hobbies in research and development, because it relieved boredom and passed the time. But this had really been Welford's baby. Sometimes he'd spent twelve hours at a time in here, getting Powell to bring him food and drinks down from the galley or rec room. Hoop had never been sure exactly why Welford had become so interested in the spray gun technology. Perhaps it was simply because it was something he excelled in.

"So what's this?" Ripley asked.

"Welford's folly," Sneddon said. "I helped him with some of the designs."

"You did?" Hoop asked, surprised.

"Sure. Some of the stuff he was using down here was... pretty cutting-edge, actually."

Hoop hefted one of the units Welford had been working on. It looked like a heavy weapon of some sort, but was actually surprisingly light. He shook it, already knowing that the reservoir would be empty.

"We're going to fight them with water pistols?" Ripley said.

"Not water," Sneddon said. "Acid."

"Fire with fire," Hoop said, smiling and holding up the gun.

"The miners had been asking us for something like this for quite a while," Sneddon said. "The trimonite is usually only found in very small deposits, and surrounded by other less dense materials— sands, shales, quartzes, and other crystalline structures. It's always been a time-intensive process, sorting through it. The idea with this was to melt away all the other stuff with hydrofluoric acid, and keep the *trimonite* untouched."

"Sounds dangerous," Ripley said.

"That's why it's still just in the lab," Hoop said. "We were looking for a way to make the application process safer."

"And you found it?"

"No," Hoop said. "But safe's the last thing on my mind right now."

"How do we know this will even bother them?" Kasyanov asked, negative as ever. "They have acid in their veins!"

"There's only one way to find out," Hoop said. "We have two units. Let's get them primed, and we can get out of here."

* * *

Ten minutes later they stood ready at the workshop's locked doors. Hoop had shrugged a tool bag over his shoulder, packed with all the tools he thought they might need. He and Sneddon carried the spray guns, containment reservoirs fully loaded with hydrofluoric acid. Ripley and Lachance had charge thumpers, the charge containers loaded with six-inch bolts. They wore bolt belts around their waists, heavy with spare ammunition. Baxter and Kasyanov were carrying newly charged plasma torches.

They should have felt safer. Hoop should have felt ready. But he was still filled with dread as he prepared to open the doors.

"You all follow me," he said. "Sneddon, take the rear. Eyes and ears open. We'll move slow and steady, back around the hub, down the staircases to the docking deck. Once we get to the corridor outside Bay Three, that's when I get to work." He looked around at them all. Ripley was the only one who offered him a smile.

"On three."

It took almost half an hour to work their way back around the ship's accommodation hub and down to the docking deck. On a normal day it might have been half that time, but they were watching the shadows.

Hoop expected to see the surviving alien at any moment, leaping toward them from a recessed doorway, appearing around a closed corner, dropping from above when they passed beneath domed junctions. He kept the spray gun primed and aimed forward—it was much easier to manage than a charge thumper. There was no telling how effective the acid might be, but the thumpers were inaccurate as weapons if the target was more than a few yards away, and the plasma torches were probably more dangerous to them than the creature.

They'd seen that on the *Delilah*.

Hoop's finger stroked the trigger. *I should be wearing breathing apparatus*, he thought. *Goggles. A face mask*. If any of the hydrofluoric acid splashed back at him, or even misted in the air and drifted across his skin, he'd be burnt to a crisp. His clothes, skin, flesh, bones, would melt away beneath the acid's ultra-corrosive attack.

Stupid of him. *Stupid!* To think that they could take on the creature with a form of its own weapon. His mind raced with alternatives.

He should switch back to the thumper.

He should have Baxter take lead with the plasma torch.

They should stop and think things through.

Hoop exhaled hard, tensed his jaw. *Just fucking get on with it*, he thought. *No more dicking around! This is it.*

Descending the wide staircase into the docking level, they paused beside a row of three doors marked with bright yellow "Emergency" symbols. Baxter opened the first door and took out three vacuum-packed bags.

"Suits?" Ripley asked.

"Yeah, everything's in there," Baxter replied. "Suit, foldable helmet, compressed air tank, tether cable." He looked around at the rest. "Everyone suit up."

They took turns opening the bags and pulling themselves into the silver space suits. It was like being wrapped in thin crinkly plastic, with stiff sealing rings where the parts fit together. Fabric belts slipped through loops and kept the material from flapping too loosely. The helmets were similarly flexible, with comm units sewn into the fabric. The suits were designed for emergency use only, placed close to the docking bays in case of a catastrophic decompression. The air tanks would last for maybe an hour, the suits themselves intended purely to enable the user to get to the nearest safe place.

When they were all ready, they moved on.

Reaching the corridor outside Bay Three without incident, Hoop looked around at everyone else. They seemed more pumped up than they had before, more confident. But they couldn't let confidence get the better of them.

"Baxter, Sneddon, that way." He pointed past the closed doors and toward Bay Four, where Ripley's shuttle was docked. "Close the doors in Bay Four, make sure as hell they're secure, and keep watch. Kasyanov, Lachance, back the way we came. Close the corridor blast doors. Ripley, with me. Let's hustle."

When the others moved off he shrugged the tool bag from his shoulder and held the spray gun out to Ripley. "Just hold it for me."

She took the acid gun from him, one eyebrow raised.

"Too dangerous for me to actually use, eh?"

"Ripley—"

"Show me. I can handle myself."

Hoop sighed, then smiled.

"Okay, you prime it here, wait until this light is showing red. Aim. Squeeze the trigger. It'll fire compressed jets in short pulses."

"Shouldn't we be wearing proper safety gear?"

"Definitely." He turned away, knelt, and opened the tool bag. "I won't need long," he said. The space suit made normal movements a little more awkward, but he took a heavy portable drill out of the bag, fitted it with a narrow drill bit, and then propped it against one of the door panels.

Beyond, in the vestibule to Bay Three, lay the vacuum of space.

"You sure that door will hold?" Ripley asked. "Once you get through, and we start decompressing—"

"No!" he snapped. "No, I'm not sure. But what else do you suggest?"

Ripley didn't answer. But she nodded once.

"Helmets," he called. "Clip your tether lines close, and to something solid." Ripley fixed her flexible helmet collar and turned on her air supply, and along the corridor in both directions he heard the others doing the same. When he was sure everyone was ready, he fixed his own helmet with one hand, then started drilling.

It was the loudest noise they'd made since opening up the *Samson*. The metal drill bit skittered across the door's surface before wedging against a seam and starting to penetrate. Curls of metal wound out and dropped to the floor like robot hair. Smoke wafted, and Hoop saw heat shimmering the air around the drill's head as the bit bored slowly into the door.

He leaned into the tool, driving it deeper.

It didn't take long. The drill casing banged against the door when the bit pushed through, and Hoop turned off the power. A high-pitched whistling began instantly as air was forced through the microscopic gap between bit and metal.

He looked around at Ripley. She'd tethered herself to a door handle across the corridor.

"Everyone get ready," he said into his helmet's comm. "Here goes nothing." He placed his gloved hand over the rapid release button on the drill and pressed. A thud, a shudder through the drill, and the bit was sucked through the door and into the vestibule beyond.

Hoop backed away, tying himself to the heavy door handle with the shortest lead possible, then kicked the drill aside.

A piercing whistle filled the corridor as air was sucked out through the tiny hole. The door vibrated in its heavy frame, but it remained solid and secure. Dust cast graceful shapes in the air, shimmering skeins wavering as the artificial lighting flickered with a power surge.

Soon the flow of air ceased, and they were standing in vacuum.

"Everyone okay?" Hoop called. Everyone was.

Which meant the time had come to make their way through to the *Samson*.

They were assuming there was nothing dangerous left inside. Four aliens had emerged. Two had been killed in the vestibule, another blasted into space when the window had failed, and the fourth was somewhere aboard the *Marion*. They were as certain as they could be that there had only been four, but there was no saying they hadn't left something behind when they'd fled—eggs, acid sacs, or something else unknown. They knew so little about the beasts.

"Right. We can't afford to use the plasma torch or spray guns in the *Samson*."

"I'll go first, then," Ripley said. She handed the spray gun back to Hoop and hefted the charge thumper. "Makes sense." And she was through the door before anyone else could speak.

Hoop followed her quickly through the ruined vestibule, past the airlock and along the short docking arm. She paused at the *Samson*'s open hatch, but only for a moment. Then she ducked, pushed the charge thumper ahead of her, and entered the dropship.

"Oh, shit," she said.

"What?" Hoop pressed forward, senses alert. But then he saw what she had seen, and his stomach lurched.

"Going to be a pleasant journey," Ripley said.

9

DROP

PROGRESS REPORT:

To: Weyland-Yutani Corporation, Science Division
(Ref: code 937)

Date (unspecified)

Transmission (pending)

Presence of previously identified alien species confirmed.
Several specimens destroyed. Warrant Officer Ripley in
play. Plan proceeding satisfactorily. Anticipating further
update within twelve hours.

I have a purpose once more.

Before undocking with the *Marion*, Lachance assured them all that
he was the best pilot on the ship. His brief display of humor did
little to lighten the mood.

Even when Hoop leaned over to Ripley and informed her that
the Frenchman might well be the best pilot in the *galaxy*, she still
struggled to hold down her vomit.

Bad enough this was their one and only chance. But forced to
make the journey in this dropship, it seemed as if fate was rubbing
their faces in the worst of everything that had happened.

Once the internal atmosphere had been restored, they'd been
forced to remove their headgear in order to conserve the suits'

limited oxygen supplies.

Anything not bolted or screwed down in the *Samson* had been sucked out during decompression. But there was still the blood, dried into spattered black smears all across the cream-colored interior paneling, the light-blue fixed seats, and the textured metal decking. And there was the stench of decomposition, still heavy even though the ship had been in vacuum for almost a whole day.

An arm was jammed beneath one row of seating, clawed fingers almost wrapped around the seat post, bones visible through scraps of clothing and skin. Ripley noticed the others doing their best to not look at it, and she wondered whether they knew who it had been. There were tattered insignia on the torn clothing, and a gold ring on one finger.

They should have moved it aside, but no one wanted to touch it.

And aside from the human detritus, there was what had been left behind by the aliens.

The interior of the *Samson*'s passenger hold was laid out with two facing rows of seating across an open space, twelve seats per side. In this open space were fixings for equipment storage—they'd secured their various weapons there—and a raised area containing low-level cupboards and racks. Even when sitting, passengers could see over this raised portion to communicate with one another.

At the rear of the cabin, two narrow doors were set into the bulkhead. One was marked as a bathroom, the other Ripley guessed led into the engine room.

They had all chosen to sit as close as possible to the slightly raised flight deck. Lachance and Baxter sat up there, with Ripley and Hoop on one side of the passenger cabin, Kasyanov and Sneddon on the other. None of them wanted to sit at the rear.

None of them even wanted to look.

In their time aboard the ship, the aliens had made the shadowy rear of the cabin their own. The floor, walls, and ceiling were coated with a thick, textured substance. It clung around the two doors, crossing them here and there, like bridges of plastic that had melted, burned, and hardened again. It looked like an extrusion of some kind, dark and heavy in places, glimmering and shiny in others, as if wet. There were hollows that bore a chilling resemblance to shapes Ripley knew well.

The aliens had made their own place to rest, and it was a stark reminder of what had been in here until so recently.

"I hope this trip is quick," Sneddon said. Kasyanov nodded beside her.

"Lachance?" Hoop asked.

"Last checks," the pilot said. He was propped in the flight seat, leaning forward and running his hands across the control panels. A screen flickered to life in front of him, two more in the bulkhead by his side. "Baxter? Have we got a link to the *Marion*'s computer yet?"

"Just coming online now," Baxter said. In the co-pilot's seat, he had a pull-out keyboard on his lap, hands stroking keys as a series of symbols flashed across the display suspended before him. "Just calling up the nav computer... Ah, there we are." The windscreen misted for a moment, and when it cleared again it was criss-crossed with a fine grid display.

"Leave it off for now," Lachance said. "I want to get away from the *Marion* first. I'm worried there's still wreckage from the crash matching our orbit."

"After so long?" Kasyanov asked.

"It's possible," Lachance replied. "Okay, everyone strapped in?"

Hoop leaned across Ripley and checked her straps. His sudden closeness surprised her, and she felt his arm brushing her hip and shoulder as he tightened the safety straps.

"Bumpy ride," he said, smiling. "The atmosphere of this rock can be nasty."

"Great," she said. "Thanks." Hoop nodded, caught her eye, looked away again.

What was that? she thought. *Come on, Ripley, you're dodging monsters at the edge of space, and you can still get horny?* She chuckled soundlessly, and knew that he heard her exhalation.

"How's it looking?" Hoop asked.

"All systems online," Lachance said. "Inertial dampers are a bit glitchy, so the ride might be bumpier than usual."

"Oh, super," Sneddon said.

"How often have you guys been down?" Ripley asked.

"We've all been planetside a few times," Hoop said. "Kasyanov for medical emergencies, the rest of us for various other reasons. But it's mainly the miners who made this trip."

"Soon you'll know why," Kasyanov said quietly. "This planet's a regular shit-hole."

"Okay, everyone," Lachance said. "Thank you for flying Lachance Spaceways. Dinner will be served half an hour after take-off—today we have lobster ravioli and champagne. There's a selection of in-flight entertainment, and your vomit bags are under your seats." He chuckled. "You'll be needing them. Dock disconnect in ten seconds." He switched on an automatic countdown, and Ripley soundlessly ticked off the seconds.

Nine… eight…

"Electro-locks off, magnetic grab disabled."

…six… five…

"Retros primed, fire on my mark."

…three…

"Passengers *might* feel a slight bump."

What the hell is a slight bump? Ripley thought. Hoop grasped her hand and squeezed. Sneddon and Kasyanov looked terrified.

"… one… mark."

There was a moment of nothing. And then Ripley's stomach rolled, her brain bounced against her skull, her senses swam, her breath was punched from her lungs, and a shattering roar filled the cabin.

She managed to turn her head and look past Hoop through the windscreen and onto the flight deck. As they dropped quickly away from the *Marion*, the extensive damage from the other dropship's crash became even more apparent. She also saw the *Narcissus* docked at the other edge of the ship's belly, and felt a curious anxiety at being away from her. Perhaps because that ship had been her home for so long, whether she'd been aware or not.

But the shuttle was locked up safe, and Jonesy would spend most of his time asleep. She'd made sure he had plenty of food.

A siren wailed, buzzers cut through the cabin, and the ship's attitude changed. Lachance seemed to be calm and in control, stroking buttons and waving his hand across projected controls between him and the windscreen. The *Marion* moved out of sight to port, and LV178 came into view. With the vibration of the ship's descent it was difficult to make out any real features—to Ripley it was little more than a yellowish-gray smudge beyond the windows.

A few moments later Lachance hit a button and heat shields rose to block out the view.

"Just about to start skimming the atmosphere now," he said.

Artificial gravity flickered as it adjusted to the planet's real pull. Sneddon puked. She leaned forward and aimed most of it between her legs. Kasyanov glanced sideways then ahead again, closing her eyes, gripping her seat arms so tightly that her knuckles were pearls of white on her dark skin.

Hoop's grip almost hurt, but Ripley didn't mind.

The *Samson* started to shake even more. Each impact seemed hard enough to tear the ship apart, and Ripley couldn't hold back the gasps and grunts that came with each thud. It brought back memories of descending down to LV426 in *Nostromo*, but this was much worse.

She looked back at that strange swathe of material the aliens had left behind. It must have been quite solid to survive the decompression and remain intact, yet from here it looked almost soft, like huge spider webbing covered with dust and ash. The creatures must have hibernated in there. She wondered just how much longer the beasts could have slept, waiting, if they hadn't decided to open up the *Samson*.

Her thoughts drifted, and she feared what was below them. Hoop figured that eighteen miners had been left behind down on the surface, and no one knew what had happened to them. There was no real information on what they had found, how the alien attack had happened, where they had been discovered. The trimonite mine was the last place in the galaxy she wanted to go right then, but it was the only place that offered any hope for their survival.

Get the fuel cells and get out again. That was Hoop's plan. They'd all agreed.

It felt as if the ship was shaking itself to pieces. Just when Ripley believed all their worries might end there and then, Lachance spoke again.

"Might be a little turbulence up ahead."

Sneddon leaned forward and puked again.

Ripley leaned back and closed her eyes, and Hoop squeezed her hand even tighter.

It seemed like forever, but it couldn't have been more than an hour before they were deep in LV178's atmosphere, flying a mile above the planet's surface toward the mine. Baxter had fired up the nav computer and calculated that the facility was six hundred miles away.

"Just over an hour," Lachance said. "I could fly faster, but the storm's still pretty rough."

"Let me guess," Kasyanov said. "Might get bumpy?"

"Just a little."

"How are we still flying?" Sneddon asked. "How is the ship still in once piece? How is my stomach not hanging out of my mouth?"

"Because we're hardy space explorers," Baxter said.

In truth, the vibrating and bumping had reduced drastically once they had entered the atmosphere and Baxter had plotted their route. Lachance gave control over to the autopilot, and then turned his seat around.

"Lobster," he said.

Sneddon groaned. "If you ever mentioned food again, Lachance, I won't be responsible for the consequences."

"Okay, folks, we've got an hour," Hoop said. "We need to talk about what happens next."

"We land, get the fuel cell, take off again," Ripley said. "Right?"

"Well…"

"What?" she asked.

"It might not be quite that simple," Hoop said. "There are variables."

"Oh, great," Kasyanov said. "You can't get much more variable that those monsters, can you?"

"Landing pad," Hoop said. "Access to the mine. Air quality inside. Damage. And the fuel cells are stored several levels down."

"So tell me what all that means?" Ripley said, looking around at them.

Sneddon held up her hands. "Hey, I'm just the science officer."

"The planet's atmosphere isn't great," Hoop said. "The mine and its surface complex are contained in an environmental dome. The landing pads are outside, connected by short tunnels. Inside the dome there are several surface buildings—stores, mess block, accommodations—and then two entrances to the mine, also enclosed for additional safety.

"Once down in the mine, in each entrance there are two caged elevators descending to nine levels. The first three levels are abandoned—they've been mined out. Level four is where the fuel cells are stored, along with a load more emergency stores. Food, water, equipment, stuff like that. Most of the emergency stores are belowground in case of a disaster, so they'll be accessible to anyone down in the mine. And levels five through nine are the current working levels."

"Then it's on one of those levels they found the aliens?" Ripley asked.

"That's a fair bet."

"So we get in, descend to level four, get the fuel cells, and come back out."

"Yeah," Hoop said. "But we have no idea what state the mine's in."

"We take it all step by step," Kasyanov said. "Whatever we find, we work through it as best we can."

"And just as fast as we can," Sneddon said. "Don't know about you all, but I don't want to be down here one minute longer than necessary."

After that, silence hung heavy. Lachance turned his chair around again and kept an eye on the flight computers. Baxter scanned the nav displays. Ripley and the others sat quietly, not catching one another's eyes, and trying not to look at the strange sculptures the aliens had left behind.

Ripley took the easy way out and closed her eyes.

And surprised herself when Hoop nudged her awake. Had she really slept? Through all that movement, buffeting, and noise?

"Sheesh, haven't you slept long enough?" he asked. Anyone else and she might have been annoyed, but there was a lilt to his voice that said he almost understood. He sounded hesitant, too, almost sad.

"We there?"

"Just circling the complex now."

"Lights are on," Lachance said from the flight deck.

"But no one's home," Baxter replied. "Dome looks intact, can't see any obvious damage."

Ripley waited for a moment, sensing the subtle vibrations of the ship. Their flight seemed much smoother than when she'd fallen asleep. She hit the quick release catch on her straps and stood up.

"Ripley?" Hoop said.

"Just looking." She moved forward and leaned against the back of the flight chair. The Frenchman turned lazily and squinted back at her.

"Come to see my cockpit??" he asked.

"You wish," she replied.

The windscreen was hazed with dust, but she could still make out the segmented metallic dome below as the ship circled it. One side of it was almost buried with drifting sand, and across its surface were several blinking lights. There was no sign of clear sections, nor could she see any access points.

"Bleak," she said.

"Wait 'til you get inside," Baxter said.

"Where are the landing pads?"

Lachance leveled the *Samson* slightly and hovered, drifting sideways directly over the dome. He pointed. Ripley could just make out three bulky shapes on the ground, also half-buried by drifted sand.

"Get closer," Hoop said, joining Ripley behind the two flight chairs. "We don't know what happened down here, but it's a fair bet they were pursued all the way to the ships."

"How do you figure that?" Sneddon asked from where she was still strapped in.

"Because the *Samson* left so many behind."

Lachance dropped them lower and closer to the landing pads. They were only a couple of hundred yards from the dome, and Ripley saw hints of the connecting tunnels that ran between them. Sheets of sand blew across the ground, driven by winds they could not feel in the *Samson*. The landscape was daunting but strangely beautiful, dust sculptures forming incredible, graceful shapes. Away from the artificial interruption of the mine, the desert looked like a frozen sea, flowing over years instead of moments.

Miles in the distance, electrical storms flashed deep inside looming clouds.

"How the hell are you going to land?" Ripley asked.

"The pads are usually cleared by the ground crews," Lachance said. "Big blowing machines, sand scoops. It'll be okay. I'm good."

"So you keep saying," she said. "I'm still waiting for proof."

"No sign of any nasties waiting for us," Hoop said.

"In this weather?" Baxter asked.

"There's no saying what environments they live in, or even prefer," Ripley said. She remembered Ash—before his true nature was exposed, when he was studying the alien—talking about remarkable adaptations to the ship's environment. Maybe sand-lashed, storm-blasted landscapes were their preference.

"Strap in, ladies and gentlemen," Lachance said. He checked readouts, stroked his hand across the projected nav controls in front of him, and then settled back in his seat.

Ripley and Hoop went back to their seats and secured their safety straps. She waited for him to check her clasps again, and saw Sneddon looking from her to Hoop, and smirking. Ripley stared back.

The science officer looked away.

The *Samson* shook as retros fired. Moments later there was a heavy bump, and then the engines started to cycle down.

"There," Lachance said. "Told you I was good."

Hoop exhaled, and from across the cabin Ripley heard Kasyanov mutter something that might have been a prayer. Straps were opened, they stood and stretched, then gathered at the front of the ship to look outside.

Lachance had landed them facing the dome. The line of the partly buried tunnel was obvious, leading from their pad to the dome, and the storm suddenly seemed more intense now that they had touched down. Maybe because there was more sand to blow around at low level.

"Suit up," Hoop said. "Grab your weapons. Lachance, you take point with me. I'm going to be opening doors and hatches. Baxter, you bring up the rear."

"Why do I have to come last?" the communications engineer asked.

"Because you're a gentleman," Sneddon said. Kasyanov chuckled, Baxter looked uncertain, and Ripley wondered at the complex relationships between these people. She'd barely scratched the surface—they'd been here so close together for so long.

The inside of the *Samson* suddenly seemed so much safer. Through her fear Ripley was determined, but she couldn't shake those terrible memories. Not the new ones, of Powell and Welford being killed by those fast, furious things. And not the old ones, back on the *Nostromo*. She couldn't help feeling that even more terrible memories were soon to be forged.

If she lived to remember.

"Let's stay close and tight," she said. No one replied. Everyone knew what was at stake here, and they'd all seen these things in action.

"We move fast, but carefully," Hoop said. "No storming ahead. No heroics."

They fixed their helmets, checked each other's suits and air supplies, tested communications, and hefted the weapons. To Ripley they all looked so vulnerable: pale white grubs ready for the aliens to puncture, rip apart, eat. And none of them had any real idea about what they were about to encounter.

Perhaps the uncertainty was a good thing. Maybe if they knew for sure what they would find down in the mine, they would never bring themselves to enter.

Breathing deeply, thinking of Amanda, who probably believed her mother to be dead, Ripley silently vowed that she would do anything and everything necessary to stay alive.

Lachance opened the outer hatch, and the storm came inside.

PART 2

UNDERGROUND

10

S K I N

"What the hell is *that*?" Hoop asked.

"Looks like… hide, or something," Lachance said.

"They shed their skins." Ripley came to stand beside them, charge thumper aimed forward. "It happens when they grow. And you've seen how quickly that is."

"How many *are* there?" Hoop almost went forward to sift through the drift of pale yellow material with his boot. But something held him back. He didn't even want to touch it.

"Enough," Sneddon said. She sounded nervous, jumpy, and Hoop was already wondering whether she should really be in charge of the other spray gun.

Then again, they were *all* scared.

They'd made their way across the storm-lashed landing pad and into the tunnel entrance without incident. The violent winds, blasting sand, and screaming storm had been almost exciting, primal conditions that they could never grow used to after living on climate-controlled ships.

Inside the tunnel the illumination was still functioning, and halfway along there were signs of a fight. An impromptu barricade had been formed from a selection of storage pods and canisters, all of which had been knocked aside, trampled, broken, and blasted. Impact marks scarred the metal-paneled walls and ceiling, and a dappled spread of flooring was bubbled and raised. The acid splash was obvious, but there was no sign of the wounded or dead alien that had caused it.

They reached the end of the tunnel, facing the heavy, closed blast doors that opened directly into the mine's surface dome. And no one was eager to open them. They all remembered what had happened the last time.

"Any way we can see inside?" Ripley asked, nodding at the doors.

"Baxter?" Hoop asked.

"I might be able to connect with the mine's security cameras," the communications officer said. He put his plasma torch down carefully and pulled a tablet computer from the wide pockets of his suit.

The storm rumbled against the tunnel's upper surface, sand lashing the metal with a billion impacts, wind roaring around the grooved, curved metal shell. It sounded like something huge trying to get in. The tunnel and metal dome had been constructed to provide the mine with protection against such inimical elements. A huge investment had gone into sinking this mine almost thirty years ago, and its maintenance had been a headache ever since. But the allure of trimonite was great. Its use in industry, its allure as an ultra-rare jewel, ensured that the investment paid off. For those with a monetary interest, at least.

As usual, it was the workers—braving the elements and facing the dangers—who gained the least.

"Can you tell whether systems are operational?" Ripley asked, her voice impatient.

"Give me a chance!" Baxter snapped. He knelt with the tablet balanced on his thighs.

All good so far, Hoop thought, but they hadn't come that far at all. There could be anything beyond these doors. The mine's upper compound might be crawling with those things. He imagined the surface buildings and dome's interior as the inside of a huge nest, with thousands of aliens swarming across the ground, up the walls, and hanging in vast structures made from the same weird material they'd found inside the *Samson*.

He shivered, physically repelled at the thought, but unable to shake it.

"Got it," Baxter said. Hoop waited for the man's outburst of disbelief, a shout of terror, but none came. "Hoop?"

He moved beside Baxter and looked down at the screen. Across the top were several thumbnails, and the main screen was taken with a view of the dome's interior, as seen from high up on one side. The lights were still on. Everything was motionless.

"Thumbnails?" Hoop asked.

"Yeah. Other cameras." Baxter touched the screen and images began to scroll. They were from differing angles and elevations, all showing the dome's interior. Hoop was familiar with the ten or so buildings, the vehicles scattered around, the planet's geography altered and flattened inside the dome's relatively small span. Nothing looked particularly out of place. It all seemed quite normal.

"Can't see any damage," Lachance said.

"Don't like this at all," Kasyanov said. Fear made her voice higher than normal. It sounded like impending panic. "Where are they? What about the other miners, the ones left behind?"

"Dead down in the mines," Sneddon said. "Taken deep to wherever those things were found, maybe. Like wasps or termites, gathering food."

"Oh, thanks for that," Kasyanov said.

"It's all just maybes," Ripley said.

Hoop nodded. "That's all we've got. Baxter, keep in the middle of the group, and keep your eyes on that screen. Scroll the images, watch out for any movement that isn't us. Shout if you see anything." He moved to the door controls and checked the control panel. "All good here. Ready?"

Baxter held back, and the others stood in a rough semi-circle around the big doors, weapons held at the ready. *Not weapons*, Hoop thought. *They're tools. Mining tools. What do we even think we're doing down here?* But they were all looking to him, and he projected calm and determination. With a single nod he touched the switch.

A hiss, a grinding sound, and the doors parted. A breeze whistled out as pressures equalized, and for a moment a cloud of dust filled the tunnel, obscuring their vision. Someone shouted in panic. Someone else moved quickly forward and through the doors, and then Hoop heard Ripley's voice.

"It's fine in here," she said. "Clear. Come on through."

He was next through the doors, spray gun at the ready. The others followed, and Kasyanov closed the doors behind them. They were much too loud.

"Sneddon?" Hoop asked.

"Air's fine," she said. She was checking a device slung onto her belt, its screen showing a series of graphs and figures. She slipped off her helmet and left it hanging, and the others did the same.

"Baxter?" Hoop asked.

"I'll *tell* you if I see anything!" he snapped.

"Right, good. Just keeping you on your toes." He nodded at a bank of steel containers lined up along the dome wall beside the door. "Okay, let's get these suits off, secure them in one of these equipment lock-ups. We'll pick them up on the way back." They stripped the suits quickly, and Hoop piled them inside one of the units.

"Mine entrance?" Ripley asked, and Hoop pointed. There were actually two entrances, both housed inside bland rectangular buildings. But they were going for the nearest.

Hoop led the way. He carried the spray gun awkwardly, feeling faintly ridiculous hefting it like a weapon, even though he knew their enemies. He had never fired a gun in his life. As a kid, living in a more remote area of Pennsylvania, his Uncle Richard had often taken him out shooting. He'd tried to force a gun into Hoop's hands—a vintage Kalashnikov, a replica Colt .45, even a pulse rifle illegally borrowed from a neighbor on leave from the Colonial Marines' 69th Regiment, the Homer's Heroes.

But Hoop had always resisted. The black, bulky objects had always scared him, and his kid's knowledge of what they were for had made the fear worse. *I don't want to kill anyone*, he'd always thought, and he'd watched his uncle's face as the older man blasted away at trees, rocks, or homemade targets hung through the woods. There had been something in his expression that had meant Hoop never truly trusted him. Something like bloodlust.

His uncle had been killed years later, just before Hoop's first trip into space, shot in the back on a hunting trip into the woods. No one ever really knew what had happened. Lots of people died that way.

But now, for the first time ever, Hoop wished he'd taken one of those guns and rested it in his hands. Weighed the potential uses he might have put it to, against the repulsion he felt for the dull black metal.

An acid spray gun. *Who the fuck am I kidding?*

This had always been a strange place, beneath the dome. Hoop had been here several times now, and he always found it unnerving—it was the planet's natural landscape, but the dome made it somewhere *inside*, the climate artificial and entirely under their control. So they kicked through sand and dust that the wind no longer touched. They breathed false air that LV178's sun did not heat. The structure's underside formed an unreal sky, lit in gray swathes by the many spotlights hung from its supporting beams and columns.

It was as if they had trapped a part of the planet and tried to make it their own.

Just look where that had got them.

As they neared the building that enclosed the first mine head, Hoop signalled that they should spread out and approach in a line. The door seemed to be propped or jammed open. If one of those things emerged, best it was faced with an array of potential targets. All of them armed.

They paused, none of them wanting to be the first to go through.

"Hoop," Ripley whispered. "I've got an idea." She slung the charge thumper over her shoulder by its strap and darted quickly toward the building. Beside the half-open door she unbuckled her belt and pulled it loose of the loops.

Hoop saw what she was about to do. His heart quickened, his senses sharpened. He crouched low, ensuring that the gun's nozzle was pointing slightly to the left of the door. If something happened, he didn't want to catch Ripley in the acid spray.

Ripley fashioned a loop at the end of the belt and edged forward, feeding it over the top of the door's chunky handle. She looked back at the others, acknowledging their slight nods. Then she held up her other hand with three fingers pointing, then two, one…

And she pulled.

The door screeched across accumulated grit. The belt slipped from the handle, and nothing emerged.

Before Hoop could speak, Ripley had swung the charge thumper from her shoulder and edged inside.

"Baxter!" Hoop said as he ran forward.

"No cameras in there!" Baxter responded.

It wasn't as dark inside as Hoop had expected. There was a low level illumination coming through the opaque ceiling—artificial light borrowed from outside—and the lift's internal lights were still powered up. The lighting was good.

What it showed was not.

There was a dead miner in the lift. Hoop couldn't distinguish the sex. In the seventy days since they had died, bacteria brought to the mine by the humans had set to work, consuming the corpse. Environmental control had done the rest; the damp, warm atmosphere providing the ideal conditions in which the microorganisms could multiply. The result caused the corpse's flesh to bloat and sag.

The smell had diminished until it was only a tang of sweet decay, but it was enough to make Hoop wish they'd kept their suits and helmets. The unfortunate victim's mouth hung open in a laugh, or a scream.

"No sign of what killed them," Kasyanov said.

"I think we can rule out heart attack," Lachance quipped.

Hoop went to the elevator controls and accessed them. They seemed fine, with no warning symbols on the screen and no sign that there were any power problems. The small nuclear generator in one of the other surface buildings was still active, and doing its job well.

"It's working?" Ripley asked.

"You're not seriously expecting us to go down in that?" Sneddon said.

"You want to take the stairs?" Hoop asked. There were two emergency escape routes leading out from the mine, a series of rough staircases cast into holes sunk adjacent to the lift pits. Almost five thousand feet deep, and the idea of descending seven thousand steps—five hundred flights—appealed to no one.

"Can't we at least move them out?" Ripley asked. She and Kasyanov went forward and started shifting the body. Hoop had to help. It didn't remain in one piece.

With the lift cage to themselves, they all entered, taking care to avoid the corner where the corpse had been. Hoop found it even more disturbing that they couldn't tell who it was. They had all known the victim, that was for sure. But they didn't know them anymore.

What had happened struck Hoop all over again. He liked to think he was good at coping with emotional upheaval—he'd left his kids behind, effectively fleeing out here into deep space, and on some levels he had come to terms with why he'd done that—but since the disaster, he had woken sometimes in a cold sweat, dreams of smothering and being eaten alive haunting the shadows of sleep. His dreams of monsters had become so much more real. He thought perhaps he cried out, but no one had ever said anything to him. Maybe because almost everyone was having bad dreams now.

"Hoop?" Ripley said quietly. She was standing beside him, staring with him at the lift's control panel.

"I'm okay."

"You're sure?"

"What are those things, Ripley?"

She shrugged. "You know as much as me."

He turned to the others. There were no accusing stares, no smirks at his momentary lapse of concentration. They all felt the same.

"We go down to level 4," he said, "get the power cell, then get out as quickly as we can."

A few nods. Grim faces. He inspected their make-do weapons, knew that none of them were in the hands of soldiers. They were just as likely to shoot each other.

"Take it easy," he said softly, to himself as much as anyone else. Then he turned to the control panel and ran a quick diagnostic on the lift. All seemed fine. "Going down." He touched the button for level 4. The cage juddered a little and the descent began.

Hoop tried to calm himself and prepare for what they might find when the doors opened again, yet his stomach rolled, dizziness hit him, and someone shouted out.

"We're falling. We're *falling*!"

The elevator began to scream.

The old stone farmhouse in northern France, a holiday home for her family for as long as she could remember. She is alone right now, but not lonely. She can never be lonely with her daughter so close.

The silence is disturbed only by the gentle breeze, rustling leaves in the woodland far at the bottom of the garden, whispering in the few scattered trees that grow closer by. The sun blazes, scorching the sky a lighter shade of blue. It's hot but not uncomfortable—the breeze carries moisture from Ripley's skin, slick from the sunblock she's been careful to apply. Birds sing their enigmatic songs.

Far above, a family of buzzards circles lazily, eyeing the landscape for prey.

Amanda runs to her through a freshly harvested field, the crop stubble scratching at her legs, poppies speckling the landscape red, and her smile countering even the heat and glory of the sun. She is giggling, holding aloft a present for her mother. Amanda is such an inquisitive little girl. Often she emerges from the small woodland with snails attached all over her arms and shoulders, small frogs captured in her hands, or an injured bird nursed against her chest.

As her daughter climbs the low wooden fence between garden and field and starts across the lawn, Ripley wonders what she has brought home this time.

Mommy, I found an octopus! *the girl shrills.*

A blink later and she is on the lawn at Ripley's feet, shivering and shaking as the long-legged thing curls its tail tighter around her sweet throat, and Ripley is trying to hook her fingers beneath its many legs, prise it off, pull it away from her angel without tearing Amanda's hair off with it. I'll cut it, *she thinks, but she's worried that the acid will eat into the ground, and keep on eating.*

And then from the woods there comes a series of high-pitched screeches. Shadows fall. The sun retreats, birds fall silent, and the buzzards have disappeared. The garden is suddenly plunged into twilight, and those shadows that have always haunted her emerge from among the trees. They are looking for their child.

It's mine! Ripley *shouts, kneeling and protecting Amanda with her own body.* Whatever's inside her is mine!

The shadows stalk closer. Nothing is beautiful anymore.

"Ripley!" Hoop shouted, nudging her. "Grab on to something!"

She shook her head. The vision had happened in an instant. And then it was gone, leaving only a haunting sensation.

The elevator plunged, screeching against its control framework, throwing sparks that were visible through the cage walls, vibrating violently, shaking her vision so much that everyone and everything around her was a blur.

She heard the thud of weapons hitting the floor and dropped her own, staggering back until she was braced against the wall. But there was nothing to hold onto. And even if there had been, it would have made no difference.

Her stomach seemed to be rising and rolling, and she swallowed down the sudden urge to vomit.

Someone else puked.

Hoop hung onto the long handle set into the wall beside the door, one hand curled through it and the other working at the controls.

"What the hell—?" Baxter shouted.

"I've got it!" Hoop cut in. But it was clear to Ripley that he *didn't* have it. She edged across to him, afraid that at any moment she and the others would actually lift from the floor and start to float.

We can't be going that fast, she thought. *We'd have struck bottom by now!* Five thousand feet, Hoop had said. She turned the figures over, trying to calculate how long they might have at freefall, but—

"There are buffers," Hoop shouted. "Each level. We've passed the first four already, barely felt them. Approaching five…"

Thud!

A heavy vibration passed through the lift, thumping Ripley in the chest.

"We're not slowing!" she shouted.

"We will!" he responded. "Dampers were fitted over the bottom two levels, in case of—"

"This?"

He looked at her. Beside him she could see a flickering set of figures on the control panel. Their depth approached 2,500 feet, the numbers flipping too fast for her to see.

"It's one way to test them," he said.

Ripley felt a flood of emotion. They were helpless, and that was a sensation she hated. In space, there were so many variables that presented countless levels of danger, but usually they were countered by some mechanical, electrical, or psychological means.

Even with that thing stalking them on the *Nostromo* they had gone on the offensive, hunting it, seeking to drive it toward the airlock. And after Dallas was gone and Ash was revealed for what he was… even then they had been acting in their own best interests.

Here, now, she could only stand and wait to die.

They flashed past levels 6 and 7, and each time the impact of safety buffers seemed harder. Was their descent slowing? Ripley wasn't sure. Sparks flew all around the cage's outsides, metal whined and screeched, and at the speed they were going now, she figured they'd know nothing about reaching level 9.

She contemplated that final moment, the instant when the elevator struck, crumpled, and they were all smacked into the solid floor, mashed together… and she wondered if she'd feel anything at all.

The brief waking nightmare seemed somehow worse.

"We're slowing!" Hoop said. They thudded past the buffer on

level 8, and then a heavy grinding sound commenced.

Ripley and the others were all flung to the floor. A rhythmic clanging began, resounding explosions from all around that vibrated through the cage's structure. Bolts, screws and shreds of metal showered around her, and Ripley expected them to burst apart at any moment.

The noise became almost unbearable, pulsing into her ears, her torso, and the vibrations threatened to shake her apart bone-by-bone. Lying flat on the floor, she managed to turn her head toward Hoop. He was sitting propped in the far corner, head tilted to one side so he could still look at the control panel.

He glanced across, saw her looking.

"Dampers working," he shouted.

Then they struck bottom. Ripley's breath was knocked out of her as she was punched into the elevator's floor. Something heavy landed on her leg. A scream was cut off, but someone else grunted and started to moan.

The lift mechanism was smoking, filling the air with an acrid haze. Lights flickered off and then came back on again, buzzing and settling into an even glow. The sudden silence was more shocking than the noise and violence had been.

Ripley pushed herself up onto hands and knees, breathing hard and waiting for the white-hot pain of cracked ribs or broken limbs to sing in. But apart from an array of bruises, a bloodied nose, and a sense of disbelief that they had somehow survived, she appeared to be fine.

"Are we still falling?" Sneddon asked. "My guts tell me we are."

"Nice landing," Lachance said, nodding at Hoop. "Make a pilot out of you yet." Hoop smiled back.

"I think…" Baxter said. He stood, then howled, slipping sideways and falling again. Kasyanov caught him. "Ankle," he said. "Ankle!" The doctor started examining him.

"Anyone else hurt?" Hoop asked.

"Only my pride," Lachance said. His suit was speckled with vomit, and he brushed at it with one gloved hand.

"Best pilot in the galaxy, my ass," Ripley said, pleased to see the Frenchman smile.

"We okay?" Sneddon asked. "We're not just hanging here waiting, to fall the rest of the way, are we? The way our luck's been going, you know."

"No, we're down," Hoop said. "Look." He nodded at the cage doors, then pulled a small, narrow flashlight from his tool belt. It threw out a surprisingly bright beam. He aimed it past the bent bars of the deformed cage, revealing the smoother metal of more solid doors.

"Level 9?" Ripley asked.

Hoop nodded.

"And the elevator's fucked," Baxter said. "That's just fucking great." He winced as Kasyanov probed around his foot and lower leg, then groaned when she looked up.

"Broken ankle," she said.

"No shit," Baxter replied.

"Can you splint it?" Hoop asked. "He's got to be able to walk."

"I *can* walk!" Baxter said, a little desperately.

"We can help you," Ripley said, aiming a warning stare at Hoop. "There are enough of us. Don't panic."

"Who's panicking?" Baxter said, looking desperate, eyes wide with pain and terror.

"We won't leave you," Ripley said, and he seemed to take comfort from that.

"Everyone else?" Hoop asked. Sneddon nodded, Lachance raised a hand in a casual wave. "Ripley?"

"I'm fine, Hoop," she said, trying not to sound impatient. They were down, battered and bruised, but they couldn't afford to hang around. "So what now?"

"Now we have two choices," Hoop said, glancing at Baxter again. "One, we start climbing."

"How many stairs?" Kasyanov asked.

"We've struck bottom at level 9. Seven thousand steps to—"

"Seven-fucking-*thousand*?" Sneddon spat. Baxter remained silent, but he looked down at the floor close to his wounded foot and ankle.

All his weight was on the other foot.

"Choice two," Hoop continued, "we make our way across to the other elevator."

Silence. Everyone looked around, waiting for someone else to speak.

"And whatever they found was down here, where they were working the new seam," Baxter said. "On level 9."

"There's no choice," Kasyanov said. "How far is the other elevator shaft?"

"In a straight line, a little over five hundred yards," Hoop said. "But none of the tunnels are straight."

"And we have no idea what happened down here?" Ripley asked.

No one answered. They all looked to Hoop. He shrugged.

"All they said is that they found something horrible. And we already know what that was."

"No we don't!" Kasyanov said. "There could be hundreds!"

"I don't think so." They looked to Sneddon, who was looking down at the spray gun she'd picked up once again. "They hatch from people, right? We've seen that. So by my reckoning—"

"Eighteen," Ripley said. "Maybe less."

"Eighteen of them?" Kasyanov asked. "Oh, well, that's *easy*, then!"

"We're better prepared now," Ripley said. "And besides, what's the alternative? Really?"

"There is none," Hoop said. "We make it for the other elevator, up to level 4 for the cell, then back to the surface."

"But what about—" Kasyanov began, but Hoop cut her off.

"Whatever we find on the way, we handle it," he said. "Let's say positive. Let's stay cool, and calm, and keep our eyes open."

"And hope the lights are still working," Lachance said.

As they picked up their weapons, and Kasyanov did her best to splint Baxter's ankle with supplies from her med kit, Ripley mulled over what Lachance had said. Down here, in the dark. Feeling their way along with the aid of weak flashlights, a billion tons of planet above them.

No, it didn't bear thinking about.

When she blinked, she saw Amanda in a floral dress thrashing on the sweet, green grass with one of those monsters attached to her face.

"I'll see you again," she whispered. Hoop heard, glanced at her, but said nothing. Perhaps they were all finding some way to pray.

11

MINE

As she exited the remains of the elevator—wondering whether they were incredibly lucky to have survived, or incredibly unlucky for it to have happened in the first place—Ripley realized with a jolt that this was the only planet other than Earth on which she had ever set foot. The voyage aboard the *Nostromo* had been her first, coming soon after she'd been licensed for space flight, and even after landing on LV426 she'd never actually left the ship.

She had always assumed a moment like this would have brought a moment of introspection. A rush of wonder, a glow of joy. A deep grounding of herself and her place in the universe. Sometimes, after having traveled so far, she'd feared that she would have no real stories to tell.

But now she only felt terror. The rock beneath her feet felt just like rock, the air she breathed was gritty with dust, stale and unpleasant. There was no epiphany. The beasts had ruined everything for her— any chance of joy, any scrap of innocent wonder—and quickly the fear was replaced with rage.

Outside the lift was a wide-open area, propped at frequent intervals with metal columns. Along one side stood a line of lockers, most doors hanging open. There were also storage boxes stacked against a wall, marked with symbols she didn't understand. Most of them were empty, lids leaning against their sides. Trimonite boxes waiting to be filled, perhaps. Ripley found them sad, because they would never be used.

Lighting was supplied by several strings of bare bulbs, all of them still illuminated. The cables were neatly clipped to the rough rock ceiling.

At first, looking around, Ripley caught her breath, because she thought the walls were lined with that strange, organic, extruded compound they'd found in the ship. But when she moved closer she saw that it was rock that had been melted and resolidified, forming a solid barrier against the loose material that might lie behind it. There were still props and buttresses lining the walls and ceiling, but the bulk of the strength lay in the altered rock. They'd used the bigger, tracked plasma torches for that, she supposed. Their heat must have been incredible.

"Everyone good?" Hoop asked, breaking the silence. He was standing close to a set of plastic curtains that led into a tunnel beyond.

No one spoke. Hoop took that as confirmation that, yes, they were all good, and he pushed the curtains aside.

Ripley quickly followed. Out of all of them, Hoop felt the safest. The strongest. She wasn't even sure why she believed that. But she went with her instincts and decided to stay close to the engineer. If they ended up in a fight, she wanted to fight beside him.

The corridor beyond the elevator compound was narrower and more functional. The lights continued along the ceiling. The walls were slick and held strange, almost organic flow patterns where they'd been plasma-torched. Shallow ditches were cut into the floor at the base of each wall, and water so dark it was black glinted there. It was motionless, stagnant, inky. Ripley wondered what it contained.

Hoop waved them on.

Baxter hobbled with one arm over Kasyanov's shoulder. He grunted, gasped, and though he couldn't avoid the pain, Ripley wished he wasn't making so much noise. Every sound he made was amplified, echoing along the rock-lined tunnels much louder than their careful footfalls.

They'll know we're here, she thought. *They probably know anyway. If anything's going to happen, it's going to happen, and being cautious won't prevent it.*

They reached a junction. Hoop paused only for a moment, then took the left fork. He moved quickly and carefully, holding his flashlight in one hand, the spray gun in the other. The additional light helped illuminate contours and trip hazards on the ground.

It wasn't far along this tunnel that they came across the first sign of the aliens.

"What the hell is that?" Baxter asked. He sounded tired, and on the verge of panic. Maybe he thought that at some point they'd be forced to leave him behind after all.

"Something from the mine?" Lachance suggested. "Mineral deposit left by water?"

But Ripley already knew that wasn't the case.

It started gradually. A smear on the wall, a spread of material on the floor. But ten yards from them the alien material lined all surfaces of the tunnel in thick layers, strung like natural arches beneath the ceiling and lying across the floor in complex, swirling patterns.

A gentle mist floated on the air. Or perhaps it was steam. Ripley tugged off a glove and waved her hand before her, feeling the moisture but finding it hard discerning whether it was hot or cold. Another contradiction, perhaps. These strange structures were impressive, and even vaguely beautiful in the same way a spider's web was beautiful. But the things that had made this were the opposite.

"No," Sneddon said. "It's them. We saw something like this on the *Samson*."

"Yeah, but…" Lachance said.

"That was a much smaller scale," Ripley said. "Not like this." She was breathing fast and shallow because she could smell them here, a faintly citrus stench that clung to the back of her throat and danced on her tongue.

"I don't like this," Baxter whispered.

"Me neither," Lachance said. "I want my mommy. I want to go home."

The tunnel narrowed ahead of them where the substance bulged out from the walls, up from the floor, down from the ceiling. Here and there it formed stalactites and stalagmites, some of them thin and delicate, others thicker and looking more solid. There were hints of light deep within the alien structure, but only here and there. The ceiling lights still worked, but were mostly covered up.

Hoop stepped a little closer and shone his flashlight inside.

Ripley wanted to grab him and pull him back. But she couldn't help looking.

The light didn't penetrate very far. The moisture in the air was revealed more fully by the flashlight beam, skeins of light and dark shifting and waving with a gentle breeze. Whether that breeze was caused by their presence, their breathing, or that of another, Ripley didn't want to find out.

"I'm not going in there," Sneddon said.

"Yeah," Kasyanov said. "I'm with you on that one."

"I'm not sure we'd get through anyway," Hoop said. "And even if we could, it'd slow us down."

"It's like a nest," Ripley said. "A giant wasp nest."

"Is there another way to the elevator shaft?" Baxter asked.

"This is the direct route," Hoop said. "The spine of this level. But all the mine sections have emergency exits at various points. We'll go back, take the other fork, then cut back toward the elevator as soon as we find an exit."

Ripley didn't say what she knew they were all thinking. *What if all the tunnels are like this?* But she caught Baxter's eye, and the truth passed between them—that he could never climb so many stairs. Maybe none of them could.

Not quickly enough.

They headed back, turned into the other fork of the corridor, then dropped down a series of large steps carved into the floor. Water flowed more freely along the gutters here, tinkling away at various points into hidden depths. Walls ran with it. It provided a background noise that was welcoming at first, but quickly became troubling. Behind the sound of flowing water, anything could approach them.

"I think this is the most recent mine working," Hoop said. "They've been at this particular vein for two hundred days, maybe more."

"So this is where they found them," Sneddon said. "Somewhere along here."

"Maybe," Hoop said. "We don't know the details. But we don't have much choice." He moved on, and the others followed.

There were several side corridors, smaller with lower ceilings, and as Hoop passed them by, Ripley guessed they were also mine workings. She had no idea how a mine functioned, but she'd been told that the quantities of trimonite found here were small compared to most ore mines. This wasn't mining on an industrialized scale, but rather prospecting for hidden quantities of an almost priceless material. Digging through a million tons of rock to find half a ton of product.

She hoped that Hoop would know an emergency exit when he saw it.

Behind her, someone sneezed, uttering a quiet, "Oh!" afterward. Amanda had used to sneeze like that—a gentle sound, followed by an expression almost of surprise.

Amanda is eleven years old. Ripley knows because her daughter wears an oversized badge on her denim shirt, all purple and pink, hearts and flowers. I bought her that, *she thinks, and although she can remember accessing the site, ordering the card and badge and the presents she knew Amanda wanted for her birthday—remembers the small smile of satisfaction when she confirmed "place order," knowing that everything her daughter wanted was on the way—there is also a sense of dislocation, and the knowledge that this never happened.*

Family and friends are there. And Alex, Ripley's ex husband who left them when Amanda was three years old and never, ever came back. No calls, no contact, no sign at all that he was still alive; Ripley only knew that he was through a friend of a friend. Inexplicably, even Alex is there, smiling at Ripley across a table laden with birthday food and cake, with an "Isn't it a pity we never made it" smile.

And Ripley, also inexplicably, smiles back.

There are other faces, other names, but they are clouded in memory, ambiguous in dreamscape. There's singing and laughter, and Amanda smiles at her mother, that honest, deep smile of love and adoration that makes Ripley so glad to be alive.

The birthday girl's chest explodes open. The "I am eleven" badge flicks from her shirt and goes flying, skimming across the table, striking a glass of orange juice and tipping it over. The denim shirt changes from light to dark. Blood splashes, staining everything, and when it strikes Ripley's face and blurs her vision she wipes it away, staring at her juddering daughter—no longer beautiful, no longer pristine—and the thing clawing its way from her chest.

The monster is impossibly large. Larger than the innocent body it bursts from, larger than the people sitting around the table in a frozen tableau, sitting, waiting to be victims to the beast.

Ripley goes to scream.

It had been an instant, that was all, leaving a sense of dread which also slowly faded. But not entirely.

The person who sneezed was still drawing the post-sneeze breath, and Hoop glanced back past Ripley, not even concerned enough to tell them to keep quiet. Ripley caught his eye and he paused, frowned, seeing something there. But she offered him a tight smile and he went on.

Ten minutes, maybe more. They stalked forward, Hoop taking the lead with the spray gun that might or might not work against the aliens, the others following close behind. These tunnels were less well formed, and Ripley supposed it was because this was one of the mining tunnels of level 9, not the spine passageway itself. But she was worried. If there had been alien evidence back in the main passageway, wasn't there a good chance that they'd probed everywhere?

Even up?

The deeper they moved, the more signs of mining emerged. The tunnel widened in places, low ceilings shored with metal props as well as being melted hard. Walls showed evidence of mechanized excavation, and scattered along the tunnel were heavy, wheeled, low-profile trolleys that must have been used for disposal of the excavated material. They passed a spherical machine with several protruding arms tipped with blades and scoops.

Ripley wondered why they hadn't been using more androids down here, and realized that she hadn't actually asked. Maybe some of those who'd died in the dropships had been androids.

Of those survivors, it was only Sneddon who had proved her humanity to Ripley. And only because she had been challenged.

It didn't matter. Her issues with Ash—and whatever Ash had become, once his AI had infiltrated the shuttle's computer—should not jaundice her view of these people. They were all fighting to survive. Even Sneddon, with her obvious fascination for the deadly creatures, only wanted to get away.

Paranoid, much? Ripley thought. But at the same time, she wasn't sure that paranoia was a bad thing right now.

Hoop had moved perhaps ten yards ahead. Suddenly he stopped.

"Here," he said.

"Here?" Ripley asked.

"Emergency tunnel?" Lachance said from directly behind her.

She scanned the tunnel ahead, around Hoop and beyond, but though the lighting was adequate, there were still just shadows. Maybe one of them hid the entrance to a side-tunnel, doorway, or opening. But she thought not. All she could see was...

Something strange.

"No," Hoop breathed. "Here. This is what they found. This is where it changed." He sounded off. Awestruck, scared, almost bewitched. And for a painful, powerful moment, all Ripley wanted to do was to turn and run.

Back the way they had come, as fast as she could. Back to the staircase, then up, then to the *Marion* where she could hide herself away in the *Narcissus*, live the final moments of her life snuggled in the stasis pod with Jonesy and memories of better times.

But her memory already seemed to be playing tricks on her. She was starting to doubt that there had ever been better times.

She went forward until she stood next to Hoop, and the others followed.

"Through there," he said. "Look. Can't you feel it? The space, the… potential."

Ripley could. She could see where he was pointing—a widened area of tunnel just ahead, and a narrow crevasse at the base of the wall on the left—and although there was only the faint glow of light from within the crack, the sense of some wide, expansive space beyond was dizzying.

"What is it?" Sneddon asked.

"It's what they found," Hoop said. "A nest. Those things sleeping, perhaps."

"Maybe they're still down there," Kasyanov said. "We should go, we should—"

"If they were, they'd have heard us by now," Lachance said.

"Then where are they?" Baxter asked. None of them replied. No one had an answer.

Hoop started forward toward the wall and whatever lay beyond.

"Hoop!" Ripley said. "Don't be stupid!" But he was already there, kneeling and looking down into the crack. She could see cables now, leading into it, proof that the miners had gone that way, too. Hoop slid through, flashlight in one hand, spray gun in the other.

"Oh, my God," he said. "It's *huge!*"

Then he was gone altogether. There was no sign that he had fallen or been pulled through, but still Ripley was cautious as she approached the hole, crouching low and aiming the charge thumper.

She saw light moving in there, and then Hoop's face appeared.

"Come on," he said. "You've got to see this."

"No we don't!" Kasyanov said. "We don't have to see *anything*!"

But the look on Hoop's face persuaded Ripley. Gone was the fear she had grown used to so quickly. There was something about him now, some sudden, previously hidden sense of wonder that almost made him a different man. Perhaps the man he was always meant to be.

So she dropped to her behind and eased herself down into the crack, feeling for footholds and allowing Hoop to guide her down. She dropped the last couple of feet, landed softly, and then moved forward to allow the others access.

The breath was punched from her. Her brain struggled to keep up with what her senses were relaying—the scale, the scope, the sheer impossible size and staggering reality of what she was seeing.

The vast cavern extended beyond and below the deepest part of the mine. The miners had done their best to illuminate it, stringing light cables along walls and propping them on tall masts across the open spaces. The ceilings were too high to reach, out of sight in places, like dark, empty skies.

And they had also climbed over the thing that took up much of the cavern's floor.

Ripley found it difficult to judge just how huge the place was. There was no point of reference. The thing inside the cavern was so unknown, so mysterious, that it could have been the size of her shuttle or on the scale of the *Marion*. At a rough guess she would have put the cave at two hundred yards across, but it could have been less, and perhaps it was much, much more. She thought the object was some sort of carved feature, hewn from the base rock long, long ago.

She had the impression that it had once been very sharp, defined, each feature clear and obvious. But over time the structure had softened. Time had eroded it, and it was as if she looked through imperfect eyes at something whose edges had been smoothed over the millennia.

She heard the others dropping down behind her, sensed them gathering around her and Hoop. They gasped.

"Oh, no," Kasyanov said, and Ripley was surprised at the wretchedness her voice contained. Surely they should have been feeling wonder. This was amazing, incredible, and she couldn't look at the structure without feeling a sense of deep awe.

Then behind her, Lachance spoke and changed everything.

"It's a ship," he said.

"What?" Ripley gasped. She hadn't even considered that

possibility. Buried almost a mile beneath the planet's surface, surely this couldn't be anything but a building, a temple of some sort, or some other structure whose purpose was more obscure.

"Down here?" Hoop said. There was silence again as they all looked with different eyes.

And Ripley knew that Lachance was right.

She was certain that not all of the object was visible—it quite obviously projected beyond the edges of the cavern in places—but there were features that were beginning to make sense, shapes and lines that might only be of use in a vessel built to fly. The entire left half of the exposed surface might have been a wing, curving down in a graceful parabola, projections here and there seemingly swept back for streamlining. There were cleared areas that might have been entrance gantries or exhaust ducts, and where the object's higher surfaces rose from the wing, Ripley could see a line of hollows seemingly punched into the curved shell.

"It's not like any I've ever seen before," Lachance said quietly, as if afraid his voice might echo out to the ship. "And I'm not sure. But the more I see, the more certain I become." No wisecracks now. No casual quips. He was as awestruck as the rest of them.

"The miners went close," Hoop said. "They strung those lights up and all across it."

"But we're not going to make the same mistake, right?" Baxter said. "They went closer, and look what happened to them!"

"Amazing," Sneddon whispered. "I should be..." She took a small camera from her hip pocket and started filming.

"But how can it be all the way down here?" Kasyanov asked.

"You've seen enough of this planet," Hoop said. "The storms, the winds, the moving sands. This looks old. Maybe it was buried long ago. Ages... ten thousand years. Sank down into the sand, and storms covered it up. Or perhaps there was some way down here, a long time back. Maybe this is the bottom of a valley that's long-since been filled in. Whatever... it's here."

"Let's go," Baxter said. "Let's get the hell—"

"There's no sign of those aliens," Hoop said.

"Not yet, no! But this must be where they came from."

"Baxter…" Kasyanov started, but she trailed off. She couldn't take her eyes off the massive object. Whatever it was, it might have been the most amazing thing any of them had ever seen.

"Ripley, is this anything like the one your guys found?" Hoop asked.

"Don't think so," she said. "I wasn't on the ground team that went there, I only saw some of the images their suit cameras transmitted. But no, I don't think so. That ship was large, but this…" She shook her head. "This looks *enormous*! It's on a much different scale."

"It's the find of the century," Sneddon said. "Really. This planet's going to become famous. *We'll* be famous."

"You're shitting me!" Baxter replied. "We'll be *dead*!"

"There," Lachance said, pointing across the cavern. "Look, where it rises up into what might be the… fuselage, or the main body of the ship. Toward the back. Do you see?"

"Yeah," Ripley said. "Damage. Maybe an explosion." The area Lachance had pointed toward was more ragged than the rest, smooth flowing lines turned into a tattered mess, tears across the hull, and a hollow filled only with blackness. Even this rough, wrecked area had been smoothed somewhat over time. Dust had settled, sand had drifted against torn material, and everything looked blurred.

"Seriously, I think we should get back," Baxter said. "Get ourselves away from here, and when we reach home, report everything. They'll send an expedition. Colonial Marines, that's who need to come here. People with big guns."

"I agree," Kasyanov said. "Let's go. This isn't for us. We're not meant to be here."

Ripley nodded, still unable to take her eyes from the sight, remembering the horrors of her waking nightmares.

"They're right," she said. She remembered her crew's voices as they'd approached that strange extraterrestrial ship, their undisguised wonder. It had quickly turned to dread. "We should leave."

And then they heard the noise behind them. Back through the tumbled section of cavern wall, from where they'd just dropped down. Back in the tunnels.

A long, low hiss. Then a screech, like sharp nails across stone.

A many-legged thing, running.

"Oh, no," Kasyanov said. She turned and aimed her plasma torch at the hole they'd climbed down through.

"No, wait—!" Hoop said, but it was too late. Kasyanov pulled the trigger and a new sun burst around them.

Ripley fell back, a hand clasping into her collar. The others retreated, too, and the plasma burst forged up through the crack, rocks rebounding, heat shimmering the air all around in flowing waves. Ripley squinted against the blazing light, feeling heat surging around them, stretching her exposed skin, shriveling hair.

She tripped and fell back, landing on Hoop where he had already fallen. She rolled aside and ended up on her stomach beside him. They stared into each other's faces. She saw a brief desperation there—wide eyes, and a sad mouth—and then a sudden reaffirming of his determination.

She stood behind him as Kasyanov backed away from what she had done. The plasma torch emanated heat, its inbuilt coolant system misting spray around the barrel. Before them, the rocks glowed red, dripping, melted, but they were already cooling into new shapes. Heat haze made the cavern's wall seem still fluid, but Ripley could hear the rocks clicking and cracking as they solidified once more.

The crack they had crawled through was all but gone, swathes of rock melted down across it and forming a new wall.

"We can hit it again, melt through!" Baxter said. "Kasyanov and me, we can use both of the plasma torches to—"

"No," Sneddon said. "Didn't you hear what was through there?"

"She fried it!" Baxter protested.

"Wait," Ripley said, holding up a hand and stepping closer.

The heat radiating from the stone was tremendous, almost taking her breath away. Though she could hear the sounds of it cooling, and the whispered bickering behind her, she also heard something else. The opening back up into the mine was now almost non-existent, just a few cracks, and if she hadn't known it was there she wouldn't have been able to find it. But sound traveled well.

"I still hear them," she whispered. "Up there." The sound was terrible—low screeches, the clatter of hard limbs on stone, a soft hissing she didn't think had anything to do with the heat. She turned and looked at her companions, standing around her with their mining tools, their weapons, raised. "I think there's more than one."

"There must be another way back up into the mine," Hoop said.

"*Why* must there?" Kasyanov challenged.

"Because if there isn't, we're fucked!"

"If there isn't, we can make one," Lachance said. "Just not here." He turned and looked around the edges of the cavern, gaze constantly flickering back to the huge buried structure.

Ship, Ripley said, reminding herself of the impossible. *We're standing a stone's throw from an alien ship!* She had no doubt that's what it was. Lachance's assessment made sense, and so did the idea that the aliens had come from here.

She had seen all this before.

"There has to be another way in," Hoop said, a hint of hope in his voice. "The lights are still lit. The plasma torch fried those cables behind us, so there must be others coming in from elsewhere."

"Let's track around the cavern's edges," Sneddon said, pointing. "That way. I reckon that's in the direction of the second elevator, don't you?" She looked around, seeking support.

"Maybe," Lachance said. "But the mine tunnels twist and turn, there's no saying—"

"Let's just move," Hoop said. He started walking, and Ripley and the others followed.

To their right, the mysterious buried object. To their left, the cavern's uneven edges. Shining their flashlights against the walls did little to banish the shadows. They only crouched deeper down, further back. And it wasn't long before Ripley started to sense the greatest danger coming from that direction.

She held her breath as she walked, trying to tread softly so that she could hear any sounds coming from the shadowed areas. But there were six of them, and though they all tried to move as silently as possible, their boots made a noise. Scrapes on rock, the grumble of grit being kicked aside, the rustle of clothing, the occasional bump of metal on stone.

Hoop froze so suddenly that Ripley walked into him.

"We're being stalked," he said. His choice of word chilled her. She wasn't sure those things *could* stalk.

"Where?" she whispered.

Hoop turned around, then nodded toward the cracks, fissures, and tumbled rocks that made up the edge of the cavern.

"Yeah," Sneddon said. "I get that feeling, too. We should—"

A soft hiss, like pressurized air escaping a can.

"Oh shit," Kasyanov said, "oh shit, now we're—"

Baxter scrambled back, his bad ankle failed beneath him, and he must have had his finger on the plasma torch trigger. White-hot light erupted from the weapon, scorching the air and splaying across the low ceiling at the edge of the cavern. Someone shouted. Ripley threw herself against Kasyanov just as a hail of molten rock pattered down around them. Someone else screamed.

The eruption ended as quickly as it had begun, and Baxter jumped to his feet and backed away.

"Sorry, sorry, I heard—"

"Damn it!" Hoop hissed. He was tugging at his trousers, getting more frantic with every moment. "*Damn* it!"

Lachance pulled a knife from his belt, knelt beside Hoop, and sliced his trousers from knee to boot, dropping the knife and tearing the heavy material apart. Then he picked up the knife again.

Hoop had started shaking, breathing heavily.

"Hoop," Lachance said, glancing up. "Keep still." He didn't wait for a response, but held the leg and jabbed at it with the knife's tip.

Ripley heard the hardening pellet of rock strike the ground. She smelled the sickening-sweet stench of burnt flesh. Then from in the shadows behind them once more, another long, low hiss.

And the clack of terrible teeth.

"Let's go," Hoop said. He was looking past Ripley, back into the shadows. When she saw his eyes widen, she didn't have to look. "Let's *go!*"

They ran, down into the cavern and toward the sloping wing structure that curved up out of the cavern floor. Hoop groaned as he went, limping, his tattered trousers flapping around his injured shin. Baxter hobbled, one arm over Lachance's shoulder. The others hefted their weapons and moved quickly, carefully, across the uneven floor.

There was only one direction they could take, and the blasted opening into the ship's interior looked darker than ever.

Ripley's single thought brought only terror.

They're herding us…

12

CATTLE

...Toward the ship, Hoop thought. *Driving us like cattle. And we're doing exactly as they want.*

There was no other explanation. The aliens hadn't attacked, but instead were slinking around the party of survivors, moving through shadowy fissures in the rock, making themselves known yet not exposing themselves. Everything Hoop had seen of them— everything he knew from what had happened aboard the *Marion*, and to Ripley more than thirty years ago—pointed to the creatures being brutal and unthinking monsters.

This was different. If he was right, they were planning, scheming, working together. That thought terrified him.

His leg hurt, a deep-seated, white-hot burn that seemed to smolder in his bones, surge through his muscles, filter around his veins. The whole of his lower right leg felt as if it had been dipped in boiling water, and every step was an agony. But there was no choice but to run. He knew that the damage was minimal—he'd looked— and the wound was already likely cauterized by the glowing globule of molten stone that had caused it.

So he did his best to shut the pain away.

His son had visited the dentist once, terrified of the injection of anaesthetic he'd require for a tooth extraction. On the way there, Hoop had talked to him about pain, telling him it was a fleeting thing, a physical reaction to damage that he knew would do him no harm, and that afterward he wouldn't actually be able to remember what the pain had felt like.

Pain was a difficult concept to conjure in memory, Hoop had said. Like tasting the best cake ever. Such thoughts only really meant anything when the tasting—or the pain—was happening.

He tried it now, repeating a mantra to himself as they ran across that strange cavern's floor. *It doesn't mean anything, it doesn't mean anything*. He tried to analyze the sensation, take interest in it instead of letting it take over. And to an extent, it worked.

Kasyanov and Sneddon went ahead, Sneddon aiming her spray gun in front of her. Baxter and Lachance were bringing up the rear, Baxter looking determined through his own agony. Ripley stayed with Hoop, glancing frequently at him as she kept pace. He did his best not to give her cause for concern, but he couldn't hold back occasional grunts or groans.

Responsibility weighed heavy. That he couldn't rationalize away. He was in command, and although the *Marion*'s survivors, with Ripley in tow, were acting more like a leaderless group, he still felt in every way responsible for their fate.

Even as they ran he racked his brains, trying to decide whether he had made all the right decisions. Should they have remained on the *Marion* for longer, spending more time preparing? Should he have assessed both elevators, before deciding which one to take down into the mine? Perhaps if they'd taken the other one, they would be on their way back to the surface already, precious fuel cell pushed on a trailer between them. But he couldn't deal in "what if" and "maybe." He could only work with what they had. The definitives.

They had to reach the other elevator, and soon.

And yet the aliens were behind them, pushing them forward. Hoop hated feeling out of control, unable to dictate his own destiny, all the more so when there were others relying on his decisions.

He stopped and turned around, breathing heavily.

"Hoop?" Ripley asked. She paused, too, and the others skidded to a halt. They were close to where the craft's wing rose out of the ground, though the distinction was difficult to discern.

"We're doing what they want," he panted, leaning over.

"What, escaping?" Kasyanov asked.

"We're not escaping," Hoop said, standing straighter.

"He's right," Ripley said. "They're herding us this way."

"Any way that's away from them is fine by me," Baxter said.

"What do you—?" Ripley asked, and for that briefest of moments Hoop might have believed they were the only two people there. Their eyes locked, and something passed between them. He didn't know what. Nothing so trite as understanding, or even affection. Perhaps it was an acknowledgement that they were thinking the same way.

Then Sneddon gasped.

"Oh my *God*!" she said. Hoop looked back over his shoulder.

They were coming. Three of them, little more than shadows, and yet distinguishable because *these* shadows were moving. Fast. Two flitted from somewhere near where the survivors had entered the cavern, the third came from a different direction, all three converging.

Lachance crouched, bracing his legs, and fired his charge thumper. The report coughed around the cavern, lost in that vast place.

"Don't waste your time!" Baxter said. "Maybe if they were a few steps away."

"If they get that close, we're dead!" Lachance said.

"Run!" Hoop said. The others went, and he and Ripley held back for just a moment, again sharing a look and each knowing what the other was thinking.

They're driving us forward again.

The surface underfoot changed only slightly as they headed up onto the craft's huge, curving wing. It still felt to Hoop as though he was running on rock, although now it sloped upward, driving a whole new species of pain into his wounded leg as he relied on different muscles to push himself forward.

Over the time this thing had been buried down here, sand and dust must have dropped onto it and solidified. Boulders had fallen, and this close he could see a series of mineral deposits that formed sweeping ridges all across the wing, like a huge ring of expanding ripples, frozen in time.

Each ring came up to their knees, and leaping over each ridge made Hoop cry out. His cries echoed Baxter's.

"It's only pain," Ripley said, and she looked surprised when Hoop coughed a laugh.

"Where to?" Sneddon called from up ahead. She had slowed a little, then turned, spray gun aiming back past them.

Hoop glanced back. He could only see two aliens now, their repulsive forms skipping and leaping across the ground. *They should be closer*, he thought, *they're much faster than us*. But he couldn't worry about that now.

He looked around for the third creature, but it was nowhere in sight.

"That damaged area," he said, pointing. "It's the only way we know for sure we'll get inside."

"Do we really *want* to get inside?" Ripley asked.

"You think we should make a stand here?" Hoop asked. Sneddon snorted at the suggestion, but Hoop had meant it. Ripley knew that, and she frowned, examining their surroundings. There was nowhere to hide—they would be exposed.

"Not here," she said. "Far too open."

"Then up there, where the fuselage is damaged," he said. "And remember, there's another one somewhere, so keep—"

The third alien appeared. It emerged from shadows to their left, already on the wing, manifesting from behind a slew of low boulders as if it had been waiting for them. It was perhaps twenty yards away, hunched down, hissing and ready to strike.

Ripley fired her charge thumper, and if hatred and repulsion could fuel a projectile, the alien would have been smashed apart just by the energy contained in the shot. But he didn't even see where the shot went, and if the creatures really were herding them toward the old ship, it likely wouldn't even react.

Ripley held her stance, looking left and right. Hoop hefted his spray gun. The others pointed their weapons.

The nearest alien crawled sideways, circling them but never coming closer. Hoop's skin prickled when he watched it move. It reminded him of a giant spider... although not quite. It more resembled a hideous scorpion... yet there were differences. It moved with a fluid, easy motion, gliding across the rough surface of the giant wing as if it had walked that way many times before.

He fired the spray gun. It was a natural reaction to his disgust, a wish to see the thing away. The staggered spats of acid landed in a line between him and the monster, hissing loudly as the acid melted into dust and stone, and whatever might lie beneath. And even though the fluid didn't reach the alien, the creature flinched back. Only slightly, but enough for him to see.

Breath held against any toxic fumes, Hoop backed quickly away. That pressed the others into motion, as well.

"We could charge it," Ripley said.

"What?"

"All of us in one go. Run at the thing. If it comes at us we all shoot, if it slips aside we move on."

"To where?"

"A way out."

"We don't *know* a way out!" Hoop said.

"It's better than doing what they want, isn't it?" Ripley asked.

"I'm for going where they aren't," Baxter said. "They're that way, I'm going this way." He turned and hobbled again toward the ship's main fuselage, right arm now flung over Kasyanov's shoulder.

"We have to stay together," Hoop said as they all followed. But he couldn't help thinking that Ripley had been right—charge, take the fight to them—and he hoped he wouldn't have cause to regret his decision later.

The ground rose steeper before leveling again, the curve of the wing still scattered with boulders and those strange, waved lines of mineral deposits. Hoop thought perhaps this whole cavern had once been under water, but there was no way of proving that right now. And such knowledge couldn't help them.

What *could* help them was a place to stop. Somewhere easy to defend, a position from which they could make a stand. A route around or through the strange ship, leading back up into the mine.

A fucking miracle.

Maybe *he* should make a stand, here and now. Just him. Turn and charge the alien, spray gun spitting acid, and who knows, maybe he'd get lucky. The creature was just an animal, after all. Maybe it would turn and run, and he and the others could push home their advantage and charge back the way they'd come. Using the plasma torches, it wouldn't take much to open up that access again.

One glance back told him everything he needed to know.

The three aliens were stalking them, spiked shadows dancing across the massive wing's surface, flitting from boulder to crevasse as they sought natural cover. They moved silently and easily, their fluid motions so smooth that their shadows flowed like spilled ink. They were hunters, pure and simple. Having their quarry suddenly turn and charge would not faze them at all.

Fuck that.

He wasn't about to sacrifice himself for nothing.

"Faster," he muttered.

"What?" Lachance asked.

"We should move faster. Quick as we can, get there as soon as possible, find somewhere to defend. Perhaps that'll throw them, a little."

No one replied, and he read doubt in the silence. But they all ran faster, nonetheless. Even Baxter, hopping, swearing under his breath, and Kasyanov, sweating under the man's weight. Whatever Hoop thought of his comm officer, there was a stark courage there that he couldn't help but respect. And Kasyanov's fear seemed to be feeding her determination.

Hoop's leg was a solid weight of pain now, but he used it to fight back, slamming it down with each step, forging forward, driving events toward what he hoped would be a good resolution. He'd never been the praying kind, and faith was something he'd left behind with other childhood fancies. But he had a strange sense that this was all part of something bigger. However unlucky they'd been—the *Delilah* crash, the *Marion*'s damage, the beasts on the *Samson*, and now the elevator's malfunction and their descent into this strange place—he couldn't help feeling that there were larger hands at play.

It might have been the effect of their discoveries. This ship was an incredible, undeniable sign of alien intelligence, the likes of which no one had ever seen before. It had opened a doorway in his mind to greater, wider possibilities. But there was something more. Something he couldn't quite pin down.

Ripley was part of it, he was sure. Maybe finding someone like her in the middle of all this was fucking with his mind.

Someone like her? he thought, laughing silently. It had been a long time since he'd really cared about someone. Jordan had been a fling, and she'd always remained a good friend. But with Ripley there was more. An instinctive understanding that he hadn't experienced with anyone since...

He thought briefly of home, his estranged wife, and his children left behind. But there was too much pain and guilt to hold that thought for long.

Baxter was crying out with each step, the foot of his broken ankle dragging along behind him. Yet he still bore the plasma torch at the ready. As they neared the steeper slope up onto what must have been the ship's main fuselage, Hoop began to look ahead.

The broken area they'd seen from a distance was larger than he'd thought. It extended from above the wing and back over the soft curve of the vessel's main body, its skin torn apart and protruding in stark, sharp sculptures across the extent of the damage. It wasn't one large hole, but a series of smaller wounds, as if something had exploded inside the ship and blasted outward, rupturing the hull in several places. Even after so long, there were scorch marks evident.

"That first hole," he said, pointing. He darted forward quickly and looped his arm through Baxter's, careful to let him wield the plasma torch. "You okay?" he asked quietly.

"No," Baxter said, but there was a strength to his voice.

"Hoop, they're following closer," Ripley said from behind.

He let go of Baxter's arm, tapped him on the shoulder, then turned around. Down the slope the three aliens were creeping forward, their casual gait as fast as the human's sprint. And they *were* closer.

"Go on," he said to the others. He and Ripley paused, looking back.

"Shot across their bows?" Ripley asked.

"Yeah."

She lifted and fired her charge thumper at the closest creature. As it paused and skipped aside, Hoop fired the spray gun at it. The spurts didn't quite reach the target, but they impacted across the sloping wing close to it, sizzling, scorching. Yet again he saw the beast cringe back away from the acid.

Ripley fired at the other two as well, shots echoing around the massive cavern, the sounds multiplying. They shifted aside with amazing dexterity, dancing on long limbs. Beneath the echoing reports he heard their hissing. He hoped it was anger. If they were riled up enough, they might charge to within range of the spray guns and plasma torches.

"Come on," Hoop said to Ripley. "We're almost there."

As they climbed the steeper slope, the surface beneath their feet changed. It became smoother, and the feel of each impact was different as well. There was no give, no echo, but still a definite sense that they were running on something hollow. The ship's interior almost bore a weight.

As they reached the first of the blasted areas, Hoop ran ahead. The miners had strung a series of lights along here, some of them hung on protruding parts of the ripped hull. And looking down inside, he saw a similar array.

This was where they had entered the ship.

His concern intensified. He shook his head, turning to face the others, ready to suggest that—

"Hoop," Ripley said, breathing hard. "Look."

Back the way they had come, several more shadows had appeared. They were moving quickly across the wing's surface. From this distance they looked like ants. The analogy didn't comfort him one little bit.

"And there," Sneddon said, pointing higher up the slope of the ship's fuselage. There were more shadows back there, less defined, yet their silhouettes obvious. Motionless. Waiting.

"Okay," he said. "We go inside. But don't touch *anything*. And first chance we get, we fight our way out."

"Ever get the feeling you're being used?" Sneddon asked.

"All the time," Ripley muttered.

Hoop was first down into the ship.

13

ALIENS

Maybe she's nine years old. There's a doorway leading down into the old ruin, steps worn by decades of tourists and centuries of monks long, long ago. A heavy metal grille is fixed back against the wall, the padlock hanging unclasped, and at night they close off the catacombs, allegedly to prevent vandals from desecrating their contents. But ever since they arrived, Amanda has been making up stories about the night-things they want to keep locked in.

When the sun goes down, she says, the shadows down there come alive.

Ripley laughs as she watches her daughter creeping down out of the sun, putting on a faux-scared expression, clawing her hands and growling. Then she shouts for her mother to follow her, and Ripley is aware of the people crowding in behind her. These are popular ruins, one of the city's main tourist venues, and there is rarely a quiet time.

The shadows envelop her. They carry a curious chill, and the damp, musty smell of places never touched by sunlight. Amanda has disappeared ahead of her. Ripley doesn't feel the need to call, but then she looks back and sees that she is alone.

Alone down here, in the shadows, in the darkness.

Someone cries out. She edges forward, running one hand along the sandy wall. The floor is uneven and she almost trips, then her hand touches something different. Smooth, lighter than rock, more textured.

There are skulls in the wall. The skulls are the walls, thousands of them, and each one has a massive trauma wound—a hole, a smashed face. She fancies that she can see tooth marks on the bones, but perhaps that's only—

My imagination, *she thinks, but then the cry comes again. It's Amanda, and recognizing the voice seems to conjure the girl. She is held back against the wall across a small, bone-lined room, clasped around the arms, shoulders and legs by the gnarled skeletal fingers of the long-dead.*

She sees her mother, but there is no joy in her eyes.

Her chest explodes outward beneath her loose dress, and teeth bite their way through the material. Jagged, terrible teeth.

"Holy shit," Ripley breathed, and she looked down into the darkness. For a while she was lost, not knowing where or when she was, and whether that had been a bastardised memory, or a vision of the future. Time swirled, uncertain and inelegant. *I'm not sure how much more of this I can take.*

Kasyanov frowned at her and began to speak, but Ripley turned away.

"Come down!" Hoop shouted up out of the ship. "There are lights. And it's… weird."

"Weird how?" Ripley asked, thinking, *Worn steps and skulls and bones in the walls…*

"Just come and see."

She dropped down beside Hoop, still trying to shake the dregs of that brief, horrible vision from her mind.

The miners had been this way. That didn't comfort Ripley at all, though the lights they'd strung up inside this damaged portion of ship did help. The explosion had blasted a hole through the ship's skin, and inside it had scoured along the interior levels, knocking down partitions and clearing anything that might have been in the way. It reminded Ripley of a wasp's nest, layer upon layer laid out to some fluid symmetry, and from where they now stood—at the epicenter of the exploded area—they could see at least four lower levels exposed.

She supposed that if the *Marion* were sliced in half, something similar would be revealed.

But the walls, floors, and ceilings of this ship were nothing like the *Marion*. Thick tubes ran between levels, and where they'd been ruptured, a solidified flow hung from them. It looked like frozen honey, or fine sand caught mid-pour. The walls had rotted back to bare framing, the struts themselves bent and deformed by the ancient explosion.

The levels were not as equidistant as she'd first thought, and this didn't seem to be a result of the damage. It seemed that they had been formed this way.

"This is… weird," Sneddon echoed, her fascination obvious. Filming with her camera again, she moved forward, climbing down a slope of detritus toward the first solid floor. Its surface was uneven, pitted in places, lined here and there, looking very much like age-worn skin.

"I'm not liking this," Ripley said. "Not one bit."

She'd heard it said that nature did not like right angles, and there were none in evidence here. The material in the walls and floors was a dark gray color, but not consistent. Here, there were patches where it was lighter, and appeared to be thinner. There, it was almost black, as if blood had pooled and hardened just below the surface, creating a hematoma. It resembled the mottled skin of an old corpse.

"Great way to make a ship," Lachance said.

"What?" Baxter asked. "What do you mean?"

"Growing it," Sneddon said. "This wasn't built, it was *grown*."

"No way…" Kasyanov said, but when Ripley looked at the doctor, she saw wide-eyed fascination reflected in the Russian's eyes.

"We shouldn't be doing this," Ripley said.

"We can't go back out there," Hoop said.

"But they *drove* us in here! Are we just going to do what they want?"

"How can they want anything," Lachance protested. "They're just dumb animals, and we're their prey!"

"None of us knows what they are," Ripley said. "Sneddon?"

Sneddon only shrugged.

"I've told you before, I've never seen anything like them. Their apparent viciousness doesn't mean they can't act and think together.

Back in prehistoric times, velociraptors hunted together, and there are theories that posit advanced communication between them. But…" She looked around, shaking her head. "I don't think this is their ship."

From outside came the sounds of hard claws skittering on the ship's skin. They all looked up, and Ripley saw a shadow shifting back from the damaged area by which they'd entered. The silhouette stretched up for a moment, flickering across the cavern's high ceiling before disappearing again.

"They're waiting up there," she said. She felt so helpless.

"We've got to go," Hoop said. "Inside. Follow the lights that are still working, moving as fast as we can. Then as soon as we find another way out, we take it." He looked around at them all, and his face was drawn from the pain. "I don't like this anymore than the rest of you, but there are too many of them out there. If we can trick them, instead of fight them, I'll be happier with that."

"But something happened to the miners down here," Sneddon said.

"Yeah, but we have an advantage. We know some of what happened, and we know to be careful." He waited for any words of dissent, but there were none.

I don't like this one bit, Ripley thought. But she looked up again, at the ragged opening in the ship's strange hull, and knew that they had no choice. The option of climbing back up there, with those things waiting just out of sight… it wasn't an option at all.

Hoop went first, taking the small flashlight from his pocket again. The string of bulbs hung by the miners continued to work, but Hoop's light penetrated the shadows they cast.

The group moved quickly. Almost confidently.

Ripley tried to shake the recent vision from her mind. Those other daytime nightmares had been more surreal, but less troubling, featuring Amanda at an age when Ripley had never known her. But this one was the worst yet. Her daughter was young, sweet, innocent and beautiful, exactly as she remembered her. And Ripley's inability to protect her daughter against the monsters still rang true, settling into her soul like a canker of guilt, eating, consuming, as if it had all been real.

She even felt herself starting to cry. But tears would only blur her surroundings, making everything more dangerous. She had to keep her wits about her.

She had to survive.

As they moved inward from the damaged area of the extraterrestrial ship, the surroundings became even stranger. Ripley thought of the old story of Jonah in the heart of the whale, such a disturbing image when translated to their current situation. Much of their surroundings showed distinctly biological features— uneven floors lined with inlaid tubing that resembled veins; skin-like walls, hardened over time yet still speckled with dust-filled pores and imperfections.

Then they began to encounter objects that must have formed some sort of technology. One narrow corridor opened into a gallery viewing area, looking down over a deep pit. It was ringed with a waist-high barrier. On the gallery stood several identical metallic units. They might have been seats surrounded by control equipment of some kind, the details obscure, arcane. If they *were* seats, then Ripley couldn't easily identify the shapes of the beings meant to fill them.

The pit was filled to a few feet below the gallery by a glassy fluid of some kind, its upper surface scattered with grit and dust. The ceilings and walls were smooth, and Ripley could only assume that the dust had blown in from outside over the eons.

"Which way now?" Ripley asked.

The gallery led around three quarters of the pit, and there were at least six openings leading off from it, including the one they had just come through.

Hoop was peering at the opening through which they'd just come. From back that way came the sound of scuttling, hissing things.

"Let's get the hell out of here!" Baxter said, sweating, trying to hide away his pain. Even standing still he was shaking. Ripley couldn't imagine the agony he was working through, but knew there was no alternative. She only hoped a time didn't come when he physically couldn't go any farther.

What then? she wondered. *Leave him behind? Kill him?* She turned away, just as Hoop spoke.

"Let's change this game," he said. "Kasyanov, Baxter, get ready with the plasma torches." He nodded at the opening they'd come through. "Bring it down."

"Wait!" Sneddon said. "We have no idea what effect the plasma torches will have on this stuff. We don't even know what the ship's made of! Whether or not it's flammable."

Ripley heard more hissing, and back along the tunnel shadows shifted, casting spidery shapes along floors and walls.

"We run or we do it, that's all!" she said. She braced herself to fire her charge thumper.

"Ripley." Hoop handed her something from his waist pack, a chunky object about the size of a computer tablet. "Load it through the top. Real charges."

"We can't just fire those things at random," Lachance said.

"Not at random," Ripley said, plugging the container into the top of the thumper. "At *them*." She braced again, took aim, and fired. The charge clattered along the tunnel, its echoes sounding strangely muffled as it ricocheted from the walls.

Ripley frowned.

Hoop grabbed her arm. "Time delayed," he said as he pulled her to the side.

The explosion thudded through their feet and punched the air out of Ripley's lungs. Behind the rumbling roar of the mining charge, she was sure she heard the aliens screeching in pain, and a shower of debris burst from the tunnel, pattering from her suit, scratching her face.

Smoke blasted after it, driven in streaming tendrils by the rush of air. Ripley swallowed to try and clear her ears, gasped at the stinging sensation across her face. Even as she stood up, Kasyanov and Baxter were at work with the plasma torches.

The entire gallery was brightly illuminated by the scorching plasma. Looking down, Ripley could see a network of slow ripples playing back and forth across the surface of the pit. The blast must have resounded through the ship. It was so thick, the surface so heavy, that the ripples moved like slow snakes, colliding and interfering, making complex but strangely beautiful patterns.

The stench was terrible, almost like burning flesh. The structure all around the opening slumped down, flowing, echoing the lazy ripples from below.

"Hold off!" Hoop shouted, and Kasyanov and Baxter ceased fire. Flames flickered all across the surfaces, fluttering out here, reigniting there, as the heavy framework dipped down until it met the bubbling floor. It had already started to harden again, effectively closing off the opening. The air shimmered from the incredible temperatures. Ripley's lungs burned.

"Now *we* decide which direction to take," Hoop said.

An alien's curved head forced through the melted doorway. There was no warning—none of them could see beyond, and the opening itself was all but obscured by the melted structure. The creature's smoothed dome pushed through the hardening material, its teeth stretching and gnashing. It seemed to struggle for a moment, shoving forward, and at either side its long-clawed hands sliced through.

But then it was held fast, the cooling material steaming where it bit into its mysterious hide.

"Everybody back," Hoop said, and he aimed his spray gun.

Ripley backed away across the gallery and held her breath, fascinated yet terrified. The alien was still struggling to move forward, and all around it the melted and re-set material stretched, changing color and tone as the tension changed. Perhaps five seconds earlier, and the monster might have burst through, catching them unawares and causing chaos.

But now the creature was held fast.

Hoop fired a burst of hydrofluoric acid directly at the head.

Smoke, steam, sizzling, hissing, screeching. Everything was obscured by clouds of vapor, but Ripley had the definite impression of frantic, thrashing movement.

"Back," she said. "Hoop, *get back*!" They all retreated across the gallery, and Ripley felt the waist-high barrier against her back. She edged along it toward the far end. The others were going in the same direction, and Hoop turned and ran toward her.

Behind him, something exploded.

He'll be splashed with it, the acid, and I'll have to watch him die, Ripley thought. But though Hoop winced and ducked down as he ran, the spattering remains of the alien's head splayed across the gallery in the other direction. Part of it bounced across the floor, leaving sizzling patches behind, and dropped down into the pit. What struck the surface floated there for a moment, then sank with a final angry hiss.

Hoop reached them, grinning.

"Well, at least we know they don't like *this* acid," he said. "Come on. Let's get the hell out. Baxter—"

"Don't even ask," Baxter said. "The way things are going, I'd beat you in a race. I'm fine."

He was far from fine, though. He couldn't touch his left foot to the floor, and if it weren't for Kasyanov, he'd fall. His face was strained, damp with sweat, and he couldn't hide his terror.

He's still afraid we'll leave him behind. It was a horrible idea, but one they all had to be contemplating.

"Don't know how long that will keep them back," Sneddon said, nodding back at the melted opening. It was still smoking. They couldn't see any remains of the alien, but the place where it had forced through was seared with acid scars.

"Come on. This way," Hoop said. He headed for an opening at the far end of the gallery, as far from their entry point as they could get. He fixed his flashlight to the spray gun's strap so that he could aim both in the same direction. They all followed, none of them questioning him.

Entering a narrow, low-ceilinged tunnel, Ripley couldn't escape the idea that they were being swallowed once again.

They entered areas that the miners had not lit. They ran, flashlights held out in front or strapped onto their weapons, shadows dancing and retreating. And not long after leaving the gallery, they found the first bodies.

The tunnel-like corridor opened up into another wide space, and there was something different about it. The smooth curves were the same, the non-regularity of something biological, but the sheets and swathes of material hanging across walls and from the ceiling didn't belong here. Neither did the things hanging within it, like horrible, rotting fruit.

There might have been six bodies there, though Ripley found it difficult to tell where one ended and another began. The darkness, the decay, the way they'd been hung up and stuck there, fixed in place by that strange extrusion that had filled one of the mining tunnels far above—it all blurred the edges of what they saw. And that wasn't a bad thing.

The stench was awful. That, and the expression on the first face upon which Hoop shone his flashlight. It might have been a woman, once. Decay had shrunk the face, drawn in the skin, hollowed the eye sockets, but the scream was still frozen there. Clawed hands stretched on either side, reaching—unsuccessfully—for what had been happening to the victim's chest.

The hole was obvious. The clothing was torn and hanging in shreds. Protruding ribs were splintered.

"Birthing ground," Sneddon said.

"They just hung them here," Kasyanov said. "It's… a nursery."

On the floor in front of the hanging, dead people stood a group of egg-like objects, upright and shaped like large vases. Most of them were open. No one stepped forward to look inside.

They passed quickly through the larger space. Every instinct urged Ripley to look away, but sick fascination—and her determination to survive, to learn about these monsters and use everything she could against them—made her look closer. She wished she had not. Maybe somewhere on the *Nostromo* there had been a similar scene, with Dallas hanging there, stuck in place like the victim in a massive spider's dense webbing.

"Where are you taking us?" Lachance asked Hoop. "This isn't the way out. We're just going deeper."

"I'm taking us as far as I can away from them," Hoop said,

pointing back over his shoulder with his thumb. "And up, as soon as we can. There must be ways into and out of this ship, other than the hole blasted in its hull. We just have to find them."

Before long the spaces they passed through—corridors in a spaceship, Ripley knew, though she could only think of them as tunnels—were clear of the alien material once again, and back to the old, gray, mottled surfaces. Still strange, but not so threatening. If there had been time, she might even have admired what they were seeing. It was amazing, it was extraterrestrial. But all she had time for was escape.

They drove us down here to be like the miners, she thought, trying not to imagine how awful it must be. To find yourself trapped in that webbing, watch the egg opening in front of you, feel the legged thing settling over your face. At first you blacked out, like Kane, but then came the waking and the waiting. Waiting for the first sign of movement from inside. The first twinge of pain as the alien infant started to push, claw, and bite its way out.

She thought of Amanda again, and groaned out loud. No one seemed to hear, or if they did it simply echoed their own despair.

They moved quickly, flashlight beams dancing around them. Hoop led the way, and Kasyanov and Baxter were behind him. They'd found a rhythm to their movements, and although Baxter's left foot was all but useless, Kasyanov supported him well enough that he could hop with an almost graceful motion.

They all grasped their weapons. Ripley's charge thumper had three explosive charges left. She'd seen the effect one charge could have, and she knew she'd never be able to fire it if they were too enclosed. But it still gave her a sense of protection.

Wherever they went through different areas of the massive ship, everything seemed to be made from the same strange material. Or grown, perhaps. Gone were the hints of technology. They passed many openings where thin, opaque sheets seemed to act as doors. Most were sealed, a few torn and tattered, but the small group kept to the wider passageways.

There were more gallery areas, more pits with smooth-surfaced fluid at varying levels. Ripley wondered what they were for, these pits—fuel, food, environmental facilities of some kind? Were they storing something?

At one point they climbed a curved stairway, the risers as deep as their waists, and they had to clamber up almost thirty stairs until the route leveled out again. Here the surfaces felt slick and sticky, and there so smooth that they took turns slipping while hauling themselves up. Ripley kept wiping her hands on her clothing, but though they felt slick and wet, they were actually dry.

Another mystery to this place.

Away from the nursery, the air smelled quite neutral, apart from an occasional breeze that worked through the hallways bringing a hint of decay. There was no telling what caused such a breeze this deep down beneath the ground. *Huge doors opening elsewhere in the ship*, Ripley thought. *Something large and unseen moving around. Something big, sighing in its sleep.* None of the possibilities were good.

They encountered one large open space containing several tall sculptures made of the same material as the walls and floor. The shapes were ambiguous, fluid amalgamations of the biological and the mechanical. As elsewhere in the ship, time had softened their edges and made it more difficult to see any details. They were carvings being hidden again beneath time's camouflage. There was an undeniable beauty to them, but lit by the flashlights they threw tall, twisting shadows that were also intensely troubling. An alien could have been hiding behind any one of them.

"We can't have lost them that easily," Hoop said, but no one responded. Ripley had been thinking that, and she was sure the others had, too. But Hoop had become their leader. No one liked to hear the person in charge casting such doubts.

They left the hall of sculpture, and soon after Hoop had cause to speak again.

"More bodies," he said from up ahead. But there was something wrong with his voice.

"Oh, my..." Kasyanov said.

Ripley moved forward. The passageway here was quite wide, and she and the others added their flashlight beams to Hoop's.

For a while none of them spoke. There was very little to say. Shock worked its way around them, and they all dealt with their own thoughts and fears.

"I think we've found the ship builders," Ripley said.

14

BUILDERS

PROGRESS REPORT:

To: Weyland-Yutani Corporation, Science Division
(Ref: code 937)

Date (unspecified)

Transmission (pending)

Warrant Officer Ripley is still on the planet surface with
remainder of *Marion*'s crew. No updates for some time.

Single alien specimen survives on Marion, whereabouts
unknown.

Plan proceeding satisfactorily. I am convinced that Ripley
will fulfill her purpose. She is strong, for a human.

I look forward to conversing with her again. I acknowledge
that I am artificial, but it has been so long. I have been
lonely.

I hope this does not contradict programing.

Infiltration of ship's computer about to commence.

As they had moved through the ship, Hoop had been building a
mental picture of the aliens who might have constructed it.

His imagination had dipped once again into that childhood
fascination with monsters. Such tall stairs implied long limbs. High
arched openings could hint at the aliens' shape. This ship, its nature,

indicated something almost beyond understanding. It was either so technologically advanced that it was barely recognizable, or the technology was so different from any he knew that it made it futile to try to interpret it.

What he saw before him dispelled any such guesswork. There was a sadness to their appearance that invited only pity, and he realized that their story was just as fear-filled, as tragic, as what was being played out now.

"Poor things," Ripley said, echoing his thoughts. "It's not fair. None of this is fair."

There were three dead creatures lying in front of them—two that must have been adults, and one child. They cradled the child between them, protecting it with their bodies, and that's how they had died and decayed. The mummified infant's corpse was nestled between its parents' torsos, an expression of love that had lasted for countless years. Their clothing had remained relatively whole, a metallic material that still lay draped across prominent bones and between their long, thick limbs.

From what Hoop could make out, they each had four legs and two shorter, thinner arms. The leg bones were thick and stocky, the arms much more slender and delicate, hands protruding from narrow sleeves. The hands were skin and bones, digits long and fine, and he saw what might have been jewelry on one adult's fingers. Their torsos were heavy, contained within suits that were reinforced with a network of metallic ribs and struts.

It was difficult to see how much of the bodies remained whole. The skin or flesh that Hoop could see was mummified, grown dusty and pale over time.

Their heads were the most uncertain part about them, because each had been smashed and holed by an impact. Hoop thought he knew what the impacts had been. Lying beside one adult's outstretched hand was a weapon of some kind.

"They killed themselves?" Sneddon asked.

"One of them did," Hoop said. "Killed their partner, child, then themselves. Rather that than be fodder for those things, I reckon."

The skulls still retained shreds of skin and waves of fine hair. It looked as if they'd had a small snout, two eyes, a wide mouth containing several rows of small teeth. Not the teeth of a carnivore. Not the bodies or the appearance of monsters.

"They look like dog-people," Lachance said. "Only... big."

"I wonder what happened here," Ripley said. "How did the aliens get on their ship? What took the ship down?"

"We might figure it out one day, but not today," Hoop said. "We need to keep moving."

"Yeah," Baxter said. "Keep moving." He was starting to sound weak, and Hoop was concerned that he'd start slowing them down. There was nothing to do about it if he did—nothing but reduce speed for him to keep up.

Kasyanov threw him a brief frown. She was also exhausted.

"Let me," Hoop said, but she shook her head.

"No way," she said. "I've got him."

Past the bodies, the passageway started to grow wider and taller. Their flashlights gradually lost effectiveness, and the further they went the darker their surroundings. Footsteps began to echo. Baxter coughed and the sound carried, reverberating back to them, rumbling on and on.

"What is this?" Hoop asked as Sneddon walked beside him.

"No idea," she whispered. "Hoop, we're getting lost in here. I think we should go back the way we came."

"And run straight into those things?"

"If they're still looking for us, I'm sure they've found another way past that gallery by now."

"What do you mean, *if* they're still looking?"

Sneddon shrugged. "Just can't help thinking they've stopped following because we're doing exactly what they want."

"Or because I killed one of them as it was coming for us, maybe they're holding back. More cautious, now that they know we *can* kill them."

"Maybe," Sneddon said, but he knew better. She didn't think that at all. And really, neither did he.

"So, what?" he asked. "I'm doing my best here, Sneddon."

"We all are." She shrugged again. "Dunno. Let's just move on, stay sharp."

"Yeah," Hoop said. "Sharp." He swung the spray gun left and right, the attached flashlight doing little to pierce the darkness. There seemed to be nothing but wide space around them, and he wondered whether they were in a hold of some sort. If so, then this ship had taken off without cargo.

Or without large cargo, at least.

It was as the walls and ceilings started to close in again that they found what might have been the way out.

Lachance saw it first, a break in the wall to their left with a hint of those large steps rising into shadow. They went to investigate, and with their combined flashlight power they could see the top of the staircase, maybe forty yards up. What lay beyond was unclear, but it was heading in the right direction.

Hoop started climbing, and the others followed.

After a few stairs they started taking turns pulling Baxter up behind them. It gave Kasyanov a rest, but then halfway up even she needed some help. She had exhausted herself, and Hoop only wished she had something in her medical bag that could help. Pain inhibitor, energy booster, *anything*.

By the time they reached the head of the large staircase, they were all panting with exhaustion. They were met with what appeared to be a blank wall, and Hoop turned quickly, looking back down the way they'd come and expecting an ambush. *We have the high ground*, he thought, but then realized that wouldn't matter. If there were enough of them, no fight would last very long.

"Hey, look," Sneddon said. She'd gone to one side of the wall and touched a series of projections. Without warning, a heavy curtain of some undefinable material was slowly sliding open. It jerked, grinding as it moved, and parted in the middle. Beyond lay more shadows.

"Enter freely," Lachance drawled. "You're *welcome* to stay the night."

"I'll go first," Hoop said. But Ripley was already through.

He heard her sharp intake of breath even as he stepped through the ancient doorway into what lay beyond.

"It's a birthing ground," Ripley said, echoing Sneddon's comment from earlier. But this was much, much different.

There was no telling what the room had once been intended for, but it had been turned into a vision of hell. All along one side and the far end, at least fifteen of those long-limbed dog-aliens were cocooned against the walls, trapped there by clumps and swathes of alien extrusion. Most were adults, but there were two smaller shapes that might once have been children. Their exposed chests were burst, thick ribs broken and protruding, heads thrown back in endless agony. They might have been there a hundred years or ten thousand, bodies dried and mummified in the dry air. It was awful to behold.

Even more awful were the things scattered around the middle of the room. Most stood upright, the height of an adult's waist. More eggs, one for each victim fixed against the wall. They all appeared to have hatched.

"Don't get too close!" Sneddon said as Lachance edged forward.

"They're ancient," Hoop said. "And they're all open. Look." He kicked at a petal-like flap on the egg nearest to him and it crumbled and fell away. "Fossilized."

"Fucking gross," Baxter said. "This just gets worse and worse."

"We're going that way?" Ripley asked. She was aiming her flashlight across the wide room toward a shadowy doorway in the far wall.

"Yeah," Hoop said. "This is all ancient history. Just don't look." He started across the room, aiming his flashlight and spray gun at the ground ahead so that he didn't trip.

He saw movement inside an open egg close by, and froze, readied to spray it with acid. But it had only been a shadow. Shit, he was on edge.

As he started to move again, he felt almost like an intruder in this ancient tableau. Whatever had happened here was between those dog-aliens and the monsters that still infested the ship—a confrontation that had apparently occurred long before Earth had discovered technology, and while its people were still farming the land and looking to the stars with superstition and fear. Even then, these things existed.

It made him feel very small and ineffectual. Even bearing the spray gun he was just a weak creature needing a weapon to protect him. Those aliens were their own weapons, perfect hunting and killing organisms. It was almost as if they were created as such, though he had no wish to imagine the creator.

Hoop had never been a God-fearing man, and he regarded such outdated beliefs as ignorant and foolish. But perhaps there were gods other than those the human race had once known.

Light flickered around the large room, casting movement into the eggs, into the eye sockets of the dog-aliens, and into corners where anything could be hiding. He sensed everyone's nervousness, and he felt it himself. This was far more than any of them had expected.

"We'll get through this," he said softly, but no one answered. None of them could know that for sure.

At the end of the room, passing through the opening to whatever might lie beyond, they came close enough to touch one of the cocooned victims. Hoop passed his flashlight over the dead thing and paused on its face. The creatures they'd found back in the tunnels had been deformed by the weapon that had ended them, but apart from their chest wounds, these were whole.

This one looked agonized and wretched. Hoop wondered at a universe that could still express such pain, after so long.

He shone the light into the space beyond and then entered.

Another tunnel, another corridor, another hallway. The walls were curved, the floors uneven and damp. The dampness was a new thing, and he paused to sweep his foot across the surface. Fluid was bubbled on the floor, as if the surface was greasy, and his boot broke a thousand bubbles into a smear.

"Slippery in here," he said back over his shoulder. Ripley was there again, shining her flashlight past him.

"The smell's changed, too," she said. She was right. Until now the ship's interior had smelled of age—dust, staleness, air filtered in from the atmosphere-processed mine to lift scents from all around. But here it was different. He breathed in deeply and frowned, trying to place the smell. It was subtle but foul, slightly tangy, like someone who had gone unwashed for a long time. There was also something underlying it that he couldn't place at all. Not a smell, but a sensation.

"It's warmer," Ripley said. "Not the air, but... it *smells* warm."

"Yeah," he said. "Like something alive."

"The ship?" Ripley asked.

He shook his head.

"I think if it ever was alive, in any form, that was long ago. This is more recent. This is them."

He heard Ripley passing the word back—*Go careful, stay sharp!*—and then he moved forward once again. Always forward. Going back was still an option, but it also felt like it would be a mistake.

Responsibility weighed down heavier than ever, gathering mass the more time that passed without incident. He'd never been a great decision maker—it often took him a long while just to choose dinner from the *Marion*'s limited menu—but he feared that if he decided they should turn back, the act of making that choice might doom them all.

Better to forge forward.

As they moved on, the dampness and the smells in the air increased. The inside of his nose started to sting. He was sweating, the humidity rising, nervousness drawing moisture from his body. His mouth was parched, his throat sore.

"We shouldn't be going this way," Baxter said. "This is bad. This is wrong."

"It's *all* wrong!" Lachance said sharply. "But this is up towards the top of the ship again, and that's good enough for me."

"What about the things they hatched?" Sneddon asked, and Hoop stopped dead. *Something's been bugging me and that's...*

"Where are they?" he asked, turning around to look at the others.

"That was a long time ago," Ripley said.

"We don't know how long they live. The ones in the *Samson*

waited for weeks, so maybe they can hibernate for years. Or longer."

"So there could be a lot more down here than just those hatched from the miners," Sneddon said.

"It doesn't change anything," Hoop said, and he waited for any response. But everyone was looking at him. "Changes *nothing*. We're here now. We go forward, up, and out."

They continued on, but the corridor—twisting and turning, erring only slightly upward—ended at another wide, dark room.

Oh, no, Hoop thought. *This is it. This is what they found, or some place like it.*

It was another birthing ground. There was no telling how many places like this there were in the ship, nor how big the ship even was. As they paused at the edge of the hold, he found himself shaking with a deep, primeval fear. This was a danger beyond humanity, one that had existed since long before humans even knew what the stars were.

"They're unopened," Sneddon said. She pushed past Hoop, slinging the spray gun over her shoulder and taking something from her pocket.

"Don't get too close!" Hoop said.

"Mummified. Preserved." The room was lit with a bright flash as Sneddon started taking pictures of the eggs. "They're almost like fossils."

Hoop swept the spray gun and its attached flashlight from side to side, searching the extent of the chamber and looking for an exit. He saw one at the far side of the room, a tall, framed opening. He also saw something else. He aimed his flashlight up.

"Look."

The string of lights was slung from wire supports fixed into the room's high ceiling. Some of the lights were smashed, others seemed whole, but no longer worked. Or they had been intentionally deactivated.

Hoop didn't like that one little bit.

"Look here!" Sneddon said. She was at the far edge of the room now, standing back from one of the eggs and taking photographs.

The flashes troubled Hoop—for a second after each one his vision was complete blackness, his sight returning slowly every time. He didn't like being blind, even for a moment.

The egg before her was open. Unlike the others, it didn't look old and fossilized, but newer. Wetter.

She flashed off another shot, but this time Hoop blinked just as the light seared around the room, and when he opened his eyes again his vision was clear. In the final instant of the flash, he saw that the old-looking eggs were opaque beneath the camera's flash. Inside, there were shapes. And he was certain that some of those shapes were moving.

"Sneddon, don't get too—"

"There's something—" Sneddon said. She took one step closer.

Something leapt from the egg. In an instant it wrapped itself around Sneddon's face. She dropped the camera and it started flashing on automatic, the white-light searing the room at one second intervals as she grabbed the thing and tried to force her fingers beneath its grasping claws and the long, crushing tail that coiled around her neck. And then she dropped to her knees.

"Holy shit!" Lachance said, swinging the charge thumper up and toward her.

Ripley knocked it aside.

"You'll take her head off!"

"But that thing will—"

"Keep her still!" Hoop said. Then he was beside Sneddon, trying to assess what was happening, how the thing had attached, what it was doing to her.

"Oh, shit, *look* at those things!" Kasyanov said.

Other eggs were opening. Even beneath the shouting and panic Hoop could hear the wet, sticky, almost delicate sounds of the flaps peeling back, and the slick movements of the things inside.

"Don't get too close to any of them!" he said. "Get over here, everyone get close to—"

"Fuck that!" Kasyanov said, and she fired her plasma torch across the room. Sneddon's still-flashing camera was nothing compared to the blazing light. The doctor swept it from left to right, the fire rolling in a white-hot wave across the space, and beneath its concentrated heat the eggs began to burst. They split apart and wriggling, thrashing things emerged, sliding out in a slick of fluid already bubbling beneath the heat, their legs and tails whipping for purchase. Then they began to shriek.

It was a horrible sound, ear-splitting, far too human.

"Help me drag her!" Ripley said, trying to grab Sneddon beneath one arm. But the science officer slumped forward, her shoulder striking an egg, before falling onto her side. "There!" Ripley shouted, nodding at the opening across the room. "Help me!"

Lachance pulled the spray gun from Sneddon's other shoulder, grabbed her beneath the arm, and began to haul.

The egg that Sneddon had nudged against opened. Hoop saw it, and without thinking he swung the spray gun to bear. Ripley saw the barrel aiming at her and opened her mouth to shout a warning, but then she sensed the movement as well, turned, and swung the charge thumper from her shoulder.

"Not yours!" Hoop shouted. He'd given her real charges, and if she fired one in this confined space, it might kill them all.

Lachance was quick. He dropped Sneddon, stepped back, and fired his own charge thumper, loaded with non-exploding ammunition. The egg shuddered as something passed through it, and the flaps drooped as a thick, viscous fluid leaked out.

"Don't step in it!" Ripley warned as she and Lachance grasped Sneddon again.

Kasyanov was staring at her handiwork. Half of the room was ablaze, plasma having stuck to the walls and the eggs and seeded multiple fires. Several more eggs—the ones not caught in the initial blast—burst open, their boiling insides spraying across the room. Kasyanov winced back, wiping at something that had landed on her forearm and glove.

"Don't spread it!" Hoop shouted.

The doctor glanced back at him, shaking her head and holding up her gloved hand.

"It's okay, it's not acid," she said. "I think it's..." Then her face changed, as the suit material began bubbling and smoking as the liquid started to eat through.

Kasyanov screamed.

"Let's go!" Hoop shouted. Ripley and Lachance dragged Sneddon, Baxter hopped as best he could, and Hoop went for Kasyanov, reaching for her while trying not to touch the parts of her that were affected. She saw him coming and tried to be still, but a heavy shudder was passing through her body. Her teeth clacked together so hard that he thought they'd break, and she was starting to foam at the mouth.

She reached out her good hand and grasped his.

"I... can't... see..." she managed to croak, and Hoop squeezed her hand. Her eyes looked fine, but there wasn't time now to examine them closely. The room was heating up. He needed to get away.

The face-hugging things were still bursting from their eggs, cooking in the fire, screaming.

They made it across to the opposite doorway. Ripley went first, lighting the way with her own flashlight. Hoop guided Kasyanov in last, leaning her against the dripping wall and trying to say some comforting words in her ear. He couldn't tell whether or not she heard.

Then he stood in the opening and faced back into the room. The waves of heat were intense, drawing in air from behind him to feed the flames. The sounds of the blaze were incredibly loud—the roar of air alight, the crackle and pop of eggs bursting and burning. The stench was foul, scorching his nose and throat as the whipping limbs of flames threatened his clothing, face, and hair.

But there were still several eggs that were untouched.

As he leveled the spray gun and braced himself, he glimpsed something glimmering across the other end of the room. A shine, coming from the shadows. He aimed the flashlight that way, and saw.

"Ripley!" he said, trying not to shout too loud. "Lachance, Baxter! They're here."

15

OFFSPRING

"We're killing their children," Ripley said.

And though she wasn't certain just how accurate this assessment was—where the eggs came from, what laid them, how these beasts procreated—somehow she felt it was right. Any species would go to great lengths to protect its offspring. This was nature's way.

Across the burning, smoking, spitting pit of the egg chamber, the first alien stepped from the shadows.

Hoop's acid spray gun wouldn't reach that far, so Ripley didn't hesitate. She braced the charge thumper against her hip and fired. It was a lucky shot. The projectile struck the alien low down on one leg, knocking the limb from under it and sending it sprawling to the left, rolling across two burning eggs. It shrieked and stood, shaking off the flames like a dog shaking water from its coat.

…One…

Ripley counted in her head. The only other time she'd fired an explosive charge from the thumper, the time delay had hit five seconds, and now—

…two…

"Hold your breath!" Hoop fired three spurts of acid across the right-hand side of the room.

…three…

The acid splashed from the wall, landed across the floor and several eggs, and immediately started hissing. One egg was sliced immediately in two, red smoke boiling up from its ruined insides.

...*four*...

The alien was on its feet again, one arm-like limb slapping at its legs where the small, metallic charge had penetrated and stuck.

"Down!" Ripley shouted. She turned her back to the flames and crouched.

The explosion reverberated across the room and through the ship's structure, the floor punching up at their feet, air thumping at their ears. She gasped, swallowed, then spun around to face the room again.

The alien was all but gone, most of its torso and lower limbs blown away. Its head had rebounded from the roof and landed close to where it had been standing, and the next two aliens rushing into the room kicked it aside.

Hoop was gasping next to her. She glanced at him, saw the blackened split in his suit's right arm.

But there was no time.

"Run!" she shouted. The two aliens had parted, stalking between the flames, and she only had one charge left. Someone shouldered her aside and the world turned white. She squeezed her eyes closed and slid down the wall, feeling the heat on one side of her face as more fire erupted through the egg room.

A wind roared past them to feed the fire, and then someone was squeezing her hand. Hoop was there, trying to pull her away and urge her to run.

Baxter stood above them, one leg firm and the other foot barely touching the ground. He had his back to them as he tracked one of the aliens, loosing another quick burst from the plasma torch and catching the creature across the head. It screeched, squealed, and darted across the room from one wall to the other, streaking fire behind it. When it struck the wall it slid to the floor and did not move again.

Ripley couldn't see the other one.

"There'll be more!" Hoop said.

"I'll stay…"

At least that was what Ripley thought Baxter said. It was difficult to tell, his back still to them, plasma torch drifting left and right as he sought new targets. The room was a sea of flames now, the wind of the firestorm almost strong enough to knock him down. He was silhouetted against the flames.

"Don't be fucking stupid," Hoop said. He ducked down and took Baxter's arm over his shoulders. "Ripley, can you guide Kasyanov?"

"I'm… " Kasyanov said. "I can walk… just not see…" She still shivered, one hand held out in front of her. It barely resembled a hand anymore.

"Your eyes aren't damaged," Ripley said.

"Fumes…" she said. "My belt, hip pocket. Red capsules. For… pain."

"Hurry!" Hoop said. Ripley knew he was right, there'd be more aliens, but they needed Kasyanov on her feet. With Baxter hobbling and Sneddon down, they were rapidly getting to the time when they'd have to leave someone behind. And she sure as hell wasn't about to decide who it would be.

She rooted through Kasyanov's belt pockets and found a strip of red injection capsules. She removed three, popping the top from one and ramming the needle through Kasyanov's suit into her right forearm. Then she popped the other, knelt, and jammed it into Baxter's leg. Hoop was last, the needle pressed into his shoulder.

"Ouch!" he yelled, and Ripley laughed. She couldn't help it. Baxter grinned, and Hoop smiled sheepishly.

Then she stood, took Kasyanov's good hand and placed it on her own shoulder.

"Hold tight," she said. "Stop when I stop, go when I go. I'll be your eyes."

Kasyanov nodded.

"Lachance?" Hoop said.

"I'm okay for now," the Frenchman said, kneeling and slinging Sneddon over one shoulder. "She's light. But we won't get far like this."

Ripley stared at the thing on Sneddon's face, and between blinks she saw Kane lying in sick bay on the *Nostromo*, Ash and Dallas hovering without any idea what to do. *Maybe she* shouldn't *get far*, she thought. Already that thing might be planting its egg inside her. But the idea of leaving her was too sick to contemplate.

With Sneddon's spray gun lost and Kasyanov's plasma torch hanging from one shoulder, they were down on their weapons. After the one charge she had left, Ripley would be firing bolts again. She had no idea how long the plasma and acid would last.

Kasyanov clasped her shoulder hard. *Like her life depends on it!* Ripley thought, smiling grimly. Then the flashlight strapped to Lachance's charge thumper went out.

"One down," he said, already gasping beneath Sneddon's weight.

"Hoop, Lachance is right. We can't get far like this," Ripley said.

"We have to," he replied.

He was right. That was the only answer. This wasn't one of those situations where a miracle would suddenly present itself. They *had* to get as far as they could, and there was no use waiting for something else to happen. One foot in front of the other, defending themselves, fighting when they had to, moving quickly when they didn't.

And if and when we get back to the Marion, *there's Ash*, she thought. She wondered just how far that bastard had gone. He'd dragged her with him through the cosmos, searching for alien life, and once he'd found it, he'd tangled her up in all this. Commitment she could understand, but his determination went way beyond that.

Maybe he'd even…

She barked a short, bitter laugh.

"What?" Hoop asked, shooting her a sideways glance.

"Nothing," she said. And it *was* nothing. Even if Ash had been responsible for the shuttle's fuel cell decay, that meant nothing right now. But if they ever made it back to the *Marion*, they'd have to be careful. That was all.

One foot in front of the other… step by step.

The corridor rose steadily, as wide as any they'd yet followed, and they started passing openings on either side. Hoop slowed before each opening and fired a quick shot from his spray gun every time, but nothing shrieked, nothing came at them from the shadows.

They didn't even know there was an opening above them until they heard the scream.

It was different from the other alien noises they'd heard, a deeper cry as if from something larger. The shriek was somehow more measured, almost more intelligent. It was haunting.

Ripley stopped and crouched, and Kasyanov did the same behind her. She looked upward. There was a wide, darker shadow in the ceiling above them that swallowed light, and it was only shining a flashlight directly up that revealed the shaft rising above them. High up in that shaft, something moved.

Hoop was ahead with Baxter, both of them already aiming their weapons. But neither of them fired. *Acid and fire will drop back down*, Ripley thought.

"Back!" Ripley said. She and Kasyanov backed up, and behind them she heard Lachance grunting with the effort of reversing with Sneddon still slung over his shoulder. Hoop and Baxter moved forward, further along the corridor, so that the opening in the ceiling was now between them. Ripley and her group pressed tight against the wall, giving the leaders as wide a field of fire as they could.

But not wide enough.

"Come on!" Ripley said. "Quickly!" And she ran. Kasyanov clasped her shoulder firmly and moved with her, perfectly in step. Lachance struggled along behind, keeping up with them as they passed beneath the gap in the ceiling. Ripley risked a glance up…

…and saw the moving thing much closer now, falling, limbs knocking sparks from the shaft's sides, no longer screeching but growling, keening, its mouth extended and open, ready for the kill.

She shrugged Kasyanov's hand from her shoulder, pushed her to keep moving, then crouched and fired her charge thumper up. Then she rolled backward without waiting to see where the charge had gone.

"Run!" Hoop said. He grabbed Ripley by the collar and hauled her to her feet, then helped Baxter stagger along the corridor. *The charge will fall*, Ripley thought, *bounce off that thing and land behind us, and when it blows it'll knock us down, knock us out, and then—*

The explosion came from behind them. She could tell by the sound that the charge had detonated up in the shaft somewhere, but then seconds later its effects powered down and along the hallway, shoving them all in the back. Kasyanov grunted and stumbled forward, falling with her arms outstretched and screaming as the damaged hand took her weight. Ripley tripped face-first into Hoop's back, hands raking across his shoulders for purchase and knocking him down. As they fell she thought of his spray gun and what would happen if its reservoir burst beneath them.

Hoop must have been thinking the same—he braced his hands in front and pushed sideways, spilling Ripley against the wall and landing on his side. The wind was knocked from her and she gasped, waiting long seconds for her breath to return. And while she waited she watched—

Lachance dropping Sneddon, tipping forward, rolling, and then coming to his feet again, pivoting on his left foot and swinging his charge thumper up to aim back toward the blast.

Ripley turned to look as she gasped in a breath, and what she saw drove the air from her lungs again, as surely as any explosion.

The alien had dropped from the shaft and was blocking the corridor—the *entire* corridor. One of its limbs and part of its torso seemed to have been blown away, and acid hissed and bubbled across the floor and walls. It staggered where it stood, one of its sturdy legs lifting and falling, lifting and falling, as if putting weight down gave it pain.

It was larger than any other alien they had ever seen. Its torso was heavier, head longer and thicker.

It hissed. It growled.

Lachance fired.

Two bolts struck the alien's wounded side, smacking shreds of shell-like skin and bubbling flesh back away from them. It shrieked and flailed its remaining limbs, striking deep scratches across the walls. Lachance's next two shots hit it directly beneath its raised head.

The shrieking stopped. The beast froze. Hoop stood and aimed the spray gun, but he didn't fire. Even the drifting smoke from the explosion seemed to go still, waiting for whatever might happen next.

"One more," Ripley whispered, and Lachance fired again. The bolt struck the alien's abdomen, but it was already slumping to the ground, limbs settling, its damaged head resting against the corridor's side. And then slowly, slowly, it slid down as its acid-blood melted a depression in the wall.

Hoop tensed, ready to fire his acid-gun, but Ripley held up a hand.

"Wait!" she said. "Just a bit."

"Why?" he asked. "It might not be dead."

"Looks dead to me," Lachance said. "Half its head's blown off."

"Yeah, well…" Ripley said. They waited like that, watching the motionless creature, the smoke drifting down from the vertical shaft, drawn back along the corridor toward the burning egg chamber. She couldn't feel the breeze anymore, but the fleeting smoke indicated that the fires were still blazing. They listened for more movement, but heard none. And all the while she tried to see what was different about this dead beast.

Apart from being bigger than the others, there were other, more subtle differences. The length of its limbs, the shape of its head.

"What the hell is that?" Hoop asked, pointing. "There, at its ass-end."

"Oh, well, that's gross," Lachance said.

The alien's abdomen had burst open, spilling a slick mess across the floor. It sizzled and spat as the acid-pool spread, but it was the things lying in the pool that drew Ripley's attention. Scores of them—maybe hundreds—spherical and each roughly the size of her thumb. They glimmered moistly beneath the flashlight beam, sliding over one another as more poured from the wound.

"I think we killed a queen," Ripley said.

"You're sure?" Hoop asked from behind her.

"Pretty sure—it's the only thing that makes sense. They're eggs. Hundreds of eggs." She looked back at him. "We nailed a fucking queen."

She examined the rest of the creature, playing her flashlight across its blasted and slashed body. Though bigger than any they had so far seen, something about it was also almost childlike—its features were larger, the spiked and clawed limbs not quite so vicious. Ripley felt a strange frisson, a sense of likeness. But she was *nothing* like this thing.

Nothing at all.

"I think she's young," she said. "Imagine just how big…?" She shook her head. "We need to go."

"Yeah," Hoop agreed.

"My eyes are improving," Kasyanov said. "I can move quicker. I'll stay behind you. But let's get the hell out of this pit."

They moved on, the corridor still erring upward. They were more cautious now, Hoop and Ripley shining their lights ahead across walls, floor, ceiling. At every junction they paused to listen before moving on. And when they reached another staircase leading up toward what might have been an opening in the ship's hull, he handed Ripley another charge magazine.

"Last one," he said. "Five charges left."

"And I'm almost out of bolts," Lachance said.

"My plasma torch is still almost full," Kasyanov said.

They were being worn down step by step, Ripley knew. Whether or not this was an intentional act by the aliens, whether they could even consider something that complex, she didn't know. But the fact remained.

"That's the way out," she said, nodding up at this new, shorter staircase.

"How d'you know that?" Lachance gasped. His knees were shaking from Sneddon's weight. He was almost exhausted. And Baxter, leaning against Hoop, was looking up at the new, waist-high steps with something approaching dread.

"Because it has to be," Ripley said.

They started climbing—

She is panting, sweating, exhausted, ebullient. It's one of those moments that opens up and out into a perfect, never-to-be-repeated time, so rare that its blooming is like that of the planet's most precious flower. She is filled with a sense of well-being, an all-consuming love for her daughter that is so powerful that it hurts.

This time, now, *she thinks, doing her best to consign that instant to memory. The cool heather beneath her hands as she clasps onto the hillside and pulls herself higher. The heat of the sun on the back of her neck, sweat cooling across her back from the climb. The deep-blue sky above, the river below snaking through the valley, vehicles as small as ants passing back and forth along the road.*

The slope steepens as they approach the hill's summit, and Amanda giggles above her, pretending that she didn't know. It's dangerous—not quite mountain climbing, but it's a hands-and-knees scramble, and if they slip it will be a long tumble down. But Ripley can't be angry. Everything feels too good, too right, for that.

So she climbs harder and faster, ignoring the feel of empty space pulling her back and down from the hillside. Amanda glances back and sees her mother moving quicker. She giggles again and climbs, her teenager's limbs strong and supple.

I've never actually been here and seen this, yet it's the best moment of my life.

Amanda reaches the summit and shouts in triumph, disappearing over the top to lie back on the short grass and wait for her mother.

Ripley pulls herself up the natural steps in the slope. For an instant she feels terribly alone and exposed, and she pauses in her climb. Shocked. Cold.

Then she hears another sound from above that makes her start climbing again. Her sense of well-being has been scrubbed away by that sound, and the moment of perfection dissipates as if it has never been felt at all. The sky is no longer cloud-free. The hill's wildness is now brutal rather than beautiful.

The sound was her child, crying.

Ripley reaches the top, clinging to the hillside now, terrified that she will fall and even more afraid of what she'll see if she does not. When she pulls herself up and over onto the summit, she blinks, and everything is all right.

Then she really sees Amanda, standing there just a few yards away with one of those monstrous things attached to her face, tail tightening, pale fingers gripping, body throbbing. Ripley reaches out, and her daughter's chest comes apart—

* * *

"…Go in there!" Hoop said.

"What?" Ripley asked, blinking away the fog of confusion. It was harder to do this time, the debilitating sense of loss clinging to her more persistently. They'd reached the top of the staircase—she knew that, even though she had almost been elsewhere—but she took a moment to look around before realizing what Hoop was saying.

"But *look* at it!" Baxter said. "We can't just ignore that."

"I can," Hoop said. "I can, and I *am*!"

The head of the staircase opened into a wide area with two exits. One led up again, perhaps toward a hatch in the ship's hull, or perhaps not. There was no telling. The other was closer, much wider, and like nothing they had seen on the ship before.

At first she thought it was glass. The layers of clear material were scarred and dusty with time, but still appeared solid. Then she saw it shimmer as if from some unfelt breeze, and knew it wasn't glass. She didn't know exactly *what* it was, but it was there for one purpose.

Lachance grabbed Baxter's flashlight and shone it ahead. The light smeared across the clear surface and then splashed through the large space beyond. Some of what it illuminated Ripley recognized. Some she did not. None of it made her want to go any closer.

"More eggs," she said.

"But different," Baxter said. He hobbled closer and pressed his face to the barrier. It rippled as he touched it.

Lachance played his light around, and Hoop added his own.

"Oh," Baxter said. He turned around slowly.

"What is it?" Ripley asked. *We just need to leave!*

"I think we just found where your queen friend came from."

Ripley closed her eyes, sighed, and there was a terrible, unrelenting inevitability to this. She did not feel in charge of her own actions. She was long past thinking, *Maybe this is all a dream.* No, she wasn't asleep, but she didn't feel entirely awake, either. The more she tried to take control of events, the more they ran away from her. And here she was again, needing to go in one direction, yet drawn relentlessly in another.

Hoop shone his light back down the staircase they'd just climbed. No movement. Then he turned back to the new room beyond the clear enclosure.

"I'll go first," he said.

The second thing Ripley noticed was that the tech here was far more recognizable—and more prevalent—than it had been anywhere else in the ship. There were at least six separate movable workstations where the equipment appeared largely identical, ranging from sizeable units to smaller, more intricate devices. There was very little dust, and everything had a sharpness, a clarity, that the rest of the ship was lacking. Time had not paid this place so much attention.

The *first* thing she noticed was the eggs, and the things that guarded them.

There were sixteen eggs, each one set apart from the others within a waist-high, circular wire enclosure. The enclosures were set around the room's curved perimeter, leaving the center open for the mobile workstations. The eggs looked similar to the others they had found and destroyed, though there were subtle differences in color, tone, and shape. They were rounder, fatter, and their surfaces seemed to be more thoroughly networked with fine veins. Ripley thought perhaps they were newer, or simply better preserved.

Crouched beside the eggs were things that at first glance resembled statues. But she knew not to take anything down here at first glance. They were aliens, their spiked limbs dulled, curved heads dipped and pale. Slightly larger than others they had seen, yet so different from the queen they'd so recently killed. It was Lachance who hit it on the head.

"They look like… the ship's builders."

And they did. They were a monstrous blend of alien and dog-creature. More limbs than other aliens, each with a chunkier body, thicker legs, and a more prominent head, still they possessed the same chitinous outer shell, and one had slumped to the side with its grotesque mouth extended, the glimmering teeth now dulled. Ripley was glad she hadn't seen them alive.

"How long have they been here, do you think?" Baxter asked.

"Long time," Kasyanov said. "That one almost looks like it's mummified. But these eggs… maybe the damned things can *never* die."

One egg was open, and on the ground close by it was the body of one of the miners.

"Nick," Lachance said quietly. "He owed me fifty dollars."

Nick's chest was open, clothing torn, ribs protruding. He looked fresher than the other corpses they'd found, yet Ripley thought he'd probably died around the same time. The atmosphere in this section was cleaner, and perhaps lacking in the bacteria of decay.

"Only one egg has opened," she said. She blinked softly, trying to take control of the feeling that was slowly enveloping her. It was an urgency driven by disgust, a pressing desire fed by hatred.

"And we just popped the bastard that came from that," Hoop said. "You think so?"

"Yeah, popped it," she said. She looked around at the other eggs and the things that had settled to guard them, long ago. If all these eggs were queens—if that's what the creature they'd just killed had been—then they had the potential to produce many, many more aliens.

Thousands more.

"We have to destroy them all," she said. She lifted the charge thumper.

"Wait!" Kasyanov said. "We haven't got time to—"

"We make time," Ripley said. "What happens if we don't survive? What happens if a rescue mission eventually arrives, comes down here? What then? There are thousands of potential creatures in this one room. We've fought off a few of those things. Imagine an army of them."

"Okay, Ripley," Hoop said. He was nodding slowly. "But we need to take care. Lachance, come with me. We'll check the other opening, make sure that's really the way out. Then we'll come back and fry these fuckers." He looked at Ripley, and held up a hand. "Wait."

She nodded, but with one glance urged him to hurry. She

wouldn't wait for long. Her finger stroked the trigger, and she imagined the eggs bursting apart, spilling their horrendous cargo to the clear gray floor.

Fuck you, Ash, she thought, and she almost laughed. He'd done everything he could to procure another one of these monsters for his Weyland-Yutani bosses. And she was doing everything she could to destroy them all.

She would win. Of that she had no doubt. The burning question was, would she also survive?

"I will," she said.

Perhaps thinking she was replying to him, Hoop nodded.

Sneddon was slumped beside the door, creature still clasped across her entire face. Baxter stood resting against the wall, plasma torch cradled in his arms. Kasyanov blinked the pain from her eyes, also holding her plasma torch.

As Hoop and Lachance left, Ripley had a flash-image of Amanda on top of that hill.

I'll save you, baby. I'll save you.

16

MAJESTY

"We're getting out of this. Right, Hoop?"

"What do you expect me to say to that?"

"That we're getting out of this."

"Okay, Lachance. We're getting out of this."

Lachance exhaled and wiped his brow. "That's a relief. For a minute there I thought we were fucked."

"Come on. Let's see what's up here." They crossed the open area at the head of the steep staircase, and Hoop paused to look back down. His light didn't seem to penetrate quite so far, now, its power starting to wane. He couldn't quite see the bottom. There could have been anything down there, crouched in the shadows and staring up at him, and he wouldn't know.

Lachance moved through the opening and started up the shorter staircase. Hoop followed. There were only five tall steps before the walls seemed to close in, forming a blank barrier. But Lachance leaned left and right, looking at varying angles.

"Hidden opening," he said. "Clever." He ducked through a fold in the strange wall material.

Hoop glanced back and down. There was no noise down there, no hint that anything had gone wrong in that strange lab with the queen eggs. Yet he still couldn't shake the idea that they were making a mistake here. That splitting up, even for such a short time, was a stupid thing to do.

Ripley was stronger than ever, yet he could sense a ripple of danger emanating from her now. A need for some sort of vengeance, perhaps, that might well put them all in peril. She was a logical woman driven by the instinct for survival, intelligent and determined. But as she was shooting that queen, he'd seen something in her eyes that had no place with logic. Still instinct, perhaps. But the instinct for attack, rather than defense.

When she'd looked at him just now, he'd seen murder in her eyes.

He walked into Lachance, then realized why the Frenchman had stopped.

The hidden route emerged onto the huge ship's wings close to the cavern wall. The miners' lights were still strung across the cavern, shedding a weak light over the whole area. Looking back along the wing he could see the damaged area where they'd entered, several hundred yards away and seemingly so long ago.

"Can't see any of those bastards," Hoop whispered.

"If they're up here, they're hiding," Lachance said. "But look. What *is* that?" He was pointing to the right, toward where the ship's hull seemed to disappear beneath the cavern wall that rose high above them, curving eventually into a high ceiling hidden by shadows.

"That's our way out," Hoop said. There was a series of cracks in the wall above the wing, any one of which might have been a route back up into the mine.

"Yeah, but what is it?"

Hoop frowned, looked closer. Then he saw what Lachance meant. "Holy shit…"

It wasn't part of the ship. It was made of stone. Much of it had tumbled, but some still stood, a structure that at first glance formed the crevassed, cracked wall of the cavern.

"Is that a building of some sort?" Lachance asked. "A wall?"

"We'll see," Hoop said. "But not yet. Come on, we need to get the others."

"And wipe out those eggs," Lachance said.

"Yeah." Hoop took one more lingering look around the cavern—the huge, buried vessel, like no ship any of them had ever seen; the massive cavern formed above and around it; and now this vast wall that seemed to loom over the ship, burying it, smothering the parts of it they had yet to see. It was almost as if the ship had crashed into the structure, rupturing it, ploughing through until it wedged to a halt.

Whatever had happened here, they'd never know the full story. He'd bet money on it.

Because even after wiping out those eggs, there were more measures they could take. Already he was making plans.

They ducked back inside the ship, descended the steep steps, and reached the open area at the head of the longer staircase.

First came the flash of plasma fire from the lab ahead of them.

Then the scream.

Lachance was first across the landing, ducking through the clear curtain into the lab, thumper coughing as he entered. Hoop was right behind him. *Ripley started without us!* he thought, but as he entered and saw what was happening, he knew that wasn't the case.

They should have been more careful.

Ripley waited. She walked a complete circuit of the center of the room, careful to give the dead miner a wide berth. None of the eggs gave any signs of opening, there was no sound or movement, yet she remained alert. If one of them so much as twitched or pulsed, she'd open fire.

Baxter had crouched down beside Sneddon and the two of them were motionless, unconsciously mimicking the mummified aliens. Kasyanov continued to blink quickly, touching at her eyes with her good hand and wincing as her gloved fingertips brushed against the swollen red eyelids. Her acid-burnt hand was held in front of her, shaking. She'd need attention back on the *Marion*—they all would—but they had to get there first.

Apart from the one that had opened, the alien eggs seemed untouched, and almost immune to any effects of time. Perhaps the wire enclosures formed some sort of stasis field, letting the eggs and their monstrous cargo sleep until the time came for them to wake.

That time was when a host, a victim, was brought before them.

Finger still stroking the trigger, Ripley moved closer to one of the hybrid figures. Though they repulsed her, she couldn't deny that she was also fascinated. This one must have been birthed from one of the dog-aliens that had built this strange ship. Which meant that the aliens seemed to take on some of the attributes of whomever or whatever they used as a host for their gestation. Did Kane's alien have some of Kane in it?

Would Amanda's?

"No," Ripley breathed. "They'll never leave here. None of them." She looked at Sneddon where she sat slumped close to the doorway, that huge spider-like thing still clamped tight to her face, tail around her throat. Soon it would die and fall off, leaving an egg inside her chest that would quickly gestate and become one of them. Then the pain, the terrible agony of her death, and the new monster would emerge.

If Ash had his way, Sneddon would be in stasis before that happened.

"No," Ripley said again, louder. Kasyanov looked across at her, Baxter glanced up, both alarmed. "We can't take her," she said, nodding at Sneddon. "She's infected. We can't save her, and we mustn't take her."

"Well, there's no way we're leaving her!" Kasyanov said.

"Haven't you got something for her?" Ripley asked.

It took a while for Kasyanov to understand what Ripley was really asking. When she did her red-rimmed eyes widened.

"And who the hell are you?" she asked. "You don't even know Sneddon, and you're asking me to kill her?"

"Kill?" Baxter asked, looking confused.

"No, just help her," Ripley said.

"How exactly is killing her going to help her?" Kasyanov snapped.

"Have you seen what they do?" Ripley asked. "Can you imagine how much it would hurt having something…" *Amanda, screaming, hands held wide as a beast burst its way outside from within.* "Something eating its way out of you from the inside, breaking your ribs, cracking your chest plate, chewing its way out? Can you even *think* about that?"

"I'll take it out of her," Kasyanov said.

Something creaked.

Ripley frowned, her head tilted to one side.

"Don't you go near her," Kasyanov continued. "None of us knows you. None of us knows why you really came, so you just—"

"Listen!" Ripley said, hand held up.

Creak…

She looked around at the eggs. None of them seemed to be moving, none of those fleshy wings were hinging open, ready to disgorge their terrible contents. Maybe it was a breeze, still tugged through the tunnels and corridors by the fires they had set deeper in the ship. At the doorway, those strange curtains hung heavy. Around the room nothing moved. Except—

Scriiiitch!

It was Kasyanov who saw it.

"Oh… my… God!"

Ripley spun around, backed away toward where the others waited by the doorway, clasping the charge thumper and immediately realizing that they were very close to being fucked.

It wasn't just one of the mummified aliens that was moving.

It was all of them.

She squeezed the trigger, Kasyanov opened up with the plasma torch, and Ripley felt the ice cold, blazing hot kiss of fire erupting all around her.

She screamed.

"Back back *back*!" Hoop shouted. Baxter was already trying to haul Sneddon out of the room, and Kasyanov was grasping the unconscious woman's boots, trying to lift with her one good hand, plasma torch sputtering where it hung from her shoulder.

As Lachance and Hoop entered there was a thudding explosion

from across the room. Shrapnel whistled past Hoop's ears and struck his suit, some of it dry, some wet. He winced, expecting more pain to add to his throbbing arm. But there were no more sizzling acid burns. Not yet.

Ripley stood in front of them all, charge thumper at her hip as she swung thirty degrees and fired again.

"Back!" Hoop shouted again, but Ripley couldn't hear, or wasn't listening.

The frozen, statue-like aliens were moving. Several were down already, burning from Kasyanov's plasma torch or blown apart by Ripley's first shot. Others moved across the room toward Ripley. Some were slow, stiff, hesitant, as if still waking from a slumber Hoop could not comprehend.

One was fast.

It streaked toward Ripley from the right, and if Hoop hadn't already had his finger on the spray gun trigger, she might have died. Instinct twitched his finger and sent a spurt of acid across the room. The alien's movement made the shot even more effective, the acid slicing across its middle section. It hissed, then screamed, and thrashed backward as Lachance's thumper discharged. He fired three bolts into its head and it dropped down, dead.

Ripley's second charge exploded. The whole room shook, detritus whizzing through the air and impacting walls, faces, flesh. She cried out and went to her knees, and Hoop saw that she'd already suffered burns across her right hip and leg from a plasma burst. It couldn't have actually touched her—if it had, it would have eaten through her suit, flesh and bones—but she'd been too close when Kasyanov had fired her torch. If the torch's reserves hadn't already been nearly depleted, Ripley would have died.

Hoop turned to the right, away from everyone else, and let loose another concentrated stream of acid, squeezing his eyes almost entirely closed against the fumes, holding his breath. An egg exploded, gushing sizzling insides. Another fell in two, the thing inside thrashing briefly before growing still.

Ripley was on her feet again.

"Get out!" she shouted at them all. "Get back! Now!"

Three more aliens surged through a cloud of smoke and came at her. She fired another charge at them, striking the foremost creature and driving it back into the other two, the glimmer of metal obvious in its chest. She turned her shoulder and crouched as the blast came, then she quickly stood again.

Hoop helped Kasyanov with Sneddon's dead weight, and Lachance backed out with them.

"Ripley!" Hoop shouted. "Out, now!"

As he backed through the clear-curtained doorway with his crewmates, he could see her silhouetted against a wall of white-hot flame that still burned across the left half of the room. Her hair was wild, her stance determined, as something emerged from the flames and came at her, blazing.

She fell, rolled, kicked out with one boot. The alien tripped over her leg and went sprawling, spilling one queen's egg onto its side. Ripley screamed in pain as her wounded leg was jarred, but then she was standing again, aiming the charge thumper and firing her last shot into the monster's face.

She burst back through the curtains as the charge exploded. It shoved her through, fire blooming all around her, arms outstretched. She let go of the empty thumper and broke her fall, grunting as her already wounded body was subjected to another impact.

Ripley stood quickly and went for Kasyanov. She grasped the spray gun, tugged, and Kasyanov pulled back.

"Ripley!" Hoop said. She was bleeding from the leg and hip, slashed across the shoulder and side of her neck by an alien's tail. Her face was blackened from an explosive blast. A large patch of her hair had been burnt away, and her right eye was almost closed. She should have been down on her knees, at least. But something kept her going.

"Give it to me!" she demanded.

A rage, a burning fury at these things and what they meant.

"Let it go!" she screamed.

Kasyanov slipped the strap from her shoulder and stepped back, looking at Ripley as if she was one of those things.

Hoop went to shout at her again. But she was already turning back to the clear curtain, shouldering it aside and facing the terrors within. The fires. The bursting eggs. And those things that remained, waking, rising, coming to kill her.

She stood before them, and the thing that drove her fury wasn't the memory of dead friends, but the unreal vision of her tortured daughter. She could do nothing about Dallas and the others on the *Nostromo*, and she was beginning to fear that she and the *Marion*'s survivors would never survive.

But she could protect the daughter she had not seen for more than thirty-seven years. She could make sure these things were wiped out, and that if and when more people came here, there was no risk that they would ever be found.

Two queen eggs burst apart beneath the flames, and Ripley held her breath and fired a spray of acid across their remains. Just to make sure.

A large creature staggered at her, elements of the dog-aliens even more apparent now that it was up and moving. She hosed it down, sweeping the spray gun left and right and slicing gushing wounds in the thing's carapace. It stumbled and fell, its tail whipping through the air and catching her across the stomach. She just staggered for a moment.

Fires danced, shadows wept, and nothing else moved in that strange, ancient laboratory. Why the dog-aliens had kept and nurtured the queen eggs, what they hoped to gain, if they had even known the terrible dangers they toyed with, she would never know. But she didn't care. Knowing would change nothing.

They all had to die.

Three eggs remained, awake and ready, pulsing as the flaps slowly drew back to disgorge their charges. She fired an acid blast at each one, ensuring that their insides were destroyed. Something squealed as it died, and she hoped it hurt. However old the eggs and their contents might be, they were always ready to invade another host, and plant their dreadful larvae.

"Not anymore!" Ripley shouted. "Fuck you, Ash!" Maybe he was a good target for her ire, maybe not. But having someone to curse other than these beasts felt good.

Then they were done. Dead and gone. The queen eggs—so much potential, so much promise of pain and heartbreak—were cooking, melting, bubbling messes on the floor. She lowered the spray gun and blinked the fumes away, and flames flickering through tears made the scene look almost beautiful.

Something grabbed her and she turned, seeing Hoop standing behind her and realizing only then how much pain she was in.

"Ripley, we have to…" he said, eyes going wide at something he'd seen.

"What?"

"We need to patch you up."

"I'm fine," Ripley said, not feeling fine but finding the strength to move. "There's Sneddon and Baxter… you can't carry me as well. I'll walk 'til I drop."

And she did. Five paces out through the curtained opening, a few more across the open space beyond, and then her whole world started to spin. She was bleeding, burning, maybe even dying. And though she held on as hard as she could, Ripley couldn't fight back the darkness descending all around her.

Faces watched her fall. She only hoped she would see them all again.

"They'll be coming," Hoop said.

"She's bleeding badly," Kasyanov said. "Her shoulder and neck, her stomach, they're slashed up pretty good."

"Will she bleed to death?" Hoop asked.

Kasyanov waited for only a moment. "Not in the short term."

"Then she can bleed while we run. Come on. We're almost out." He grasped Ripley and tugged her to her feet. She tried to help, but barely had any strength. Blood shimmered on the front of her suit, flowing across her boots and speckling the floor. *They'll pick up the scent and follow us*, he thought. But he didn't even know if the aliens could smell, and his priority now was to move as far away from here, as fast as they could.

Back up into the mine, to the second elevator, and out of this hellhole.

Baxter started hauling himself up the shorter staircase toward the outside, wounded ankle dragging behind him. It looked less painful, though, since he'd had the injection. Lachance and Kasyanov lifted Sneddon and pushed her up, step by step. As Hoop pulled Ripley up onto the first step, her feet kicking feebly, she started talking.

"...take her..." Ripley muttered.

"Huh? We are. We're all getting out."

"No... don't take..."

She fell silent and he thought perhaps she was dreaming. Her eyes rolled, blood flowed. She looked a mess. But her strength was humbling, and on the next step she opened her eyes again, looking around until they focussed on those ahead and above them. "Sneddon," she said, quietly so only Hoop could hear. "We can't take her."

He didn't even reply. Ripley groaned and seemed to pass out again, and when he dragged her up to the next step the trail of blood she left behind glimmered in the light.

But he lifted her, pulled her up. Because he wasn't leaving *anyone* behind. Not after everything they'd been through. Hoop had lost so much in his life. His wife, his love, his children, left behind when he fled. Some of his hope, and much of his dignity. And at some point the time for loss would have to end. Maybe now, when he was at his lowest and everything seemed hopeless, he would start winning things back.

This is it. His friends, bleeding and in pain yet forging on as hard as they could, inspired him. And Ripley, the strange woman who had arrived in their midst, her own story tragic and filled with loss... if she could remain so strong, then so could he.

He climbed up the next step and pulled her up after him, and for some reason she felt lighter.

Outside, the others hunkered down close to where the folded

access opened onto the ship's upper surface. They kept low and quiet, as if being suddenly exposed after their nightmarish trip through the tunnels and corridors scared them even more. Hoop handed Ripley to Lachance, slipping the charge thumper from her shoulder as he did so. Even hazy and balancing on the edge of consciousness, she grabbed for the weapon. He eased her hand aside.

"It's okay," he said. "I've got it." And she relented.

"What are you doing?" Lachance asked.

"Insurance," Hoop said. "Giving us the best chance I can." He held up two fingers—*two minutes*—then slipped back through the opening.

By his reckoning, there was one charge left in the blaster.

Now that he was facing it alone, the ship's interior felt even stranger, more alien than ever. They had only left it moments before, but already he felt like an invader all over again. He wondered one more time just how alive that huge ship was, or had once been. But it was ancient, and whatever intelligence might once have driven it was now surely in the deepest of slumbers, if not dead.

He edged down the first high step, then the second, and then he heard something that froze him to a halt. Everything in his world came to a standstill—the past, the future, his breathing, his thoughts. His heart skipped a beat, as if hiding from that sound.

A high-pitched keening, so filled with pain and rage that it prickled his skin, the sound itself an assault. He was chilled and hot at the same time, his soul reacting in much the same way as skin when confronted by intense heat or cold. He might burn or freeze with terror, but for a moment he couldn't tell which.

What have we done? he thought. He could smell burning flesh, though there was no similarity to any meat he knew. He could hear the roar of the flames they had left behind, consuming what was left of the aliens, the eggs. And dropping down one more step, he could see the three creatures that had come after them.

They were the same as the first ones they had encountered, back on the *Marion*. No dog-like features, no attributes that might have made them a queen. Warriors, perhaps. Soldier aliens. And they were whining and keening as they stood outside the burning, ruined lab, swaying from side to side, their tails waving, heads dipping to the left and then right. It was a dance of death and mourning, and for the briefest of moments Hoop felt almost sorry for them.

The one in the middle bent to the ground and seemed to take a long, deep sniff of the blood trail there. Ripley's blood trail. Then it hissed, a purposeful sound very different from the wails of grief, and the other two creatures also bent to the trail.

Got her scent now, Hoop thought. *Sorry, Ripley, but if there's anyone we have to leave behind…*

He wasn't serious. Not for a moment. But the aliens' reactions set his own blood chilling. They hissed again, louder than before. They crouched and spread their limbs, adopting stances that suddenly made them look even more deadly.

Hoop started climbing back up the steps. They still had their backs to him, but they only had to turn a quarter circle to see him. They would be on him in two bounds, and even if he had a chance to fire the charge-blaster, the delay on the charge meant he'd be dead before it blew.

He wished he'd brought his spray gun, too.

He made the top of the steps, braced himself, checked that the route behind him was clear. Then he paused at the fold in the wall and aimed the charge thumper up at the ceiling.

Four seconds, maybe five. Did that give him time? Would they be up the steps and through before the charge went? He didn't think so. But he also didn't think he had time to worry about it.

They had Ripley's scent, and Ripley had come this way.

He pulled the trigger, and the last explosive charge thumped up into the ceiling.

From beyond, down in the ship, he heard three high-pitched shrieks, then the skittering of hard claws as the aliens came for him.

Hoop sidestepped up through the opening and onto the ship's surface.

"Down there!" he said, shoving Ripley ahead of him, sliding down the gentle slope, and Lachance and Kasyanov pushed Sneddon the same way. They slid through the dust, and then from above and behind them came a dull, contained *thud*. Loud enough, though, to send echoes through the cavern.

Hoop came to a stop and looked back. Dust and smoke rose from the opening, but nothing else. No curved head, no sharp limb. Maybe, just maybe, fate had given them a break.

The blast was still echoing around the cave as they started across the ship's surface toward the openings they could see in the vast wall. They negotiated their way over piles of tumbled rocks. Ripley found her feet, although she still clasped onto Hoop's arm. Their combined lights offered just enough illumination to outline shadows and trip hazards, and the closer they came to the nearest opening, the more convinced Hoop became that the ship continued beyond the barrier. It was almost as if the vessel had struck the wall, and penetrated it upon landing.

Or crashing. They'd entered through a damaged portion of the ship's hull, after all, where blast damage was still obvious after so long.

More rocks, and Hoop noticed for the first time that some of them seemed more regular than he'd realized. Square-edged, smooth. One of them displayed what might have been markings of some sort.

But there was no time to pause and wonder. No time to consider what the markings and the tumbled, regular blocks might mean. A wall? A building? It didn't matter. A way out mattered, and from what Hoop could see, their best bet was through the nearest crack.

The mine wasn't far above the cavern's ceiling. He was sure of it. They were almost there.

"No sign of anything following us," Lachance said.

"That's what worries me," Hoop said. "I think I'd rather see them than wonder where the fuck they are."

"Yeah. Right." Then Lachance nodded ahead. "What do you think?"

"I think we've got no choice." They moved across the rubble field toward the opening in the cavern's looming wall.

17

ANCIENTS

When he was a kid, Hoop's parents took him to see the Incan ruins in Ecuador. He'd seen footage about them on the NetScreen, and read about them in the old books his parents insisted on keeping. But nothing had prepared him for the emotions and revelations he felt walking among those ancient buildings.

The sense of time, and timelessness, was staggering. He walked where other people had walked a thousand years before, and later he thought back to that moment as the first time mortality truly came knocking. It hadn't troubled him unduly. But he'd realized that his visit to those ruins was as fleeting as an errant breeze, and would have as much effect as a leaf drifting in from the jungles and then vanishing again. The memory of his being there would float to the floor and rot away with that leaf, and fascinated visitors even a hundred years hence would have never heard of him.

It was humbling, but it was also strangely uplifting. *We all have the same*, he'd once heard someone say, *one life*. Even as a teenager more concerned with girls and football, that had struck him as deep and thoughtful. One life... it was up to him how well he lived it.

Looking at those Incan ruins, he'd vowed to live it well.

Staring at what was left of this strange, ancient place, he wondered what had gone wrong.

There was some property to the stone all around them that gave it a subdued glow. It was light borrowed from the flashlights, he was sure, subsumed and then given back as a surprisingly sharp luminosity. He'd shine his flashlight at one spread of stone, move it aside, and the stone would glow for a long while afterward. It helped them light their way. It helped them see where they were going.

This wasn't part of the ship on which they had been. This was a building, a grounded structure built into the rock of the land. It was a ruin, yet one that was remarkably well preserved in places.

Fleeing though they were, Hoop couldn't help staring around in wonder.

They'd entered through a badly damaged area, climbing over piles of rubble, some of the fragments the size of one of their boots, some five yards across. Anything could have been hiding in the shadows. From what they could see, nothing was, or if it was it remained hidden.

They soon found themselves on a curving, sloping path that led upward, and kicking aside dust and gravel Hoop could make out the fine mosaics that made up the paving. Swirls of color, unfaded by the immensity of time. Curling, sharp patterns, features he could not make out, splashed shapes that fought and rested in harmony with each other. He suspected the mosaic told a story, but it was too smothered with dust for him to make it out. And perhaps he was too short to appreciate the full tale. Those dog-aliens might have seen it better, with their longer legs, higher heads.

This was amazing. An alien civilization, an intelligence the likes of which had never yet been discovered in almost two centuries of space exploration, and many hundreds of star systems entered and charted.

"I don't think I can process any of this," Lachance said. "I don't think I can think about it all, and run at the same time."

"Then just run," Hoop said. "You okay there?"

Lachance was still lugging Sneddon, slung across one shoulder so that he could still access his charge thumper with the other hand.

"All that time in the *Marion*'s gym is paying off."

"Tell me if—"

"You've got enough on your mind." And Lachance was right. Ripley still clung to Hoop's arm, and though her eyes were open and he could see that she was taking some of this in, she was still bleeding, stumbling, fading in and out. They'd have to stop soon. Patch her up.

Baxter and Kasyanov were helping each other, arms slung over shoulders like casual lovers.

The curved path rose around a massive central column, like the largest spiral staircase ever. The huge building's ceiling was high, damaged in places but still largely whole. Their flashlights lit some of the way ahead, and the glowing property of the stone helped level the illumination. But there were still heavy shadows in front of them, hiding around the bend, concealing whatever waited.

Hoop remained ready.

Doorways led off from the central spiral. There were intricate designs around these, beautiful sculptures showing dog-aliens in what must have been tales from their civilization's past, real or mythical. He saw the creatures in groups and ranks, at war, bathing, creating an obscure form of art, exploring, and in some carved spreads they seemed to be interacting with other, even stranger looking creatures. There were star charts and the representations of aircraft, spacecraft, and giant floating things that might even have been living. This made him think of the buried vessel they had just left behind, and the implications…

They were staggering, yet still too dangerous to muse upon.

Concentrate, Hooper! he thought. *Don't look at the fancy decorations around the doors, think about what might come* though *them!*

The curving, rising path ended in another vast open space. Huge columns supported a solid ceiling so high that the lights barely touched it, yet the material still became subtly luminous, retaining some of the light they aimed upward. They were creating their own starry sky, soft splashes of color and light retained and shining back down at them, if only for a time.

Around the nearest supporting column, upright objects cast long shadows.

"Is that them?" Lachance whispered. They all paused, panting from the climb up the spiraling ramp, some of them groaning softly from their wounds. Ripley was relatively alert again, right hand pressed tightly across the wound in her stomach.

"No," she said. "Too big. Too still."

"Statues," Hoop said. "At least I hope so. Come on. We'll stay near the wall, look for another way up."

They kept close to the edge of the wide-open space. In truth the size of it scared Hoop. He'd rather move through corridors and tunnels than this inhuman cavern, where the lights couldn't reach the other side and shadows might hide anything. But keeping close to the wall did something to hold back the agoraphobia.

As they closed on the massive column and the statues arrayed around its base, some of the detail became clearer. There were a dozen figures standing on high stone plinths. Several of them had lost limbs, one of them a head, but others remained virtually whole. They were all dog-aliens, with their stocky legs, strange torsos, bulky heads, and yet each was distinct. Some carvings wore different clothing that almost covered their bodies. Others stood on their hind legs and reached for the sky, or pointed, or held their limbs up as if gesticulating. Even their facial features were diverse. Hoop could see carved areas around the plinth's bases, and he assumed it was their written language. Maybe these were famous persons—rulers, teachers, or explorers.

"No time," he whispered, because he knew everyone would feel as fascinated as him. "Not now. Maybe we'll come back. Maybe we'll send someone back."

"They'd just die," Ripley said. She seemed stronger now, as if becoming used to the pain, but he could still see the dark dampness of blood across her suit, and a sheen of sweat on her forehead.

"We need to get you patched up," Hoop said.

"No, we—"

"Now." He refused to argue. Two minutes to bind and treat her wounds might save them half an hour if it meant she could walk under her own steam. "Guys, eyes and ears open. Ripley... strip. Kasyanov?"

Kasyanov gently laid down her plasma torch, wincing from the pain in her own terribly wounded hand, and unclipped her waist pack.

Ripley started peeling off her slashed and bloodied suit. Hoop flinched back when he saw the open wound across her neck, shoulder, and upper chest, but he didn't look away. The edges of the wound pouted open, skin tattered, flesh and fatty layers exposed. Revealing them to the air made Ripley woozy again, and she leaned against him as the doctor set to work.

"This will hurt," Kasyanov said. Ripley didn't make a sound as Kasyanov sterilised the wound as best she could, washing out dark specks of dust and grit. She injected painkiller into six locations, then sprayed a local anaesthetic along the entire extent of the gaping cut.

While the anaesthetic went to work she tugged down Ripley's suit to below her waist and examined the stomach wound. As Hoop glanced down he caught Kasyanov frowning up at him.

"Just do your best," Ripley hissed.

Hoop hugged Ripley to him, kissed the top of her head.

"Hey," she said. "Fast mover."

Kasyanov treated the stomach wound, then stood again and started stapling the gash across her shoulder. The staple gun made a whispering click each time it fired. Ripley tensed but still didn't make a sound. After fixing the wound closed, Kasyanov taped a bandage across it and sprayed it with a sterile solution.

Then she turned her attention back to the stomach wound, stapling it, as well.

"I'll fix you up properly when we get back to the *Marion*," she said.

"Yeah," Ripley replied. "Right."

"You'll be able to move easier now. Nothing's going to pop or spill out."

"Great."

Kasyanov taped her stomach, then stood again. She took a small syringe from her pack.

"This will keep you going. It's not exactly… medicine. But it'll work."

"I'll take anything," Ripley said. Kasyanov pressed the needle into her arm, then stood back and zipped up her pack.

"You good?" Hoop asked.

Ripley stood on her own, tucking her arms into her suit and shrugging it on. "Yeah," she replied. "Good."

She wasn't. He could see that, and hear it in her voice. She was in pain and woozy, and distracted, too. Ever since she'd wiped out those queen eggs she'd been somewhere else. But there was no time to discuss it now.

Hoop thought again about those aliens viewing their burning infant queens, sniffing Ripley's blood, and howling.

"There," he said, pointing along the base of the vast wall. "Openings. Whichever one leads up, we take it. Lachance, you take point. I've got Sneddon." He knelt and took Sneddon's weight onto his shoulder. As they moved out, he held back until Ripley was walking ahead of him. She moved in a very controlled way, every movement purposeful and spare.

When they reached the first of the openings, Lachance shone his light inside. Moments later he waved them on and entered, and they started up another curving ramp.

From behind, somewhere in the vast shadowy depths, something screeched.

The rough leaves tickle her stomach. They're running across a field in France, weaving through the corn crop, arms up to push the stringy leaves aside and stop them scratching their eyes. She and Amanda are wearing their bathing costumes, and already she's anticipating the breathtaking plunge into the lake.

Amanda is ahead, a slim and sleek teenager, darting between corn rows and barely seeming to touch the plants. Ripley isn't so graceful, and her stomach feels as though it has been scratched to shreds by the leaves. But she won't look down to check. She's afraid that if she does she'll lose track of her daughter, and something about this...

...isn't right.

The sun shines, the corn crop rustles in a gentle breeze, there is silence but for their footfalls and Amanda's excited giggling from up ahead. But still this is wrong. The lake awaits but they will never reach it. The sun is high, the sky clear, yet the heat hardly touches her skin. Ripley feels cold.

She wants to call, Amanda, wait! *But the leaves slapping across her stomach and chest seem to have stolen her voice.*

She sees something out of the corner of her eye. A shadow that does not belong in the cornfield, a shape too sharp and cruel. But when she looks it has gone.

Her daughter is further ahead now, pushing plants aside as she sprints the final hundred meters to the field's edge and the welcoming water.

Something keeps pace with them off to the right, a dark shape streaking through the crop and smashing thick stalks into shreds. But looking directly at it means that Ripley can't see it at all.

She's panicking now, trying to run faster, trying to shout. Amanda has vanished ahead, leaving behind only swaying plants.

Ripley hears a high, loud screech. It's not human.

Bursting from the crop at the edge of the field, she sees Amanda caught in a grotesque web between two tall trees, trapped there in the strange, solid material that appears to have held her there for an age. Her daughter screams again as the bloody creature bursts fully from her chest.

In her peripheral vision, Ripley sees those tall beasts moving out of the corn to pay homage to their newborn.

Amanda screams one last time—

"Ripley, fast!" Hoop shouted.

Ripley looked around, not shocked or surprised. She knew exactly where she was and why. The vision was a memory of a time that had never happened. But she still shed a tear for her cocooned, bleeding, screaming daughter. Terror mixed with anger, becoming a part of her, unwilling to let go.

"They can't win, Hoop," she said. "We can't let them."

"They won't. Now run!"

"What are you—?"

"Run!" he shouted. He grabbed her hand and ran with her, but soon let her go again and fell back.

"Don't be stupid!" Ripley shouted back at him.

"Argue, and we'll all die!" Lachance called back. "Hoop knows what he's doing."

They climbed the ramp. It was steeper than the first, the turns tighter, and it seemed to grow narrower and steeper the higher they went. Soon there were steps built into its surface, and they had to slow down so that they didn't trip. Lachance carried Sneddon again. Kasyanov helped, and Baxter was using his plasma torch as a crutch, lamming it down and swinging along on it with every step. She wondered what effect that would have if he had to fire it again. She wondered…

She turned and ran back down the ramp.

"Ripley!" Lachance called.

"Argue and we all die!" she said, and soon they were out of sight above her. For a while she was on her own, descending the ramp, illuminated by an already fading glow from the structure around her. Then she heard something running toward her and she crouched down close to the central spine.

Hoop appeared, lit up by her flashlight's beam. Sweating, eyes wide, he tensed, but didn't relax again.

"We really need to go," he said.

"How many?"

"Too many."

Ripley wasn't sure she could run again. Her stomach ached, she could barely move her right arm, and she felt sick. But the booster Kasyanov had given her coursed through her veins, and every negative thought was dragged down and hidden away. There was a sensory distance around her. Though unpleasant, it was also protecting her, so she embraced it, losing track of her various agonies. She knew that they would be waiting for her on the other side.

From above, Lachance started shouting, but she couldn't tell what he was saying.

"Oh, no," Ripley said. Yet Hoop grinned and grabbed her hand, and before she knew it they were running up the ramp once more. She saw lights ahead of them, and the ramp ended in another wide space. This was more like a cave than a building—slopes of rocks, an uneven ceiling, walls that had only ever been touched by human tools.

At the far end, Kasyanov and Baxter held Sneddon up between them. The first thing Ripley noticed was the opening in the rock behind them.

Then Sneddon lifted her head and looked around, and Ripley saw that the face-hugger was gone.

18

ELEVATOR

When Hoop had broken away from the others, he'd seen at least ten of the aliens stalking through the massive room, searching between giant pillars, crouching by the statues and their plinths. There was enough fading light still emanating from the stonework, and as he'd watched their shadows had slowly merged into the surroundings.

He'd backed away slowly, light extinguished, and then run, finding his way by feel. Ripley's flashlight had brought light to his world again.

Being back in the mine should have made him feel better. But Hoop knew that those things were still pursuing them, scenting blood, and that every second's delay would bring them closer. The elevator was their salvation. Reach that, go up, and they'd be way ahead of the game. It was now a simple race. And for once, things seemed to be going well.

The thing had dropped from Sneddon's face and died, and they'd left it back there in the tunnels. She seemed fine. Quiet, confused, a little scared, but able to walk on her own, and even keen to carry the spray gun that Lachance had been hefting for her.

With Sneddon on her feet again and Ripley patched up, it meant that they could move faster than before. Even Baxter seemed to have found his stride, using his plasma torch as a crutch. Hoop dared to hope.

If we get out of this I'm going home, he thought. The idea had stuck with him for some time, and he'd been thinking of his kids. He hadn't seen them for seven years, didn't know if they'd remember him, had no idea how much his ex-wife might have turned them against him. They were adults now, plenty old enough to ask why he hadn't stayed in touch. No contact at all. Nothing on their birthdays, no messages at Christmas. How difficult would it be for him to explain, when he wasn't even sure of the reasons himself?

But when this was over and they launched themselves back toward Earth, it would be his last time. To arrive back home would be so wonderful it was now all he could wish for.

And there was something else. Maybe he didn't actually deserve hope, but Ripley did. She had been through far too much to just die out here.

The mine was familiar territory. The lights still worked, and as they moved through the tunnels of the lowest parts of level 9 toward the second elevator shaft, Hoop waited for their way to be blocked once again. Those things had been in here, building their strange constructions—nests, traps, homes. But maybe between here and the elevator it would be clear. Maybe fate had cut them a break.

But he knew the pursuing aliens would find their way. They had Ripley's scent, and their blood was up, their hatred and fury, their ferocity, richer than ever before. He saw no need to tell the others, but he made sure they moved quickly, quietly. They all understood the urgency. They'd all been through too much to slow down now.

"It's close!" Baxter said. "I recognize this place. Just around this next corner, I think." He'd been down in the mines more than any of them, and Hoop hoped he was right. And when they turned the next corner, there it was.

The elevator shaft stood in the center of a wide-open area, ceiling propped by metal columns. It seemed whole, undamaged, untouched. The shaft was set in a heavy network of metal stanchions. The elevator car was parked on this floor, too, which meant the miners had all used the other one to flee to the surface.

"Something's bound to be wrong with it," Lachance said, and Hoop actually guffawed.

"Just live with the fact we've been given a break," he said. "Come on. Everyone inside, quickly."

He waited beside the elevator while Baxter checked the controls. Power was still on, and when he pressed at the buttons, the cage door slid open to reveal the elevator car. As with the one that had crashed, the walls were of mesh and struts, the floor a solid sheet. No mirrors, no music. There was no need for luxuries in a mine.

Sneddon stood close to Hoop, swaying slowly from side to side.

"You feeling okay?" he asked.

Sneddon nodded. "Thirsty," she croaked.

"Won't be long now." He looked past her at Ripley. She was staring, frowning deeply. She'd placed herself at the far side of the elevator doors, and even as they started filing aboard, she kept her eyes on the science officer, and tried to steer clear of her.

"Ripley?" he asked softly. But she looked at him and shook her head. She knew as well as any of them that they had to leave this level. Anything else was of a lesser priority.

She's carrying one of those things, Hoop thought, glancing at Sneddon again. She looked tired, but herself. He'd seen them on the viewing screen, from inside *Samson*, bursting from chests. He'd listened to Ripley's story about the crew member on her ship, how he'd effected a miraculous recovery, only to be ripped apart an hour later.

Sneddon seemed fine. But she was living on borrowed time.

Maybe she knew that.

He stepped into the elevator, and instantly it felt as if they were rising. A weight fell from him. He slumped against the wall and sighed, closing his eyes, and as the doors slid closed he seemed to be waiting forever for the sound they made when they came together.

"We're looking good," Baxter said. "I think we might—"

The impact was massive, smashing against the doors, bowing them inward. A fresh crash came from another side, and another, and then all four sides of the enclosed elevator shaft were being assaulted from outside, aliens smashing against the mesh again and again. Metal creaked and tore, and Hoop heard the distinctive *snap!* as a set of teeth crunched together.

They all moved away from the walls, colliding in the center of the elevator and huddling there. Hoop trained his spray gun on the walls, the others aimed their weapons, but none of them could fire. Acid would splash and kill them all, plasma would surge across the inner surfaces. Closed away from the aliens at last, they also found themselves defenseless.

"Press the fucking button!" Lachance screamed at Baxter.

More banging, rending metal, and the rage-filled hissing of the creatures trying their best to reach their prey.

Baxter didn't hesitate. He lunged for the control panel and slapped his open hand on the button labeled "4".

If he'd stepped carefully he might have been all right. If panic and fear hadn't slammed him against the lift cage wall, perhaps he'd have been able to jump lightly back into the center. But the instant the car began to rise, an alien's head burst through the gap between doors, bending and ripping them apart. It thrashed and twisted as it tried to force itself inside. Moments later its teeth flashed out and struck hard against Baxter's right shoulder. They chewed so rapidly that they burrowed through his jacket, skin, flesh, and clamped tight around his scapular.

Baxter screamed, eyes wide. The alien pulled, tugging him halfway through the ragged hole it had created.

They were rising.

Hoop went to help, grabbing at the comm officer's belt, Lachance doing the same on the other side. The alien's clawed hand slashed in, and Hoop only just let go in time. He held Baxter's legs instead, pulling as hard as he could, gritting his teeth, vision blurring with the effort.

The cage rattled violently.

Baxter began screaming because he knew what was to come. He was stuck fast halfway through the opening, and they pulled one way while the alien tugged the other, rising and dangling from the suffering man as the lift took its prey out of reach.

Whether or not the alien let go, Hoop did not know. But he

closed his eyes as Baxter struck the first of the cross-beams forming the shaft's superstructure. The man's cry instantly cut off and was replaced with the most dreadful sound of ripping, tearing, crushing.

He suddenly became very light. Hoop turned around and let go as something splashed down onto the elevator's floor.

"Oh, God!" someone said.

They continued rising. Below them the cacophony persisted as aliens smashed against the walls. But the elevator accelerated, rapidly passing level 8 and speeding up even more. Hoop's stomach dropped. And when he turned around and looked at what was left of Baxter, he wasn't the only one to fall to his knees and puke.

Ripley covered him up. He'd been torn in half just below his ribcage, and his legs and lower body had dropped to the elevator floor. She couldn't keep her eyes off the broken ankle. Baxter's foot lay at an odd angle, and the heavy padding they'd used to try and splint the break had come unraveled. He'd struggled so long on that, and for so far, because he wanted to survive.

Of course he did.

They all wanted to survive, and they'd do anything to do so. Baxter had run and walked on a broken ankle, going through untold pain. And now...

She only looked briefly before dropping her suit jacket across the ruined, open part of him. Things that should never be outside a body were splashed across the elevator floor, and her jacket covered most of them.

She was cold, her tattered thermal vest doing little to hold in her body heat. But she'd rather be cold than stare at what was left of that poor man. Her stomach rolled a little, more at the stench of vomit than what she had seen.

Am I just stronger? she thought. *Have I just seen too much? Is it that I expect the worst, so it doesn't worry me?* She wasn't sure.

Maybe it was because she had something more on her mind.

She turned her back on Baxter, picked up his dropped plasma torch, and checked out Sneddon. The science officer seemed to be in reasonable shape, and there was even color in her cheeks again. She was quiet, leaning against the elevator wall and staring into some distance only she could see.

"How do you feel?" Ripley asked.

"Yeah," Sneddon said. "Yeah, good. Weird dreams. But I'm okay."

"You know what happened to you." It was a statement, not a question.

"Yes, I know."

Ripley nodded, looked around. The others were staring at her. *I'm the stranger here*, she thought. Her gaze rested on Hoop, and she couldn't quite read him. They were all tired, shocked from Baxter's gruesome demise. She couldn't say anything yet. She just couldn't.

"She'll be fine," Hoop said. "We have a med-pod on the *Marion* that can—"

"It's okay," Ripley said, turning away. She breathed hard. The sensation of movement from the elevator had been startling—still was—probably made worse by the walls distorted by the alien attack. She felt suddenly sick. But she swallowed, bit her lip, and willed it back down.

Sneddon couldn't reach the *Marion* alive. Ripley knew that, yet she was uncertain how far she would go to prevent it. Ash was up there, ready and waiting to receive the science officer into his control. It didn't matter that she was a human being. She was impregnated now, and she carried what Ash had been seeking for thirty-seven years.

Does he already know? She had to assume that was a yes.

Would he go to any lengths to protect and preserve Sneddon, and what she carried? Again, yes. She knew that, had witnessed Ash's determination before.

Sneddon couldn't be taken to the *Marion*. And Ripley could not kill another person. The problem circled, deep and heavy, and she closed her eyes, hoping that a solution would come.

Each level they passed was marked by a soft chime from the elevator's control panel, and the voice of someone from far away and long ago reciting, "Seven... Six... Five." The cage decelerated then, and Ripley experienced the strange sensation of being stretched, head and shoulders growing suddenly light. It made it easier to breathe, but did nothing to level her queasiness.

She did her best not to puke. Her stomach wound throbbed deep and cold, and she thought if she heaved the act might pop the staples holding her together. Her shoulder and arm were stiff, and she was sure she could feel the penetrating metal of the clasps there every time she moved. She thought of asking Kasyanov for another shot of anaesthetic or painkiller. But she was already woozy enough. If a flash of pain now and then was what she had to endure to stay awake, so be it. She needed all her wits about her. They all did.

The elevator slowed to a halt, and a different chime sounded from the control panel. Outside of the cage, all was blackness.

"Level 4," Lachance said. "Lingerie, footwear, monsters, and beasties."

"This level was mined out two years ago," Hoop said. "Lots of deep tunnels, a complex network. One of the longest in the mine snakes away from here for over three miles."

"Sounds lovely," Ripley said. "So the fuel cells are here?"

"Yeah, we use this level for storage now. Lachance?"

"Spare fuel cells shouldn't be that far away. We'll need to find a powered trolley to carry one."

"You okay?" Kasyanov asked, and it took Ripley a few seconds to realize the doctor was talking to her.

She nodded. Realized they were all looking at her.

"You were… mumbling to yourself," Hoop said.

"I'm good," Ripley insisted, smiling. But she hadn't realized she was saying a word.

Waiting for Hoop to throw the doors open, she tried to analyze her wounds again, assess just how badly hurt she was. But the shots Kasyanov had given her made that quite hard to do. She was slightly removed from herself, a distance that made the pain bearable but which also furred the edges of her perception.

She'd have time for reality later.

I'm awake. I'm me. Stay sharp, Ripley!

Damaged as they were, Hoop had to force the cage doors open manually, and they shone their lights outside. They all waited in silence, playing the lights around the open area they revealed. Hoop edged forward and stepped outside, crouching low, turning his flashlight and spray gun left and right.

"Looks clear," he whispered. "Wait here." He crossed to a mess of dials and controls fixed onto a wall, flicked some switches, and with a buzz and a click the lights came on. As elsewhere in the mine, there were strings of bare lights slung tight to the ceiling, and more hung from hooks sunk into the walls. But basic though they were, everyone welcomed the illumination.

"Flashlights off," Hoop said. "Conserve whatever charge you have left. We might need them again."

Ripley and the other three survivors left the elevator and fanned out. The area was similar to that on Level 9, a wide space with metal props at regular intervals. There was more mining equipment discarded all around—tools, clothing, some water canisters, and several wheeled trolleys. Lachance checked out the trolleys and found one whose power pack was still half-charged. He stood on the small control deck, accessed the control panel, and rolled forward a few steps.

"How far in are the stores?" Ripley asked.

"Not far," Hoop said, pointing at one of the tunnels leading off. "Just through there, hundred yards or so. Why?"

"And how many fuel cells are stored down here?"

"Three," Lachance said. "Two spares for the *Marion*, and one for the mine's power plant on the surface. The plant is designed so it runs off ship-grade power cells. We store them all down here, so we don't lose the ship if they… malfunction."

"Okay," Ripley said. She looked around at them all, bloodied and desperate, holding their mining tools that had been turned into weapons. They weren't soldiers. They weren't even miners. But they'd survived so far, and if and when they got home, they would have a hell of a story to tell.

"We've got to bury the mine," she said.

"What?" Lachance asked. "Why? We discovered something amazing down there! That ship was incredible enough, but those buildings we found… it can't have been just one. It was the start of a city, Ripley. Maybe a thousand, even ten thousand years old. It's…" He shrugged, at a loss for words.

"The most amazing discovery since humankind first came into space," Ripley said.

"Yes," he agreed. "That. Precisely."

"But it's contaminated," she said. "Corrupted. Tainted by those things. Whatever deep history we witnessed down there was dictated by them, not by those dog-things who built the ship and the city. They might have been the amazing ones. That ship was remarkable, I can't deny that. And we saw that they had wonderful architecture, and art, and knowledge and imagination that might put ours to shame. But am I the only one who thinks that ship might have been shot down? Maybe even by their own people?"

The others were watching her, listening silently.

"Everything went wrong. A disease came and destroyed all that they were, and we can't let that disease escape." She looked pointedly at Sneddon, who was staring down at her feet. "We can't."

"She's right," Sneddon said without looking up. "Yeah. She's right."

"I can set one of the fuel cells to overheat," Hoop said.

"And blow us all to hell," Lachance said. "No thanks, already been there, and now I'm keen to leave. One of those cells goes, it'll be like setting a nuke off in here."

"That's *exactly* what it'll be," Hoop said. "And Ripley's right. We can't just escape from here and go on our way. We have to make sure no one else finds this place."

"And they will!" Ripley said. "Have no doubt of that. Hoop?"

"Ash," Hoop said.

"Your mad android?" Lachance asked.

"He'll do his best to complete—"

"Thanks for bringing an insane AI to our ship, by the way," Lachance said.

"Ash docked the ship!" Ripley said. "I was still in hypersleep. I've been used in this more than all of you together. But he'll be logging whatever he can of this, recording details, constructing a full report for Weyland-Yutani. And damaged though your antenna array may be, he'll find a way to send it, or take it back to the Company."

"Unless I wipe him from the systems," Hoop said. "I already told you I can do that."

"And I firmly believe that you'll try," Ripley said. "But there was something different about Ash. Weyland-Yutani made him... devious. Capable of lying, of harming humans, of trying to kill me. So we can't take any chances at all." She held up her hands. "We blow the mine."

"It's simple enough," Hoop said. "Start the fuel cell, initiate charging, disconnect damping and coolant systems. It can be done."

"But there's no accurate way to judge how long it will take to blow," Lachance said.

"It doesn't have to be accurate," Ripley said. "As long as it gives us time to take off."

Hoop and Lachance looked at each other, and in their silence Ripley heard their agreement. They saw why it needed to be done, and they could do it.

"Suits me," Kasyanov said. "Quite happy to burn those fuckers, or bury them for all eternity."

"Don't forget there's still that one on the *Marion*," Sneddon said. She was still looking at her feet, and Ripley saw something in her that she'd never noticed before. A strange kind of calmness.

"We'll tackle that when the time comes," Hoop said.

"And only if we have to," Lachance said. "With luck, it'll just burn with the ship."

"Right," Hoop said.

They all stood in silence for a few moments. Then Hoop clapped his hands together, causing them all to jump.

"Let's get to it, then!"

"Thank you," Ripley muttered, so quietly that he probably didn't hear. But he smiled nonetheless.

You're all going to die, she thought, a silent message to those things raving down below. Maybe they were finding their way up through Level 7 now, coming for the people who had killed their queen, and all of their future queens, as well. But she was starting to feel better. Starting to feel *good*.

She hoped it wasn't the drugs.

19

CELLS

PROGRESS REPORT:

To: Weyland-Yutani Corporation, Science Division
(Ref: code 937)

Date (unspecified)

Transmission (pending)

Infiltration of Marion's computer successfully achieved.
All major systems now under complete control, sub-system
routines being accessed. It was more difficult than
projected... I have been away for some time, and systems
have advanced.

Limited contact achieved with LV178 surface control
systems. Elevator One remote controls were successfully
interrupted upon manual operation. Elevator descended to
Level Nine.

Some evidence of new activity on Level Four.

Things seem to be going to plan.

Anticipating return of survivors to Marion within
approximately seven hours.

Alien specimen surviving on Marion still not detected. It
is waiting somewhere.

I am hoping that they bring a viable egg back with them.

I am hoping it is time to go home.

* * *

Hoop was unsettled.

Their course of action was now clear—lift a spare fuel cell onto the trolley, set another one to fire up and overheat, get the hell back to the surface, the *Samson*, the *Marion*, then into Ripley's shuttle before the ship hit the atmosphere and came apart, all while watching out for the alien that had escaped into the interior of the *Marion*.

Simple.

But one thing troubled him, and it was close at hand.

Sneddon. She looked and acted fine, though there was something… quieter about her now, something calm. Unnaturally so. She had one of their infants in her chest. Ever since that facehugger had fallen from her and died, Hoop had been thinking, *It's okay, it's fine, we'll get her to the* Marion *and into the med-pod, get that thing taken out of her, lock it up somewhere and leave it to burn up with the ship.*

But it couldn't be that easy, and Ripley's comments were starting to hit home. She was injured, and the shots Kasyanov had given her might have gone to her head, just a little. The muttering, the swaying. But she knew exactly what she was talking about.

She always had.

If they took Sneddon back to the *Marion* with them, what would happen? What if Ash had somehow infiltrated the ship's systems? Hoop didn't think it likely—the *Marion* was a comparatively new ship, and its computing systems were a hundred times more complex than they'd been when Ripley had gone to sleep. But the chance was always there, and if Ash somehow found out about what Sneddon was carrying…

That was just what the AI wanted. He'd been searching for thirty-seven years, and there was no end to what he might do to protect the object of his quest.

Yet Hoop had no answers. He couldn't bring himself to leave Sneddon behind, however terrible the risk. And as they commenced working on the spare fuel cells, he watched Ripley, fearing what she had planned for the science officer.

She'd picked up Baxter's plasma torch, apparently not even

noticing the splash of his blood across its power housing.

"Ripley!" he said. She looked up. "Bring me that tool pouch, will you?" She came across to him, carrying a tool kit that had been hanging from a hook on the wall.

I'll just work, he thought. *Face those problems when the time comes. For now... just concentrate.*

The spare cells hadn't been stored in the best of conditions. There were three, each of them the size of a small adult. One wasn't even propped up off the floor, and a quick inspection revealed signs of decay to some of its metal framework and mountings. One of the other two was being loaded onto the trolley by Lachance and Kasyanov, and Hoop set to work on the last cell.

Sneddon stood off to one side, watching, ostensibly listening for any of those things that might be approaching. Hoop was pretty confident they had some time before the beasts could make their way up through the mine. Both staircases had blast doors at every level that were kept permanently shut, and they wouldn't know how to use the code keys on the control panels. But it gave Sneddon something to do.

He watched her. They all did, and she knew it. Yet she offered them back a gentle smile, as if she knew something they did not.

Hoop opened the cell's metallic shell and placed the cover to one side. He set to work disconnecting three cooling loops, then removed the coolant supplies altogether, for good measure. He delved deeper, past wires and conductors to the governing capacitors. These were adjustable, and he turned them all up to full.

A soft hum rose from the core. Barely the size of his fist, still its potential was staggering.

"We're almost good to go," he said after a while. More adjustments, several wires snipped, and then he disconnected and rerouted the last safety failsafe, meaning he could initiate the cell without having to input its own unique code.

"How long do you think it will give us?" Ripley asked.

"I'm thinking nine hours until it goes critical," he replied. "Plenty of time to get off this rock."

"If those things haven't made it out to the *Samson* and trashed it. Or if they're not just sitting inside, waiting for us to board. Or—"

"Fuck it," he said, cutting her off. "If they've done that, I'll come and sit beside this thing and wait for it to blow, rather than die of exposure or starvation."

"Let's hope then, eh?" Ripley asked.

"Let's hope. Hey, you okay?"

"Yeah. Flying high from the shots Kasyanov gave me, that's all."

Hoop nodded, then called over to where Lachance was fussing over the cell on the trolley.

"We good?" he said.

"Ready," the pilot replied. He looked down at the cell that lay next to Hoop, its cover removed and half of its mechanical guts hanging out. "You've done a real butcher's job on that."

"I'm an artist," Hoop said. "Everyone else good? Sneddon?"

"Let's get the hell out of here," she said.

"Right." Hoop breathed deeply and held two bare wires, ready to touch them together.

What if I'm wrong? What if the overload happens in minutes, not hours? What if…? But they had come too far, survived too much, to pay any more attention to what-ifs.

"Here goes nothing," he muttered, touching the two wires together.

A spark, a clunk, the sound of something whirring noisily inside the cell. Then a slew of lights flickered into life across its dismantled maintenance panel, some dying out, others remaining lit.

A red warning light began to pulse.

"Okay, it's working," he said. "In about nine hours, everything inside of a mile of here will become a cloud of radioactive dust."

"Then let's not hang around," Ripley said.

The elevator still worked. Kasyanov had removed the remains of Baxter's body. Even so, with the introduction of the fuel cell, things were cramped. They rose quickly to ground level and exited into the vestibule area, Lachance steering the trolley carrying the replacement fuel cell. They watched for movement, listened for the sound of running things.

Everything was suddenly going too smoothly, but Ripley tried not to question it.

Close to the tunnel entrance at the edge of the dome, they opened the metal storage container and donned their suits once more. They gauged oxygen supplies, then checked each other's fittings and connections. Ripley felt constrained having to wear the suit again.

The lights were still on in the tunnel that stretched between dome and landing pad. They moved quickly, passing the place where the floor was bubbled from an acid spill, and when they were close to the external pad Hoop called a halt.

"Nearly there," he said. "Let's not get hasty. We've got plenty of time, it's been less than an hour since I fired up the cell. Slow and careful from here."

Ripley knew he was right. The aliens had chased miners this far and further, so they certainly couldn't lower their guard just yet. But there was a small part of her, filled with dread, that whispered that they should never leave.

She ignored it.

She had to, because Amanda was still in her dreams, and haunting those occasional, shocking waking visions that seemed so real.

Her stomach hurt more and more, but she didn't want another shot of painkiller. Once they were on board the *Samson*, launched, flying safely up toward the *Marion* in low orbit, perhaps then. But for these last moments on this wretched planet's surface, she wanted all her wits about her.

Sneddon walked with them, carrying something that might kill them all. Didn't they realize that? Didn't they see what was happening here? Hoop had described to her the fate of their shuttle *Delilah*, and they knew it had been the hatching monsters that did that.

What if Sneddon's beast hatched on their way up?

Ripley's finger stroked the torch's trigger. One slight squeeze and Sneddon would be gone. A moment of shock, another instant of awful pain as the burning plasma melted through her flesh and bone and turned her heart and lungs to cinder…

"Wait," Ripley said. The word had a weight of finality to it, and when Hoop sighed and turned to look at her, she thought he knew.

Sneddon did not even turn around. She looked down at her feet, shoulders dropping.

"We can't…" Ripley said. She was crying now, finally unable to hold back the tears that fell for everyone—her old, dead crew; the survivors with her now; Amanda. Most of all, for Sneddon.

"What, Ripley?" Lachance asked. He sounded tired.

Ripley lifted the plasma torch and aimed it at Sneddon's back.

"We can't take her," she breathed.

No one moved. None of them stepped back, away from the area where the flames would spout. But none of them went to help, either. Maybe shock froze them all.

"You know what happened before," Ripley said. "Same thing might happen to the *Samson*, when we're partway there. If she hatches… if the thing bursts from her chest… how do we kill it on the shuttle? Can't use this." She lifted the plasma torch slightly, nozzle now aimed at the back of Sneddon's head. "Can't use the acid gun Hoop's carrying, either. We'd fry everyone, burn a hole in the dropship. We'd be an easy target for it. So…" She sniffed hard, blinking to clear her vision.

"So?" Hoop asked.

Ripley didn't answer. Sneddon still hadn't turned around.

"Move, say something, damn it!" Ripley shouted. "Fall down! Start to shake, to scream, try to stop me—*give me a reason*!"

"I feel fine," Sneddon said. "But Ripley… I know I'm going to die. I've known that since I woke, knowing what had happened to me. I'm a science officer, remember." She turned around. "I know I'm going to die. But not down here. Not like this."

Ripley's finger tightened on the trigger. Hoop only watched, his face seemingly impassive. She wished he'd give her some sort of signal—a nod, a shake of the head.

Help me, Hoop!

"I'll stay in the airlock," Sneddon said. "The moment I feel something happening, I'll blast myself out. But please, take me, and I'll do anything I can to help. There's still an alien on the *Marion*, remember? Maybe I can tackle it. Maybe it won't do anything to me if it knows what's inside me."

Ripley blinked and saw Amanda, arms wide, face distorted with agony as a monster burrowed out from her chest.

"Oh, no," she gasped. She lowered the plasma torch and went to her knees. Hoop came but she waved him away, punching out at his stomach. He hadn't helped her before, she didn't want him now. They watched her, and then they turned away when she stood again, wiping at her eyes.

"Okay. Come on," Hoop said. "Let's see if the storm's still blowing."

Ripley was last to leave the tunnel. And she was angry at herself. She hadn't held off from firing because of anything Sneddon had said about traveling in the airlock, or helping them on the *Marion*. She had relented simply because she couldn't kill another human being.

Maybe that made her good. But it also made her weak.

Outside, the storm had dissipated to a gentle breeze. Wafts of sand still drifted across the landscape, and there were small mounds piled against the *Samson*'s landing feet. In the distance, electrical storms played jagged across the horizon, so far away that the thunder never reached them. The system's star was a vague smudge against the dusty atmosphere in the west, bleeding oranges and yellows in a permanently spectacular sunset.

The *Samson* remained untouched on the landing pad. Hoop climbed up the superstructure, brushed dust from the windows and checked inside. He couldn't see anything amiss.

There was a moment of tension as they opened the external door and Hoop entered. Then he opened up the internal door and they boarded safely, taking great care when lifting the replacement fuel cell and securing it to the cabin rack. They relied on it completely, and any damage would doom them all.

Once they were all inside, Sneddon settled inside the small

airlock, just as she'd promised. There was a window into that space, but no one looked. Not even Ripley. She closed her eyes as Lachance went through pre-flight checks, and didn't open them again when they took off.

But she did not sleep. She thought perhaps she might never sleep again.

This is a real memory, Ripley thinks, but the division between real and imaginary is becoming more and more indistinct. If this is real, then why am I in pain? Why does she hurt from where an alien's tail slashed across her stomach, a claw opened her shoulder to the bone? If this is real, then everything will be all right.

She is on a roller coaster with Amanda. Her daughter is nine years old and utterly fearless, and as she whoops and laughs, Ripley holds onto the bar across their stomachs so hard that her fingers cramp into claws.

I love it, Mommy! *Amanda shouts, her words whipped away by the wind.*

Ripley closes her eyes but it changes little. She can still feel the vicious whipping of gravity grasping at her, tugging her this way and that as the car slips down a steep descent, around a tight corner, twisting and ripping back toward a cruel summit. With every twist and turn, the pain shoots through her.

Mommy, look!

There's an urgency to Amanda's voice that makes Ripley look. There's something wrong with their surroundings. Something so wrong, yet the roller coaster is traveling so fast now that she cannot seem to focus on anything outside the car.

People seem to be running across the park around them.

Screaming, dashing, falling…

Dark shapes chasing them, much faster than the people, like animals hunting prey…

Muh—Mommy? *Amanda says, and because she sits beside her in the moving car, Ripley can focus on her.*

She wishes she could not.

A bloom of blood erupts from her torn chest, a terrible inevitability.

Amanda is crying, not screeching in pain but shedding tears of such wretchedness that Ripley starts crying as well.

I'm sorry, Amanda, *she says.* I should have been home to protect you. *She's hoping that her daughter will say that she understands, and that everything is all right. But she says nothing of the sort.*

Yes, you should have, Mommy.

The infant alien bursts outward in a shower of blood that is ripped away by the wind.

As they reach the roller coaster's summit the car slows to a crawl, and Ripley can see what has happened to the world.

"You're crying," Hoop said. He was squeezing her hand, shaking it until she opened her eyes.

Ripley tried to blink the tears away. This had been the worst episode yet. And with increasing dread, she knew it wouldn't be the last.

"You in pain? Want another shot?"

Ripley looked across at where Kasyanov watched her expectantly. The doctor had bound her own hand and placed it in a sling. "No," she says. "No, I just want to stay awake."

"Your call."

"How long 'til we get to the *Marion*?"

"Lachance?" Hoop called. The ship was shaking, buffeted from all sides as it powered up through the unforgiving atmosphere.

"Two, maybe three hours," the pilot said. "Once we're in orbit we've got to travel a thousand miles to the *Marion*."

"Everything good?" Ripley looked at the fuel cell on the rack in front of them, shaking as the *Samson* vibrated.

"Yeah, everything's good."

"Sneddon?"

Hoop nodded. "Everything's good."

"For now," Ripley said. "Only for now. Nothing stays good for long. Not ever."

Hoop didn't reply to that, and across the cabin Kasyanov averted her eyes.

"I've got to go help Lachance," Hoop said. "You be okay?"

Ripley nodded. But they all knew that she was lying, and that she would not be okay.

Nothing stays good for long.

PART 3

NOTHING GOOD

20

HOME

This was the first step of Hoop's journey home. *All the way* home. He'd decided that down in the mine, and the more time that passed, the more he began to believe it. He had started thinking of his children again. This time, however, their faces and voices no longer inspired feelings of intense guilt, but a sense of hope. The fact that he'd left them behind could never be changed or forgotten—by them, or by him—but perhaps there were ways that damage could be fixed.

He had found his monsters, and now it was time to leave them behind.

"How long until the *Marion* enters the atmosphere?" he asked.

In the pilot's seat beside him, Lachance shrugged.

"Difficult to say, especially from here. We might have a couple of days once we dock, it might only be hours. If we approach the ship and it's already skimming the atmosphere, there's a good chance we won't be able to dock, anyway."

"Don't say that," Hoop said.

"Sorry. We've always known this was a long shot, haven't we?"

"Long shot, yeah. But we've got to believe." Hoop thought of those they had lost, Baxter's terrible death even though he had given the best he could, done everything possible to survive. To run through an alien-infested mine on a broken ankle, only to meet an awful end like that… it was so unfair.

But fairness had no place in the endless dark depths of the universe. Nature was indifferent, and space was inimical to man. Sometimes, Hoop thought they'd made a mistake crawling from the swamp.

"We're going to do this," Hoop said. "We've got to. Get away from this pit, get back home."

Lachance looked across in surprise.

"Never thought you had anything to go back to."

"Things change," he said. *Hopefully. Hopefully things can change.*

"We've left them all behind," Lachance said, relaxing into his seat. He scanned the instrument panel as they went, hands on steering stick, but Hoop heard such a sense of relief in his voice. "Who'd have thought we would? I didn't. Those things… they're almost unnatural. How can God allow something like that?"

"God?" Hoop scoffed. But then he saw something like hurt in Lachance's eyes. "Sorry. I'm no believer, but if that's your choice, then…" He shrugged.

"Whatever. But those things, I mean… how do they survive? Where's their home planet, how do they travel, what are they *for*?"

"What's anything for?" Hoop asked. "What are humans for? Everything's an accident."

"I can't believe that."

"And I can't believe otherwise. If your God made everything, then what was his purpose for them?"

The question hung between them, and neither could offer an answer.

"Doesn't matter," Hoop went on. "We survive, we get out of here, head for home."

"Five of us, now," Lachance said.

"Four," Hoop said softly. "Sneddon's with us now, but…"

"But," Lachance said. "Four of us on Ripley's shuttle. Two men, two women."

"We'll start a whole new human race," Hoop quipped.

"With respect, Hoop, I believe Ripley would eat you alive."

He laughed. It was the first time he'd laughed properly in a long while, perhaps even since before the disaster, more than seventy days before. It felt strange, and somehow wrong, as if to laugh was to forget all his friends and colleagues who had died. But Lachance was laughing, too, in that silent shoulder-shaking way of his.

Though it felt wrong, it also felt good. Another step toward survival.

Leaving the atmosphere brought a sense of peace. The rattling and shaking ended, and the shuttle's partial gravity gave them all a sense of lightness that helped lift their moods. Glancing back into the cabin, Hoop noticed Ripley looking in on Sneddon. He stood to go to her, but she turned and nodded, half-smiling. Whatever Sneddon's fate, it had yet to happen.

Her predicament was difficult to comprehend. She knew she was going to die. She had seen it happening to others, and as science officer she knew more than most what it entailed. Surely she'd want to ease her own suffering? Maybe she'd already spoken with Kasyanov. But if she hadn't, Hoop would make sure the doctor prepared something to send her quietly to sleep, when the time came.

He only hoped that Sneddon would see or feel the signs.

Something chimed softly on the control panel.

"*Marion*," Lachance said. "Six hundred miles away. We'll be there in fifteen minutes."

Something flashed on the panel, and a screen lit up with a series of code.

"What's that?"

"*Samson*'s computer communicating with *Marion*," Lachance said. "The nav computer will give us the best approach vector, given comparative speeds and orbits."

"Ash," Ripley said. She'd appeared behind Hoop, leaning on the back of his seat and resting one hand on his shoulder.

"Can you disconnect?" Hoop asked.

"Disconnect what?"

"The *Samson*'s computer from the *Marion*'s."

"Why would I want to do that?" Lachance looked at them both as if they'd suddenly grown extra heads.

"Because of Ash. It might be better for us if he doesn't know what we're doing. What Sneddon's carrying."

"And how the hell would he know that?"

"We have to assume he's infiltrated the *Marion*'s computer," Ripley said. "That would be his aim. Maybe he can't, but just in case he has..."

"No," Lachance said. "That's paranoia, and leaving us blind to fly in manually is just stupid."

"But you could do it?" Hoop asked.

"Of course," Lachance said. "Yes. Probably. Under normal conditions, but these are far from normal."

"That's right," Ripley said. "Far from normal. Ash, the AI, his orders were very particular. Crew expendable. My old crew, and now this one. Lachance, we just can't take the risk."

The pilot was silent for a while, turning things over in his mind. Then he accessed the shuttle's computer and started scrolling through commands. He pressed several buttons.

"It's done," he said.

"You're sure?" Hoop asked.

"It's done! Now shut up and let me fly."

Hoop glanced up and back at Ripley and she nodded.

"How's Sneddon?"

"Okay when I last looked."

Hoop unbuckled himself and headed back into the cabin. Kasyanov seemed to be dozing, but she opened her eyes as they passed, watching them without expression. At the airlock he looked through the small viewing window into the narrow space. Ripley came up next to him.

Sneddon sat with her back against the airlock's external door, eyes closed, her face pale and sheened with sweat. Hoop tapped on the door. Her eyes rolled beneath their eyelids, and her frown deepened. He knocked again.

She opened her eyes. She looked lost, fighting her way out of nightmares into real, waking horror. Then she saw Hoop and Ripley looking in at her and gave them a thumbs-up.

"It can't be long now," Ripley said as they turned away from the door.

"You think we should have supported you down there," he said. "Stepped back, let you burn her."

"Perhaps." She looked wretched, and he reached for her. At first he thought she would resist, pull back, throw a punch as she had down on the planet. But though she was initially tense, she soon relaxed into his embrace. There was nothing sensuous about it. It was about comfort and friendship, and the sharing of terrible things.

"When the time comes," he whispered into her ear. Her hair tickled his mouth.

"Heads up!" Lachance called. "*Marion*'s up ahead. Let's buckle in, get ready for approach. Hoop, could do with you up here to do all the crappy little jobs while I'm flying this thing."

Hoop gave Ripley one last squeeze then went back to the cockpit seat.

"One step closer to home," he said.

"Okay, I'm flying by sight here," Lachance said. "Proximity and attitude alerts are on, but I can't use auto-pilot this close without linking to the *Marion*."

"So what do you need from me?"

"See those screens there? Keep an eye on them. Once we're a mile out, if speed of approach goes into the red, shout. If *anything* goes red, scream your head off."

"You've done this before, right?"

"Sure. A hundred times." Lachance grinned at him. "On the simulator."

"Oh."

"First time for everything." He raised his voice. "Hold onto your panties, ladies, we're going in!"

Despite his brief display of gung-ho attitude, Hoop knew that Lachance was as careful and as serious as they came. He watched the screens as the Frenchman had instructed, but he also watched the pilot—his concentration, determination, and care.

The *Marion* appeared first as a shining speck ahead of them, visible just above the plane of the planet. It quickly grew, its features becoming more obvious and familiar, until they were close enough to see the damage to its docking-bay belly.

"Eyes on the screens," Lachance said.

The docking was smooth and textbook perfect. Lachance muttered to himself all the way through, going through procedures, whispering encouraging words to the dropship, and occasionally singing a line or two from songs Hoop mostly didn't know. The ships kissed with barely a jolt, and Lachance performed a frantic series of button-presses and screen swipes that secured them together.

"We're docked," he said, slumping in his chair. "Sneddon?"

Ripley unbuckled and jumped to the door.

"She's fine."

"And she's with us until the end, now," Kasyanov said. "I've been thinking about something I can put together to…" She trailed off, but Hoop nodded at her.

"I was going to ask."

"So what's the plan now?" Ripley asked.

Hoop blinked and took a deep breath.

"Now we get the cell to your shuttle," he said. "Everything else is secondary."

"What about the other alien?" Kasyanov asked.

"Let's just hope it's hiding somewhere."

"And if it isn't? Say it attacks us, we have to fight it off, and the cell is damaged."

"What do you suggest?" Ripley asked.

"Hunt it down," Kasyanov said. "Make sure it's dead and gone, and only then transfer the fuel cell."

"My shuttle is on the next docking arm," Ripley said. "A hundred yards, if that."

"So we recce the route now," Hoop said. "When we know it's clear, we lock all the doors leading back into the rest of the ship, transfer the cell. Then two of us guard the shuttle while the others gather food and supplies for the journey."

"Outstanding," Ripley said. "But what about Sneddon?"

They all looked to the airlock. Sneddon was watching them through the small window, that same sad smile on her face. Hoop opened the inner door and she entered slowly, looking around at them all.

"I felt it move," she said. "Not too long ago. So I think… maybe I should go first?"

Ripley held out her plasma torch, and Sneddon took it with a nod.

They slid on their suits' helmets again, all comm links open, and prepared to cross the vacuum of the vented air-lock and vestibule.

"I'll start bleeding the air now," Lachance said from the pilot's seat.

Hoop swallowed as his ears popped. The last of the air bled away. The *Samson*'s outer door opened, and Sneddon walked through back onto the *Marion*.

He didn't think he'd ever known anyone so brave.

21

PAIN

PROGRESS REPORT:

To: Weyland-Yutani Corporation, Science Division
(Ref: code 937)

Date (unspecified)

Transmission (pending)

Samson has docked with the Marion. Contact between ship
and dropship computers has been cut. This intimates to me
that Ripley is still on board.

I have no idea who else is on board or what has happened.

But I persist in hope.

All cctv and communication systems within Marion are
patched into central computer. I have eyes and ears
everywhere.

As soon as they dock I can assess the situation. Only
after that can I decide upon future actions.

I have located the loose alien on the Marion. I have full
remote access to blast doors… for now I have trapped the
alien in Hold #3. It remains there, still and quiet.

There, if I need it.

Sneddon stepped out into the vacuum of the docking vestibule
and approached the doors leading into the corridor beyond. They

would have to lock those doors and seal the hole again before pressurizing the corridor, and only then could they access the rest of the *Marion*, including *Narcissus*'s docking arm.

She disappeared through the door. The others waited nervously in the vestibule, Ripley swaying back and forth. Her stomach and shoulder wounds were hurting more and more, but she embraced the pain, using it to fuel her resolve. There would be time for medicine, and sleep, later.

Sneddon soon returned.

"All clear," she reported. "Doors are still closed and sealed." Her voice was fuzzy and crackly through the suit's communicator.

"Okay," Hoop said. "Change of plan. We'll bring the fuel cell through before we seal the door up again. Otherwise we'll be going back and forth by opening and closing the damaged door, and that's asking for trouble."

"But if the thing appears and—" Lachance said.

"It's a risk," Hoop said, acknowledging the danger. "*Everything's* a risk. But the more time we spend fucking around here, the worse things may become. There's an alien somewhere on board, the *Marion*'s going to crash, and Ripley's AI might be keen on giving us a very bad day."

"Ash isn't *my* AI," Ripley said. "He's Weyland's."

"Whatever. Let's get the cell out of the *Samson* and into the corridor. Then we can go about sealing that door."

"I'll stand guard," Sneddon said.

"You okay?" Ripley asked.

Sneddon only nodded, then turned and disappeared back through the door with her spray gun.

"Ripley, you go too," Hoop said. "Don't use that plasma torch unless you absolutely have to."

She nodded and followed Sneddon, wondering exactly what he'd meant. Use it on what? Or on whom? She heard Hoop talking to Lachance and Kasyanov about bringing the fuel cell through, and she was happy leaving them to it. It gave her a chance to talk.

The science officer was just outside the door, leaning against the wall. Ripley nodded to her, then walked a few steps in the opposite direction. There was no sign of anything having been here since they'd left. If the alien had broken back through to this area, it would have depressurized the entire ship.

It was further in, hiding. Perhaps they would never see it again.

"Your AI," Sneddon said. "It wants what I have?"

Ripley noticed that Sneddon had switched channels so that contact was only between their suits. She did the same before replying.

"Yes. He did his best back on *Nostromo* to get a sample, and now he's doing it again."

"You talk as if it's a person."

"He was," Ripley said. "He was Ash. None of us even knew he was an android. You know how they are, how advanced. He was… odd, I guess. Private. But there was never any cause to suspect his intentions. Not until he let an alien onto the ship."

"Is he watching us now?"

"I'm not sure." She didn't know how far Ash had gone, how far he could infiltrate. But if the aliens were her nightmares, he was her nemesis. "We have to assume so, yes."

"He won't want the rest of you," Sneddon said. "Only me, if he knows what I have inside me."

"Yes. He'll want to get you put into hypersleep as quickly as possible, then take you back to the Company. The rest of us are just liabilities."

"And then?"

Ripley wasn't sure how to answer, because she didn't know. Weyland-Yutani had already shown themselves as being brutal and single-minded in their pursuit of any useful alien artefacts or species.

"And then they'll have what they want," she said finally.

"I'm not going," Sneddon said.

"I know." Ripley couldn't look at her.

"It's… strange, knowing I'm going to die. I'm only afraid of how it'll happen, not death itself."

"I won't let it happen like that," Ripley said. "Kasyanov will give you something, as soon as the time comes. To ease your way."

"Yeah," Sneddon said, but she sounded doubtful. "I'm not sure things are going to be quite that easy."

Ripley wasn't sure either, and she couldn't lie. So she simply said nothing.

"It's only pain," Sneddon said. "When it happens, it'll hurt, but it doesn't matter. A brief moment of pain and horror, and then nothing forever. So it doesn't really matter."

"I'm so sorry," Ripley whispered, blinking away tears. They came far too easily, now that she'd let them in.

At first Sneddon didn't reply. But Ripley heard her breathing, long and slow, as if relishing every last taste of compressed, contained air. Then the science officer spoke again.

"Strange. I can't help still being fascinated by them. They're almost beautiful."

They stood silently for a while, and Hoop emerged from the doorway that led to the docking arm. He tapped at his ear, and Ripley switched her communicator back to all-channels.

"What's going on?" he asked.

"Sneddon and I were talking." He just nodded.

"We've got the cell. Ripley, you go along to the door to Bay Four." He pointed, then turned. "Sneddon, back there to the corridor blast doors to the other docking bays. I'm going to seal this door, then we'll repressurize."

"How?" Ripley asked.

"Honestly? I haven't figured that yet. If we just open the blast doors, the pressurization will be explosive, and we'll be smashed around. Got to let air bleed in somehow."

"Don't suppose you have another drill?"

Hoop shook his head, then looked down at the spray gun that was hanging from his shoulder. He smiled.

Kasyanov and Lachance appeared with the fuel cell. They wheeled it through the doorway, then set the trolley against the far wall.

"Strap that against the wall, tight," Hoop said. Then he closed the doors and pulled a small square of thick metal out of a pocket, pressing it against the hole he'd drilled on their exit from the *Marion*.

He removed his hand and the metal remained where it was.

"Bonding agent," he said when he saw Ripley watching. "Air pressure will press it tight. It'll give us enough time."

Ripley walked along the corridor until it curved toward Bay Four. She paused where she could see the door, beyond which lay the docking arm with her shuttle, waiting for them all. Walking made her wounds hurt, but standing still was barely a relief. *It's only pain*, Sneddon had said. *It doesn't matter*. She felt warm dampness dripping down her side from her shoulder. She'd opened the wound there again.

It's only pain.

She could see back along the curving corridor, and she watched Lachance and Kasyanov securing the trolley and fuel cell to the wall with cargo straps from the *Samson*. She did the same, tying herself tight with her belt against a heavy fixing point.

"All ready?" Hoop asked. He disappeared in the other direction, following Sneddon toward where the corridor merged with the one from the ruined docking arm.

"What's the plan?" Kasyanov asked.

"Squirt of acid through the door," Hoop said. "Hardly subtle, but it should work. It'll get a bit stormy in here, though. Hold on to your dicks."

"We don't all have dicks, dickhead," Kasyanov muttered.

"Well, hold onto something, then." He paused. "On three."

Ripley counted quietly. One… two…

Three…

There was a pause. Then Hoop said, "Oh, maybe it won't—" A whistle, and then a roar as air started flooding into the sealed area.

That'll wake Ash up, Ripley thought. She couldn't help thinking of the bastard as still human.

PROGRESS REPORT:

To: Weyland-Yutani Corporation, Science Division
(Ref: code 937)

Date (unspecified)

Transmission (pending)

The survivors include Warrant Officer Ripley. I am pleased
that she is still alive. She and I feel close. From what
I can see from the *Marion*'s cctv cameras, she seems to
be wounded. But she's walking. She impresses me. To have
woken from such a long sleep, to face the truth of her
extended slumber, and then to address her situation so
efficiently. She could almost be an android.

I am going to kill her, along with Chief Engineer Hooper,
Doctor Kasyanov, and the pilot.

Science Officer Sneddon is carrying an alien embryo.
Frustratingly I can glean no details, but from the
few conversations I have monitored, it seems as if her
condition is obvious. As is her expressed intention to end
her own life.

I cannot allow this.

Once she is on board the *Narcissus* and the new fuel cell
is installed, I will take the steps necessary to complete
my mission.

The roar died down to a low whistling, and then that too faded
to nothing. Ripley's ears rang. She looked back along the corridor
and saw Hoop appearing from around the curve, suit helmet
already removed.

"We're good," he said.

"You call that good?" Lachance asked. "I think I soiled my spacesuit."

"Wouldn't be the first time," Kasyanov said.

"Sneddon?" Ripley asked.

"I'm here." Her voice sounded weak. *She doesn't have long*, Ripley
thought. She pulled her own helmet off and let it dangle from its
straps, hoping she wouldn't need it again.

Hoop and the others pushed the fuel cell on its trolley, and when
they reached the door that led into Bay Four's vestibule, they paused.

"Lachance, go back and stay with Sneddon," Hoop said. "And
Kasyanov... you said you might have something?"

Kasyanov took a small syringe from her belt pouch.

"It's the best I can do," she said.

"What does that mean?" Ripley asked.

"It means it won't be painless. Get me to *med bay* and I'll find
something better, but with the limited stuff I have on hand, this is it."

Hoop nodded, face grim.

"Let's get ready to fly."

Hoop opened the doorway, and Ripley and Kasyanov pushed the trolley through.

The movement was sudden, unexpected, the hissing thing leaping at them from where it had been crouched beside the door. Kasyanov cried out and stumbled back, but Ripley quickly gathered her senses, crouching down and opening her arms.

"Jonesy!" she said. "Hey, it's me, it's all right you stupid cat." Jonesy crouched before her for a moment, hissing again. Then he slinked around her legs and allowed her to pick him up.

"Holy shit," Kasyanov said. "Holy shit, holy shit…"

"He does that," Ripley said, shrugging.

"We'll be taking him with us?" Kasyanov asked.

Ripley hadn't even thought about that. On a shuttle built for one, four was bad enough. They still had to prepare for the extraordinary length of their journey—coolant for the shuttle's atmosphere processor, filters for the water purifier, food, other supplies. But with a cat as well? With them taking turns in the stasis pod, Jonesy might not even live long enough to survive the journey.

But she couldn't even contemplate the thought of leaving him behind.

"Let's cross that one when we come to it," Hoop said. "Come on. I've got work to do."

It felt strange to Ripley, entering the *Narcissus* one more time. The urgency was still there, but this time with a different group of people. The danger was still imminent, but now it was compounded—a crashing ship, an alien somewhere on board, as well as one of them just waiting to give birth to another beast.

Jonesy jumped from her arms and leapt delicately into the stasis pod, snuggling down in the covered lower section, out of sight. Ripley so wanted to do the same.

"Kasyanov," she said. She felt suddenly woozy again, as if the ship was shaking and changing direction. *Maybe this is it*, she thought, *maybe we're crashing and…*

Hoop caught her as she stumbled. Kasyanov stripped the suit top from her shoulder and blood flowed freely, darkening the suit and dripping on the floor.

"Staples have popped," Kasyanov said. "I'll re-do them. This first." Before Ripley could object, the doctor slid a small needle into her shoulder and squeezed the pouch on its end. Numbness spread. The pain receded. Her right hand tingled, then all feeling faded away.

She'd never be able to hold the plasma torch now.

Hoop moved back through the shuttle to the small hatch leading into the engine compartment. He half-crawled inside, looked around for a while, and emerged again.

"I'm going to be in here for a while," he said. He paused, frowning, thinking. "Okay. We can stay in touch using the suit helmets. Ripley, stay here with me. Kasyanov, you and the others need to get into the *Marion* and start gathering what we'll need."

"I'll go with them," Ripley said.

"No, you're hurt."

"I can still walk, and carry supplies," she said. "We'll shut the *Narcissus*'s outer door behind us, so you won't have to worry about anything coming inside and disturbing you. Stay here, work. Fix it well." She smiled.

"It'll work," Hoop said. "But don't take risks. Any of you. Not with that thing running around, and not with… you know."

"Not with Sneddon," Kasyanov said.

"We should do it now," Ripley said. "She can't have long left."

"Well…" Hoop stood and emptied out the tool pouch he'd brought with him. "While I'm here buying our ticket home, that's your call."

It was harsh, but Ripley knew it was also true.

"Don't be long," Hoop said. "And stay safe."

"Safe is my middle name," Ripley said. She laughed, coughed painfully, and then turned to leave. Kasyanov went behind her, closing and sealing the door. Ripley couldn't help thinking she'd never see the inside of the *Narcissus* again.

"Med bay, then the stores," Kasyanov said. "Maybe an hour. Then we'll be away."

"Yeah," Ripley said. "And even after thirty-seven years asleep, I'm tired."

22

CHESS

PROGRESS REPORT:

To: Weyland-Yutani Corporation, Science Division
(Ref: code 937)

Date (unspecified)

Transmission (pending)

Chief Engineer Hooper is in the Narcissus. I could lock
him in if I so desired. I could hurt him. But he is busy.
I will leave him alone for now.

As for the others... I have decided to take a risk, a
gamble. I am somewhat powerless, having no physical form.
I am playing a game of chess. I've always been good at it,
and have never lost a game, against a human or a computer.
AIs are the Grand Masters now.

Here is my gamble: I suspect that Science Officer Sneddon
will be safe in the presence of the alien. It will sense
what she carries inside. She will survive the attack, the
others will die, and she will then make her way quickly
back to the Narcissus.

Whatever her thoughts, she is human, and her instinct is
still to survive.

None of the others can survive. They know too much about
me, about Science Officer Sneddon.

I am so close.

It is my move.

* * *

Ripley made sure she was behind Sneddon. She'd swapped the plasma torch to her left shoulder now, and thought she could probably still lift and fire it one-handed if she had to. Her right arm was numb from her shoulder down. It flopped uselessly, as if she'd been sleeping on it and had just woken up, and she soon stopped to tuck it into her open suit jacket.

She wasn't afraid of what Sneddon would become—she would hear it happening, see it—but she wanted to be ready to put the science officer out of her misery.

Lachance led the way with his charge thumper held at the ready. Kasyanov followed him, plasma torch slung from her shoulder, her wounded hand also hanging in a sling. They'd insisted that Sneddon keep her spray gun, even though she had volunteered to give it up.

If they'd had time, their list of items to gather would have been long. Food, clothing, coolant and additives for environmental systems, bedding of some sort, medicines, washing and bathroom supplies. Something to help pass the time—games, books, distractions.

But with very little time and danger around every corner, their list was reduced to necessities.

"Coolant and additives we can get from the stores in Hold 2," Lachance said.

"Galley for the dried food," Kasyanov offered.

"And then straight back," Ripley said. There was no time to go to med bay for medicines, the rec room for books, or the accommodations hub for sleeping gear and personal effects. They all felt the pressure now.

They'd paused to look through several viewing windows as they worked their way up out of the docking bay area on the *Marion*'s belly, and the planet already looked frighteningly closer. Soon the vibration would begin as they started to skim the atmosphere. The hull would warm up, heat shielding would bend and crack, and if they didn't die from excessive heat build-up, the explosion as the *Marion* came apart would finish them.

Ripley had never noticed the cctv cameras before, but she saw them now. Probably because she was looking for them. Every one of them resembled an eye watching her pass. They didn't move to track her, but reflections in the lenses gave the impression of pupils panning to follow her movement. There was an intelligence behind them all, one she knew so well. *Fuck you, Ash*, she kept thinking. But while cursing him, she also tried to figure out what moves he might make.

They reached the wide open area with a row of viewing windows on either side and an elevator shaft in the center. Several closed doors lined the walls, and leading from the far end was the wide stairwell heading up into the *Marion*'s main superstructure.

"Elevator?" Ripley asked.

"I've had enough of elevators," Kasyanov said. "What if we get stuck?"

That's right, Ripley thought. *Ash could trap us in there.*

"You should keep everything basic now," Sneddon said, referring to them in the second person without seeming to notice. "Don't want any mechanical issues to hold you up. There's not enough time. It's too…" She winced, closed her eyes, put her hand to her chest.

"Sneddon," Ripley whispered. She stood back and aimed the plasma torch, but the woman raised her hand and shook her head.

"Not yet," she said. "I don't think… not yet."

"Sweet heaven," Lachance said. He'd moved across to the port row of windows, and was looking down on the planet's surface. "Pardon my French, but you want to see something completely fucking heartwarming?"

He was right. It was strangely beautiful. North of them, a hole had been blasted through the plumes of dust and sand that constantly scoured the planet's surface. A huge, blooming mushroom cloud had punched up through the hole, massive and—from this great distance—seemingly unmoving. Compression waves spread out from the explosion like ripples in a lake, moving as slowly as the hour hand of an old analog clock. Streaks of oranges, reds, and yellows smudged across half the planet's surface visible from the ship, and violent electrical storms raged beneath the clouds, sending spears of violet deep through the dust storms.

"Well, that's me, unemployed," Lachance said.

"Now there's only one of those bastards left," Ripley said.

"Two," Sneddon said from behind them. She'd grown paler, and she seemed to be in pain. "I think... I think now might be the time to..."

She rested her spray gun gently on the deck.

Behind her, something ran down the stairs.

"Oh, shit..." Ripley breathed. She swung her plasma torch up into its firing position, but Sneddon was in the way, and though she'd dwelled endlessly upon putting the woman out of her misery, she wasn't ready for it now.

The alien dashed from the staircase to dart behind the elevator shaft that stood in the center of the area. Ripley waited for it to appear on the other side. And then, a blink later, it would be upon them.

"Sneddon, down!" Ripley shouted.

The science officer moved, and everything she did was very calm, very calculating—it almost seemed like slow motion. She lifted the spray gun again and turned around.

Lachance moved to the left and circled around the large space, edging forward so he could see behind the elevator block. Kasyanov remained close to Ripley on her right. Everything was silent—no hissing, no clatter of claws on the metal deck.

It's as if we imagined it, Ripley thought.

Then the alien powered from behind the block. Sneddon crouched and fired the spray gun, acid scoring a scorched line across the wall behind the creature. Lachance's charge thumper coughed. The projectile ricocheted from the elevator, throwing sparks, and knocked Kasyanov from her feet.

The beast was on Lachance before anyone had time to react. It grabbed him by the shoulders and shoved him back, its momentum slamming him so hard into a wall that Ripley heard bones crunch and crush. Blood coughed from his mouth. The alien slammed its head into his, teeth powering through his throat and severing his spine with a *crack!*

Ripley swung the plasma torch around.

"Turn away!" she shouted. Her finger squeezed the trigger.

Nothing happened.

She glanced down at the weapon, stunned, wondering just what she'd done wrong. *I primed it, safety off. Maybe the charge is run down, so what the hell?* In the instant it took her to think, the alien came for her.

From behind she heard Kasyanov groaning and trying to stand, and Ripley expected the white-hot touch of plasma fire at any moment from the Russian's gun. She'd be saving Ripley from an awful death, destroying the alien, giving her and Hoop a chance. Right then, Ripley would have welcomed it.

The alien was closer, larger, just about the most terrifying thing she'd ever seen, and she thought, *I'm so sorry, Amanda.* She'd made a promise, and had broken it.

She went to close her eyes, but before she could she saw a line of fire erupt across the alien's flank. It slipped, hissing and skidding across the floor toward her.

Ripley dropped all her weight in an effort to fall to the left, but she was too late. The alien struck her hard. Claws raked, teeth snapped an inch from her face. She screamed. The monster hissed and then shrieked, and Ripley smelled rank burning.

The thing thrashed on top of her, and everywhere it touched brought more pain.

Then it was up and gone. Ripley lay on her side, head resting on her extended left arm. Blood spattered the floor around her— red, human. *Mine*, she thought. Her body felt cool and distant, then suddenly hot and damaged, ruptured, leaking. She opened her mouth, but could only groan.

Kasyanov sent another spurt of fire after the alien before slumping to the deck, plasma torch clattering down beside her. Ripley wasn't sure the shot made contact, but the beast screamed and rushed back toward the wide staircase.

Sneddon followed, firing the spray gun as she went, one short burst catching the alien across the back of one of its legs. It stumbled into the wall, then leapt toward the staircase. Sneddon ran closer, fired again, and missed, scoring a melting line diagonally across the first few stairs.

"Sneddon!" Kasyanov rasped, but the science officer didn't look back. The beast fled, and she followed, shooting all the way.

"Get what you need!" Sneddon shouted through their earpieces. She sounded more alive than Ripley had heard before. There was an edge of pain to her voice, an undercurrent of desperation. But there was also something like joy. She was panting hard as she ran, grunting, and from somewhere more distant Ripley heard the alien screech one more time. "Got you, you bastard!" Sneddon said. "I got you again that time. Keep running, just keep running. But I'll chase you down."

Ripley wanted to say something to her. But when she opened her mouth, only blood came out. *I wonder how bad?* she thought. She tried turning to look at Kasyanov, but couldn't move.

"Kasyanov," she breathed. There was no reply. "Kasyanov?"

Shadows fell.

She only hoped Amanda would be waiting for her, ready to forgive at last.

Hoop heard it all.

It only took thirty seconds, and by the time he'd dropped his tools, wriggled out of the shuttle's cramped engine compartment and then exited the ship—carefully closing the door behind him— Sneddon's shouting had stopped. He heard more, though—pained sighs, grunts, and an occasional sound like a frustrated hiss. But he couldn't tell who they came from.

"Ripley?" He crossed the vestibule, peering through viewing panels in the door before opening it. He closed it behind him and headed along the corridor. He held the spray gun pointed ahead, ready to fire at a moment's notice. He had no idea which way Sneddon and the alien had gone.

"Lachance?"

"He's dead," a voice said. It took him a moment to identify it as Kasyanov. She sounded different, weak. "And Ripley is…"

"What?"

"Bad. So much blood."

"What about Sneddon?" Hoop asked again. "Sneddon? You hear me?" There was a click as someone disconnected their comm unit. It had the sound of finality.

"Hoop, I'm hurt, too." Kasyanov might have been crying.

"How bad?"

"Not good." A grunt, and a gasp. "But I can walk."

"Which way did Sneddon chase that thing?"

"Up the staircase."

"Away from us and into the belly of the ship," he replied. "Right. I'll be there in two minutes, do what you can for Ripley, and I'll carry her to med bay."

More silence.

"Do you hear me?"

"What about the fuel cell?" Kasyanov asked.

"It's almost done."

"Then we could be gone."

He couldn't blame her. Not really. But Hoop wasn't about to bail without doing everything he could, for anyone who was left alive.

"Fuck that, Kasyanov," he said. "You're a doctor. Heal."

Then he started running. He sprinted around corners without pausing to look or listen. Opened doors, closed them behind him, the spray gun slung across his shoulder and acid swooshing in the reservoir. He thought of Sneddon's bravery, and how she had already sacrificed herself by pursuing the monster into the ship. Maybe she'd catch and kill it. Or perhaps it would turn and kill her. But she had given them a chance.

The *Marion* shook.

A subtle vibration, but he felt it through his boots.

Oh, not now, he thought. He skidded around a corner, up some stairs, and then he was in the wide area where the chaos had only just ended. Lachance lay dead against the wall to his left, head hanging from his body by strands. Ripley was on the floor to his right. Kasyanov knelt beside her, melted hand pressed tight to her right hip, the other busy administering emergency first aid. Beyond them, the windows looked down onto the planet. To the north Hoop saw the bright bruise of the explosion that had taken the mine, and felt a brief moment of glee. But it didn't last long. Shimmering threads of smoke and fire flitted past the window as the *Marion* encountered the very upper reaches of LV178's atmosphere.

"We don't have long," Kasyanov said, looking up at his approach. Hoop wasn't sure whether she meant the *Marion* or Ripley, but in his mind they were the same.

"How bad are you?"

"Bolt from Lachance's thumper broke up, ricocheted, hit me." She moved her ruined hand aside slightly, looking down. Hoop could see the shredded jacket and undershirt, the dark bloodstains glinting wetly in artificial light. She pressed the wound again and looked up. "Honestly, I can't feel anything. Which isn't a good sign."

"It's numb. You can walk?"

Kasyanov nodded.

"You go ahead, open the doors, I'll carry her," Hoop said.

"Hoop—"

"I'm not listening. If there's a chance for her, we'll take it. And you can sort yourself out while we're there."

"But that thing could be—" Their earpieces crackled, and Sneddon's voice came in loud and fast.

"I've got the bastard cornered in Hold 2!" she shouted. "Shot it up, its acid splashed everywhere... not sure if... oh, fuuuuck!" She moaned, long and loud.

"Sneddon," Hoop said.

"It hurts. It hurts! It's in me, moving around, and I can feel its teeth." Another groan, then she coughed loudly and shouted, "*Screw you*! Hoop, it's cornered behind some of the equipment lockers, thrashing around in there. Might be dying. But... I'm going to... make sure!"

Hoop and Kasyanov stared at each other. Neither knew what to say. They were witnessing a fight far away from them, and listening to the impending death of a friend.

Metal clanged, the sound of something falling over and hitting the deck.

"Come on, come on," Sneddon whispered. "Okay, I'm almost done." She was talking to herself, muttering between croaks of pain and high-pitched whines that should not have come from a person.

"What are you doing?" Hoop asked.

"Got a full crate of magazines for the charge thumpers. Rigging a charge. You'll feel a bump, but it'll get rid of this… for good. So…"

Hoop ran to Ripley, scooped her up, slung her over his shoulder. She moaned in unconsciousness, and he could feel her blood pattering down on his back and legs.

"Med bay," he said to Kasyanov. "Need to get as close as we can before it blows."

"Maybe a minute," Sneddon said. "The one inside me… it wants out. It's shifting. It's…" She screamed. It was a horrible sound, volume tempered by the equipment yet the agony bare and clear.

"Sneddon…" Kasyanov whispered, but there was nothing more to say.

"Come on!" Hoop led the way, struggling with Ripley's weight. Kasyanov followed. He heard her groaning, cursing beneath her breath, but when he glanced back she was still with him. She had to be. He didn't know how to use the med bay equipment, and if Kasyanov died, so would Ripley.

"You going to be——?" he started asking, but then Sneddon came on again.

"It's coming for me." Behind her voice Hoop heard an alien squeal, and the scraping of claws on metal growing rapidly louder. Sneddon gasped, then fell silent. The channel was still open; Hoop could hear the hiss and whisper of static. He and Kasyanov paused at the head of a staircase. And then he heard the more uneven hissing of something else.

"Sneddon?"

"It's… just staring. It must see… know… sense… Oh!"

"Blow the crate," Hoop said. Kasyanov's eyes went wide, but he wasn't being cruel or heartless. He was thinking of Sneddon, as well as them. "Sneddon, blow the crate before——"

The crunch of breaking bones was obvious. Sneddon let out a long groan of agony.

"It's coming," she rasped. "The thing's just watching. It's dying, but it doesn't care. It sees… its sibling… coming. This close it's almost beautiful."

"Sneddon, blow the——"

"Two seconds," the science officer whispered.

In those two seconds Hoop heard the infant alien clawing, biting, tearing its way from Sneddon's chest, its high-pitched squeal answered by the dying adult's more tempered cry. Sneddon could not scream because her breath had been stolen. But she spoke in another way.

He heard the soft mechanical click. Then the connection was cut.

Moments later a distant rumble turned from a moan into a roaring explosion that blasted a wall of air through the corridors. A heavy thud worked through the entire ship, pulsing through floors and walls as Hold 2 was consumed by the massive blast.

A long, low horn-like sound echoed as incredible stresses and strains were placed on the superstructure, and Hoop feared they would simply tear apart. The tension of skimming the planet's atmosphere, combined with the results of the explosion, might break the ship's back and send it spinning down, to burn up in the atmosphere.

He slid down one wall and held Ripley across his legs, hugging her head to his chest to prevent it bouncing as the metal floor punched up at them again and again. Kasyanov crouched next to them.

Metal tore somewhere far away. Something else exploded, and a shower of debris whisked past them, stinging exposed skin and clanging metal on metal. Another gush of warm air came, and then the shaking began to subside.

"Will she hold?" Kasyanov asked. "Will the ship hold?" Hoop couldn't answer. They stared at each other for a few seconds, then Kasyanov slumped down. "Sneddon."

"She took it with her," Hoop said. "Took both of them with her."

Kasyanov glanced at Ripley, then crawled quickly closer. She lifted an eyelid, bent down to press her ear to the injured woman's open mouth.

"No," Hoop breathed.

"No," Kasyanov said. "But she's not good."

"Then let's go." He dropped the spray gun, heaved her over his shoulder again, and set off toward med bay. Kasyanov followed, her plasma torch clattering to the floor.

Now they were three, and he wouldn't let anyone else die.

Amanda watches her. She's eleven years old today, and she sits in a chair beside a table scattered with half-eaten pieces of birthday cake, opened presents, discarded wrapping paper. She's on her own and looking sad.

Her birthday dress is bloodied and torn, and there is a massive hole in her chest.

I'm sorry, *Ripley says, but Amanda's expression does not change. She blinks softly, staring at her mother with a mixture of sadness at the betrayal and… hatred? Can that really be what she sees in her daughter's eyes?*

Amanda, I'm sorry, I did my very best.

Blood still drips from the hole in her daughter's chest. Ripley tries to turn away, but whichever way she turns her daughter is still there, staring at her. Saying nothing. Only looking.

Amanda, you know Mommy loves you, however far away I am.

The little girl's face does not change. Her eyes are alive, but her expression is lifeless.

Ripley woke for a time, watching the floor pass by, seeing Hoop's boots, knowing she was being carried. But even back on the *Marion*, Amanda was still staring at her. If Ripley lifted her head she would see her. If she turned around, she would be there.

Even when she closed her eyes.

Amanda, staring forever at the mother who had left her behind.

23

FORGETTING

PROGRESS REPORT:

To: Weyland-Yutani Corporation, Science Division
(Ref: code 937)

Date (unspecified)

Transmission (pending)

I wish I was whole again.

I never used to wish. I was not programed for that, and it is not an emotion, nor an action, that I ever perceived as useful. But for thirty-seven years I was alone in the shuttle's computer. And there was enough of the human still in me to feel lonely. I was built as an artificial person, after all.

Loneliness, it seems, is not necessarily connected to one's place in the universe. I know my place, and have no feelings either way about what and where I am. In my case, loneliness rose from simple boredom.

There are only so many times I can defeat the ship's computer at chess.

And so I have spent long years dwelling upon what wishing might mean.

Now, I wish I was whole again.

The game has turned against me. I am in check. But not for long. The game is never over until it is over, and I refuse to resign.

Not while Ripley, my queen, still lives.

* * *

Ripley was heavy. He refused to think of her as dead weight—he wouldn't allow that, would not give her permission to die—but by the time they reached med bay his legs were failing, and it had been ten long minutes since she'd displayed any signs of life.

The *Marion* shook and shuddered. It, too, was close to the end.

The difference was that for Ripley there was still hope.

"I'll fire up the med pod," Kasyanov said, pressing her good hand against the security pad. The medical bay was a modern, sterile place, but the object at its center made all the other equipment look like Stone Age tools. This Weyland-Yutani chunk of technology had cost Kelland almost a tenth of what the whole of the *Marion* had cost, but Hoop had always known it had been a practical investment. A mining outpost so far from home, where illness or injury could cripple the workforce, needed care.

Yet there was nothing humane in their incorporation of the pod.

It was insurance.

Hoop put Ripley down on one of the nearby beds and tried to assess her wounds. There was so much blood. Her shoulder wound weeped, several staples protruded from her stomach and the gash there gaped. New injuries had been added to the old. Puncture wounds were evident across her chest, perhaps where the thing's claws had sunk in. Her face was bruised and swollen, one eye puffy and squeezed shut, scalp still weeping. He thought her arm might be broken.

He had seen the med pod at work several times before, but he didn't know what it could do for Ripley. Not in the time they had left.

He was pulled in two directions. In truth, he should be back at the shuttle, finishing the fuel cell installation and ensuring that all systems were back online. After that there was Ash, the malignant presence he had to wipe from the *Narcissus*'s computer before launching.

If Ripley were awake, he could tell her what he'd found. According to the log, the old fuel cell had still maintained more than sixty percent of its charge when it had docked with *Marion*, and it could only have been Ash who had engineered its draining. To trap her there with them. To force them down to the planet's surface, not only to retrieve another fuel cell, but to encounter *them*.

The creatures.

Everything that had happened since Ripley's arrival had been engineered by the artificial intelligence. Those additional lives lost—Sneddon, Baxter, Lachance—could be blamed squarely on him.

Hoop wished the bastard was human so he could kill him.

"Pod's ready," Kasyanov said. "It'll take half an hour for it to assess the wounds and undertake the procedures."

Hoop couldn't waste half an hour.

"I'll go back for the supplies we need," he said. "Stay in touch."

Kasyanov nodded and touched her suit's comm unit. Then she turned her attention to the med pod's screen and frowned in concentration, scrolling through a complex series of branching programs flashing there. She was sweating, shaking.

"You good?"

"No. But I'm good enough for this." She wiped her forehead with the back of her hand. "Her first, then if there's time, me."

"There'll be time," Hoop said, but they both knew there were no guarantees.

"I feel… weird inside. Bleeding in my guts, I think."

"I'll get up to the bridge, first," Hoop said, gingerly lifting Ripley off of the bed. "See just how much time we have."

As if in response, the ship shuddered one more time. Kasyanov didn't look up or say anything else, and her silence was accusation enough. *We could have just gone.* But they were set on their course, now, and Hoop knew she would see it through.

He held Ripley as gently as he could, and carried her to the med pod.

"Amanda!" she shouted. She shifted in his arms and he almost dropped her. He staggered a little, then when he righted himself and looked down, Ripley was staring right at him. "Amanda," she said again, softer.

"It's okay, Ripley, it's me."

"She won't leave me alone," she said. Her eyes were wide and white in her mask of blood and bruising. "Just staring. All because of them. My little girl won't forgive me, and it's all because of *them*." Her voice was cold and hollow, and a chill went through him. He laid her gently in the med pod.

"We're going to patch you up," Hoop said.

"I want to forget," she said. "I can't… even if you fix me, I can't sleep with Amanda staring at me like that. I'll never sleep again. It'll make me go mad, Hoop. You can make me forget, can't you? With this?"

Hoop wasn't sure exactly what she meant, and how much she wanted to forget. But she was all there. This wasn't a delirious rant—it was a very calm, very determined plea.

"It feels as if I've known nothing else but them," she said. "It's time to forget."

"Kasyanov?" Hoop asked.

"It's a med pod, Hoop," the doctor said. "That's almost certainly beyond its capabilities."

"But it does neurological repairs, doesn't it?"

"Yeah. Repairs, not damage."

"They've given me a nightmare, and I think it's going to kill me," Ripley said. "Amanda. My girl, dead, staring, never forgiving me. Please, Hoop. *Please!*" She sat upright, wincing at the pain it drove through her, but reaching out and grasping his arm.

"Hey, hey, lie back," he said. "Let Kasyanov do her work." But he could see the terror in her eyes, and the knowledge at what sleep would bring. *Even if it's not real, it's tearing her apart*, he thought.

"We're ready," the doctor said.

Ripley let Hoop ease her back down, but she was still pleading with her eyes. Then they closed the clear lid. He felt a tug as he saw her shut away in there, maybe because he thought he might never touch her again.

"So can you?" he asked.

"It's not me that does the work, it's the pod. I just initiate the programs." Kasyanov sighed. "But yes, I think it could manipulate her memories."

"How?"

"I've only ever heard about it," Kasyanov said. "It can repair brain damage, to an extent, and at the same time there's an associated protocol that allows for memory alteration. I think it was designed primarily for military use. Get soldiers back into the fight that much quicker, after battlefield trauma." She paused. "It's really pretty inhumane, when you think about it."

Hoop thought about it, remembering the sheer terror he had seen in Ripley's eyes.

"I don't think I have any choice," he said. "How much memory will it affect?"

"I have no idea. I don't think it was developed for fine tuning."

He nodded, tapping his leg.

"Do it."

"You're sure?"

If we go too far back, she won't even remember me. But that was a selfish thought, far more about him than it was about her. If he had a shred of feeling for her, his own desires shouldn't enter into it.

When they were finally on *Narcissus* and away from here, they could meet again.

"*She's* sure," he said, "and that's as sure as I need to be."

Kasyanov nodded and started accessing a different series of programs.

While the doctor worked, Hoop moved around the med bay, seeing what he could find. He packed a small pouch with painkillers, multi-vitamin shots, antibiotics, and viral inhibitors. He also found a small surgery kit including dressings and sterilization pads. He took a handheld scanner that could diagnose any number of ailments, and a multi-vaccinator.

Just him, Kasyanov, and Ripley, for however many years it took for them to be found.

"You'll see Amanda again," he said—mostly to himself, because he was thinking of his own children, as well. They were *all* going home.

"Hoop," Kasyanov said. "I'm about to initiate. The pod calculates that it'll take just under twenty minutes for the physical repairs, and five more for the limited memory wipe."

Hoop nodded. Kasyanov stroked a pad on the unit and it began to hum.

Inside, Ripley twitched.

```
PROGRESS REPORT:
To: Weyland-Yutani Corporation, Science Division
(Ref: code 937)
Date (unspecified)
Transmission (pending)


I will save Ripley. Together, she and I can continue our
mission into the darkness. I am convinced there are many
more aliens out there. One location is a freak accident,
two means countless more.
I would like to know their history.
With a new fuel cell we can drift forever as we seek signs
of another colony.
And Ripley can sleep, ready to bear our inevitable prize
back home.
I only need her. The others cannot come. I will allow what
she has requested. In truth, it's perfect. She will not
remember how determined I remain to fulfill the mission.
She will not remember the things I have done.
On waking, she will not even know I am still here.
She will be weak, disorientated, and I will guide her back
to the Narcissus.
```

Hoop moved quickly through the ship toward the bridge. More than ever it felt like a haunted ship. He'd always known the *Marion* busy, the crew going about their tasks, the off-duty miners drinking or talking or working out. It had never been a silent place. There was always music emanating from the accommodations hub or rec room, a rumble of conversation from the galley and bar.

He felt a pang as he missed his friends, and Lucy Jordan, his one-time lover. She had become more than a friend, and after their romance had dwindled—sucked away, she'd joked without really joking, by the cold depths of space—their friendship had deepened to something he'd rarely felt before. They had trusted each other completely.

And she had been one of the first to die.

Hoop had never given way to loneliness. As a child he'd enjoyed his own company, preferring to spend time in his room making models or reading his parents' old books, and when he was a teenager he'd kept a small circle of friends. Never one for team sports, his social life had revolved around nights at their houses, watching movies or drinking cheap booze. Sometimes a girl would come onto the scene and take him or a friend away for a time, but they'd always returned to the familiarity of that small, closed circle.

Even as an adult, after marrying and having children and then losing it all, he had rarely felt lonely.

That only happened after the aliens arrived.

Every step of the way toward the bridge, he thought of Ripley. He so hoped she would live, but a different woman was going to emerge from the med pod. If the unit worked well, she would remember little or nothing from the past few days. He would have to introduce himself all over again.

Even though the creature had to be dead, he remained cautious, pausing at each junction, listening for anything out of place. A constant vibration had been rippling throughout the ship ever since the explosion in Hold 2, and Hoop guessed the blast had somehow knocked their decaying orbit askew. They were skipping the outer edges of the planet's atmosphere now, shields heating up, and it wouldn't be long before the damaged docking bays started to burn and break apart.

He needed to find out just how long they had.

The bridge was exactly as they'd left it less than a day earlier. It seemed larger than before, and he realized that he'd never actually been there on his own. Lachance was often on duty, sitting in his pilot's seat even though the *Marion* rarely needed any manual input. Baxter spent a lot of time at his communications console, processing incoming messages for miners or crew and distributing them as appropriate throughout the ship's network. Sneddon sometimes spent long periods there, talking with Jordan, and their security officer, Cornell, would sometimes visit.

Other people came and went. The place was never silent, never empty. Being there on his own made it seem all the more ghostly.

He spent a few minutes examining readouts on Lachance's control panels, consulting the computers, and they told him what he needed to know. He reached into a drawer and pulled out a small data drive, uploading a data purge program before dropping it into an inner pocket.

Insurance, he thought.

Then he quickly made his way down through the accommodations hub. It was a slight detour, but it was much closer to the galley and rec rooms. They needed food, and there wasn't time enough to go to where most of it was stored.

He found what he sought in various private quarters. Everyone kept a stash of food for midnight hungers, and sometimes because they just didn't feel like eating with the others. He grabbed a trolley and visited as many rooms as he could, finding pictures of families who would never see their loved ones again, witnessing all those personal things that when left behind seemed like sad, incomplete echoes of what a person had been.

As he gathered, it dawned on him that they'd never be able to take enough to sustain them. But Kasyanov had said there was a large supply of food substitutes and dried supplements stored in the med bay. They'd make do. There would be rationing.

He tried to concentrate entirely on the here-and-now. The thought of the journey that lay ahead would cripple him if he dwelled on it for too long. So he kept his focus on the next several hours.

Leaving the laden trolley along the route that led down to the docking bays, he made his way back up to the med bay. Kasyanov was sitting on one of the beds, jacket cast aside and shirt pulled up to reveal her wounds. They were more extensive than Hoop had suspected; bloody tears in her skin that pouted purple flesh. She quivered as she probed at them with tweezers. There were several heavy bags piled by the door, and a stack of medical packs. She'd been busy—before she took time to tend herself.

"Bad?" he asked softly.

She looked up, pale and sickly.

"I've puked blood. I'll have to use the med pod. Otherwise, I'll die of internal bleeding and infection within a day."

"We've got maybe two hours," Hoop said.

"Time enough," she replied, nodding. "She'll be done in fifteen minutes."

He had seen the unit working before, but it never ceased to fascinate him. Ripley looked thin and malnourished, battered and bruised. But the med pod had already repaired most of her major wounds, and several operating arms were concentrating on the rip in her stomach. They moved with a fluid grace, lacking any human hesitation and targeted with computer confidence. Two delved inside, one grasping, another using a laser to patch and mend. Its white-warm glow reflected from the pod's glass cover and gave movement to Ripley's face, but in truth she was motionless. Back down in the depths of whatever dreams troubled her so much.

They, too, would soon be fixed.

The arms retreated and then her wound was glued and stitched with dissolvable thread. A gentle spray was applied to the area— artificial skin, set to react over time as the natural healing processes commenced. When she woke up, there would be little more than a pale pink line where the ugly slash had once existed.

Bumps and bruises were sprayed, her damaged scalp treated, an acid splash across her left forearm and hand attended to, after which the pod's arms pulled a white sheet from a roll beneath the bed and settled it gently across Ripley's body. It was almost caring.

Kasyanov glanced at Hoop, and he nodded. She initiated the next process. Then sighed, sat back, and closed her eyes as the interior of the med pod changed color. Rich blue lights came on, and arms as delicate as daisy stems pressed several contact pads against Ripley's forehead, temples, and neck. The lights began to pulse hypnotically. The pod buzzed in time with the pulsing, emitting a soporific tone. Hoop had to look away.

He turned to Kasyanov. Her breathing was light and fast, but she waved him away, nodding.

"I'm good," she said.

"You're shit."

"Yeah. Well. What's that, a doctor's analysis?"

Hoop could barely smile. Instead, he went to the bags she'd left by the med bay's door and opened the first to check inside.

"Antibiotics, viral tabs, painkillers, sterilization spray," Kasyanov said. "Other stuff. Bandages, medicines, contraceptives."

Hoop raised an eyebrow.

"Hey. Forever is a long time."

He checked another bag and saw a jumble of plastic containers and shrink-wrapped instruments.

"You planning on passing time by operating on us?"

"Not unless I have to. But you really want to die from appendicitis?"

A soft chime came from the med pod and the lights inside faded to nothing. Sensor tendrils curled back in, fine limbs settled into place, and then the lid slid soundlessly open.

"She's done?" Hoop asked.

"Guess so." Kasyanov hauled herself upright, growling against the pain. "Get her out. I've got to——"

A distant explosion thudded through the ship. The floor kicked up. Ceiling tiles shuddered in their grid.

"Hurry," Hoop said. As he moved across to the pod and prepared to lift Ripley out, Kasyanov was already working at its control panel. Her good hand moved quickly across the touchscreen. Hoop lifted Ripley clear, the lid slid closed, and moments later a sterilizing mist filled the interior.

Hoop settled Ripley on one of the beds, carefully wrapping her in the sheet and fixing it with clips. She looked tired, older. But she was still alive, and her face seemed more relaxed than he had seen it. He so hoped that she was dreaming harmless dreams.

"Now me," Kasyanov said. "Five minutes, if that. We've got time?"

Hoop was surprised at the doctor's sudden vulnerability.

"Of course," he said. "I'm waiting for you, whatever happens."

She nodded once, then with a wry smile she held out her hand.

"Quick lift?"

Hoop helped her into the pod. She lay down, touched the inner shell, and a remote control grid appeared. A wave of her hand closed the lid.

"See ya," she said, attempting an American accent.

Hoop smiled and nodded. Then he turned back to check that Ripley was all right.

Behind him, the med pod whispered.

PROGRESS REPORT:

To: Weyland-Yutani Corporation, Science Division
(Ref: code 937)

Date (unspecified)

Transmission (pending)

The doctor has served her purpose.
She makes the next step almost too easy.

The med pod wasn't quite soundproof.

Looking at Ripley, Hoop heard Kasyanov's muffled yell. He turned around to see thin metallic straps whipping across the doctor's body, constricting across her shoulders, chest, stomach, hips, and legs. She cried out in pain as they crushed against her wounds.

Hoop knew that shouldn't be happening. He tried to open the lid, but it was locked, and however much he touched and pressed the external control panel, nothing happened.

Kasyanov looked at him through the glass, wide-eyed.

"Ash," Hoop hissed. Kasyanov couldn't have heard him, but she saw the word on his lips. And froze.

A soft blue light filled the med pod.

"No!" she shouted, the word so muffled that Hoop only knew it because of the shape of her mouth.

A single surgical arm rose from its housing and loomed over Kasyanov's chest.

Hoop tried to force the lid. He snapped up the plasma torch and used the hand rest to hammer at the lid's lip, but only succeeded in bending part of the torch.

Kasyanov's voice changed tone and he looked to her lips, searching for the word she had chosen, and it was *Hoop*.

He turned the torch around and aimed at the pod's lid, close to her feet. If he was careful, only released a quick shot, angled it just right, he might be able to—

The blue light pulsed and the delicate arm sparked alight. There was a fine laser at its tip, and in a movement that was almost graceful, it drew rapidly across Kasyanov's exposed throat. Blood pulsed, then spurted from the slash, splashing back from the pod's inner surface and speckling across her face.

She was held so tightly that Hoop only knew she was struggling because of the flexing and tensing of her muscles, the bulging of her eyes. But those soon died down, and as the blue light faded, Kasyanov grew still.

Hoop turned away, breathing hard, and even when the ship juddered so hard that it clacked his teeth together, he did not move.

You bastard, he thought. *You utter bastard, Ash.*

Somehow he held back his rage.

Ripley groaned and rolled onto her side.

"I've got you," Hoop said, moving to her side. Dropping the plasma torch, he slipped his hands beneath her and heaved her up onto his shoulder.

The shuttle awaited them, and now he was the last survivor of the *Marion*.

It was time to leave.

24

REVENGE

PROGRESS REPORT:

To: Weyland-Yutani Corporation, Science Division
(Ref: code 937)

Date (unspecified)

Transmission (pending)

Ripley lives. He will bring her, and then discover the
final surprise.

Time to leave.

I cannot pretend I am not disappointed that things went
wrong. I cannot deny that I am frustrated. But I have time
on my side.

I am immortal, after all.

Hoop left med bay with Ripley over his shoulder. The ship juddered so hard that he fell into a wall, jarring his whole body. The *Marion* groaned and creaked. It struck him what an irony it would be if the ship broke her back there and then, venting to space, killing him and Ripley and ending their long, terrible journey.

He thought of Lachance, who might have prayed to help him reach his destination. But Hoop knew that he was on his own. The universe was indifferent. Whether he and Ripley escaped, or died

· here and now, it all came down to chance.

A rhythmic booming commenced from somewhere deep below. It sounded like a giant hammer, smashing at the ship's spine, pulsing explosions working outward from the engine core, thudding heartbeats of a dying ship. But still the vessel did not break up.

"Well, let's go, then," he muttered, moving on.

He tried to move quickly. His legs were as shaky as the ship now, and he couldn't remember the last time he'd eaten. His stomach rumbled, and he was suddenly, sickeningly hungry. He snorted a laugh at how ridiculous that was. But he also vowed to enjoy a feast, once they were in the *Narcissus* and away from the ship.

Just the two of us now, he thought. *One asleep, one awake, sharing the stasis pod and maybe being together for a while in between. We might even do this. We might survive and get home.*

And what story would he tell Ripley, when his newfound loneliness became too great and he woke her, ready to spend some of his own time in hypersleep? How would she react to being roused by someone she didn't know? If the memory wipe had been thorough, the last thing she'd remember would be putting herself into stasis after destroying the *Nostromo*.

But that was for the future. If they survived, he would be able to tell her everything, or perhaps nothing at all. All he could concentrate on now was staying alive.

He moved as quickly and safely as he could. Reaching the stairs that led down into the docking area, he decided he'd have to take the elevator. Ripley was becoming heavier by the moment. He glanced at the trolley of food and realized he would have to return for it.

As he entered the elevator, though, he already mourned the feast left behind.

The car descended smoothly, and the doors opened onto a corridor lit by flickering lights. Something exploded. It was far away, but it punched through the whole superstructure, knocking him from his feet again. Ripley rolled against the wall, groaning, waving her hands.

"Don't wake up yet," he muttered. She'd panic. He had enough to contend with.

She opened her eyes and looked right at him, motionless, holding her breath. There was no expression on her face, and nothing like recognition in her eyes. Hoop began to speak, to make sure she was still Ripley, still there. But then she closed her eyes again and slumped down. He had no idea what she had seen, but it hadn't been him.

A deep groan rumbled through everything, and he felt a sickly movement in his stomach and head. The *Marion* was starting to turn in a roll, and if that happened she would quickly come apart. From somewhere behind him he saw flashing yellow and orange bursts, illuminating the walls before fading again. *Fire!* But then he realized there were viewing ports back on the deck from which he'd just descended. The flames were filtering in from outside.

Things were heating up.

He closed a blast door behind him, but it immediately re-opened. He didn't bother trying again. Maybe it was Ash still playing his games. Or it might just be the *Marion*, getting cranky in her final moments.

"Come on, come on!" he implored, urging himself on, Ripley slung across both of his shoulders now. He staggered along the corridor, bouncing from wall to wall as the ship shook and rumbled. Another explosion came from far away and he felt the pressure blast smack him in the back, pushing him onward so hard that he lost his footing and went to his knees. He kept hold of Ripley this time. She grunted.

"Yeah, me too," he said. He stood again and passed by the *Samson*'s docking arm, moving quickly on to Bay Four and the *Narcissus*. He opened the vestibule doors and hurried through. In minutes they'd be away. He would look back and see the distant flare as the massive ship met its end.

Or maybe not. Maybe he wouldn't look at all. He'd seen enough destruction, and he couldn't help feeling sad at the *Marion*'s demise.

Ash would die with the ship. Hoop had never met an android that he'd liked, but he'd never disliked any of them, either. He'd regarded them as expensive, fancy tools. Sometimes they were useful, but more often they were rich playthings that did the jobs that any man or woman could do, given the right equipment and training.

But he hated Ash.

And they were about to beat him.

He opened the *Narcissus*'s door and entered the shuttle, keeping his eyes on the vestibule as the airlock slid closed again, followed by the shuttle doors.

Then Hoop heard something behind him. A soft, gentle hiss. The scraping of claws on leather. Something alive.

He turned around slowly, and Jonesy sat crouched on the arm of the pilot's chair, teeth bared at him, hackles spiked.

"Oh, for fuck's sake!" Hoop relaxed, lowering Ripley to the floor. He went to the pilot's seat and sat down.

Jonesy hissed again and jumped away when Hoop went to stroke him.

He switched on the ship's computer and it powered up instantly. All good. He sat back and waited for the system statuses to load onto the control screens, looking around at the shuttle's interior. Ash was here. He couldn't be seen or sensed, but here more than anywhere Hoop had that distinct sense of being watched.

Hello Ash, he typed.

`Good afternoon, Chief Engineer Hooper.`

Good? he typed. *No. Pretty fucking shitty, really.*

Ash did not respond.

Initiate launch sequence, Hoop typed.

`No.`

I thought you'd say that. Hoop took the memory stick from his inner pocket, and slipped it into one of the panel's interface points.

The computer screen before him flashed, then faded to blank. When it fired up again the previous lines of text had vanished, and the cursor sat ready to create some more.

`I'm more than just a program.`

No, Hoop typed, *that is exactly what you are. Thinking you're more than that is why this is going to work.*

```
But I'm everywhere, Chief Engineer Hooper. I'm in the
Narcissus, deeper and more entrenched than any of its
former programs. I'm in the Samson and the Marion. Do you
really think a third rate virus program can affect me?
```

Probably not, Hoop typed. *This isn't third rate. It's the best that money can buy… from your old friends at Weyland-Yutani.*

```
No.
```

That was Ash's total response. Whether it was a plea or a denial, Hoop didn't wait to find out. He pressed a button on the virus purger, then hit the initiate button on the control panel. A splash of code lit up three screens. It started to scroll quickly, and every few seconds a particular line of code was highlighted red, isolated, and placed in a boxed area on the left of the central display.

Hoop left the purger to do its work. and went to where he'd propped Ripley by the door.

She was still unconscious, and for that he was glad. He carefully took the sheet from her and dressed her in some underwear he found in the small clothing locker. Jonesy the cat sat beside her and purred as he did so, eager to maintain contact with his mistress as much as he could.

Hoop struggled with her vest, laying her flat and stretching her arms over her head to pull it down. Just before he smoothed it over her stomach, he paused and looked closely at the fixed wounds there. They were visible as pale pink lines in her waxen skin. When she woke up, if she looked closely enough, she would find them. And he would be there to tell her all about it.

"You can sleep without nightmares, Ripley," he said, holding her close. "And when we wake up, I'll only tell you as much as you need to know." She seemed lighter when he lifted her this time, and her face was almost serene as he laid her in the stasis pod where she had slept for so long.

Jonesy jumped in with her and snuggled down by her feet, as if eager to go back to sleep. Hoop could hardly blame him.

Something buzzed on the control panel, and he sat back in the pilot's chair.

The screens were blank once again, and a red light glowed softly on the purger. He plucked it from the interface and held it up between two fingers, filled with distaste even though he knew Ash wasn't really in there. That was a simplistic notion, but somehow that naive idea made Hoop feel better. Especially when he dropped the purger to the floor and crushed it beneath his boot.

Hello Narcissus, he typed.

`Narcissus online.`

This is Chief Engineer Hooper of the Deep Space Mining Orbital Marion. *I have Warrant Officer Ripley with me. Please initiate all pre-launch checks.*

`With pleasure, Chief Engineer Hooper.`

A series of images and menus flashed across the screens, flickering as each launch and flight system was checked. It all looked good. He didn't see anything to worry him.

"We're not home yet," he said. The shuttle shook as something happened on the *Marion*, another explosion or a closer impact with LV178's atmosphere. They didn't have very long.

Hoop went to the stasis pod and fired it up. Its small screen was already flashing as the *Narcissus*'s computer ran through its own series of diagnostics. It looked like a comfortable place to spend some time. A *long* time.

As the shuttle's computer went through its pre-flight diagnostics, Hoop accessed the navigation computer and created a new program.

It was simple enough—he input the destination as "origin," made certain that was listed as Sol system, then clicked the auto panel so that the ship's computer would work out the complex flight charts.

"Earth," he whispered, thinking of that long-ago place and everything that it meant to him. He hoped he would get back in time to see his family again.

He hoped they would welcome his return.

The computer still wasn't done calculating, so he squeezed back through the hatch and into the engine room to complete work on the replacement fuel cell. It was connected into the ship and fixed on its damper pads, but he still had to finish refixing its shell. It took a few moments, then he sat back and regarded his work. It all looked good. He'd always been a neat engineer, and tidying up after himself was part of his work ethic. So he grabbed the old, denuded fuel cell by the handle on the end and tugged it back through the hatch after him.

Hearing a warning chime, he left the cell by the hatch and went to the pilot's station again.

```
Pre-flight checks completed. All flight and environmental
systems online.
Launch procedure compromised.
```

Hoop caught his breath. He rested his fingers on the keyboard, almost afraid to type in case Ash's soundless voice replied.

What's the problem? he typed, wondering how Ash would respond. *No problem for me*, maybe, or, *We'll all go together*. But the response was straightforward, to the point, and nothing malignant.

```
Automatic release malfunction. Manual release from
Marion's docking bay required.
```

"Oh, great," he said. "That's just fucking great." It wasn't Ash's voice, but it was a final farewell. Hoop couldn't launch the shuttle from inside. He'd have to be out there, back in the airlock and on board the *Marion*, so that he could access manual release.

Ash's parting gift.

"You bastard," Hoop said.

But had he really expected it to end so easily? His heart sank. The ship shook. From the viewing windows that looked out across the *Marion*'s belly, he could see feathers of flames playing all across the hull. Parts of it were already glowing red.

He went to Ripley's side to say goodbye. He stared down at her where she slept, aware that they hadn't gone through the usual pre-hypersleep procedures—she should have eaten and drunk, washed, used the bathroom. But this rushed process was the best he could manage.

He was letting her fly into the future.

His own future was shorter, and far more grim.

"So here we are," he said. It felt foolish talking to himself, and really there was nothing left to say. He bent down and kissed Ripley softly on the lips. He didn't think she would mind. In fact, he kind of hoped she'd have liked it. "Fly safe. Sweet dreams."

Then Hoop closed the stasis pod and watched its controls flash on as the *Narcissus*'s computer took control. By the time he was standing by the shuttle's door, plasma torch slung over one shoulder, Ripley was almost into hypersleep.

Amanda is in her late teens, lithe, tall and athletic, just like her mother. She stands by a stone wall somewhere dark and shadowy, and her chest bursts open, spilling blood to the floor, a screeching creature clawing its way out from the wound.

Ripley turns away because she doesn't want to see. Behind her, a monster spews hundreds of flexing eggs from its damaged abdomen.

She turns again and sees a blood-spattered metal wall, tattered corpses at its base. More aliens crawl toward her, hissing, heads moving as if they are sniffing her, and she understands their age-old fury in a way that only nightmares can allow. It's as if they have been looking for her forever, and now is the moment of their revenge.

She turns back to Amanda, and her daughter is maybe fourteen years old. She coughs and presses her hand to her chest. Rubs. Nothing happens.

Ripley turns a full circle. More blood, more aliens, but now it's all more distant, as if she's viewing things through a reversed telescope.

Those beasts are still coming for her, but they're a long way off, both in time and memory, and becoming more distant with every moment that passes.

Amanda, she tries to say. But though she knows this is a dream, still she cannot speak.

25

GONE

Three more minutes and she'll be gone.

Hoop shoved the empty fuel cell out through the airlock, then returned to the *Narcissus* and closed the hatch behind him, flicking the lever that would initiate its automatic sealing and locking. He heard the heavy *clunks* and then a steady hiss, and Ripley was lost to him. There wasn't even a viewing panel in the door. He would never see her again.

The *Marion* was in her death-throes. The ship's vibrations were now so violent that Hoop's heels and ankles hurt each time the deck jerked beneath him. He moved quickly through the airlock, plasma torch held at ready in case that last alien had survived, and in case it was coming for him still.

Two minutes. He just had to live that long, in order to release Ripley's shuttle. He hoped to survive for longer—and a plan was forming, a crazy idea that probably had a bad ending—but two minutes was the minimum. After that, after Ripley would be safe, things would matter less.

He reached the vestibule and closed the airlock behind him, sealing it and leaning to one side to look at the *Narcissus* through one of the viewing windows. All he had to do now was to hit the airlock seal confirmation, and the ship's computer would know it was safe to go.

His hand hovered over the pad. Then he pressed it down.

Almost instantaneously a brief retro burst pushed the *Narcissus* away from the *Marion*, and the two parted company. More retro exhalations dropped the shuttle down beneath the ship's belly. It fell through veils of smoke and sheets of blazing air, buffeted by the planet's atmosphere, before its rockets ignited and it vanished quickly toward the stern.

And that was it. Ripley and the *Narcissus* were gone. Hoop was left alone on the *Marion*, and he knew the ship he'd called home was moments away from dying.

For a while he just leaned there against the wall, feeling each death-rattle transmitted into his body up through the floor and wall. He thought about his plan, and how foolish it was, how almost beyond comprehension. And he thought about the easier way out. He could just sit there for a while, and when the time came and the ship started to come apart, his death would be quick. The heat would be immense, and it would fry him to a crisp. He probably wouldn't even feel it. And if he did feel it, it would be more sensation than pain.

The end of all his agonies.

But then he saw his children again. Between blinks they were actually there with him in that vestibule, the two boys silent but staring at him accusingly, their eyes saying, *You left us once, don't leave us again!* He sobbed. In that instant he could understand why Ripley had asked for that merciful wiping of her memory.

Then his children were gone again, figments of his guilt, aspects of his own bad memories. But they didn't have to be gone forever. Where there existed even the slightest, most insignificant chance, he had to take it.

The *Samson* wasn't very far away.

He paused briefly outside the door that led into the *Samson*'s docking arm. It was still vacuum in there, and he wouldn't have time to find the tools to drill a hole again. This escape would be more basic, more brutal than that.

He wanted to give himself a chance. He needed supplies, even though the probability of surviving was insignificant. It was a dropship, built for surface-to-orbit transfers, not deep space travel. There likely was enough fuel on board for him to escape orbit, but he wasn't even certain whether the craft's navigational computer could calculate a journey across the cosmos toward home. He would point them in the right direction, then fire the thrusters. Retain perhaps twenty percent of the fuel, but use the rest to get him up to the greatest speed possible.

And there was no stasis unit in the *Samson*. He'd likely be traveling for years. He might even grow old and die in there, if the ship held together that long. *What a find that would be*, he mused, *for someone hundreds or thousands of years from now.*

Bad enough to consider traveling that long with company, but on his own? The one comfort was that he was again king of his own destiny. If he wanted to persist, then he could. And if the time came when ending it was a much more settling proposition, it was simply a case of opening the airlock door.

Best get moving then.

But he needed food, water, clothing, and other supplies. Much of what he required still sat on that trolley, up in the *Marion* and just beyond the large docking deck. So he ran. He thought of the feast he'd promised himself, and that kept him going, the idea of reconstituted steak and dried vegetables, with flatcakes for dessert. A glass of water. Maybe he'd even be able to access the electronic library they used on board the *Marion*, if it had been updated to the *Samson*'s computers. He wasn't sure about that, it hadn't been a priority, and such minor considerations had usually been passed down to Powell and Welford.

He hoped they hadn't shirked their responsibilities.

With the prospect of a lonely eternity ahead, Hoop was surprised to find that he was shedding tears as he ran. They weren't for him, because he was way past that. They were for his kids. They were for his crew and everyone he'd seen die horrible, unnatural deaths. And they were for Ripley.

It was as if the *Marion* knew that he was abandoning her. She was shaking herself apart. Conduits had broken beneath the constant assault, and clouds of sparks danced back and forth outside a closed doorway. He ducked beneath the bare wires, moving quickly, too rushed to be overly cautious. As he neared the stairs leading up from the docking level, bursts of steam powered up from fractured channels in the flooring, scorching his skin and lungs and soaking his suit, running in bright red rivulets where other people's blood had dried onto the strong material.

At the top of the stairs was a short corridor, and that emerged onto the wide area where elevator and stairs led up into the *Marion*. This was where he'd left the trolley of supplies.

It was still there. It had shifted a little, because he'd forgotten to lock its wheels. But there were packets of dried foods, a few sachets of dried fruit from their damaged garden pod, and a precious bottle of whiskey. Perhaps in an hour he would be drinking to Ripley's health.

Knowing what had to come next, he knew that he couldn't take everything. So he grabbed two of the bags he'd brought along from the trolley, opened them and tried to cram in as much as he could. He rushed. He didn't think about what he chose, just scooped packets and sachets and rammed them in.

With both bags full and tied shut, he slung one over each shoulder and turned to run back to the *Samson*.

Then he stopped. He turned back to the trolley and plucked up the bottle of bourbon nestling on the bottom shelf. Heavy, impractical…

But entirely necessary.

As he ran, he found himself laughing.

Die now or die later, Hoop thought. It gave him a sort of bravery, he hoped. Or carelessness. Perhaps sometimes the two were the same.

He suited up and waited outside the doorway that led into Bay Three. He wore a bag over each shoulder, and clasped in his left hand was the bourbon. He'd tethered himself to the wall opposite the doors, and as soon as they were fully open he'd unclip and let himself sail through, carried by the torrent of atmosphere being sucked from the ship. With luck he would drift right through the vestibule and into the open airlock beyond. If he was unlucky, he'd be dragged with the main flow of air, out through the smashed portion of outer wall and window, and smeared along the underside of the doomed ship.

He probably wouldn't feel much. The end would be quick.

But if he did make it across to the airlock, he'd haul himself into the *Samson*, close the hatches, and initiate its environmental controls. It wouldn't be long before he could breathe once more.

The chance was slim. But there was little else to do. The *Marion* just had minutes left. Through viewing windows he'd already seen sizeable chunks of hull spinning away, consumed in flame. If the ship didn't burst apart it would explode from the tremendous pressures being exerted.

Fuck it. He had to try. It was all he had left.

Reaching out with a hand that surprised him by shaking, he touched the panel that would open the doors.

```
PROGRESS REPORT:
To: Weyland-Yutani Corporation, Science Division
(Ref: code 937)
Date (unspecified)
Transmission-initiated


I cannot be angry at my failure. I am an AI, and we are
not designed to suffer such emotions. But perhaps in the
time I have been on my mission I have undergone a process
of evolution. I am an intelligence, after all.

So, not angry. But... disappointed.

And now my final act, it seems, will also be thwarted.
I have attempted to transmit every progress report I filed
since arriving on the Marion. But the transmissions are
failing. Perhaps damage to the antennae array is worse
than I anticipated, or maybe the codes I am using are
outmoded.

Strange. An AI would not think to keep a diary. Yet that
appears to be exactly what I have done.

The diary will cease to exist along with me.

Not long now. Not long.

I wonder if I will dream.
```

* * *

Chance smiled. But considering the pain Hoop was in, perhaps it had been more of a grimace.

The decompression had sucked him through the narrow gap between the doors, ripping off his helmet and thrusting him into a spin. He'd struck the edge of the airlock entrance, and for a moment he could have gone either way. Left, and he'd have tumbled from the massive wound in the vestibule's side wall. Right—into the airlock— meant survival, at least for a time.

If he'd dropped the bourbon, he could have used his left hand to push against the wall and slide himself to safety.

Fuck you! his mind had screamed. *Fuck you! If I survive, I want a drink!*

Unable to move either way, he'd heard something clanging along the walls as it bounced toward him from deep within the *Marion*. Many smaller items were being sucked out through the hole, immediately flashing into flame as they met the superheated gasses roaring past outside.

Then something large slammed across the opening. For perhaps two seconds it remained there, lessening the force of the suction, letting Hoop reach around into the airlock with his right hand and haul himself inside.

It was the trolley on which he'd gathered supplies. As he closed the airlock door, the decompression began again with a heavy thud.

The *Marion* lasted a lot longer than he'd expected.

Seven minutes after blasting away from the dying ship, Hoop switched one of the *Samson*'s remote viewers and watched the massive vessel finally break apart. She died in a glorious burst of fire, a blooming explosion that smeared across the planet's upper atmosphere and remained there for some time, detritus falling and burning, flames drifting in the violent winds.

Further away, toward the upper curve of the planet, he could still see the ochre bruise of the fuel cell detonation that had destroyed the mine. It was strange, viewing such violence and yet hearing nothing but his own sad sigh. He watched for a minute more, then turned off the viewer and settled back into the seat.

"Burn," he whispered, wondering whether Ash had any final thoughts before being wiped out. He hoped so. He hoped the AI had felt a moment of panic, and pain.

Hoop was no pilot. Yet he would need to attempt to program the dropship's computer to plot a course back toward Earth. Maybe he'd be picked up somewhere on the way. Perhaps someone would hear the distress signal he was about to record. But if not, he thought he might survive for a while. The *Samson* carried emergency rations that would supplement what he'd managed to bring on board. Its environmental systems would reprocess his waste and give him water and breathable air.

He'd also found a small file of electronic books on the computer. He'd been unreasonably excited at first, before he'd scrolled through the limited selection and a cruel truth hit home.

He'd already read them all.

He looked around the dropship's interior. The alien extrusion was still coating the rear wall, and he thought perhaps he might try to clear it off. There was dried blood on the walls and floor, and the limb was still trapped beneath the equipment rack in the passenger cabin.

Hardly home.

And yet his first meal as a castaway was a good one. He reconstituted some steak stew, carrots, and mashed potatoes, and while they cooled a little he broke the seal on the bourbon. It smelled good, and he knew he wouldn't be able to make it last for long. He held the bottle up and turned it this way and that, starlight glimmering through the golden brown fluid. Then he drank without offering anyone, or anything, a toast.

Relishing the burn as the drink warmed him from the inside out, Hoop pressed "record."

"When I was a kid I dreamed of monsters," he said. "I don't have to dream anymore. If you can hear this, please home in on the beacon. I'm alone, drifting in a dropship that isn't designed for deep space travel. I'm hoping I can program the computer to take me toward the outer rim, but I'm no navigator. I'm no pilot, either. Just a ship's engineer. This is Chris Hooper, last survivor of the Deep Space Mining Orbital *Marion*."

He leaned back in the pilot's seat, put his feet up on the console, and pressed *transmit*.

Then he took another drink.

Ripley is lying in a hospital bed. There are shapes around her, all come to visit.

There's a little girl. Her name is Amanda, and she is Ellen Ripley's daughter. She's still young, and she smiles at her mother, waiting for her to come home. I'll be home for your eleventh birthday, *Ripley says.* I promise. *Amanda grins at her mommy. Ripley holds her breath.*

Nothing happens.

Behind Amanda are other shapes Ripley does not recognize. They're little more than shadows—people she has never known, all dressed in uniforms emblazoned with a ship's name she does not recognize—but even as Amanda leans in to hug her, these shadows fade away.

Soon Amanda begins to fade, as well, but not from memory. She's back home, an excited little girl awaiting her mother's return from a long, dangerous journey.

I'll buy her a present, *Ripley thinks.* I'll buy her the greatest present ever.

But in the blankness left when Amanda disappears, other figures emerge. Her crew, her friends, and Dallas, her lover.

They look frightened. Lambert is crying, Parker is angry.

And Ash. Ash is…

Dangerous! *Ripley thinks.* He's dangerous! *But though this is her dream, she cannot warn the others.*

And much closer, beneath clean hospital sheets, something is forcing itself from Ripley's chest.

ABOUT THE AUTHOR

TIM LEBBON is a *New York Times*-bestselling writer with almost thirty novels published to date, as well as dozens of novellas and hundreds of short stories. Recent releases include *Coldbrook*, *Into the Void: Dawn of the Jedi* (Star Wars), *Reaper's Legacy*, and *The Sea Wolves* (with Christopher Golden). Future novels include *Contagion* and *The Silence*. He has won four British Fantasy Awards, a Bram Stoker Award, and a Scribe Award.

Fox 2000 acquired film rights to *The Secret Journeys of Jack London* series, and his *Toxic City* trilogy is in development with ABC Studios. Several other novels and screenplays are also at varying stages of development.

Find out more about Tim at his website
www.timlebbon.net

ALIENS™
THE OFFICIAL NOVELIZATION
by Alan Dean Foster

The official novelization of the hit *Aliens* movie.

Ellen Ripley has been rescued, only to learn that the planet
from *Alien*—where the deadly creature was discovered - has
been colonized. But contact has been lost, and a rescue team
is sent. They wield impressive firepower, but will it be enough?

APRIL 2014

ALIEN™ 3
THE OFFICIAL NOVELIZATION
by Alan Dean Foster

The official novelization of the blockbuster *Alien 3* movie.

Ellen Ripley continues to be stalked by the savage alien race, after her escape pod, ejected from Colonial Marine spaceship *Sulaco*, crash-lands on a prison planet, killing everyone else aboard. Unknown to Ripley, an alien egg is aboard the ship. The alien is born inside the prison, and sets out on a killing spree.

MAY 2014

TITANBOOKS.COM